AMETHYST COUNTRY

To Marian,

Best Wishes

Mary Lennon

AMETHYST COUNTRY

Mary Lennon

Matador
Unit E2 Airfield Business Park,
Harrison Road, Market Harborough,
Leicestershire. LE16 7UL
Tel: 0116 2792299
Email: books@troubador.co.uk
Web: www.troubador.co.uk/matador
Twitter: @matadorbooks

ISBN 978 1803131 887

British Library Cataloguing in Publication Data.
A catalogue record for this book is available from the British Library.

Printed and bound in the UK by TJ Books, Padstow, Cornwall
Typeset in 11pt Minion Pro by Troubador Publishing Ltd, Leicester, UK

Matador is an imprint of Troubador Publishing Ltd

For Ken

Prologue

Grace stands on Dooagh Bridge. Dusk, a small breeze has taken up, she tightens her scarf. Around her a hum of voices from the cottages, the bang of a pail, a baby cries, someone whistles a tune, sheep bleat.

This is the cusp: rest before sleep, dusk before dark, shadows before ghosts. For days she's been unsettled, uncertain. Go or stay? If she goes, what will become of them? Her husband is captivated, compelled to stay – a marriage neither here nor there?

This place is alien – stunning, fearsome. Ahead the ocean, still lighting the land, behind her, the mountain, Sliabh Mór, in shadow. In this place, the sea, sky, land, come and go, never one colour for long.

Now with the light fading, she sets up her easel, looks hard, begins to paint the shifting shades and shadows – pale blue, grey, navy, indigo, a flittering carmine, a yellow streak over Clare Island – all there if she can work fast, if she can catch it, hold it.

Is this her hour?

1

The bus crossed the Michael Davitt Bridge onto the island, came to a wheezing halt outside a pub and all passengers were asked to leave. Helen stepped out into dizzying space, a high, open sky, the dark rocky shoreline of the Sound and in the distance, blue mountains. She leaned against the pub wall, until the cold hard brick pressing at her back steadied her.

She looked to right and left: a supermarket, shops, pubs, a Hotel. Achill Sound was bigger and more modern than she remembered. People moved in and out of the supermarket and a trickle of cars crossed the bridge. It was a frontier post, servicing travellers before they ventured into the hinterland and she suddenly wished she could stay here, close to the bridge. But she'd paid a deposit and a month's rent on a house someplace further from the bridge, so how could she?

Hugging the wall, she went into the pub, empty apart from two men at the bar, ordered a toasted cheese and tomato sandwich, pot of tea. Through the window she saw the bus, still parked across the road, knew she could take it back to Westport, get the train to Dublin and … what then?

Arrive, suitcase in hand, at Fiona's door? Book herself into a Hostel on Gardiner Street…and what then?

She ate her sandwich slowly, nobody bothered her. Time ticked down, she couldn't move herself. An hour passed before it came at her like on a sudden breeze: *One foot, another, watch the path below. One foot, another…*

Djouce Mountain, years before, a group of them climbed to the top on a bright morning, ate lunch, lay watching the views, when suddenly, a wind whipped up, dragging with it spitting rain. They became an anxious, scrambling bunch, until Philip, wannabe commander, grabbed the reins: *One foot, another, watch the path below…* The whole way down, he repeated it, urging them on, Helen and Sheila muttering, "Shut up, Philip."

But he'd landed them, drenched but safe.

One foot, another… Christ, was wannabe commander Philip all she had now?

She pushed herself up, crossed to the supermarket where she bought basic stuff to keep her going a few days. There she enquired about a taxi as the landlady had advised and twenty minutes later an older man with a mud splattered car drove up. He looked like a farmer who'd left a field, pulled a jacket on and changed his shoes when the call came.

"You visiting the House of Prayer?" he asked, ten seconds after she sat in.

Every time she returned home, she had to readjust to Irish inquisitiveness. "I don't know the House of Prayer" she said. In the mirror, she saw his eyes widen at her ignorance.

"Used to be the Convent. People visit for Retreats and such like."

2

A House of Prayer sounded restful. Perhaps she could stay there? Then the car turned left and they were on a road with the waters of the Sound on one side, hills on the other.

"A Mayo woman set it up some years back," he continued, "they say she has wounds in her hands and feet like Padre Pio … you know, stigmata."

His eyes held hers in the mirror, noting her surprise. She'd not envisaged Achill as a place with stigmatists, but before she could ask more, they were turning right down a side road towards the hill and through a gate where a few dormer bungalows stood, with a green space in front. It was deadly quiet, the only sign of life, one parked car.

Helen saw *Teach na Farraige* on the first house, knew she'd no escape. The driver was now all business, out the door, lifting her case from the boot, while she sat, slowly opening her purse. She'd a sudden urge to get him talking again, about anything, but he was a busy man, a farm to mind, was gone with a beep of his horn.

Keeping her back to the sea, she footered for the key. A whiff of pine disinfectant met her when she stepped inside, then the cool chill of an unlived in house. At the end of the hall, there was a combined kitchen-sitting room, separated by a counter. The room looked towards the hill at the kitchen end and towards the Sound at the other. The pine cabinets and mock grey marble surfaces seemed newish, clean, the décor standard modern, cream walls, black leather sofa, coffee table, TV. Upstairs were two bedrooms, she decided she'd sleep in the one looking out at the hill. It had a double bed, pine wardrobe. She dumped her case.

Downstairs she closed the blind on the front window to block out the sea, made tea, sat. Her body was still in motion from hours of travel: a flight from Heathrow to

Dublin airport through which she slipped like a fugitive onto a sleek coach bound for Heuston Station. She kept her eyes closed until they passed O'Connell Bridge, where the sun shone on people watching the river.

"A single ticket to Achill," she asked at the Station.

"There's no train to Achill."

"No train?"

The woman eyed her wearily, "Not since the 1930's. Train to Westport and a bus will take you out."

A man behind her sighed.

"Okay."

On the train a thread began to unravel but mercifully she slept until hanging baskets of fuchsia met her at Westport. The Achill bus was waiting so all she saw of the town was the Mall with its bridges and weirs, before they turned onto the Newport Road. She sat alone. It wasn't hard, there were only a few locals and half a dozen September visitors. The road was narrow and winding which the driver took with flying verve; she was grateful for the seat belt.

Past fields, bungalows they flew until they stopped at Mulranny, where the sea and wide open sky appeared. Dizzying space. She kept her eyes at hedgerow level, as they flashed onward through bogland, fields, dead quiet villages and finally the bridge.

She'd have made it to Crete in less time.

The buzz of the doorbell startled her. It was Joe McGreal, the landlady's cousin, arrived from Castlebar.

"Welcome to Shraheens," he said shaking her hand, then told her about fuses, bin day, hot water and handed her his phone number in case of emergency, another man in a hurry.

She managed to stall him long enough to ask about bike hire and buses. He said a neighbour, Mrs Kilbane could lend her a bike for a small sum and bus details could be got at the Sound.

As he waved from his black jeep, it crossed Helen's mind that it used to be the visitors from England who came in the smart cars, while the natives went on bikes.

She stretched out on the sofa, the humming silence finally broken by sounds: a car, children's voices, and soon after, another car, with adult voices, then movement in the house next door. Relief: half-past six, rush hour.

Hunger drove her to cook a toasted cheese sandwich then she turned on the television to blot out the falling darkness. There was a soap opera, *as Gaeilge*, with troublesome teenagers and a family feud.

She texted the same message to Isla, Fiona and Kate: *Made it, house fine, striking location. Will ring soon. X*

At half eleven, lights out in the other houses, she bolted doors and windows, checked them twice, pushed herself upstairs to bed. She tossed, turned, startled at every creak, tried to recall what she remembered of Achill. Not much except for their annual outing during holidays spent the other side of the Bay, when they'd come like pilgrims, for the spin around the Atlantic Drive. She remembers the silver VW taking on the cliff, rising higher and higher, knowing a lapse of concentration by her father would send them plummeting onto black rocks and swirling foam. Fiona kept her head at the open window like a bird catching air, whooping, while Helen held on tight, eyes pinned to her father's hands on the wheel.

Achill was Mayo, but not the Mayo she knew, not the Mayo Shane knew either; here, she'd have no traces to kick over. On Crete, where they drank ouzo, walked Samaria Gorge, snapshots would stalk – a café in Hania talking about the wonder of grapevines – fruit, edible leaves, shade, Shane interrupting to ask if she'd marry him. His skin was tanned, Shane the Greek, he looked nervous, did he think she'd refuse? He produced a blue stone ring, her favourite, they drank raki to celebrate, strong, hot, a portent for their future.

She sat up. No. For God's sake, not here; she turned the light on, reached for her book.

*

The sound of cars moving woke her out of a late doze. Eight-thirty. She surfaced groggily and through the window saw that the hill was gone, swallowed by mist. She pulled her Peruvian throw tighter, its bold pink and purple patchwork defying it. Camden Market, two years ago… another life ago. She closed her eyes.

At three o'clock, hunger forced her to the kitchen to heat soup, after which she lay and read, heard the rush hour around six, ate toast and cheese, watched television until darkness fell then crawled back to bed. Her sister Fiona and Isla had phoned.

Helen texted: *Thanx for calls. Signal poor, I'm okay.*

Through the night she slept a bit, read a bit, lay listening, every sound a threat, finally dozed. At five, she woke to Hampstead Heath, a glorious day, half of North London on its meadows, hills and ponds: babies, pensioners, teens with sound systems, dogs, bikes, skateboards. Picnics on pop up tables and blankets gobbled the grass. A group of them were celebrating Karl and Maria's twins' birthday. Helen swam in the pond with Shane and Kate, dried off under the sun.

6

Chloe, a friend of Maria's, arrived late wearing a striking vintage dress, but at opposite ends of the circle, she and Helen didn't meet. That day, Helen was hugging a secret – she and Shane had decided to have a baby. On such a bounteous day, how could she think they'd fail?

"For Christ's sake," she shouted, forced herself up, pulled the curtains. The mist was gone and through the window, a bare greenish-brown hill stood, too close. She watched clouds move back and forth above it. Downstairs, she had tea and toast, willing away hatred.

*

Another night of sleep a bit, read a bit…and then it dawned. She'd go to Galway, the bustle of a city would give her cover and it was close enough to Achill for the research. She could leave immediately, tomorrow, or the day after. This chink of light got her out of bed, to check accommodation in Galway. She couldn't arrive with no roof over her head, that much she'd learned, but as fast as her energy rose, it seeped away… a taxi to the bus, a bus to Westport, another bus to Galway, standing in Eyre Square, bag in hand, looking for some hostel, a deposit and month's rent here down the drain. She turned off her laptop, went back to bed.

She sensed the waters of the Sound in the distance, had chosen this house because it was within earshot of the sea, something she'd always yearned for. Now it terrified her. She was an isolated atom on the edge of a continent, surrounded by deep, dark water.

Achill would be hard, too hard.

2

Finn woke early, showered for ten seconds, the time his mother's boiler would permit before leaving her with tepid water all morning. He'd things to do, Jimmy Egan wanted an insulating job priced, so it would take a phone call with Tommo Gaffney, the supplier, beginning with weather and sports results before prices were tackled. This is what city types loved about the West when they came for their fortnight's holiday.

He hit the road at nine forty, with the gift of a blue sky above. Since his return from Spain, lots of people said the same thing, "How could you leave all that lovely weather behind?"

"You can get too many blue skies," he'd say, and they assumed he was joking. He wasn't, because the truth was, of course – complicated. Relentless blue skies had worn him thin, made him long for cumulus or cloud streaks but the low grey cloud which sometimes settled above Achill, wore him thin too.

He'd loved those Spanish blue skies off-season, sitting outside the Alicante bar with Tim Burke, sipping coffee and Soberano – the good old days, firm friends then. Isabel liked that bar too, sometimes joined them. She and Tim got on well. *La Guapa*, Tim called her, as she was.

Tim, the subcontractor who'd head hunted Finn, had fierce energy for driving jobs, Finn, the Quantity Surveyor, his main man. But once it all downturned, things went sour. The banks were snapping at Tim's heels and the underworld of building got murky: crap materials, shortcuts, general hit and run.

They'd finally squared up on the steps of a half built villa on a Monday morning, Finn thinking how ugly it looked, knowing he'd hit his limit. "I won't put my name to it," he said.

"Fuck's sake, you've gone soft," Tim shouted, white with anger, "lily livered."

By then Finn didn't care what names he called him. "I'm out," he said and walked.

They hadn't laid eyes on each other since.

Sadly, not that long afterwards, Isabel was calling Finn names too, "*Bastardo, Bastardo*," which he did mind, a lot.

To distract himself from morbid thoughts, he took the Atlantic Drive. Below him white topped waves punished the cliffs, in the distance Clare Island and ahead, Ashleam Bay. Once there was visibility, winter or summer, he loved this road. The slowly building curve and the power of the ocean bashing at the stoic rock was pure drama. He'd missed this in Alicante, missed too having the coastline all to himself.

Dooega was dead quiet, nothing moved except turf smoke curling from a few chimneys. He spent half an hour with Jimmy discussing insulating options and knew quickly that Jimmy, on a shoestring, couldn't manage the price. Problem was, Finn also on a shoestring, couldn't go any lower, so he left it with him. This pricing could have been done over the phone, but that wasn't the way hereabouts – well not for a local – not for Thomas Kilbane's son.

He drove back along the low road, wondering which version of Finn's return Jimmy subscribed to. He knew stories were woven about him: broken heart, broken health, broken down… grist to the gossip mill for winter evenings. They didn't believe he'd returned to look after his mother and they certainly didn't believe he was a QS, or presumed that made him a class of carpenter-roofer-builder. At first he'd wasted time explaining: surveyors do costings, contracts, spend their time on computers, not roofs – but eyes glazed over and they still wanted a sink or collapsed sidewall fixed. The shortage of trades on Achill meant locals grabbed anyone who could swing a hammer, so he abandoned explanation, shredded pride and with no better offers, became a-jack-of-all trades, apart from his no-go areas: electrics and gas. "Get a professional," he had to insist, repeatedly.

His father would be gob smacked at this turn of events: manual skills in higher demand than farming and his useless-with-his-hands son, filling the gap.

"They must be hard up, to hire you," Finn could hear him say, and he'd enjoy explaining that – actually – he was quite good with his hands and that the decline in farming had given rise to a new ascendancy – holiday homers, artists, surfers, retirees – all needing property maintenance.

Kevin, his older brother, had assumed the mantle of farmer at age six, so his father wanted Finn, given his deficiencies, to become an Agricultural Inspector, the next best thing. But Finn had disappointed again, preferred Lego to farmyards and his father had given up, relegating him to hosing down barns and tractors until at seventeen he'd escaped to Galway to study.

"A book learner," his father said in a voice dry as a wind whipped bone. He was a great man for labels – Finn and Maura, "book learners", Kevin, "born to the land," Sinead, "good with her hands." And, surprise, surprise, the labels had determined destiny: he and Maura got degrees, Kevin took over the farm, (until he couldn't hack it any longer) and Sinead became a nurse.

He sighed; he should have defied destiny – joined a circus.

Thoughts of his father often stirred gloom so he reached for Santana, the reliable antidote, the driving drum beat, taken on by the organ, then the guitar slowly asserting itself, until all three throbbed. It was his mate Phil who'd forced him to watch *Woodstock Live* and Santana's combo of Latin beat with American rock grabbed him by the balls. He'd introduced Isabel to the band, and she'd loved it too, a small gift, forgotten in their bruising ending. "*Bastardo, Bastardo.*"

"For fuck's sake lighten up," he shouted, as he drove through the hills and bogland.

*

At the Sound he stopped to pick up his mother's prescription and ran into Martha Mulherne from the History Group. He liked Martha, warm, straight up, and a woman of courage, retiring to Achill after years in London. They exchanged pleasantries then she mentioned the Group, wondering if he'd be coming soon.

"Work's busy," he lied. He wasn't in the right frame for it. They were planning future projects, not his forte.

He'd joined the Group to kill off the dark evenings and found himself in the company of a quirky bunch, mainly older, passionate, knowledgeable people. In fact, he'd felt undereducated; little of the history he studied at school related to his birthplace. They were in the throes of a *Letters Home* project which was inventive, using old letters from emigrants, so he'd offered to create visual backdrops for their exhibition. It had forced him to take his camera out, something he'd stopped doing.

"Don found out about an Irish-American Trust," Martha said, eyes bright, "set up by someone with Mayo roots. Apparently they fund projects of historical interest."

"Sounds good."

"We're discussing a memorial on Achill for tattie hokers, including those who died in Clew Bay and in Kirkintilloch. It's early stages of course," Martha added, closing her bag.

"Isn't there a memorial at Cill Damhnait cemetery?"

She shrugged, "There are headstones there, not the same thing."

He digested this.

"Anyway," she said with a wry smile, "some think it wouldn't be of enough interest."

She had his attention now, "Why not?"

"Oh," she grimaced, "there's so much competition for funding, etcetera. Meeting's next Thursday in Eilis's house if you're free?"

He nodded, said goodbye.

On the drive home he pondered Martha's words, tattie hokin was no longer of interest? He'd grown up with the story of the Clew Bay drownings, the thirty-two young people dying before they even boarded the boat to Scotland for the potato harvest, one a cousin of his mother's family. He knew it by heart, but hadn't thought about it in years and now he racked his brain to picture some marker, but other than the headstone in Cill Damhnait, couldn't think of one. And the same was true of those tattie hokers, burnt to death in Kirkintilloch, in the thirties.

A thought struck him. The Clew Bay drowning only predates the Titanic by… about twenty years and everyone's interested in that. The public obsession with the Titanic had always puzzled him until one night, in the College Bar he'd had a drunken conversation with Rachel Thornton, a History student he fancied.

"The Titanic disaster is a snapshot of early twentieth century society," she said like he was an eejit, "the haves and have-nots – bound for America in their strict social castes. Add to that, the arrogance of Empire, total belief in the infallibility of Engineering against Nature's forces …and what have you got?"

A disaster.

In every sense, since her tone had killed off any attraction he'd felt, but nevertheless, he remembered what she'd said. The Clew Bay disaster was a snapshot too he reckoned – of late nineteenth century Achill – an event which told a bigger story: poverty, land rents, migration, child labour, a snapshot which recurred up until the 1950's. If the Titanic was anything to go by, people responded to snapshots. By the time he reached home, he began to think that a tattie hokin memorial of some kind was an interesting idea, hadn't it kept the island going for generations, deserved recognition? Then he paused, was Martha reeling him in?

Watch your step, he told himself as he parked, he couldn't create false expectations. Unlike Martha and the other group members, he wasn't here to stay, was only on temporary licence. As soon as the building industry cranked up again, he'd be on his way.

3

Day four, Helen ran out of bread, milk, cheese, knew she was back at the point of misery she'd left London to escape. She'd no option but to push herself out the door, along the Sound to get food. The road was quiet, only the odd car and the sound of birds she couldn't see. Passing a modern bungalow, she noticed a raised garden bed, similar to the one outside Westgrove School, with deadly dull, low maintenance shrubs – but a surge of longing to be standing outside her school clamped her chest.

She waited for it to pass, trudged on, counting the weeks until November. *Remember, remember the fifth of November* – Guy Fawkes – burning bonfires, the smell of ash in the London air – a fitting portent for her return.

After ten minutes walking, still a long way from the Sound, she knew she'd never manage the return trip. It was either a taxi…but where on earth would she get one…or that bike. Now. She rang Mrs Kilbane's number. The woman was unfazed, if Helen wished to collect the bike, she lived further along the road in the Dooega direction. Teeth gritted, she retraced her steps.

Twenty-eight minutes later, she was on the path up to

the house, the row of fuchsia bowing under its weight of scarlet bells. A small, wiry lady shook her hand and led her into the high ceilinged blue kitchen where a range pumped out heat. It felt tropical after the walk. To Helen's immense relief, she offered tea.

Left alone, she studied the photographs, on one wall the Sacred Heart, St. Bernadette at Lourdes, on the other, photographs of children in Communion outfits and wedding attire. A large studio portrait hung at the centre – Mrs Kilbane, her husband, with four adult children, two boys, two girls, all in Sunday best and studied smiles. On a side wall was the next generation, pictures of babies and toddlers.

Mrs Kilbane returned with a tray and asked about her reasons for visiting Achill. Helen scrabbled together a mention of "research" about Grace Henry, the painter.

The woman had not heard of Grace, but knew of her husband, Paul Henry. "He's well known around these parts."

She'd been living alone since her husband's death ten years ago, but recently, her youngest son, Finn, had returned from working in Spain. "I don't know how long he'll stay," she said, shrugging her small shoulders, "he's between things."

The warmth of the woman made Helen feel at ease for the first time in days and suddenly, overcome by heat and tiredness, she longed to sleep a while in the deep chair. But the tea finished, Mrs Kilbane led her to the barn where an old tractor, farm stuffs were stored and in the corner, the bike, the newest item there – a wine coloured ten-speed Raleigh in good condition, tyres firm, and a front basket. Helen's heart lifted.

"My daughter Sinead bought it a few years back, but hardly gets up on it when she comes, so she's happy to have it used."

When Helen offered payment, she was adamant. "No, I wouldn't hear of it."

"I couldn't –"

"– it's on loan," she said firmly, "be careful on the roads round here, some drive like they own them."

Helen thanked her profusely.

Mrs Kilbane stood at the door watching her progress to the gate, so Helen didn't dare mount until clear of it, too nervous of wobbling or falling, putting the heart crossways in the older woman. At the bottom she waved then pedalled away.

*

It took Helen fifty minutes to ride to the supermarket, a severe test. She hadn't ridden a bike for months and sleeplessness had wreaked havoc on her body. About halfway there, she stopped to rest for several minutes, at inclines she had to get off, push the bike into the rising slope, gasping. Thirty–three years old, she was a wreck.

The few shoppers in the supermarket exchanged talk about weather and families; afterwards, Helen went to a different pub for coffee and scone, fortification for the return trek. A group of Italians ringed the fire, drinking Irish coffees, talking animatedly, as if arguing, the way Italians did.

In Florence, when they dived into cafes to escape the heat, Shane became hooked on watching this animated talk. August – one and a half years ago. What had she not seen then? What had she missed? Christ! She'd fled as far west as she could go to escape this; she finished, left.

*

Next morning brought a blue sky. She lay watching the hill, saw boulders dotted here, there, pockets of rushes further up, a few skinny trees clinging to life. On a morning like this it was a homely hill, nothing hateful about it, but not one she would come to know.

Then guilt began to hum, Isla must have begged, borrowed the research job from Clive. Why else give the job to an English Teacher, clueless about Art?

Isla said they were desperate: Clive had hired Thea, with an Art History Degree, who'd high tailed it off to Thailand with new boyfriend, leaving them in the lurch. "Clive has a thing about English Roses," Isla said wearily, "she looked like Kate Winslet."

"But researching what?" Helen asked.

"Digging around for a woman painter who lived on Achill in the early twentieth century."

"I don't know much about painting."

"This is a lightweight Biography, for a book about modern Irish artists, coffee table stuff. All I need is a general hoofer with a feel for the place."

"I… haven't been on Achill for years."

"You don't have to base yourself there, just visit. Thea did some preliminary work you can have. There's very little written about this woman, so if you could dig something up, talk to people, see how she was regarded … that sort of thing."

"What's her name?"

"Grace Henry."

"I've heard of Paul Henry … is she related?"

"Yes, his wife. But his fame almost eclipsed her unfortunately, hence the research."

By the end of the conversation, Helen had agreed to give it a go. But she hadn't yet lifted a finger and after breakfast, she faced Thea's plastic folder – *Grace Henry* – written in fancy italics.

Instant weariness, a woman painter, obscured as wife of… did anybody care a damn? Could Helen make herself care a damn?

One foot, another… stalker Philip again, still giving orders from behind his Bank desk no doubt.

She began sifting through a mish-mash of Internet printouts and pages of notes in messy handwriting – unreferenced! Thea's mind was clearly elsewhere, the most coherent part was information about Paul Henry, who, well known, was presumably easier to trace. Quickly, Helen knew she'd be near the starting line.

She spent an hour chasing an internet connection. When it finally settled, she sent the same email to everyone:

House is between a hill and the sea, with all mod cons, including dodgy internet connection. Weather variable, as expected, met a friendly neighbour. Holding up, miss you all, Helen xx

She said nothing about Galway – yet.

She closed Thea's folder, lay on the sofa. After a while she heard a car, voices, spotted a middle-aged couple go into the third house along. She ate beans on toast and as darkness drew in, the glint of lights coming from the neighbouring houses helped. She watched a BBC drama about a missing teenager, until sleep overtook her.

She slept for six hours, woke with a dream clinging, Chloe Howard wearing her green and orange vintage dress, dancing in a sunny garden, arms extended. These dreams were like goblins, chasing her, mocking her.

She forced herself up, walked out the road to get air. It was dry but cool, two cars passed, she took a side turning towards the hill which quickly ran out, had to turn back. When she returned, two girls were playing on the swing, and catching sight of Helen, showed no reticence.

"What's your name?" the older one asked in a strong Mayo accent.

"Helen."

"Do you live here?"

"No… staying a little while."

"I'm Róisín, she's Lena, my sister," she said.

They didn't look alike, Róisín, dark haired, Lena, fair Irish skin with ash blonde hair.

"Would you push us?" Róisín asked, formalities over.

For the next ten minutes she pushed – in strict rotation, thirty pushes each – one trying to outdo the other reaching towards the sky, a contest Róisín won easily, since she was taller. At one point Helen spotted a woman at their upstairs window, who nodded in her direction. She was probably late twenties, with a weary air.

"See you later alligator," they called when they went in.

"In a while crocodile," Helen replied, grateful for their company.

*

Desperate to hold on to some energy, she returned to her Grace Henry search. Little of any depth seemed to exist in the obvious places, or, where she found references, they referred to her primarily in relation to Paul. Maybe she'd been hard on Thea.

Slowly, hopping between sources, she managed to cobble together a picture of Grace's early life: born Scotland, 1868, in the Manse of Kirktown St Fergus, near Peterhead, the second youngest of ten, her father a Minister in the Church of Scotland, her mother a Londoner of good connections. Some of her early paintings were exhibited and sold through the Artists Society, when the family moved to Aberdeen. None had been traced.

A joint history of Paul and Grace offered more. In her early thirties, she went to Europe to study Art, first Brussels, then Paris, the Mecca. She went alone, which seemed brave. At the turn of the century, many Art schools and studios didn't admit women, except as artists' models and when, in the 1890's, professional schools opened their doors to them, they were barred from life drawing and anatomy classes.

Grace enrolled in the Delecluse Academy and lived in the Latin Quarter and it was there she met Paul Henry, a painter from Belfast, and by all accounts, they became soul mates. Both were influenced by the methods of Whistler, whom Helen had heard of, but knew nothing about.

Similarities in background between the two were remarked upon, both had Protestant clergymen fathers, both were emigrés and committed artists. They moved to London, where they married in 1903. The Henrys' move to Achill Island in 1910 was documented in several sources. It was planned as a two week holiday, on the recommendation of friends – but they stayed for nine years. Some detour!

By all accounts, Paul fell in love with the place instantly; however, each source focused on his decision to stay, making no reference to Grace's thoughts on the matter. Did she fall in love with Achill too or view it as a temporary phase? Clearly she agreed to stay and began to paint its landscape and people, but no source touched on her decision.

Helen spent another couple of hours browsing, turning up mainly the same information, until weary, she stopped. What she had established was available to anybody who tried site hopping, what the next steps were, she'd no idea. She knew nothing of Art History, hadn't a clue how to proceed. She was out of her depth, couldn't deliver on this. Before more time was wasted, she'd have to tell Isla.

She phoned Isla's office.

"She's at a Book Fair in Germany," Tanya said.

Shit. She'd forgotten.

"If it's urgent…?"

"No, I'll wait until she gets back."

*

Helen dreamt about Galway, but it looked like New York, with skyscrapers and traffic filled streets. When she got up, she googled it, but hardly recognised the place after a seventeen year gap. Was this another wild goose chase? God almighty, her mind shifted like a weather vane.

To rescue herself from her agony, she rang her sister Fiona, told her she was moving to Galway at the end of the month.

"Thanks be to Jesus, Helen!"

4

After the Friday shop at the Sound, Finn and his mother repaired to Shay's pub for scones and coffee. She liked to spread her money round the various establishments, irrespective of quality. He didn't argue.

They settled by the window and she instantly recognised someone he'd never seen before.

"Hello Helen," she said, to a young woman sitting alone at the next table.

The woman looked puzzled, then recognition dawned, "Oh, hello Mrs Kilbane."

His mother introduced her to Finn, "This is the lady who borrowed Sinead's bike."

They shook hands. She was different to expected, younger, attractive, long brown hair, green eyes. He'd assumed somebody older, more nerdy looking, when he heard researcher. Obviously, he was out of touch.

"Will you join us?" his mother said, pointing to a chair.

Helen hesitated, then nodded, "Thank you."

Young Deirdre interrupted with the delivery of their order and a brief chat ensued about her grandfather's health. Finn was still learning to readjust to chat – the oil which kept Achill's social wheels turning.

Talk over, his mother turned to Helen, "How's the research going?"

She paused, chewed her lip, "Slow-ly."

"Oh I'm sure something will turn up," his mother said.

Helen didn't look sure, asked Finn about his work.

"I do handyman stuff ... an out-of-work Quantity Surveyor, fled the building bust in Spain."

She looked surprised, "Which part of Spain?"

"South-East. I followed their boom a few years back, went with a contractor friend. Bad timing, they were as hard hit as here."

Then his mother intervened, "Finn's been planting my kitchen garden after it lying idle for years."

He registered that his mother had begun mentioning this frequently, a worrying sign.

"Oh, just winter veg, summer salad," he said to minimize it, "horticultural therapy."

Helen smiled then tentatively asked if he'd ever heard of Grace Henry?

"Yeah," he said, "definitely heard of her, but don't think I've seen her work. I've seen Paul's for sure, he's very famous round here."

"So I gather," she said grimacing, "Grace is hard to track down."

Finn thought of Martha. "I know someone, Martha Mulherne, involved in the local History Group, who might be of help?"

"There's a History Group?"

Why was she surprised? "Sure."

"I think Martha helps out in the Library too," his mother added.

"Westport Library?" Helen asked anxiously.

"Yeah, you could call in. Martha's a lovely person."

"If that fails," Finn said, "I could mention your name to her?"

"Thanks a lot," she said gratefully, "I've been a bit at sea…"

Finn glanced out the window at the heavy clouds, "Not hard round here!" He offered to put her bike in the van, drop her back, but she declined, said she needed the exercise.

*

On the road home his mother said, "She's warm, that girl, and clever I'd say, doing a research job."

"Yeah." He'd noticed how the two women got on and also how well his mother looked today, regaining her old self. Her heart attack had knocked them all sideways, she was the family's anchor, the bright side to their father's gloomier character. Her recovery had been slow but steady allowing Finn to get to know her all over again for which he was grateful. Finn is between things, she'd begun telling people, which touched him.

"Helen's very pretty don't you think?" she said.

He nodded vaguely. Helen was attractive, but not his type. Introverted he reckoned, but his mother was a great one for waifs and strays, as well as an inclination towards match making.

"Her research will be uphill," he said, "everyone knows about Paul Henry, but not much about Grace."

Finn suspected that research notwithstanding, Helen might be a refugee, running from something. She had an air of … uncertainty, that fragile edge he'd seen in outsiders who came down the years. Islands were magnets for people needing an escape. Still, coming here alone showed pluck, and if she lasted the winter, triple pluck. Lots of people managed a summer, but ran out of it when the crowds thinned and the winds blew in.

"There's something lonesome about Helen," his mother said wistfully.

"Yeah." Never underestimate his mother he reminded himself; a good listener, she sized people up well, but he was extremely wary of a two-lonely-souls scenario she might favour. Lonesome was a contagious disease in rural parts, he was steering well clear of lonesome.

*

Saturday, Finn set out for a much needed evening in Westport with his old mate, Sean. He hoped to make it before the downpour which was brewing in the dirty clouds to the East, got to Newport before raindrops splattered his window.

As soon as he walked into Molloy's Pub, Sean was on his feet to order him a pint and another for himself. He looked like a man hell bent on enjoyment. He and his wife, Tina, had twin boys eighteen months ago and he'd been confined to barracks since. "I've got a gate pass," he'd joked when he rang.

The pub was crowded, noisy, and Sean knew most of them. While Sean worked the room, Finn moved closer to the musicians, a fiddle, concertina and a guitar, two men, one woman, all young, all part of the thriving new guard keeping the old music going. He hadn't heard live music for months, it was a treat, despite the background clatter.

By closing time, Sean was all set for the night club in one of the hotels.

The thought appalled Finn. "Naw, they'll all be in their teens!"

Sean wouldn't take no for an answer. "No wonder your social life is woeful amigo, you need to live a little!"

How could Finn argue?

As feared, it was awful: the music too loud, boring, the crowd a mix of teens, twenty-somethings and some thirty-somethings who kept a safe distance from the rest. Again, Sean seemed to know everyone and after a while, disappeared into the crowd, while Finn, fish out of water, made feeble efforts – random chats with random people, then bored and boring, decided to leave. He was staying overnight in Sean's, needed his key so went looking for him.

A twenty minute search and Sean was nowhere to be found. Where the hell was he? Irritated, Finn went for air into the hotel garden, watched the stars glittering like chips of polished metal; now there was a job, polishing stars he thought, then sighed, recognising the symptom of fear ticking below the surface of his life: fear he'd lost his path and would never regain it. He drew cold air into his lungs to lift himself.

As he looped the corner to go back in, he noticed a couple in the gazebo. Hard not to be impressed by their indifference to cold, until suddenly he registered Sean's leather jacket, in a clinch with a woman. What the hell?

He called out his name, saw the two of them startle, look around.

"Be there in a minute," Sean shouted,

Finn walked into the foyer, waited six minutes, before Sean appeared.

"Sorry amigo," Sean said drunkenly, "met someone I hadn't seen for a while."

"I'm going, need your key," Finn snapped.

"Jesus, Finn-"

"-don't ever use me as your cover with Tina."

"What d'ya mean?" Sean was having trouble focusing.

"I mean if you want to cheat, don't drag me into it."

Sean's expression changed to annoyance. "What are you now, a Preacher? I'm on a night out, what's the harm in a bit of fun?"

Finn didn't reply and within a few minutes, they were both walking away, in silence, over the bridge towards Sean's house. Sean had insisted on leaving too. As they turned into the estate, he finally spoke, "Look, I don't get out much, just letting my hair down…"

"Tina's a friend of mine, so keep me out of whatever games you play!"

Sean dug himself further into his jacket, walked ahead.

*

The following morning Finn left early to avoid meeting Tina who'd want all the news of their night out. After a few chores in Westport he drove home, still pissed off. He thought Sean and Tina were solid, he also wondered if Sean ringing him had anything to do with keeping in touch. My old buddy – my arse!

"It's good to be back home…" he sang as he drove. But by Newport, he was less angry. Had he overreacted?

One of the problems of reconnecting with people after years, was not knowing how they'd lived in between. Maybe a snog in the gazebo was always part of Sean's social life and Finn was a tight arse who'd spoiled his fun. His years away had loosened his footing; he was no longer on firm ground.

Then a different thought – had he taken out some resentment about his own life on Sean? Childhood and college pals, Sean was now a County Planner, with nice house, wife, twins, while Finn's life showed no such gains. He didn't think so. Sean's wasn't the life Finn sought, but his alternative wasn't clear, to say the least. At thirty-five he was living a temporary life – between things – as his mother so aptly put it, which required patience (not his forte) and self-belief, (wobbly under pressure) that he would, in time, find his path.

Deep in ruminations, Finn nearly missed them, Gawina from the History Group and her son, trying to hitch a lift at Mulranny. They scrambled into the front seat next to him, chilled to the bone.

"Thanks so much," she said, "Simon has the van, he got delayed." She rubbed Wim's hands to warm them. "My friend's been ill, we were visiting her."

He smiled, "True kindness on this cold day."

"Her son is Wim's friend too."

"He's called Fergal," Wim said seriously.

Finn nodded, the boy always seemed bright as a button.

Finn first met Gawina and Simon, her partner, at the History Group, Gawina the more committed one. Finn had been impressed by her knowledge of the flora and fauna of Achill, understood later that for a weaver and knitter, such knowledge was part of her trade. He also liked her work, had bought scarves for his mother and sister from her. Originally from Eindhoven, she and Simon, a Mancunian, were alternative life-stylers, who'd met in West Cork, but finding it overcrowded, moved to Achill.

Simon was the island's new age smithy, bringing a skill in short supply, mending iron gates, fences, as well as making sculptures. Both worked from an outhouse beside their home, an old schoolhouse they'd refurbished in the Valley.

Gawina insisted on making him coffee when they arrived. Inside was warmer than Finn expected, the wood stove glimmering, "It's doing a good job," he said.

"It has made such a difference," she said, unlooping the hooks on Wim's duffel and helping him into his slippers.

"Coffee, decaff, chicory?" she asked.

"Coffee please."

Wim removed a dinosaur from a trunk which he launched onto various surfaces. "Jump, jump, higher, higher," he commanded.

The open kitchen-cum-living room had a black range at one end and a wooden stairs at the other which wound up to the converted landing and bedrooms. They had used recycled materials wherever possible and the feature he particularly liked was a long, narrow stained glass window at one end, which threw soft colour into the house. Simon had been driving past a church in the Midlands, which was being refitted with double glazed windows and bargained with the vicar for the green and blue stained glass. "Got it for a song," he said.

Finn didn't doubt it, Simon was a hustler, not one he was keen on. He'd helped him with the insulation a few months back, given him a knockdown price, but once finished, Simon tried to haggle further and then dragged his feet with payments. He didn't believe Gawina was party to it.

The tray arrived, coffee and pear tart, home-made. She had pulled her long blonde hair into a bunch behind her head, held in place by a knitting needle "It works better than most crap you buy in shops," she said.

She was one of those women who could look beautiful or plain at different times, which made her interesting. Short, stocky, with Nordic blue eyes, her hair was her standout feature: long, white-blonde, thick, a colour rare in Ireland. Like Samson, he reckoned, the hair was her source of strength.

"So," Gawina said looking at him in her direct way, "when are you coming back to the History Group?" Then without waiting for an answer added, "There's a good project, which will suit you Finn, to put up a memorial to the potato pickers, a memorial which will remember all of those who went."

Why did she assume it suited him? He stayed cagey, "Martha mentioned it."

"I think it would be very good to mark that history, for locals and visitors too?"

He nodded.

She studied him a moment, "Not everyone wants it. Maureen wants a book about traditional crafts, says there's memorials in the graveyard, so it would be hard to get money. Also Heritage targets…?" she raised her eyebrows

"What are they?"

She shrugged, "Something connected to tourism…I didn't understand."

"So, what type of memorial?"

"Oh, no suggestions yet, but a lot of people have old fashioned attitudes to memorials."

"Meaning?"

"They think it has to be a stone or statue, but many interesting things are possible. Lateral thinking is needed, Finn."

"Lateral thinking?"

She nodded vehemently, "A memorial can be a house, a mural, a window, a walk, a sculpture… so much scope."

Finn nodded, remembering stunning Spanish sculptures, murals in public spaces, sensed that Gawina would be a valuable group member in those discussions, but didn't want to get drawn in. He was wary of being press ganged.

The wind was now kicking up, time to go, which he did without making any commitment to the next meeting.

On the drive home, he recalled hearing a rumour that Gawina and Simon were splitting up. That would be rough. The refurbishment job had been a labour of love, every beam, nail, stitch belonged to them both. You couldn't divide that out like cutlery and bedding. He hoped for Gawina's sake it wasn't true.

It struck him that twice this week he'd had to avoid questions about the History Group, from Martha and Gawina, people he liked, respected. Dodging them made him feel slippery, evasive, but unlike them, he wasn't committed to living on Achill.

The island, pared to the bone for so long, could offer him no future. He was awaiting a sign… from the Achill skies… a head hunter… God himself? And if all those failed, he was setting hopes on Phil, who'd mentioned glimpses of an upturn in London building. London would suit him fine.

But soon, please, before Achill's mist and bogland reclaimed him.

5

At two in the morning, a sound startled Helen awake. It was different to the sounds she'd begun to know – sharp, loud voices rising and falling, a man and a woman rowing. She slid from bed, saw a light on in the girls' house. A short lull before it rose again; she couldn't hear words, just angry sounds. A light came on upstairs in the house the other side. That helped, she'd ring their bell if it blew up.

A shout was followed by a scream and then silence. Her heart galloped, she watched the other house for signs of movement – nothing – they must be holding their breath too. Then the silence was broken by a slamming door, a man heading to his car, the noise of the revving engine enough to wake anyone who'd managed to sleep through it. She stayed sitting by the window until the lights went out in the other houses. Now, wide awake, she thought about Róisín and Lena, in their beds, while that storm raged round them. Did they sleep or lie trapped, listening ?

Little chance of Helen sleeping now, she reached for her book, knowing she'd another good reason to leave this place.

*

But the weather Gods took over: rain for two full days, obliterating land and sky, a reconnoitre trip to Galway, too daunting. In London, rain was an inconvenience, but you still went about your business, on Achill, without a car, it was a controlling force, trapping her indoors. The house became a tunnel, visibility beyond the front window for about six feet and about two feet through the kitchen window behind. She kept the fire going, read, watched TV, dashed out for turf, raincoat over her head.

She spotted Róisín and Lena return from school, jumping in puddles before rushing indoors. No sign of the father's car, thankfully. Behind a curtain of rain, the only evidence of life was the hum of cartoons when she put a bag in the bin. As the hours passed, she remembered Mayo rain in childhood – endless games of cards, then hide and seek in the barn and she decided to do what they did then, stop wishing for the rain to finish – it was doomed – stay occupied, until someone would say, "Oh, the rain's stopped," and they'd race outside, maybe in time to catch a rainbow.

She began reading a short history of Achill, Ireland's largest island, which she'd bought hastily. The book began with early settlements and flew though waves of dramatic change, Anglo–Norman invasion, Tudor Conquest, the Penal Laws, the Famine – the same trajectory as for Ireland as a whole. Her attention was grabbed by a section about a Protestant Mission established in Achill, in 1830, when its leader, the Reverend Edward Nangle came to proselytise. Nangle was an effective organiser, the settlement built schools, a hotel and a hospital at Dubhgort. This was the first Helen had heard of it – a Protestant Mission on a

34

Gaelic speaking, primarily Catholic island? The man had not lacked nerve. And that wasn't all – he was committed to proselytising through the medium of Gaelic, which he had learned. The Mission, also known as the Colony, prospered, as neglect of the islanders by all, including the Catholic Church, was long standing. It was estimated that during 1847, the worst year of Famine, 5,000 of 7,000 islanders were depending on food relief. However, battles ensued between the Colony and the Catholic Church, a battle for souls, with soup as weapon – starving people pawns in the battle of Gods. Still going on she thought gloomily.

Later over rice and beans, she wondered why she was ignorant of Achill history and why she hadn't tried reading about Achill before coming? She knew the answer: stuck in her tunnel of misery, she'd failed to see what she needed to do.

As she'd failed to see clearly, that evening she asked Shane if something was going on between him and Chloe.

"We're trying for a baby and you ask me that?" he said outraged. "You don't know me if you ask me that."

He refused to speak to her for days, his anger filling up the flat and she'd been cowed. She'd failed to hold her ground, face the truth – he was right, she didn't know him.

*

Next day, she attempted to get air, but the front door strained against her and she knew she'd be driven back, saturated. She was stuck, so continued her history book, and Bingo – a mention of the Henrys, well Paul, with brief reference to Grace, his wife – also a painter – reduced to an addendum. They were described as part of the early twentieth century trail of language learners, writers and painters, drawn by Achill's stark beauty, its Gaeltacht and traditional life, which were, at that point, newly valued. This trail was aided by the arrival of the steam train to the Sound. Where the hell was it now?

Apparently the London, Midland & Scottish Railway Company reproduced a Paul Henry painting of the West for their tourist poster in the 1920's which became a huge success and thereafter an iconic image, leading to further commissions for Paul.

Caught up, she didn't notice when the wind dropped and the rain eased. When she eventually opened the door, it was dark, air damp, musty, with the sound of rivulets of water dripping from all directions. She was alone in a water world.

*

Next morning, Shraheens was a stranger: bright and green. For the first time, she felt in sympathy with her surroundings, all pawns to Nature's will. Without lingering, she set out on the bike for the Sound, determined to get the bus to Westport Library and find Martha Mulherne, the woman Finn Kilbane had mentioned who might know about the Henrys. She owed it to Isla. A car passed her, Róisín and Lena waved out the window, going to school.

Unfortunately Martha wasn't at the Library, but the Librarian offered her help.

"Grace Henry?" she asked, surprised.

"Paul Henry's wife," Helen said reluctantly, "also a painter."

"Let me look," and she tapped into her keyboard.

She printed off a brief biography, one Helen had already seen, then located a site about artists on Achill, Paul Henry, Robert Henri, Sean Keating, Derek Hill and a contemporary woman painter, Camille Souter, but nothing about Grace.

Isla wasn't wrong: Grace had been eclipsed, despite nine years painting on Achill. How unfair.

The Librarian suggested she try Paul's biography which Helen reluctantly agreed to. It was out on loan, but she reserved it.

She went to the Health Food shop then crossed the bridge. The sudden sound of claps and cheers caught her attention and there was a just married couple emerging from the church. The bride wore an off-the-shoulder white dress with a frothy veil, tenacious in the face of the wind chill factor, but she was beaming, oblivious to cold, as were many of the female guests, dressed in stylish, light outfits.

For her wedding, Helen had worn a pale blue silk dress she'd bought in a Chiswick boutique. The omens had been good that June day: the sun shone, the Surrey countryside was verdant.

Both sets of parents had overcome resistance to the Registry Office and attended, her mother looking dashing in a peacock feather hat. The celebration was held in a converted farmhouse, belonging to a friend's grandparents: prosecco on the lawn, dinner inside, followed by music and dancing until dawn.

"A brill-y-ant wedding," Fiona said, more drunk than Helen had ever seen her. "Thought it might be a damp squib, y'know what I mean?"

Her sister wasn't one to keep thoughts to herself, drunk or sober. Helen concentrated on holding her upright.

"Goes to show you Sis...better off without a lot of that wedding crap!"

So Helen thought that day too.

Shane had wanted "a public commitment" and she'd been persuaded.

"We'll do it differently," he'd promised.

Differently? They'd fooled everyone. Their wedding was full of crap – vows made, vows abandoned.

*

Back at the house, Helen fought off gloom by trying the Achill artists' site the Librarian had located, knew that searching for Grace Henry would require checking between the lines and chasing down boreens and byways.

In one of Thea's notes, there'd been mention of Paul being inspired by J.M. Synge's play, *Riders to the Sea*, and how it had captured a life unwritten. The West was viewed as the spiritual heart of Ireland, but Grace was Scottish, what did that mean for her? And what did the locals make of Grace and Paul, wandering round with easels? Were they eccentric outsiders or a welcome splash of colour on a dull day? And a harder question: what were the tensions of a husband-wife artist couple? When Paul's painting became a famous poster, how did Grace feel: happy for him; disheartened by lack of recognition for her own work or both?

Questions, questions – all she could do was list them. This job needed a sleuth not a researcher. When the Westport librarian rang to say the Paul Henry biography was in, she decided she'd pluck up energy and go. She needed to give Isla something new about Grace Henry, however small, before deserting her post; maybe Paul's biography would yield it.

Isla was a true friend, despite their unlikely start. When she arrived in Westgrove School, she stood out, dressed in smart striped trousers, white shirt and a string of pearls. Business Studies, Helen assumed and asked no more. She was dead wrong, Isla taught History and French. Their first encounter was at the copier, when Isla asked in a strong Scottish accent if she taught 2C?

"Tuesday and Thursday," Helen said, "they're bruising."

Isla looked relieved. "I appreciate your honesty."

"They're known as the horrors, if that helps?"

"It does." She smiled, "And you know, I'm not going to let those wee shits spoil my day!"

Helen was impressed by the combination of pearls and guts and later, crawling into bed, after two hours prep and marking, decided she needed more of that fighting form.

Without Isla, she might have gone under in the lambs-to-slaughter early years teaching. They were opposites: Isla pragmatic, self-accepting; Helen intense, needing to prove herself. Over their first bottle of wine, Helen told Isla that she admired her combative energy, while Isla said she admired Helen's powers of analysis. They'd become fast friends

"You save me time Helen, doing all that thinking," Isla once told her.

Painful to recall: Helen had failed utterly to do the hard thinking about Shane when it mattered most; when it would have saved her much, much more than time.

*

She walked out the road, lonely for Westgrove, noticed orange-red rosehips here and there among the straggling bushes, yellow and russet leaves along the ditch. She'd been oblivious to Autumn, *Season of mists and mellow fruitfulness …*

Class 5B, moans and groans about Keats' poem, "It's too long Miss."

Daniel Cappardi, so young, so dismissive, "What's he on about?"

Nevertheless, it was the key question.

Telling them it was the most anthologised English poem cut no ice, she failed with Keats until she brought in *La Belle Dame Sans Merci.*

The image of the knight-at-arms, alone and palely loitering, grabbed their attention.

"He sounds like he's on something, Miss."

"He is in a way."

"Opium?" Daniel's eyes hungry.

"Not exactly."

"Then what Miss?"

You could hear a pin drop.

"Something that takes you over – love, poetry, illness? He died of TB when he was twenty-five."

A short silence, broken by Natalie Dixon, old beyond years: "That TB was a killer wasn't it Miss, like AIDS?"

"It was."

Keats: a poet for all ages. Helen sat on the low bank, consumed with loss for 5B, Isla, Kate, her flat.

She could… pack her bags right now, ditch Achill, ditch Galway, take bus to train, train to city, bus to airport. Who'd stop her? Nobody would; nobody at all.

And that was the worst of it. She couldn't, couldn't face turning a street corner, bumping into them, arm in arm, their hideous happiness, their false concern, "Helen, how are you?"

And her tongue knotting with fury or spewing out bile.

"Why don't you sell your flat and move?" Fiona suggested. "Start over in a different area?"

Helen refused; it was her only home, bought with money from the sale of their parents' house. She loved it – near a park, the river, friends, work. Shane had taken everything else, this she would not let him take.

But it condemned her to this awful loneliness. It dawned on her now that she'd thought loneliness was a hole, a void, you could eventually fill. Wrong, wrong. Loneliness was a lump, a tumour, which gnawed and sucked her dry.

6

Sunday, Finn took his camera out of the back press and drove along the road to Cloughmore, the departure pier for the tattie hokers. Once a busy pier, only a few boats fished out of it now and in summer, holiday boats anchored. To the left, was Cill Damhnait Tower, of Grainne Mhaol fame, ahead the tiny island, Achill Beg, no longer inhabited, but there was nothing at the harbour to mark that annual journey to Scotland by generations. Why not?

He tried to recall when he first heard the story of the drownings, it was like he'd always known it, but one voice came through, his grandmother's, who talked of it as if she'd been there, always beginning the same way: "On a June morning, in 1894, about four hundred *grisheens* gathered on the pier, ready to get into the currachs which would take them out to the hookers, in the Sound. The hookers would then convey them to Westport Quay, where the Scottish steamer was anchored, waiting… "

There were a few hookers, that day, Finn recalled, four was it – yes – instead of five or six, part of the tragedy. The first one, the one which sank was Healy's, he knew that for sure, from her telling of the story.

Healy's was the biggest and loaded first, the young ones

scrambled on, impatient to get on their way. The tattie hokers were mainly young teenage girls, setting out to harvest potatoes in the mucky Ayrshire fields, some going for the first time. They were following a well-worn path, seasonal workers who would bring back their wages, sorely needed for rent, seed rate, debts. By all accounts, it was a fine day, a grand day for the journey.

Finn began to take photographs of the pier, Achill Beg, the Sound and a thought crossed his mind – maybe their journey round the bay could be photographed, stage by stage, as the basis for something? It was the same journey for generations. By boat would be best… Sean had a boat, but he'd probably lie low for a while, given their recent row. Could it be done from land? Then he copped onto himself, he was in temporary exile here, steady on!

If the truth be told, the History Group, especially Gawina, Martha, Michael, often overpowered him – Movers and Shakers – people firmly planted in this place, unlike himself, despite an undertow he sometimes felt sucking him back in. All the same, it was good to have the camera out again. Didn't it kill time, if time can be killed?

When he arrived back, May, his mother's cousin, his favourite relative, was visiting. The two women were discussing local news, their voices a melodic hum from childhood. On a whim he mentioned the Memorial idea.

"Who's this History Group?" May demanded.

"Michael Gallagher, Don, Eilis and others."

Well, it's about time," she said, "generations of us went tattie hokin and it shouldn't be forgotten."

It was one of the many things he liked about May, that she spoke her mind.

"Those were different times May," his mother said, "there wasn't money for anything."

"True," she said, "but there's money now, with them big computer companies up in Dublin and statues for the likes of Molly Malone!"

Finn and his mother smiled.

"You've a point there May," his mother conceded.

*

During the week his mother asked him to drop a bag of vegetables to Helen Bradshaw, since he'd be passing near her house. Before he'd time to answer she took off on a rap of sorts: Annie Reid had dropped a whole sack in; her vegetables were a lot fresher than the shop-bought ones; Helen probably didn't have much money and looked too thin.

All that for a bag of veg? "How could I say no after such persuasion Mam?"

She flicked the tea-towel in his direction like in his teens, when she thought he was being *too shmart*.

He called at Helen's house, in paint stained overalls and she looked thrown. His attire or she didn't remember him? "I'm not selling insurance I promise," he said, "I've a vegetable delivery from my mother."

The penny dropped and she invited him in. He was in two minds, but thought maybe she was as deprived of company as he was, accepted. She wore an oversized woollen jumper which emphasised her slightness, looked paler with her hair tied back. Maybe she was scrimping on food?

She peered into the bag, green topped carrots, potatoes, a few leeks, "They're lovely, tell her thanks so much."

"A cousin over supplies us and my mother's a great believer in sharing surplus."

A smile, then, "Tea, coffee?" and she ushered him into the dining room while she escaped to the kitchenette.

He sensed her awkwardness, so sat, studied the room – a typical new build, bought for holiday rental, solid enough, good windows, décor pre-IKEA, but in good nick. Quiet spot for someone alone though. "Any neighbours?" he asked.

"There's a family next door and an older couple, Anne and Paddy, in the house after, who seem friendly but aren't around much."

"Better than nobody."

She grimaced, "The family have two kids but seem… troubled. There was a heavy row recently, shouting, screaming."

"Be careful," he advised, "call the Gardai if it kicks off." He wondered if he should offer her his phone number, decided to, given the circumstances.

She looked reassured. "Thanks for that," then poured tea, apologising for only three biscuits.

A short silence so he went for an ice-breaker: "Have you Mayo connections?"

"My mother's from Lecanvey, we used to spend summer holidays there on my grandparents' farm. She moved to Dublin in her youth, met my father and that was that."

"Married a Dub?"

"Afraid so … I rarely mention it round here." When she smiled her face looked less thin. "How about yours?"

"Both Achill natives, though my mother spent a couple

45

of years in Glasgow, to see the world, before she settled down with my father who waited faithfully for her return."

Then talk turned to the Henrys and what he remembered of them growing up.

"Paul's paintings were dotted round the place, in pubs, hotel lounges, the school hall maybe" He paused, "A few of his paintings, the one of Croagh Patrick, men pushing out a currach were very familiar, like those old style John Hinde postcards were, though doubt Paul Henry would appreciate the comparison".

She smiled, "Probably not."

"There are loads of his paintings I never saw. I heard Grace's name, knew she'd painted here, but never saw her work, or wouldn't have recognised it." He paused, "So what's her painting like?"

"Well..." she looked suddenly anxious, "I haven't seen much of it, yet, that's my problem, tracking her down." She threw him a glance, "I'm an English teacher on a career break, a friend needed someone, so I took it on."

She sounded uncertain, as she had when they met in the pub.

"Interesting gig."

She sighed. "Someone qualified will write it up for a coffee table book about Modern Irish Artists or some such..." A pause, then, "Achill certainly draws artists doesn't it?"

"Yeah, the landscape's impressive."

"I read that there's a mystery attached to islands, y'know, they beckon people?"

"Hmm, with a bridge for easy exit."

"You don't agree?"

"Far more people leave than ever come to stay. It's hard

46

to make a go of it, a rock in the Atlantic, the neglected periphery for generations. All my family left."

"But you're back?"

"Temporarily. My mother was ill last winter, I was the only one able to come."

"Where are the others?"

"Australia, England, Galway."

She refilled his tea, looked directly at him, "You don't see yourself staying?"

He grimaced, "No. It's too hard to swim against the tide." He didn't want to get into this, turned to her, "Yourself, how long will you stay?"

She hesitated, "Not sure…depends on how the research goes."

As he drove away, he thought it was some lonesome set-up for a woman alone, and someone unused to it. What induced her to live in Shraheens on the brink of winter? Surely she could have based herself in Westport, Castlebar or even at the Sound? His instinct that she was a refugee of some sort was strengthened. But why do it the hardest way; what was she fleeing?

*

Back home, his mother said he'd missed a call from Kevin, that the weather in Perth was lovely.

It was always bloody lovely in Perth he thought.

"Kevin was sorry he missed you," she added.

A lie; it was something Kevin would never say, was part of his mother's attempt to deny, (patch up as she would have it) their rift. For Finn, each missed call was a dodged bullet.

When he'd first returned to Achill he'd repainted their old shared bedroom, furniture included, because it needed doing and to wipe out all traces. But he'd had a job persuading his mother to send Kevin's clothes to the Charity shop.

"He might need them sometime," she kept saying.

"Not in Perth Mam, and there's others could use them here."

She'd finally agreed, after asking Kevin first.

Right now Finn was hungry, the last thing he needed was a Kevin conversation, so he steered her into chat about his visit to Helen Bradshaw.

Before he fell asleep, he contemplated his isolated existence. Relief was what he felt after talking to Helen, social contact with someone new, someone his age, someone … uncertain… and she wasn't introverted he decided, more like shy. He missed that kind of contact more than he'd allowed himself admit, missed female contact, not just sex which he sorely missed but closeness, that interchange between men and women. He knew that his track record with women over the last ten years would be deemed poor by some. He seemed to have specialised in Bad Endings: with Alison after seven years, "You bastard"; with Isabel after six months, "*Bastardo.*"

A bastard in two languages?

It wasn't all my fault, your Honour. I swear.

He thumped his pillow to revive it, but it didn't clear his mind of depressing thoughts – the pared down existence he currently lived. All his friends, except Sean, lived elsewhere, so he'd settled for the odd GAA match with pints afterwards or the occasional mountain hike with his cousin, Phelim. The History Group was the only local group he'd joined and he was one-foot-in, one-foot-out, from the start.

In his defence he could argue that he'd planned to leave once his mother was back on her feet but the recession had blitzed his options. A ghastly thought now occurred – to an outsider did his life look perilously close to the lonely hill bachelor, living with mother? Christ, was it possible some locals saw him that way?

Deep down what was his worst fear? He knew the answer – being diverted from his purpose: leaving to find his new path. Meanwhile, had his life become one in waiting, one of killing time? Shit. He needed to shake things up, before it passed him by, while he waited for it to happen.

7

An envelope bearing Helen's name lay inside the door.

Helen, My mother would like you to join us for roast Achill lamb on Sunday about three if you are free? If you're vegetarian, we can also accommodate. Finn Kilbane.

Free? Hell yes, she thought, yes to sitting somewhere else, with people, chatting, eating food together… the extent of her deprivation dawned on her, replaced quickly by a flood of gratitude.

With a lighter step, she took herself to Westport library, sat within earshot of the weir and perused Paul Henry's biography. It was a large, beautifully produced book, and the irony of reading about Paul's life and work, because he was Grace's husband, pleased her.

There were early drawings from his London days but she quickly moved to the Achill work. Even to her totally uneducated eye, the way his painting transformed once he arrived seemed astonishing. The work seemed a total love affair with a place, landscapes and people pouring out, views of mountains, lakes, cottages, turf stacks, potato digging, fishermen, women, then later, landscape after landscape after landscape. There was no question but that Paul Henry had found his source of inspiration, and how satisfying that must have been.

According to his biographer, his reaction on arrival was intense and decisive, Achill talked to him and he decided to stay, but again no mention of Grace and whether she felt the same, although mention was made of Grace's slower pace of settling into Achill and of the difference in their artistic output. A whole body of work poured from Paul, while Grace's paintings moved more gradually.

To settle in such a remote place in 1910 was a daring act for both, an act likely to impoverish them – which apparently it did – and isolate them from friends and contemporaries in the art world – which it also did. When they exhibited jointly in Belfast a year later, the paintings were praised for their conviction, lack of sentimentality, (discarding chocolate box style) and their lack of stage Irishry! They were praised for their abandonment of the formulaic approach to rural life – whatever that was? Another question for her list.

A year later, writer and critic, AE Russell, invited them to exhibit in Dublin. Grace exhibited over twenty paintings, but their work was less well received, critics considered it overly influenced by Post–Impressionism. Helen had no idea how to assess that view, or why it would be considered a bad thing. Who could she ask?

She skimmed through Paul's many paintings, stopping at one of a bog, the knotty texture of the turf so lifelike that she touched the surface of the page to feel it. But all her fingers met with was the smoothness of a shiny page. This painting impressed her very much.

She had seen so little of Grace's work, she had no way of comparing or contrasting them but what she did grasp was the fierce commitment to painting they both possessed.

After 1912, it seems Grace became increasingly frustrated with the isolation of Achill, began visiting Galway and Dublin regularly while Paul preferred to stay put. This impacted on their marriage. According to the writer, they moved to Dublin for a while in 1915, Grace wanted to travel abroad, missed contact with European Art, especially Spain, but that plan didn't come to fruition and they returned to Achill. Probably an uneasy compromise.

In 1916 they exhibited in Dublin again. 1916 – the year of the Easter Rising, burning of the GPO, executions of the leaders – what did Paul and Grace think of it and how did that affect the Irish Art world? Was a line drawn between Art and Politics? Surely there were Volunteers on Achill? Disappointingly, the book made no reference to these events, gave no clues.

All too soon, Helen needed to move, get coffee, then the bus. She crossed the bridge and decided to try a small café called Gardenia. The coffee was reasonable, carrot cake mediocre but apart from the young waitress and her friend, it was empty. These café visits were a lifeline, where she frequently eavesdropped on chat, speculated about lives, but the two young ones barely talked, focused mainly on their phones. Roll on Sunday.

*

She arrived bearing a bottle of red wine and a bunch of lifeless, scentless pink carnations, the best of a bad lot at the Sound. Nellie opened the door, shook her hand. Inside, the table was set with a white linen tablecloth, a candle in the centre. Finn, wearing an apron, also shook her hand and took her coat. She felt suddenly shy, but once the three were seated and the food served – lamb, carrots, cabbage and leeks – she began to relax.

"They're Finn's leeks and cabbage," Nellie said.

"You're still amazed my vegetables haven't poisoned you, aren't you?" he asked, raising his eyebrows.

She shook her head, "I always knew you had it in you Finn."

He turned to Helen, "My father wouldn't let me near his kitchen garden, thought I was useless."

Helen was surprised, assumed everybody growing up on a farm learned how to grow things.

The meal was delicious, everything nicely cooked, she couldn't remember when she'd last had a roast dinner. Talk looped around: weather, Finn's work then Helen's research.

"It's going a bit better," she said, then asked Finn if he would mention her name to Martha Mulherne as he'd offered.

"I will, of course."

"Martha will be able to tell you about Miss Eva O'Flaherty, the woman who came and set up the knitting factory in Dooagh probably around the time Paul Henry and his wife were here," Nellie said. "My grandaunt Mary Aggie, worked for her. It was so badly needed round these parts. Like up in Donegal, the Board gave women the wool to knit and helped them sell their jumpers, socks, without the wool being supplied, they could only knit for their own families."

Helen made a mental note of Miss O'Flaherty's name, asked Nellie what Board it was, feeling another well of ignorance opening up before her.

"The Congested Board, I think they called it."

Talk stopped for the arrival of dessert, a Spanish trifle, which Finn had made with dried fruits soaked in brandy, topped with home-made custard and flaked almonds. Delicious.

"He's a great cook since his travels," Nellie said. "When he was a young fella, t'was all I could do to get him to wash some spuds." She raised her finger to him, "Should have sent you tattie hokin to learn about hard work!"

He raised eyes heavenward, took dishes to the kitchen.

Helen was trying to dig in her memory's recesses for tattie hokin, recalled Patrick McGill's book about hiring fairs and children going to Scotland to pick potatoes, but had never heard it in a Mayo context. She seized the moment, asked Nellie if tattie hokin had happened on Achill.

Nellie looked shocked at the question, leaned forward, "Yerra of course. Didn't Achill live off it for years and years, when there was no money to be made round here at all."

Treading carefully, Helen asked her if she'd ever gone.

"Not me, my eldest sister and cousins went, June to October, picking potatoes in Ayrshire. There was a local gaffer in charge of each squad of young ones, made sure they did their labouring, ten hours a day. That money was a lifesaver for families, with a wee bit for themselves maybe to get some clothes or yarns of wool to bring back." She paused, "'I'm glad I didn't have to go, t'was no holiday, a rough old journey, and hard mucky work." She paused, gave a rueful smile, "But when I saw a girl at school wearing a new dress from money she'd earned, I wished I'd gone too. Wasn't I the innocent one?"

Helen smiled, nodded, asked the question still puzzling her. "I thought it was only people from the North, Donegal and thereabouts, that went?"

Nellie shook her head firmly, "From Donegal, north Mayo and Achill. My mother and her sisters all went, my husband's brother, aunts and uncles. They were keen on having relatives going together, they'd look out for each other." She sighed, "It was just the way it was, for a fierce long time, right up 'til after the war was it?" she paused, looked at Finn who'd reappeared.

Finn nodded, "Yeah, it started to change then." He took orders for tea, coffee and left again – a busy host.

"After the war," Nellie continued, "less went to Scotland, more to England where they could get better work, all year round jobs, not just summers."

"How old were the tattie hokers when they went?"

"Yerra, from age eleven, twelve, into their teens."

Helen tried to picture her niece, Clodagh, setting off on that journey: unimaginable.

"It was a part of life," Nellie said, in that matter-of-fact voice Helen remembered from her own Mayo grandmother. How could she get more of that for herself?

"Did they always come back?"

"Some stayed if they were sixteen, or if a few from the same family went, the younger ones came back. Agnes, our eldest, stayed after one season, went to work as a maid in Glasgow. That's where she met her husband Stewart, who's Scottish, and she married over there. Others stayed, maybe moved to work in Lincolnshire, Lancashire or saved up their passage to America."

"Do you think the tattie hokin put them in the way of leaving for good?"

"Arra, of course it did," Nellie said, "and sure what choice had they? There was next to nothing here, not even a secondary school on the island until the 1940's and that took some getting. T'was a local man who got it off the ground to try and stop the emigration, but of course, you had to pay for secondary school then, no such thing as free secondary!"

Finn appeared bearing two Irish coffees and a tea for his mother.

"Have you been down to the Cill Damhnait cemetery?" he asked Helen.

"Not yet," she hedged.

"There's two large gravestones there to tattie hokers who died. One to those who drowned in Clew Bay in 1894, the other is from 1937, when a fire broke out in a bothy in Kirkintilloch, and ten of them were burnt alive."

"Twas locked at night, they'd no way out," Nellie added.

She looked wan now, Helen thought, realised that she'd pushed the mood in a melancholy direction.

Finn obviously thought so too, "Well," he said lightly, "here we are, good company, food, drink, warm fire, and we're talking sorrows."

Nellie smiled, rested back in her armchair and the cloud seemed to pass.

Helen also leaned back in the armchair, and for the second time, longed to fall asleep and not have to leave the warmth of this house.

*

Next morning she wrote notes from what Nellie had told her about tattie hokin, Eva O'Flaherty, the knitting factory at Dooagh, for fear those details would get away from her. Later she began sifting through memories of Galway: where she'd gone at eighteen with her friend, Sheila, for a week-end. A packed hostel – Americans, Dutch, French girls – all up early to travel on to Connemara, doing Ireland. She remembered buskers on the streets, a great bookshop, fish and chips someplace; later a smoke filled pub where they met two Australians who looked like characters from *Home and Away*. She'd fancied the dark one, Brad. They'd kissed and parted. Even Sheila was distant now, married to a French man, in Brussels.

Was Galway a pipe dream, demanding more energy than she possessed? She counted up the number of people she now knew on Achill, Nellie, Finn, Róisín, Lena... maybe Martha Mulherne, four more than she knew in Galway, then counted the things she'd known nothing about before coming here, the trail of artists, writers, language learners discovering the island, women knitters, Reverend Nangle's Colony, tattie hokin by children to Scotland, deaths by drowning and fire, all making dents in her ignorance of this island.

Galway was a city, mainly a dot on a map, another place altogether where she knew nobody at all. Was it another wild plan to escape a fractured life? Had she the energy to start all over and so soon?

She walked out the road, to clear her head. Truth was she felt daunted by Galway: arriving alone again, meeting new people again, finding her way around again. Slowly it dawned, she couldn't bear to move again. Right now she'd nowhere else to stay... except this corner of this island, the last stop before Amerikay.

She'd stay – no other option for now.

8

Ciaran Cooney, builder, offered Finn a job overseeing a
kitchen-diner extension in Kilgeever. Finn jumped at it –
work for two months. As he drove to meet the owners, the
first thing that struck him was the view of the Sheffrey Hills
in the distance, misty, magnificent. But once through their
gate, an ugly trench came into view and his heart sank. It
was the hallmark of a reckless DIY-er. He sighed, reminded
himself that work, the curse of the drinking classes, was the
saviour of the impoverished, so got out, rang the bell.

Finola Kerrigan led him into the current kitchen/
diner, which faced the road. It was beyond him why they'd
turned their back on the Sheffrey Hills, but he didn't ask.
The conversation was tricky from the outset, her husband
Will, had made a "stab at it", hence the trench. Finn nodded,
knew many Mayo men who believed they could turn their
hand to any aul job.

"The kids are getting bigger, we need it sooner rather
than later," Finola explained.

Sooner suited Finn, so the discussion began.

Finola wanted a new design, facing the Sheffrey Hills,
Will was reluctant because of costs.

Finn wondered why they hadn't sorted this out beforehand, but knew that relationship mediation was often part of house design. Over a long hour he watched Finola listen to Will's suggestions, nod, then suggest a revised version, sometimes pulling him along with her. Laborious love.

They broadly agreed on size and shape, but not which way it should face, and so Finn left with no estimated start date, which wouldn't please Ciaran.

"We'll ring you in a week,"Finola promised.

Finn sincerely hoped so; this could keep him afloat through Christmas and New Year.

On the drive back, to lift his spirit, he reached for Miles Davis' *Sketches of Spain*. Antonio had played it for him driving to Almeria, and Davis' trumpet was a revelation. The sweetest trumpet he'd ever heard, sweeter than he'd known a trumpet could be. His favourite was *Concierto de Aranjuez*, written by the blind composer Rodrigo to celebrate the bird song and gushing fountains of the palatial gardens. This track had everything: light and shade, joy and longing, a balm at the end of a day of costings, arguments with builders, suppliers, in half-baked *Ingles-Espagnol*.

He dug down for snapshots: a day in Guardamar, siesta time, the others asleep, wandering down to the sea, a long, clean, empty beach, pale green water with shards of silver, too good to miss – he stripped to his jocks and plunged, only him and two sail boats tilting further out. This is why I came, he thought.

Another one… driving alone near San Javier, he took a detour off the main road, found himself in an area of large open fields, all tilled. The white-grey, dry soil was alien, like soil beyond redemption, but a crop of artichokes flourished, their spiky heads reaching above splendid leaves. He'd eaten artichokes once, at Phil's birthday bash in some upmarket restaurant, wondered what all the fuss was about, but here, in all their leafy splendour, he loved them, felt like one of those urban kids, on a Jamie Oliver programme, who'd never seen a head of broccoli outside of an Iceland frozen pack. Then the crop changed to citrus orchards – glossy green leaves, yellow and orange globes. He wished he could have walked his father along here, just once, and watched his face as he tried to fathom how this arid soil could produce such bounty.

*

On Thursday evening, after much dithering, Finn pushed himself out to the History Group meeting in Eilis and Don's house. The house overlooked the sea at Saulia, a refurbished, extended cottage on Don's family home-place. A nice job, past and present combined well, befitting two historians.

He was late, the group deep in discussion: Eilis, Don, Martha, Gawina, Michael, Maureen. While Don poured him tea, Eilis recapped: they'd made contact with a Trust, interested in funding projects of historical interest. There were two Achill proposals from the group, a book about traditional crafts and, currently under discussion, a memorial to tattie hokers, which would recognise its long history and include reference to the Clew Bay Drownings and Kirkintilloch deaths. Eilis' summary was as neat as she was: hair in place, clothes pressed, shoes polished.

Within minutes the discussion moved into heated debate, with two clear battle lines: Martha, Gawina, Michael, passionate proponents of the memorial, Eilis, Don unsure, Maureen the most vocal in opposition. Finn was used to their forthright debates but this seemed more polarised, three versus three. High stakes, he decided, and the book lined room added a claustrophobic atmosphere.

Maureen, who worked with a Tourism organisation, spoke about trends in heritage funding, argued that the Memorial stone erected for the centenary of the Drownings at Westport Quay, made another tattie hokin memorial obsolete.

Finn didn't even know the stone existed, stayed silent.

Don, ever the accountant, agreed. "The Westport Quay memorial would probably scupper any chance of funding."

But the Gang of Three were not deterred.

"It's a striking stone marker, bearing their names," Gawina said, "but gives no information about tattie hokin, so there's no context!"

Next up was Michael, who'd never left Achill, on principle, a local teacher for thirty years. "For all an outsider can tell from that," he said, "the thirty-two victims could have been out for a boat trip. Context is everything."

"If tattie hokin was a key part of the island's survival system, surely that makes it worthy of remembrance?" Martha asked.

Round it went, tension rising, falling, rising again.

Finn had stepped into a pressure cooker, didn't know how to participate. Martha's next contribution helped: she drew a comparison with the Famine Walk, the other side of the bay, Delphi Lodge to Louisburgh, initiated in memory of those who died along that road, and making links with global famines. "It's really well supported every year, people want to remember," she said.

Nobody disagreed with that, until Maureen fired an arrow, "But the key question is, do Achill locals want the history of poverty and migration memorialised at this point in time?"

Perhaps this was the nub of the conflict, Finn thought.

Michael took it on, spoke calmly, seriously. "Locals I've talked to see tattie hokin as a badge of pride, it kept this island alive for a long, hard century! Isn't it important for us to own it? The quay at Cloughmore hasn't a hint of the hundreds and hundreds who passed through it on route to Scotland, though the Council are planning something down there to remember Grainne Mhaol. Why is only Grainne to be remembered? Don't we need to remember the ordinary people's history too? And wouldn't it be interesting for visitors? A memorial could be integrated into the Achill Tour, Scoil Acla Festival, into a walk. Besides, wouldn't we consult the local people?"

A silence settled on the room, until Maureen broke it. "I wouldn't argue with anything you've said, Michael, my concern is about funding. I think a memorial is an ambitious, complicated project. A book about traditional crafts would stand a better chance, easier to put together, could be sold at home and abroad, and at least we'd end up with something!"

Don nodded, "Unfortunately I think that's true."

Eilis suddenly put Finn on the spot, requesting his opinion. He said it surprised him there was no memorial, and thought it was a good idea. Tattie hokin, in his view, was a snapshot of an era, and people seemed to relate to historical snapshots, the new Titanic Museum in Belfast an example of that.

Then time was up, Eilis proposed the discussion be continued at the next meeting and asked members to bring provisional ideas for what type of Memorial they'd suggest.

Everyone looked relieved, except Maureen who looked unhappy.

On the drive home, he thought about Martha and how her intervention about the Famine Walk to Louisburgh had helped him join up the dots. She was something of a mystery to him, born in Dublin she'd spent thirty years working as a Social Worker in London, work which had burned her out, she said. When she retired early, instead of putting her feet up or taking a cruise, she moved to Achill to make a new home for herself and became an active part of the community.

"Did you not consider Westport," he'd asked her once, "more people, more options?"

"It's a bit trendy for me," she said with a grin, which he wasn't sure how to interpret.

He put on Nigel Kennedy's *Gershwin's Preludes*, let it wash over him. He needed distraction from a nagging fear that his presence at the meeting had created expectations. Yes, he wanted to shake himself out of his rut, but… he wasn't going to be around for long… so a fine balancing act was required.

*

Back home, his mother was on the phone, "He's just in now Kevin," she said, and with no more ado, handed the phone to Finn.

Kevin was in talkative form after a few beers, filled Finn in on work, kids, Lou, then asked, "You moving on soon?"

Finn kicked to touch. "Hopefully, but the downturn is still down this side of the globe."

"So what are you up to besides the kitchen garden Mam keeps telling me about?"

"An extension job," he lied, since it wasn't in the bag yet, then to deliberately stir it, said, "just been to a meeting of the local History Group – Michael Gallagher and a few others."

"History Group – Jays, isn't there too much history there already?"

Kevin never failed to talk shite.

Finn expanded. "They're interested in putting up a Memorial to tattie hokers."

"They'd be better off looking forward instead of back, if you ask me."

He couldn't resist, "Well you know what they say, those who ignore history are doomed to repeat it."

"Bit deep for me Finno! Don't get stuck in the past is more my kinda thing."

Always the last word, Finn knew if he didn't let it go, they'd be here for an hour. "Each to their own," he said, "my regards to all," and finished the call. This head butting never ended.

His mother came in from the kitchen, "That's good ye had a chat!"

"As you know Mam, we don't see eye to eye," he said, unwilling to play along.

"It's a shame," she said, "yous should try harder."

He didn't respond. When he first returned, Finn had tried to talk to her about Kevin but hit a closed door. Family was sacred: blood, land, loyalty – superseded all disagreements for her.

Then she asked him if Kevin had told him his "news"?

Finn shook his head.

"They're planning to visit us in Spring or early summer."

It was the *us* which worried him; Spring, early summer were other seasons altogether.

"Oh right."

*

In the bedroom he was left with that wired feeling which Kevin always provoked. Music, he thought, the punch of the eighties – Smiths or Radiohead? He opted for Morrissey, lay on his bed singing along with *This Charming Man*, the title belying his current state of mind.

9

Helen was at home, wearily skimming internet sites in her search for Grace, about to abandon it, when she stumbled on a reference she'd not come across before. Grace Henry was in a catalogue of artists who'd exhibited in two Dublin exhibitions and furthermore... the catalogues of these exhibitions could be viewed in Dublin's Pearse Street Library. Dear God, she'd not been paying close attention, could have missed it as easily as found it. A light in a tunnel, the first one, she gave a loud sigh of relief.

And then it dawned, she'd have to go to Dublin to see them... and what was the point of doing that since she wasn't qualified for this job anyway? But, she couldn't waste this opportunity to pass a new reference to Isla, who could pass it to whoever took the research over, a person who knew what they were doing. Surely Isla would understand?

*

Two days later, she woke at first light, Shane sitting across the table in the flat, his face pale in the candlelight, his mouth moving with words she refused to hear. Christ. She batted him away, got up. Movement was her only hope, she'd go to Pearse Street tomorrow on the early train, look for Grace, then she bit the bullet and rang her sister Fiona, suggesting a meal together in the evening.

Fiona was cool, disappointed she hadn't been in touch but agreed to a meal, offered her a bed. Helen had delayed ringing her because Fiona would want her to talk it all over – again. Her sister still believed that talking helped.

Next morning she cycled to the Sound, caught the bus and once on board the train, watched wet fields and sheep flash by before drifting off to sleep.

The Dublin sky was grey-dull, people staring blankly through the Luas windows as it bore them to the city centre. She moved quickly through the IFSC, passing three young women smoking in a huddle outside their office, despite the drizzle.

On the Sean O'Casey Bridge, a man on a damp blanket was begging with a cup from Insomnia. She averted her eyes, nervous of stopping to search her purse. Below the bridge, big, bedraggled seagulls standing on the steel legs waiting for food paid her no heed.

In Pearse Street Library, Helen became a member instantly. The mood of quiet industry was like pre-exam days at Belfield, when feverish study sweated the walls and it warmed her. Within ten minutes she had obtained the two catalogues. The first: *Irish Women Avant Garde Painters*, included Grace Henry, but disappointingly, had no visuals, only a list of works. The title however, alerted her to another gap in knowledge, which she added to her list: Avant Garde painting.

The second catalogue was a much larger gift: *The Poetic Art of Grace Henry H.R.H.A*, an introduction, by Antoinette

Murphy, written for a joint exhibition with Paul at the Hugh Lane Gallery in 1991, the first joint exhibition since the 1930's. Some gap, she thought. But, yes – finally – copies of her paintings.

Now that they were before her, Helen paused. What if she didn't like them? No matter, she was resigning the job. She opened the catalogue, perused each work, once, then a second time.

The range of work hit her first – Mayo landscapes, people, a luminous sunset in the West, paintings from Italy, France, in vivid Mediterranean tones, a Dublin dockland painting – rows of dockers' cottages in an area a stone's throw away from where Helen was sitting. It was a social document of another era, the area now unrecognisable with its glass walled offices, hotels and two new bridges.

The second revelation was the bold use of colours, though she didn't know why. She sat back, they were lovely – absolutely lovely – strong, interesting, varied.

It had taken her two weeks to find any of this woman's work – she'd dithered, doubted, dragged her heels, and here they were, only a train ride away! She'd been a dosser, a wastrel.

The writer of the article admired Grace's work, saw her as a prime example of a "forgotten for a time" artist and referred to her "large body of beautiful, intimate pictures." She also referred to Grace's lack of talent for "autobiography or self-publicism, unlike her husband, Paul, which helped to keep his reputation alive and his prices firm."

Helen sat back, let out a long exhalation. Finally, finally, an Art commentator offered commentary on a number of the paintings in the exhibition. It was a wonderful gift and Helen gulped it all in.

It also mentioned her later years, as impoverished, nomadic, although still painting and praised some of her late flower paintings as, "of tender beauty."

What had befallen Grace in later life to leave her poor and rootless?

Helen perused the paintings one last time, knew, even to her untrained eye, Grace Henry was worthy of attention, should be returned to the light, but… she couldn't do it, someone else had to. It needed an Art Historian, who understood painting, someone fit for purpose.

*

From a café Helen rang Isla with the good news.

"Wonderful," Isla said. "The book deadline is pushed back to May," she added, "so, there's less pressure on you."

Helen couldn't do it, couldn't bear to spoil the first bit of good news by resigning. Maybe, extra time would help her cobble more bits together and she'd exit with some pride.

"Clive's farting about as usual," Isla complained, "he has a good nose for stuff, but doesn't know what a deadline means!"

Helen knew all this about Clive, but found it comforting to hear it again, a slice of life other than her own diminished one.

"Enough of me," Isla said, "how are you girl?"

"OK."

"OK enough?"

What to say? "Yeah."

They settled for that.

*

The two sisters met at an Italian restaurant in Temple Bar and as always, Fiona looked snazzy in a stylish black coat with silvery-green velvet trim.

"Great coat," Helen said as they embraced, conscious of her own ageing black one, stylish once, now worn. Is that how she looked herself?

Over dinner they talked about Robin, the kids, Achill, but Fiona was cool, brittle. Helen knew she was angry with her but she concentrated on her tasty spinach and ricotta pasta hoping the wine might soften Fiona's edge.

When the topic turned to their parents, Fiona said, "Dad's talking about giving up his golf!"

"That would be disastrous," Helen said, "I didn't know."

The implication of that hung between them.

"I told him – no way," Fiona continued, "Maria can come in another morning." She raised her eyes to heaven. "They've enough money for that. He agreed, to shut me up!"

"Well done," Helen said, swamped with guilt. Their father had become more and more their mother's carer since their move to Spain, and bogged down in her own misery, Helen had neglected them, left Fiona to carry the can. "I'll ring him," she said, a paltry offering.

"So," Fiona asked, turning a serious gaze on Helen, "how are you?"

"I'm y'know… alright. Been doing the research, day by day, it's …occupying."

Fiona refolded her napkin. "Are you doing any better?"

She bit back from saying that being here meant better, but knew prolonged misery was hard for people to bear. She offered some progress, "It's better away from London."

"Good," Fiona poured them both more wine, "even in the wilds of Achill?"

Helen nodded, no reason to disagree.

"Shane turned out to be such a bastard!" Fiona said.

Helen nodded again, no reason to disagree with that either. It was the most frequent, well intentioned comment she'd heard since the split. At first it helped, comforted, like she wasn't a fool, but now it made it worse. Why hadn't she got over the loss of a bastard?

"What's happening about Galway?" Fiona asked.

"Well, it feels like starting over again, doesn't make sense, I'm going to stay on Achill until I'm ready."

"Thanks for telling me!" Fiona raised her voice, "What am I – the big bad wolf? "

"Of course not, when push came to shove I realised that I know some people on Achill now, but nobody in Galway."

"Are you absolutely sure about that?" Fiona looked disbelieving.

She nodded.

They ordered coffee, but Fiona couldn't let it rest, "I worry about you Helen."

Helen wished for any other conversation, but Fiona would take it personally. "I know," she said, "but people worrying about me is unnerving."

Fiona looked instantly frustrated, "It's because you're important to us."

"I appreciate that, honestly, but it makes me fear I won't get through it…" She was tired, stumbling for words. "That's why I had to get out of London." Then like a small light at the end of a passageway, Helen saw it. "I needed a break from all that tragedy – to be anonymous, live in the present and on Achill there is nothing but the present."

Fiona was stirring her coffee round, giving nothing away.

Helen ploughed on, "Strangers, the few I've met, take me as they find me, I've no past for them. It's easier." The truth of what had been instinct in London was now dawning.

Fiona leaned forward, "Aren't you very lonely?"

She nodded, "That's the flip side ... but for a while, it's the best I can do." She held Fiona's stare, "Does it make sense?"

A shrug, "I guess."

They sat in silence a minute and Helen thought about another truth she could not tell: in her depleted state she needed to keep Fiona at bay, something she'd done since childhood – when the force of her sister's personality, her certainty, threatened to overwhelm. Fiona had always seemed good at everything, except knowing when she should hold back – let Helen fall off the bike, drink cheap cider, date dodgy Liamo, burn dinners; fail – yes – but try.

She went to the Ladies, it wasn't the time for that conversation.

Over breakfast next morning, she had fleeting encounters with Clodagh and Stephen and the changes in them threw her. She'd seen photos but hadn't seen them in the flesh since last Christmas which she'd spent with them. She was in rag order then, depressed and no fun. Clodagh was a teenager now, tall, slim and wearing her uniform shorter than she used to, Stephen was shy with her. She'd forgotten how time mattered with kids, how long a year was in their lives.

Left alone briefly with Clodagh she apologised for the gap in time.

Clodagh shrugged, "Sorry to hear you and Shane split up ...are you OK? " she said, which seemed very grown up to Helen.

"I'm OK," she said," and then they were gone out the front door with Fiona on one of those family winds which lifts everybody at the same time, leaving Helen alone in the kitchen.

With time to spare before the train, she walked up Grafton Street, past a jazz saxophonist busker and headed for Stephen's Green. The day had brightened, though the willow trees looked woebegone, weeping their troubles into the pond. The ducks floated by, impeccably groomed. On Sundays she and Shane used to sit in the Green watching the ducks, reluctant to part after spending the night together in Joe Byrne's borrowed flat, lying on the same grey unwashed sheets and duvet as Joe and others, wishing for silk, like in some novel, but settling for what they could get.

Soul mates – Shane said, keen on the transcendental then.

"Full of shit," she said aloud, which nobody heard, or if they did, didn't care a damn.

The melancholy of the willows was contagious, she left.

*

At the Sound she retrieved her bike. It was getting dark, she had to cycle slowly, her puny light not up to the job. Each bend of the road dragged, until finally, exhausted, she reached the house, ate, watched darkness envelop Corraun. But slowly, the satisfaction of discovering Grace's paintings began to fade and a seam of sadness ripped her open. Shane was back, dragging her down that hateful tunnel to the last Saturday night, in the flat. The order of his telling was still blurred – he'd sidestepped, gone around, back, forth, before the hatchet fell. She'd been slow on the uptake, stuck in her own groove, fearful he no longer wanted to try for a baby, that he wanted a break from the temperature monitor, ovulation charts which had taken over their sex life. He'd been avoiding her, overworking, so Saturday evening, she'd cooked dinner, lit a candle, determined she'd make him talk, believing herself brave. Instead, she'd sharpened the knife, handed it over.

At first it was talk of the baby, the pressures, all that, and then he wasn't talking about the baby, somehow Chloe Howard was in the conversation, how she'd moved to London from Brighton and Helen was thinking what has she to do with the baby? Slowly jagged words began to pierce through, Shane talking about meeting Chloe Howard for a drink and about Helen's week-end in Suffolk with Isla and thinking what has Suffolk to do with the baby and Shane saying he'd slept with Chloe Howard that weekend – and then he was talking about feelings – feelings – he had for Chloe Howard and a scream began to build inside her – suddenly she was on a high wire with yawning gaps opening on both sides – and she knew she was going to fall, down, down, and she held onto the edge of the table thinking, don't look down, don't look down, as though that would save her. But then it was impossible to hold on any longer, nothing was solid and she was plummeting and the scream inside her head was pouring out of her mouth, "Bastard, you fucking bastard," and hitting him with the green cushion which broke over his head, all the time screaming, screaming. Then she was running to grab her coat and bag and away from her flat while he stood, stunned, in a haze of feathers. She took a taxi to Isla's and on her way felt her heart cracking, believing that the worst imaginable thing had happened.

Now the current had her, no point thrashing against it, for it would pull her downwards, regardless of effort, to where there were only moments, this moment, then another, all bleak, all blocked of light. Over months, she'd come to know she couldn't escape its force; must stay still, hold on, until finally, emptied out, she would be dumped back where she'd started.

10

Finn woke to icy window panes and dots of sheep huddling on the hill. By afternoon, a blanket of mist had vacuum packed itself around the house. He stayed close to home, reading, listening to music until he wearied of that. Desperate for some company, he wondered who he could ring to share a good bottle of Chianti: Sean was a no-go, Gawina possibly…but he didn't know the set-up with Simon and Phelim didn't drink wine. Sean had hit the nail on the head about Finn's "woeful social life". Then he thought of Helen Bradshaw. Would it seem odd if he rang her? Jesus, might she be feeling vacuum packed too?

He dithered, then chanced it, asked how she was, and then, if she was free Saturday evening to help him drink some very good Chianti, a gift from a client.

An awkward pause, she was taken off guard and then an unexpected answer, "Eh…sure. I'll get some cheese."

The mist must be getting to her too.

*

She looked different when she opened the door, her hair

loose, longer than he thought and a nice nutty brown colour but she was distant, led him in then busied herself with cheese and crackers. Was she having second thoughts he wondered while he took his rain gear off?

The Chianti proved a great ice-breaker – ruby colour with a warm deep taste. Helen said it had been a long time since she'd had really good wine.

"Is it a thanks from a client?" she asked, sitting opposite, cheese and crackers spread between them.

"I wish! More like the last five percent of the bill! The guy owns a restaurant – just keeping his head above water – so I settled for a half dozen."

"Barter?"

He nodded, felt himself relax. The wine, cheese and warm fire reminded him of evenings he used to have in Galway and Manchester, when he had a social life.

After chat about Achill, they unexpectedly began talking about themselves. In response to her questions, Finn gave the summary of his adult life: college and work in Galway, move to Manchester, then to Spain, apartments going up like Lego blocks, halted by the building crash. He planned to work on a South African housing project but was stalled by his mother's heart attack and returned to Achill.

"She seems so well now," Helen said,

"She is, thankfully."

"Is South Africa still an option?"

"No I missed that boat," then speaking more truthfully than she could know. "Now I'm a man in waiting."

"For…?"

"A sign from the Holy Ghost?"

She smiled, "Anything so far?"

"No, but my mother believes it will come."

Then in response to his questions, she gave him her summary: Dublin, college, moving to London with boyfriend, later husband, staying ten years; highs and lows of teaching; parents leaving Dublin for mother's health, to Torrevieja, Spain, (a place he knew, a random, surprising, connection) now a career break in pursuit of Grace Henry.

He registered the gaps, no mention of the husband, didn't know whether to ask, chanced it, sideways. "You wanted time out of teaching?"

She hesitated, threw some coal on the fire, then said she'd split up with her husband, needed to get away.

As he suspected. "Were you together long?"

"Twelve years, married four." Then in a twisted voice, she said, "He met someone, fell in love, left: Hop-Skip-Jump." She grimaced, "Sorry, that's the wine talking!"

"*In vino veritas*?"

She shrugged, seemed on the edge of upset and to level the playing field he mentioned his own long term relationship with Alison and their break-up after eight years.

She was looking into the fire, turned to ask, "Why did you break up?"

He told her about moving to Manchester, Alison to do a much sought after Masters in Social Policy, he to a bog standard job in an architect's office, so they could be together. A two year deal. "But the best laid plans went awry. Alison was head hunted for a dream job there, by which time I couldn't wait to get out of it."

"Difficult."

"Yep. She took the job, I went to Alicante – a trial break – in reality a slow death. Irreconcilable differences, as they say in the Law courts … she didn't want to leave Manchester, I didn't want to go back." He topped up their glasses, "Even our versions of the ending were irreconcilable! Alison insisted I left her, whereas I know she left me – for the job." He paused, "So, what next for you?"

"I'm here to put the sea between me and him. That's as far as I've got." She described the small world problem, her husband's new partner a friend of friends, they'd moved in together nearby, so staying in London was impossible, until she could manage... the proximity.

He looked at his glass, "I wonder if Chianti is the wine for broken hearts?"

She gave a small smile, "Suitably Italian, like those tragic operas."

"Hmm." Then a short silence which he broke. "Just think, we could have spent the evening talking about something important, like ... Art ... which I know very little about and gone home a more cultured man?"

She entered into the spirit, "Or football," she suggested, "which I know nothing about but millions think extremely important and I'd have become ..." she scrunched her face, "football crazy?"

"Doubt it. So," he said, "next topic?"

"One last question to complete the tragic opera, and then Art or football ...did you see the breakup coming with Alison?"

It surprised him. Who does? "God no," he said ..."though the seeds were there when I looked back."

"Is that because you saw what you thought was there, not what was in front of your eyes?"

"Whoa, deep!"

She shrugged, waited for an answer.

"Don't most breakups blindside someone! Isn't that the essence of tragedy?"

She shrugged, "I suppose."

And there they left it, talked for a while about Helen's discovery of Grace Henry's work in Dublin, and he heard a new energy in her voice.

At midnight he rose to go, refused to take the unopened bottle home. "Sure, maybe we can drink it another time... when we have that conversation about football."

"Okay, a deal!"

At the door, he thanked her for her hospitality, kissed her on the cheek. She stiffened at the touch, like a scared rabbit.

He walked home, under a clouded sky and it seemed to him it was the mist, as well as the wine, that allowed them exchange bits of their intimate lives – strangers stuck in a stalled train, with only talk to pass the time and some ... necessity to do it?

But it also stirred up Isabel, and sadness. A whirlwind romance with an operatic ending: three months in Alicante, no mates, little social life, (was a pattern emerging?) Antonio, the architect, had introduced them, and a couple of weeks later, they'd gone to bed together. Isabel, younger by eight years, had brown eyes, brown skin, spoke English and was beautiful – he'd been instantly attracted – but the urgency, the strength of the sex took him by surprise. And so it had been for months. Week in, week out, he couldn't wait to be with her, and she likewise. But gradually...the sex had levelled out, and their differences heightened under the blue skies. With the certainty of youth, she wanted them to move in together, while he, feeling old for her then, didn't. It broke her heart, she believed he'd used her, like a holiday romance! *Bastardo*.

It wasn't true; he'd loved her for a while, but the love had run its course. He had regrets, he shouldn't have jumped in so quickly. Unfair to her, he realised later, he and Alison had just finished after a long time, so how emotionally stable was he?

In their bitter bust-up, Isabel told him she'd imagined him as her future husband, *mi marido*. It gutted him; he wasn't ready to be anybody's husband.

That night his dreams were full of high cranes on the Alicante skyline and Spanish minarets along Achill Sound.

*

His Chianti evening with Helen lingered, he'd enjoyed it, found her attractive, but her break-up sounded heavy so attraction was best parked. Something unsettling about what she'd said: You see what you think is there.

He and Alison had been the perfect couple – according to his sisters and Phil, though he was no judge. Finn recalled the night Alison had rounded on Phil and his girlfriend, Sheila, a couple who specialised in rowing and making up, publicly and privately. A foursome night out in the pub, but with too much drink taken, a row started. Finn couldn't remember why Sheila was offended by something Phil said, or was it the other way round? Either way, it was tedious, annoying. But the bit that stands out, that he remembers vividly was Alison's reaction.

She rounded on them, "You two are up your own arses, spoiling everyone's evening," she said in a lethal voice. "I'm not being your audience any more, I'm finished!" Phil and Sheila went silent, eyes shocked. Finn was truly impressed, and equally impressive was how she stuck to her guns afterwards.

He admired that certainty about herself and her limits, until she exerted it against him in Manchester. After a delicious dinner one evening, she reached for his hand, "I can't turn this job down, Finn," she said, without a shred of agitation, "an offer like this won't come again."

Her calm shook him. "I see." he said, heart sinking, "which leaves me high and dry!"

"Only…" she paused, still calm, "only if you view it that way."

He was astounded. "What? You get to call the shots and also decide how I should view them?"

She pulled back, spoke quietly, "Three years Finn, that's all I'm asking."

"Creative accounting Alison – five years you're asking! I've already done two."

Alison's determination to get him to stay – in a place he didn't like, with few prospects – rocked him. She believed her choice should become his, for her sake. He never expected that of her.

You see what you think is there.

*

The Kerrigan's job got the go-ahead, Finola got her way, the extension would face the Sheffrey Hills. Finn was relieved about that but much more relieved about his finances.

False security: two weeks into it, a Monday morning, Finola stood white as a sheet on the doorstep when he and Ciaran rolled up.

"The Bank's being stupid," she said, "they won't release the next portion of the loan, even though the money was agreed."

Ciaran's face darkened, "For what reason?"

"Someone at their end didn't get us to fill some form in, and they're insisting it must be done before the money is released, even though they're the ones who made the mistake!"

"How long will it take?" Finn asked.

"They won't say," she said, close to tears. "I've got my solicitor onto them this morning…"

Finn looked at Ciaran: no money, no work.

"We can't go ahead until it's cleared," Ciaran said in his no-argument voice.

"I'll ring you as soon as the solicitor phones," she said, "he might sort it out today!"

Finn and Ciaran sat gloomily over sandwiches in Westport.

"I've a bad feeling about this," Ciaran said, "timing couldn't be worse, Santa Claus coming to four kids."

Finn felt for the man, he'd no Santa Claus worries, but had turned down several small jobs, so he'd be back on the Dole, his savings bleeding out.

At six pm, Ciaran phoned. "We're high and dry Finn, paperwork could take a few weeks. My Belmullet cousin can take me on … don't even like the fucker, but I'm grateful."

Finn rang a few people he'd turned down, might get two small jobs back, thought of ringing Phil, then remembered he was in the Pennines refurbishing an old mansion, what could Phil do for him there?

The next day Ciaran texted: *My in-laws want their hall, kitchen, dining room repainted for Xmas. You want the job? Decent money.*

His heart sank, he hated decorating around people, the way they expected you to be a trapeze artist. But a gift horse it was. He texted back: *Sure. Send me details.*

Later gloom descended. This was no life, scrounging bit jobs to get by, wasn't he in his prime with strong skills to offer? It was time to stop waiting for Godot, his mother was well again, time to move on and Phil in London probably his best bet.

A new year was coming – new page, new place.

11

Helen kept a promise made to herself in the Kilbane's house and cycled to Cill Damhnait cemetery. The wind was at her back, but the journey much longer than she'd hoped. She part cycled, part pushed, part walked, arrived heaving, in a lather of sweat. The original stone church, a substantial ruin, established by Saint Damhnait, stood at the entrance, and after a brief look at it, she picked her way through the graveyard which sloped down towards the shoreline of the Sound.

This was as close to the water as she'd come. Today, it looked benign, lapping the edge of the graveyard. Hard to imagine those waters claiming lives. She picked her way around grave stones, noting local names, Kilbane, O'Malley, Patten, Geilty, Gallagher, then spotted the large headstone, which marked the grave for the tattie hokers drowned in Clew Bay, in 1894.

Thirty-two names were listed, including two families who'd lost three children each, and three families who'd lost two children each.

There were eight girls called Mary, three Bridgets, two Honors, two Winifreds, two Sebinas, two Catherines, two called Pat and Joseph, and other names…Nancy, Martin, Margaret, Thomas, Mary-Anne, Mrs Molloy, Mrs Doogan, Maggie, Annie – almost all were young, on their way to make life better for their families.

What devastation in a small place. Everybody would have known someone who drowned, and so many young people would have left gaping holes in villages all over the island. She read through the names again, slowly, repeating them aloud.

Set against this story, her own troubles seemed not worth all the time she'd wasted, nor the tears she'd shed. She felt too sad to visit the Kirkintilloch gravestone, left it for another day and began the slow journey back.

Tired out, she went to sleep quickly, but within the hour was startled awake by the sound of glass breaking. Her heart seized, somebody had broken in, she waited, limbs frozen. Then there were shouts, from outside. Maybe glass was exploding from a fire? This thought unlocked her, she couldn't see from her window, so dragging a jumper and coat on, she rushed out. No smoke but a pane of glass had been shattered in the front door of the girls' house, by a large bowl, lying beneath the door, and from inside, the voices of a man and woman, rowing loudly.

Helen stood, fearful, then heard children's voices crying and stumbled towards the door where she encountered Anne and Paddy, the middle aged couple, from the house the other side.

"Hello Helen," Anne said, her face grim, as she rang the doorbell.

The voices stopped, Helen counted seconds, thirty, before the door opened, and the girls' mother stood there, hair dishevelled, a bloody cut over her eye.

"Yeah?" she demanded, voice hostile.

"Are you OK?" Anne asked.

"Yeah," she said, beginning to close the door.

Anne put her hand on the door. "Are the girls alright?"

"Of course they're alright," she snapped, then closed the door so sharply, glass fragments shook loose onto the path at their feet making them step back.

"I sincerely hope so," Anne called out. The three stood huddled until Anne turned to Helen, "Will you come in for a cuppa?"

"Thanks," she said, unable to stop shivering.

They led her into their cosy sitting room.

"It's shameful," Paddy said, while Anne went to the kitchen, "that kind of violence around children."

Helen nodded, couldn't speak. It took a cup of scalding tea, fortified with whiskey to warm her up.

Anne and Paddy had moved back from England nine months before, expecting to move into their new house in Castlebar, next to their daughter and her family. But best laid plans went askew, the house wasn't ready, they'd sold up in Birmingham so they began renting in Shraheens.

"It was very pleasant to be in the countryside after years in a big city," Paddy said, "until the neighbours-from-hell moved in." He wiped his forehead with a handkerchief.

"It's a regular thing?" Helen asked.

"Fairly," Anne said. "We thought of mentioning it to you Helen, but we didn't know how long you'd be here and," she frowned, "to be honest, didn't want to frighten you. Sometimes it's verbal rows and he goes off for a while, sometimes it's physical like tonight, but it's always loud and nasty." She poured tea, continued the story. They'd rung the police the first couple of times, but they took ages to arrive, usually Head-banger husband was gone by then and the woman, Cathy, wouldn't make a complaint, said she'd fallen.

The whiskey was helping Helen, "Has she ever… looked for help?"

"The opposite," Anne said, with a sigh. "I tried talking to her, mentioned places she could ring, she told me to mind my own business. I was a nurse in Coventry, I've seen all this before."

That explained Anne's fearlessness.

"We're the enemy for calling the Gardai," Paddy said, "he warned us off – mind your own effing business or you'll be sorry!"

"Heavy," Helen said.

"Yeah," Anne nodded. "We reported it, in case! Then the kids stopped talking to us, under orders." She grimaced, "It's them I feel for."

Paddy nodded. "We thought of moving out but they kept telling us the house would be ready in a month or two. At least we're in Castlebar every day helping Sadie with her Gift Shop, and we'll definitely be gone by Christmas."

Suddenly Helen felt fearful they'd leave before she did.

A car engine startled them. Paddy checked through the blinds, "That's him, scarpering, as usual."

Helen felt relief flood through her.

"He works away as a builder," he said, "comes and goes. She's stuck here with the kids, wants to live in Castlebar near her mother."

"She can't afford it," Anne said, pouring everyone a second cup of tea. She suddenly looked serious, "Don't do anything on your own Helen, he's a complete nutter. Knock or ring us," and she handed Helen her number. "If we're not around, call the Gardai."

Helen was grateful for the warning. Then as they all eased, Anne asked Helen about herself. She gave a brief summary of her career break and her Grace Henry research. Neither had heard of Grace.

"We're not very well up on Art."

Finally, Helen bid them goodnight and Paddy walked her to her door. The lights were off in the girls' house, cardboard now replacing glass.

Helen was too wired for sleep, her house now seemed unsafe. She was thrown back to primary school days, and broken glass in the upstairs window of Moran's house on their way to school. A gaggle of them stopped to gawk, until Brendan Moran appeared, shouting, "Feckin nosey parkers," and they scurried off. Nobody messed with Brendan Moran.

After school Moran's window was boarded with a piece of wood, like an eye patch. The window looked sad, embarrassed. The neighbour's boarded hall door had the same wounded look.

After Shane left, Helen's face looked wounded: shocked eyes, dark circles underneath, staring back at her in the mirror and she sometimes saw shock in other people's eyes when they met her.

As she grew sleepy, she thought about people's dreams: Anne and Paddy's peaceful retirement; the girls happy childhood; Helen's dream of a baby with Shane, hoped for month by month… The odds were shit on dreams.

Unease after the bust-up was now added to Helen's general gloom. Two days later, to get away, she decided to return to Pearse Street Library to study Grace's paintings again and spend the night at Fiona's. She watched trees passing by the train windows, wished she could be like a tree…free of memory.

In the Library, she opened the file again, studied Grace's paintings one by one, decided that Grace was a completely different kind of painter to Paul. Her shapes were different, less exact, more circular, more …suggestive of places and things, rather than representing them. What was that called? What did it signify? She was desperate for someone to talk to, reread everything for glimmers of light.

There appeared to be a strong presence of women in the modern Irish Art movement, amongst Grace's contemporaries were Mary Swanzy, Norah McGuinness, Mainie Jellett, Evie Hone. Helen was cheered by this discovery and in the middle of an article, happened upon a reference to Grace Henry's work and – unbelievably – a footnote listing a thesis written about Grace, held in the Irish Art Research Centre in Trinity College, known as TRIARC.

A blessed thesis! Had she really missed that the first time? She reread it slowly to make sure. How on earth had she not feckin seen it?

She sat back, feeling like Miss Marple, happening upon the glove in the library, the key to the whole case. But her pleasure evaporated when she realised it was four pm, too late to find that library and she'd no idea how easily she could access it.

Damn. She'd have to go hunting tomorrow.

She had dinner with Fiona's family, caught up on their news, slept soundly surrounded by others and after a quick breakfast with Fiona and the kids, phoned Trinity Art History Library, where a kind woman said she could call in. She had a spring in her step until she cut through the university grounds and was wrenched back – she and Shane took this short cut to their respective buses after a day at college. If the weather was good, they'd linger, sit in the sun, by the cricket field.

How? How could Shane walk away from it all? How could he do that?

Stricken, she turned, walked out under the arch, along Westmoreland Street and onto O'Connell Bridge, where she propped herself up watching the river moving towards the sea.

Someone spoke, interrupting her misery. An older Romanian woman, sitting on a skimpy towel, was holding out a paper cup, saying, "Please…"

To have come all the way from Eastern Europe to sit on O'Connell Bridge with a Centra budget cup seemed a terrible journey. Helen berated her own self-obsession, gave her some money, and pushed herself back to Trinity.

The Library was a converted old stone building at the back of the college, the staff welcoming, and she was led to the Grace Henry thesis. The author was called Rosarii Moran, who no doubt had sweated over this work for months, years maybe, little knowing how useful it might be to a stranger, desperate for leads, on a winter morning.

She skimmed the text, until she reached a series of colour copies of Grace's work at the back. Lots of them: Achill landscapes, portraits, Mediterranean scenes, still life studies. She let out a long breath – a feast lay before her.

But it was a profusion of riches, she flicked through text, scanned pictures, then back to text, felt panicked about how best to use the precious time, decided, finally, she'd read and look at the paintings as they came up. The author had them grouped in stages of Grace's painting life. And so she began – as they say you always should – at the beginning.

The writer's admiration for Grace Henry was stated at the outset – her tenacious commitment to her art throughout her life. She also mentioned the lack of written record about her and how Paul's memoir contained no mention of Grace. An acrimonious split was referred to.

What had befallen them Helen wondered again? Then she had an uncomfortable thought: could she do it to Shane? Wasn't that what she now longed for, to erase him from memory?

She shoved these thoughts away, returned to the text. The early part of Grace's life in Scotland was familiar, but there was new detail of their period in London: Grace painting landscapes, flower studies, Paul, doing charcoal illustrations which were commercially successful. When they exhibited together, a critic remarked upon Grace's "exquisite sense of colour" and on "a vision and mind of her own". Strong praise Helen thought.

In 1908, before Achill, they exhibited together in the Ulster Arts Club, where Paul's brother was a member. Grace's work included eighteen flower studies, and the Northern Whig reviewer was impressed by her "exquisite emotional sense of colour."

What is an emotional sense of colour, Helen wondered?

During this period, one of Grace's paintings, "*The Girl in White*", possibly a self-portrait was included in an International Art Exhibition in Santiago, Chile, a sign of her growing stature as an artist. Helen allowed herself time to study this painting: a young woman, sandy hair pinned up, was seated on a sofa in a long dress, hands folded in her lap, looking directly out, composed, thoughtful. But the most striking aspect of the work was that it was painted almost entirely in white, apart from the hair and skin colour. The dress, sofa, door behind her, were all white, creating an ethereal atmosphere. It seemed such a daunting task for a painter to set herself, but guided by the writer's commentary, Helen began to see that many colours had been used to convey and vary the whites – green, greys, blues, even pink. It was Helen's first lesson in painting appreciation, forcing her to open her eyes to how a sense of colour could be created.

The longer Helen looked, the more she saw: Grace had also used patterns to create variation in this white world – the criss-cross pattern of the sofa, the straight lines of the inlaid wood behind, the lighter shading to create the delicate, loose fabric of the dress. In Helen's humble opinion, the painting was a knock-out.

The next stage of Grace Henry's career was on Achill. The writer suggested it was safe to assume from the evidence that the decision to stay was more Paul's than hers. At last, someone who actually referred to this! Therefore, it made sense that her painting developed more slowly than Paul's. For both, the island became their subject matter, but Grace had to find her own distinctive approach.

She took to painting at night, standing in her painter's smock often at the old bridge at Dooagh, under moonlight. In these paintings, from what the writer called her early phase, the composition was simple, scenes reduced to their simplest element – and blue, grey, purple, black were used to capture the nocturnal mood.

Roads, rivers were a regular feature, symbols of journeys, directions in life, as well as landscape – *The Long Grey Road of Destiny* – a painting of the road which ran up to Sliabh Mór, a striking example.

Helen suddenly grasped how small rivers in Achill had a distinct presence, which would have taken Grace's interest.

The little river by Helen's house had recently grown in size and speed after rain, was now an audible background hum. In a city, such activity happened underground, except when rivers flooded and shocked everyone with their presence.

The island's roads were also potent markers – not numerous – but each one vital, carving out the way: across and back, up and down, on and off the island. On Achill you didn't take roads for granted, Helen knew, you needed to learn them.

Occasionally the writer made comments which Helen didn't understand – that Grace's work had a modernist approach to realism. She added them to her *Find Out More List*.

In 1911, one year after settling in Achill, they had a joint exhibition in Belfast, *Paintings of Irish Life*. She remembered this from Paul's biography. But here it was expanded on: the difference in the couple's styles also remarked upon, one critic suggesting Grace's was more original, in being less representational. Helen wondered again how couples handled reading reviews of their joint work over tea and toast next morning?

This writer echoed the view mentioned by Paul's biographer, that Grace became frustrated and depressed by the isolation of Achill, but that Paul did not share these feelings.

Then, alas, Helen's time was up, taking notes made progress slower than she'd hoped for. Reluctantly she placed the thesis back on its shelf. She needed to catch her train.

*

On the bus back to Achill, she watched the changing colour palette of the countryside: beige, tan, light brown – mellow colours – beautiful in their own way, wondered how Grace Henry would paint them? Finding the thesis had made her feel hopeful, but hope began seeping away as she neared the island. Could she see it through? Could she find the will?

Hope was fickle terrain, eight months she'd spent trying to conceive, hope rising, fading, rising again, until, finally, hopes were thrashed. Hope was dangerous ground.

12

To maintain a cautious distance Finn sent apologies to the next History Group meeting. He would read the Minutes, keep in touch that way. Or so he thought, but three days later Gawina phoned to give him a detailed report-back.

It had been a good meeting, she said, with lots of lateral thinking. Six ideas were placed on the table: a mural or tapestry, from herself, a Trail and/or Memorial Garden from Michael, a symbolic sculpture or set of life-size tattie hoker figures from Martha.

These people were unstoppable, Finn thought, asked if any proposals were being considered by the other three members.

She sighed. "Not yet. Doubts were voiced about the proposals, too ambitious, too expensive, the cart placed before the horse, which I think is strange, but we said it was brainstorming … necessary to the process."

He could well imagine the cut and thrust, the steam rising, guessed that the point about process came from Gawina, wondered about Don, Eilis and Maureen's degrees of uncertainty, but knew it would be impossible to progress without at least one of them on side. The suggestions were interesting, he thought, life-size figures put him in mind of a sculpture of a woman on a bench in Torrevieja, scanning the sea for sight of a fishing boat's return and how effective it was. But his QS mind kicked in too, getting any memorial was an uphill task – even a rock, a plaque, and that was before the problems of finding a location.

"Hopefully, next time you can come, Finn?" Gawina asked.

Was that a statement or a question? Generally, he liked her directness, it cut through crap, but sometimes she overstepped.

"Not sure, "he said, "but thanks for filling me in."

On Saturday his mother and May were making Christmas puddings, the house like a sauna, so he decided to take himself to Westport for a mooch around. He'd almost escaped, when his mother mentioned that Kevin was ringing at five, and would he be back for that?

He kicked to touch, "Don't know, I'm meeting someone in Westport about materials."

Her eyes took on that worried look, so he conceded a fraction, "Say hello to them all for me."

He resented her pressure. He and Kevin had nothing to say to each other except what couldn't be said and the tit-for-tat nature of their conversations left him with a sullied feeling.

An hour mooching around Westport was enjoyable, but long enough. To avoid going home, he wandered into the Library to see if they had a copy of the *Westport Historical Journal* which contained an article about the drownings, including the *Enquiry into the Clew Bay Drownings*, recommended by Michael. They had it, and before he knew it, he was immersed.

One account was compelling, that of a young boatman called Edward O'Malley who along with his fellow boatman, Thomas Burke, had been working at the Quay on that June day in 1894. Both men were later awarded the gold medal of the Royal Humane Society for their bravery.

Edward O'Malley rose early that morning, knowing the Scottish steamer, SS Elm was in Westport Quay. He and Thomas Burke had a boat and brought goods back and forth to the large steamers anchored in the Bay. At half past noon, Mr Burke of the town asked them to take a message to Captain Carsell on the Elm which had run aground on the flats off Annagh Head, awaiting the tide. When they got there, they tied their boat up and boarded, lingering to watch the crew unloading boxes, barrels and sacks onto Anthony Gill's lighter. The sailors worked fast: hauling and hiking the ropes, making the knots quickly adjust to the weight, tighter or slacker as needed.

Around that time, Healy's hooker came into view, with some of the tattie hokers on board and Edward heard them before he saw them, for the *grisheens* from Achill were singing like it was a holiday they were going on and the sound travelled across the water. A lot of the young ones had never seen a steamer before and began to stand up as it came into view. He knew at a glance there were too many on it and he heard Healy shouting at them to sit, but they were paying no heed, all eyes intent on the big ship they'd be boarding before long. Edward couldn't pull his eyes from the sight, for he knew for certain that with the wind ahead, the boat would jibe. Healy needed to lower the mainsail.

Too late.

In a flash, the boom and sail were bending, straining, and the boat was over on its side. The shouts now turned to shrieks of fear, and the water suddenly became a screaming mass of human beings. He saw hands fighting with the water, trying to grab for the boat, trying to grab others, heads bobbing up and down, gasping for air, screeching for help. He saw one body grab another, both going under.

As fast as they could recover from the shock of it, Edward and Thomas jumped back in their boat and were rowing towards the people, not knowing where to start, just moving towards the heaving mass of desperation. They hooked a girl's arm, then a boy's and the two were in the boat. One man tried to grab their oar, they had to pull it from him before dragging him into the boat too. And they kept hauling as many as they could out of the water, until they had over two dozen in, with others hanging onto the side. Suddenly, he realised their boat was in trouble from the weight on board, water was pouring over the gunwales and it was almost awash. They would go over too, he feared, but Thanks Be to God, O'Malley, the stevedore from the steamer, saw their plight, jumped in a boat and began rowing fast and strong towards them. Once alongside, he took some of the people off the boat and some of the ones clinging to the side. In the space of a few minutes, O'Malley's boat would have gone down too, for his boat was filling up so fast and straining, and but for swift action by John Gibbons of Innishlyre, they might have toppled. Gibbons' boat had been coming up the bay a quarter of a mile behind Healy's hooker and came to O'Malley's help.

By now, boats from the steamer had made it onto the water and the crewmen were grabbing hands, shawls, sleeves, anything they could grip, to fish the living out of the sea. Edward saw some sailors grappling with the hooker's sails, trying to get to those trapped beneath, but it was in vain, for the weight of the sodden cloth and the press of the water couldn't be overcome. He saw O'Malley land his boatload at Rosmally and go back out to help the crew who were bringing survivors on board the Elm where Captain Carswell and others tended to them.

Edward knew he had to turn and head back to the Quay to land the survivors, for there was room for no more. At the Quay, Edward and Thomas helped the saved ones off their boat. More boats were now striking out from the Quay, heading to the hooker, taking in those hanging to the hull and trying as best they could to get at those in the hold. With the hull free, the boat righted itself a little so they pushed in hooks to those who were lying in there. But to no avail – those trapped in the hold never had a chance.

By then the other hookers, one after another began arriving from Achill and those grisheens on board watched in horror at the scene before their eyes.

News of the tragedy had reached Westport and crowds of people arrived at the Quay, relatives weeping and wailing as they recognised their own among the bodies of the young girls and boys now being delivered onto the Quay. Some of the young ones who'd arrived from Achill were crying to go home Nothing could bring warmth to Edward's freezing body, nothing stop the shaking from head to toe, as he watched the scene around him.

Like Edward O'Malley, Finn felt chilled when he finished it and to get warmth into himself, went for a coffee, then walked briskly out to Westport Quay. He stood looking seaward, trying to re-imagine the scene but it was impossible to match the present day Quay with the drawings of 1894. There were a few fishing boats moored and a couple of trawlers advertising fishing trips around the bay, but light miles away from the working harbour it had once been, thronged with people, boats, cargo loading and unloading. The old wharves were gone, the warehouses rehabilitated into modern apartments, a hotel, shops and pubs; at least they'd had the sense to save the old stone buildings, the only testament to the Quay's past.

He walked on, studied the stone memorial mentioned at the meeting, which was erected for the centenary of the drownings. It was cut in the shape of two sails, which he liked, and listed all thirty-two names of those, accidentally drowned – but as Gawina had said, it made no mention of tattie hokin or the context for the drownings. Why not?

He was pleased it was there, but agreed with the others, it wasn't enough. It marked the place of their deaths; an Achill memorial could mark the background to their lives.

Tattie hokin was specific to Achill, North Mayo and Donegal, a history not known to a lot of Irish people, never mind tourists, it needed to be more visible on Achill.

But he was caught in his one-foot-in-one-foot-out dilemma. What he could do, he decided, to still his mind, was assist from time to time, as he had done with the Letters Home project, skirt the periphery, avoid getting pulled in.

*

Helen Bradshaw phoned him to say she needed to leave Shraheens, the neighbour trouble had escalated and Anne and Paddy were leaving at Christmas.

"I don't feel safe any more," she said.

"Heavy stuff, you're wise to get out!"

She asked if he knew of any properties to rent, then

became apologetic... hoped he didn't mind her asking, didn't know who else?

"That's OK." he said. "Y'know Keel would probably be a better place, more facilities, more people around. I'll ask about."

He rang a few people, drew blanks, lots of empty houses but many were stand-alone which would be more isolated than Shraheens, then remembered Sally, the estate agent he'd met at a Pucini concert in Westport a while back. A second-generation Irish returnee, her Aunt Brid was a relation of his mother's and they'd joined up for a drink after the concert.

Finn and Sally had Manchester in common, she was born there, Finn a temporary resident.

"Maybe we passed each other beneath the Town Hall's gothic splendour," Sally said, grinning.

"Ye might have and now ye meet again," Brid said, "isn't that a fine coincidence?"

His mother nodded brightly.

Sally locked eyes with Finn. "Does match making run in the blood?" she asked her aunt.

"Sally, I was only commenting ..." Brid said, embarrassed, "Where's the harm?"

Finn liked Sally's straight-up style, more of it was needed round these parts.

When he got hold of her at her office, she asked how his mother's matchmaking was progressing?

"Nothing to report, I'm afraid."

"My Aunt Brid says there's someone for us all out there!"

"Good to know."

Sally was smart as well as humorous and within a couple of hours she'd come up with several winter-let options, all on estates and as she ran through them, Finn heard Martha's estate; that would be a good fit if the price was right.

When he rang Helen she sounded mightily relieved, said the price was similar to her present house, so they arranged to go as soon as possible. Helen sounded so grateful Finn felt like the hero of the hour – such a rare things these days – he decided to savour it, while it lasted.

13

When she woke, Helen saw Shane standing in their dining room, face rigid, feathers from the broken cushion floating round his head, pulled the duvet over her head. How long… how long more… would he keep stalking? It leeched her, over and over. She lay, eyes clenched, praying for sleep. It wouldn't come, finally hunger pangs pushed her out of the bed.

Downstairs the room was gloomy. She rarely opened the blinds, preferred to block out the waters of the Sound. Now she slowly raised the slats and the hill across the Sound, called Corraun began to reveal itself, a scattering of houses, sheltered by clumps of dark trees at its lower level, then a yellowish meadow, all rocks hacked out of it with blood, sweat, tears. Further up the hill it became bare, harsh, dry stone walls and shale covered ridges. She made breakfast, sat watching Corraun brighten then darken, cloud and sunlight battling, like ancient warriors. It was the universal story, she thought, light and dark battling, over and over.

*

Later a chink of light appeared on her laptop – an email from Martha Mulherne. Finn Kilbane had mentioned her research and she was including suggestions for tracking Grace Henry: back copies of Mayo News, Western People, Westport Historical Journal and Scoil Acla, a cultural festival, with which Paul Henry had been involved, so perhaps Grace was too?

Dear Lord. Helen was embarrassed she hadn't thought of newspapers herself, the woman must think her an eejit.

Then Martha mentioned that her brother James knew of Grace Henry's work and was happy to talk, if she was free to come to Keel on Friday morning?

She was stunned by the invite, then elated.

"Yes," she shouted, replied immediately.

*

Friday morning she set out by taxi, driven by Declan Gallagher, who talked little and drove carefully. Martha welcomed her warmly, showed no sign of thinking her an eejit. She was stylishly dressed in a light green wool top and skirt with chunky silver necklace which made Helen conscious of her own dull uniform, jeans and jumper. She led Helen into a colourful living room, with warm thick curtains, paintings on the wall and two stuffed bookcases.

Helen looked out at the cliffs, "What a great view."

"It's a gift. In five years, I've never got used to it," Martha said.

And then James appeared, shook her hand. He and Martha had the same thick grey hair, but in other respects looked different: he tall, thin, older, Helen guessed, Martha short, heavier set.

Martha then excused herself, had to leave.

James served tea and light-as-air scones with bilberry jam, all made by Martha.

Helen asked what bilberries were.

"*Fraochán*," James explained, "wild blueberries – Martha gathers them on the hill above."

Martha was a woman of many parts Helen thought, her admiration for her rising by the minute.

James was obviously keen to get down to business, "I think Grace Henry is a much neglected artist," he said as an opener.

Helen almost gulped, "You've seen her work?"

"In Hugh Lane and the National Gallery but it isn't exhibited enough." He'd been introduced to her painting by a friend, Oliver, who has a keen interest in Art and a small collection of paintings. "One of Paul's," he said, "none of Grace."

James had first seen her work at the Henrys' Joint Exhibition in Hugh Lane Gallery in 1991. "It was a revelation."

Helen knew about this exhibition, from the article by Antoinette Murphy, was able to look knowledgeable. "What did you like about her painting?" she asked.

He sipped his tea, pondered. "I think her use of paint was adventurous, skilled. The landscapes were different to Paul's, very much her own. More Modernist," he smiled, "although I'm no expert, I rely on Oliver for that." He paused, "There are some similarities in their Achill work, but it fascinated me that two artists, a couple, could paint the same landscape and people, differently."

"Do you think she has been overshadowed by Paul?"

He didn't hesitate, "Definitely."

She waited, willing him on: anything James, anything.

"Some people might say her connection with Paul helped at first, they had joint exhibitions in Belfast in the early years, which his brother facilitated and that brought her to public attention, and I suppose a husband and wife team has a certain appeal, especially, if they've similar subject matter."

"Sure."

"But… ultimately his fame grew more than hers with his West landscapes and she seemed to fall under that shadow." He tilted his head to one side, "An added factor, of course, was that all women painters of the time faced huge prejudice. I suppose too, that after the marriage collapsed he was more in the spotlight." He paused. "She travelled to Europe, he stayed in Ireland, was friends with Seán O'Faoláin and others, did radio broadcasts, and wrote memoirs."

She tried not to interrupt, to keep up by scribbling, but had to ask. "I read that he didn't mention her in his memoir?"

He nodded. "What do you make of that?"

She spoke carefully. "I find it hard to understand. He could have mentioned her briefly, but nothing after thirty years of marriage seems… punitive? Or maybe it was denial – like she was a closed chapter he couldn't acknowledge."

He nodded. "I suspect it was more acceptable during that period to avoid mentioning your wife, even if she was an artist, private life viewed as your own business! I doubt he was challenged about it, like he would be nowadays."

That seemed fair comment, she jotted it down.

"Another scone?" he asked. She accepted.

After a couple of bites he continued, "Getting recognition in a man's world was an uphill battle for women artists, however good. They were expected to confine themselves

107

to craft, porcelain painting and such like, not bold modern painting."

"Do you think being Scottish made it harder for her?"

"Hmm, I never thought of that… she lived and painted most of her life here." He paused, "Paul's Irish roots were secure, I suppose, plus he became the iconic painter of the West with his tourism poster." He glanced her way, "He was a good painter too."

"I agree." They got that out of the way, but she was now worried that he was moving to a close, so quickly asked about other women artists of the time.

"What a talented group," he said, "Mary Swanzy, Mainie Jellett, Norah McGuinness, Letitia and Eva Hamilton, Estella Simons, Muriel Brandt … the list goes on, an artistic revolution really."

"One I never heard of!"

"Me neither, until Oliver enlightened me."

"Why," Helen asked, "were so many of them drawn to the avant garde movement do you think?"

"Phew…perhaps by its nature, it was open to newcomers? The movement was innovative, so more open to those outside the establishment walls?"

She kept scribbling, not wanting to stem his flow.

"I attended an Art History course in Trinity after I retired, … learned that avant garde painting not only challenged the style of painting, but also the subject matter."

She nodded, trying not to look too ignorant.

"It opened a debate about what subject matter was worthy of art which fascinated me! Ordinary working people, not just Gods, aristocrats, were being painted by the likes of Courbet, which was a move towards realism and away from romanticism."

She coughed to give herself a minute's break. "Sorry, could you explain that a bit…?"

"Oh I ramble on, well, in choosing ordinary subjects, painters were opting for the real world instead of the romantic ideal! Millet did the same, painting peasants at work, *Angelus* or *The Gleaners*, which you probably know?"

Helen nodded, recalled people pausing in a field for the Angelus. Phew!

"Their approach had huge influence on Impressionists, Surrealists and into the twentieth century, on Expressionism, Fauvism, Cubism."

At that moment, luckily for Helen, James' phone rang and he stepped out to take the call. She badly needed a breather, her hand stiff from scribbling, all the time fearing she was barely keeping up. Fauves rang a bell. Ding-dong – Rosarii Moran mentioned the Fauves impact on Grace, but she couldn't remember what she'd said.

Isla's advice about research came back: keep the target in focus, like a hunter tracking its quarry. Her target was Grace Henry, stay focused on her. Panic subsided.

Then James was back, apologetic. "I should finish soon," he said. "So, where were we… yes, Irish female and male artists were influenced by these avant garde developments, Grace and Paul too. Also, Hugh Lane was vital in promoting modern art, when you think that the Dublin Gallery was the first public location of modern art – though it had a rough ride!"

Helen knew about this from Yeats' poem, *September 1913*, in which he expressed his anger at Dublin Corporation's rejection of Hugh Lane's offer of his modern collection. Phew again!

James pulled her back, "You're probably exhausted, Martha said not to overtax you!"

"I'm loving every minute," Helen replied, "I've been so…alone with it."

"Good. So I'll add one last point, the new Irish realism reclaimed Irish subject matter: paintings of everyday life, rural landscapes, working people, especially in the West, became a big inspiration for the Henrys, Jack Yeats and others.

She nodded.

"Needless to say, there were differing views amongst them about style and subject matter," he checked his watch, "but that's for another day."

"Yes please."

He leaned back, "I'm off to Dublin tomorrow and will see Oliver while I'm there."

Her heart sank. "You're leaving Achill?"

"No, I'll be back in a week or two."

Relief, relief.

He shook her hand, "It was a pleasure meeting you and discussing Grace Henry. I'll ring when I return."

*

Before phoning her taxi driver, Helen walked Keel Beach, brimming with gratitude. James was a gift blown onto her path, like a long lost relative, providing missing links in a story. She'd ring Isla with the good news. The closer she got to the cliffs, the more rugged, impressive they looked and … familiar? Was it from summer trips, postcards, paintings, possibly Paul's? Were Art and reality fusing? Well, that suited her fine; she'd had a bellyful of reality.

But reality was never far away, Fiona rang Sunday morning, veering between fury and tears: Clodagh had gone missing for five hours the previous night.

"Missing?"

"Yes, apparently she has a boyfriend … went with him to a free gaff in Rathfarnham. Robin had to drive round for two hours to locate her – found her drunk!"

Clodagh's safe, was Helen's thought, realising she hadn't heard Fiona cry since Maurice Glynn dumped her at sixteen.

"Clodagh and her friends drank a bottle of vodka," Fiona continued, fury reigniting. "She's damn lucky she didn't need her stomach pumped!" Pause, "Or maybe that's what she needed, to frighten her."

"How is she?" Helen managed to interject.

"Sleeping off a hangover," Fiona's voice broke.

"I'll come up," Helen said, "I can make a dinner or wash dishes to give you a breather!" For once Fiona didn't argue.

How ironic, Helen thought afterwards, recalling how Fiona used her to cover her tracks, when she was in her teens and came home late from the Scouts Disco. Helen had to parrot excuses to their mother: she has to walk Carmel home; she has to pick up her runners at Ruth's house … etcetera. Then Fiona would scrape in just before their mother unleashed her wrath. She'd remind her of this … later.

*

When Helen arrived, Fiona's house was a boat after a storm, the crew bruised and exhausted. Fiona was grimly making dinner, Robin, normally upbeat was subdued. Clodagh, puffy eyed, hugged Helen like a lifeline, then sat holding onto the dog, her only friend, while Stephen blocked it out with his PlayStation.

Dinner had none of the usual chat, and everyone went to bed early. Helen couldn't help but think the impact of the event was disproportionate, but knew it wouldn't help to say so.

She stayed a few days, shopped, cleaned, forced Fiona and Robin out for evening walks while she watched TV with the kids until the battered boat began to resettle. She couldn't get to TRIARC but made it to the Hugh Lane Gallery to stand in front of one of Grace's paintings, mentioned in the thesis.

Finally, there it was, *Evening, Achill*, hanging on a gallery wall, amongst other Irish paintings. It was a study in blues, light blue sky with a single star shining, and light from cottage windows spilling warm reddish light across the scene. According to a note she'd read it was a tonal study. Helen didn't understand that fully but didn't care, she was deeply moved by its depth and blueness and by its sheer existence …the first painting of Grace Henry she'd seen in its original form. Eventually she had to pull herself away.

*

She took the train back to Westport after four days, leaving the family to themselves. With time to think, it occurred to Helen that Clodagh, a shining star at school and at home, was trying out bad girl, for a change. Helen was sympathetic, swamped with regret that she hadn't tried it more often herself: gone to India when she wanted to; fought with Shane more; and most of all, left him for Alex Bertell.

Alex, best looking man she ever fell for, brown eyes, smart, funny, they'd hit it off at Kate's party, when Shane was visiting Ireland. Instant attraction, talking under a starry sky, and by the end of the evening, they'd kissed. For a week, they'd had a mini affair – without sex – but full of lust and unmet desire. They walked in Regent's Park, went for a meal in Paddington, a film, until their final meeting in a Chapel Market cafe, where they faced each other and she said, "I can't leave Shane."

He looked her in the eye, "Why not?"

"I love him…we're together years…"

"You don't have to leave him," Alex said slowly, "you and I can see how it goes?"

"I couldn't lie, pretend …"

"You could tell him, see where that takes it?"

Alex was well ahead of her, "Have you done that?" she asked trying not to sound shocked.

"No, but I know people who have."

She couldn't imagine suggesting a trial threesome to Shane, felt suddenly anxious: she and Alex were still strangers, unknown entities with unknown loyalties. She couldn't take that leap.

Afterwards she missed him, the intensity, the excitement of someone totally new, different, felt she'd lost out on an experience she'd wanted.

Shane noticed her preoccupation.

"Work pressures," she said, which he settled for.

Now…how she wished she'd taken that chance with Alex and changed her history. Later she would have revealed it all to Shane, over a candlelit dinner, watched him reel in shock, stumble and fall.

14

Another storm: the wind moaning outside Finn's house like a keening. All evening it ebbed, flowed, sometimes building to a crescendo, then pausing wearily. He liked the way the winds broke the silence but by midnight it was clear they weren't falling away, the howling and keening assaulting the windows, pushing to get in. He lay listening, hoping he'd battened down the shed and barn enough. He had a love-hate relationship with winds, awed by their power, wary of getting trapped in their path. They moved closer, rolling round the walls and in the background the waters of the Sound churned. He got up, went to the window, the fuchsia along the pathway bent in subservience while the tall pampas danced frantically to the whirling tune, like Dervishes. He was glad of the hill behind, a defence. No sound nor light from his mother's room, she was well used to it.

Kevin loved storms, measured his courage against the howling winds: standing on the shed roof howling back, climbing the hill on hands and knees, to find a ledge or hole to park in, while they whipped round him. Sometimes Finn woke to see him leaning out the window, face blasted by the force, holding up a fist, reckless, like a young Lear, "C'mon, get me if you can!"

His superior physical strength and will power were so well established between them, Finn never tried to compete, but Kevin had a wildness to him, which resembled their cousin Tom's untrained colt, which could kill you if you got in its way. Finn feared Kevin's wildness for as long as he could remember, ducked and dived to avoid it.

In later years, their geographical distance had guaranteed minimal contact but once back in Shraheens, Kevin's presence had moved closer, summoned up unwelcome memories.

The beginning of the end was the water barrel. Finn and Kevin were playing Hide-and-Seek in the yard, Finn to hide, Kevin to seek, a game Kevin always won. But that day Finn hit on a brilliant hiding place, climbed into the barrel, replaced the lid above his head and stood to his shins in water. Kevin never thought to look, passed back and forth, twice. Finn heard his footsteps, doors swinging open, the barn, cow shed, the old horse stall, the tractor shed, then Kevin swearing, "Fuck him." Not long after, he heard him beating the bushes along the side of the field, to flush Finn out. He was glad he hadn't hidden there, he'd have got a right walloping.

Then Kevin's footsteps were back in the yard, close, Finn tensed, but they moved away. His brother still hadn't sussed him and for once he would win the game. He waited, waited, until it was safe to climb out and surprise him. Suddenly, the barrel went totally dark, the lid had let in a thin line of sky through a hole, but the hole had disappeared, something had fallen on top of it. His chest tightened, he hated the dark, raised his hand to budge the lid but it wouldn't move. Something heavy had fallen on it.

He wanted out now, began calling, "Kevin, help me, I'm in the barrel."

No reply, he shouted louder, twice, but no sound, no footsteps. He raised his voice, "Kevin, I'm stuck in the barrel, help."

Suddenly a sound, but not footsteps – water – it was coming into the barrel from the hose which fed it. He tried to push the lid again, couldn't move it, screamed, "Kevin, I'm in the barrel, help, help!"

No answer. The water was slowly filling up from the side, he was almost wet to his knees now, didn't understand why the water was coming in. Someone must have turned the tap on, his father must be in the barn, having no notion where Finn was.

He screamed, "Dad, help, help, I'm stuck in the barrel… Dad, I'm stuck in the barrel", but neither footsteps nor voice responded. Cold terror grabbed him, nobody could hear him, he would drown. He kept screaming, then bawling at the same time, his nose running snot, as the cold water reached his thighs.

"Help, help me, somebody…"

Nothing; nobody. Kevin must have gone in home, his father couldn't hear him, so he goaded himself on desperately, pushed again and again against the lid, but it wouldn't budge. What was jamming it down, it felt like a rock.

He would drown. "Heelp," he screamed, hysterical, "Heelp…"

And finally, footsteps, then Kevin's voice, "Where the fuck are ya?"

"In the barrel," he screamed.

Slowly the lid was moved and above him Kevin's face,

grinning. "You dope, you dopey eejit, are you trying to kill yourself hiding in there?"

Finn grabbed Kevin's arm, didn't care what he called him, was pulled out over the top and dragged to the kitchen like a wet rat.

His mother told him off severely, sat him by the fire, dried him, forbade him to ever get into the barrel again, while Kevin told her the story, a tale of an eejit, who could have drowned himself.

Later when his father came in, Finn said, "I was calling out to you Dad, when you turned on the tap," still shivering, despite extra layers.

"Sure I was up the field, nowhere near the barn," his father said, "how could I hear you?"

In his shocked state, it made no sense, until later. They were watching the nine 'o clock News, when it hit him. "It was you, Kevin, you turned the tap on to scare me," Finn said.

Kevin's face turned livid, "You're trying to blame me for your dopey plan. Why did you even get in there?"

Finn remembered his mother looking hard at Kevin, "Did you turn on the tap?" she asked.

"No, I didn't," he said scorn in his voice, "the tap wasn't on when I found him."

"The barrel was filling up, it couldn't do that itself!" Finn shouted back.

His mother asked Kevin again, very seriously, "Did you turn on the tap?"

Kevin scowled, "No. He panicked, lost the head, now he's is trying to blame it on me."

She sighed heavily, turned to Finn, "Jesus, Mary and Joseph, never again, never go near that water barrel or I'll take the switch to you!"

And so it entered family lore as the tale of Finn the eejit boy. But Finn knew what he knew, the tap couldn't turn itself on, knew the lid had a rock on it, gone when he looked for it the next day

That day changed everything. Until that day, Finn thought Kevin enjoyed teasing and tormenting him because he was older, and that was what older brothers did, but for weeks afterwards Finn believed that Kevin wanted to kill him. Fear, as cold as the water that came pouring into the barrel, took him over. Each day, he avoided or hid from him, didn't sleep at night until he knew from his breathing that Kevin was asleep.

Who could he tell? His mother? But how could he use the word, "kill" to her? She'd never believe that. He told Maura, his big sister that Kevin kept, "picking on him" and whatever she said, seemed to warn him off for a while. He ignored Finn disdainfully at every chance, which suited Finn perfectly. Months later, Kevin moved into Secondary school and lost all interest in him for a few years.

Looking back Finn knew for certain that Kevin had turned the tap on and lodged the barrel top with a rock, there was no other explanation, but he didn't believe that Kevin wanted to kill him, just frighten the life out of him, which it did. Like Tom's colt, Kevin's wildness was dangerous, drove him to extremes, which could, might have, accidentally killed Finn that day.

In his late teens he did confront Kevin about it. They'd unexpectedly coincided in the kitchen, both quite pissed after the pub.

"You turned on the tap into the barrel that day didn't you, to give me a fright?" Finn said.

Kevin's face darkened. "Jesus, not that crap again. You scared yourself shitless and wouldn't admit it. You were always chicken."

Finn held his ground, "And you were always a bully and won't admit it."

"Grow up," Kevin said, giving him one of his baleful looks as he banged out of the kitchen.

But Finn got his answer, knew he'd rattled him.

Christ, it was now past midnight, no more Kevin shit, he thought, giving his pathetic pillow a good punch. He'd worked hard to get him out of his life, he'd no intention of letting him back in.

*

Gawina phoned next evening, agitated, wondering if they could meet in Westport.

He'd never heard her agitated before. "Is something up?"

Silence, then tearfully, "Things are very difficult here…I don't think I can work out a Memorial proposal." Another silence, like she might be crying.

"I could meet you tomorrow in Westport, round three," he said. "I've to pick up supplies."

"Thank you… all I'll have is two hours?"

"Fine." He figured the shit had hit the fan with Simon.

Along the road to Westport the countryside was woebegone after the high winds, branches strewn, streams swollen, to lighten the journey, he put on the Gloaming, let Iarladh's voice waft round him, singing of summer coming, *"Samhradh, Samhradh…"*

They met in the Hotel lounge. She looked drawn, tense, with notebook and ring binder at the ready. They embraced, then she said despondently, "Simon will be dropping Wim back here at five."

"Two hours is good, two heads better than one, no?"

A glimmer of a smile. He'd only ever seen a determined, competent Gawina, this was worrying.

"You don't want to know my problems Finn," she said, while they sipped coffee, "but Simon is like a teenager … what he wants, what he feels, is all he talks about. I don't know this man."

She looked bleak, then shrugging her shoulders, "I really want to do a Memorial proposal but …don't think I can get the time."

Finn figured she needed the project more now than ever, also believed the project needed Gawina. "Isn't it too early for proposals, I thought it was more rough ideas at this stage?"

She shrugged, "I'm interested in the theme of charting the journey to the steamer in Westport…physically, emotionally," she chewed her lip, "but ideas take so long to turn into designs."

"Sure." Then he had a thought, "I plan on taking some photos around the Corraun, to keep my camera warm, it hasn't changed much since the nineteenth century so I can pass them to you if that would help."

She looked less despondent, until she asked, "But maybe you'll need them for a proposal yourself?"

He dithered, then told her, he wasn't planning any proposal, didn't know how long he'd be staying on Achill because of lack of work.

She looked stunned. "You're leaving?"

Shit, should he have held off – but too late now. "Not immediately, but a job closed down so I have to keep an eye out."

"Finn, you could be such an asset to the Group. And this is your home, your island, can't you stay until we at least get a proposal on paper?"

"Gawina, I have to earn my living and it's damn hard on Achill!"

She sank back into the chair. "I expect too much…that's what Simon says."

He didn't like the comparison, "I don't think I've much in common with Simon."

She glanced at him. "Sorry, I'm not in a good state, I'll concentrate on what we came for."

"Okay." He paused, "Y'know, you're entitled to expect a lot of life Gawina, you put a lot into it."

She squeezed his hand quickly, then turned to her notebook and they began work.

By the end of the two hours, she'd worked out a rough outline of what her proposal could be – a tapestry or a mural, made in parts, which could be fixed or mobile. Both could cover similar ground – the journey – drawings could be adapted to suit the medium, the costs, the time factor.

She let out a sigh of relief, "Thanks very much, I'm sorry to be so emotional…"

And then Wim was skipping across the room with Simon following. Finn greeted them and said his goodbyes.

On the drive back, he realised that telling Gawina he might be leaving had lifted weights off his shoulders, he'd been carrying some burden of guilt about not making that clear.

Then his thoughts turned back to the uphill struggle ahead for her. Separating from Simon would be tough, the man would drive a hard bargain.

To lift his mood, he sang along, *Thugamar féin an samhradh linn.*

Summer would come, as it always did and hopefully by then, both he and Gawina would be in better places in their lives.

*

Sally phoned Finn a few days later, she had keys for a few Keel rentals, so he collected Helen on Saturday morning for viewings. The first was in Martha's estate, the house further up the slope, the front seaward, the back facing Sliabh Mór. He wouldn't mind living there himself, Finn thought. It was clean, bright, more sparsely equipped than Shraheens, but Helen didn't seem to mind. Unfortunately Martha's car was gone, so they couldn't pop in to say hello.

The rent would be renegotiable in the summer months, Sally explained, because of holiday lets, standard on Achill. Helen nodded, clearly she'd no long-term plan to stay. She stood watching the Minaun Cliffs as if dazed, while Finn checked taps, switches, boiler.

"There's a couple of permanent residents living on the estate," Sally said, "a shop, post office and a pub-restaurant is open in Dooagh most of the year."

"It's a metropolis," Helen said, "I'll take it."

"Don't you want to look at a few others?" Finn asked. Her decision seemed rash.

She was adamant; she'd fallen for the view, cliffs and ocean.

"There's one snag," Sally said, "the owner wants to do some maintenance over the next three to four weeks so it won't be available until then."

Helen looked worried, "By Christmas?"

"Should be."

"I have to give notice anyway," Helen said relieved.

At the gate, Sally whispered to Finn, "Thought you'd nothing to report?"

He shook his head, "She's a friend."

"That's what they all say," and with a wry smile she was gone.

*

Before leaving Keel, Finn suggested they walk across the road to the old Amethyst Hotel where the Henrys had lodged for a while.

"Grace painted it," Helen said, pleased she remembered the name, *Country of Amethyst*.

The old hotel was on the main road, backing onto the sea, quite substantial, two storey, but in serious decline, walls peeling, broken windows. "A local bought it for redevelopment, then hit the downturn," Finn said, "new plans are afoot, I'm told."

Through the cracked windows they could see chairs and tables left to rot. Helen said she could picture Grace, sketchbook in hand, facing towards the sea. "Has Achill a connection with amethyst?"

"There was an amethyst mine above in the hill, towards Keem," he told her. "They mined it for a number of years while it was profitable. My mother says kids used sell bits of amethyst along the roads in the 60's, which they called, "diamonds".

"I never heard of it."

"Sure haven't we everything here."

She half smiled, "You sound like one of my Mayo cousins, full of it!"

He shrugged, turned the corner, called out, "There's a plaque here."

They read that Paul Henry had lived here during his years on Achill. Not a whisper of Grace, who lived there with him.

"Shit," she said, "how many times in her life was she blanked like that?"

"At a rough guess…often?"

When he dropped her back she invited him to dinner at the Hotel on Saturday evening, by way of thanks, "If you're free?"

"I'll have to check my social calendar…"he said, then grinned, "damn sure it's empty."

*

The Hotel restaurant was comfortable, candles and white linen, but not very lively for a Saturday night. He and Helen both opted for the Hake on a bed of leeks which was nicely cooked, and came with a decent side salad. Helen seemed more upbeat, talked about Grace Henry, her sister's troubles and then about Keel.

"I hadn't seen those cliffs for years," she said, "forgot how dramatic they are."

"They're that alright," he said, "And Martha would be a good neighbour, someone you could call on but wouldn't be intrusive."

She nodded, "I took to her straight away when I visited with James."

When he dropped her back Helen invited him in for a brandy and they sat companionably talking about Achill. Now she was staying until March she wanted to know about winters on the island.

He described whirling winds, dramatic storms, eye bending starry skies and sometimes snow. "We used pray for the school heating to freeze, then got bored at home having to go chasing sheep!"

She smiled, "School closing was a rare gift in Dublin. We made icy slides where we could, before people threw salt on them!"

Somehow, their first impressions of each other came up: she confessed to surprise, expecting more of a mountainy man; he admitted to thinking her standoffish.

While they talked he felt an urge to reach over and hold her hand which was near him on the arm of the sofa, a ritual of sorts like a handshake. But she might flinch, not see it that way. Instead, he hugged her when leaving, and this time she leaned into him a little. On his way home, he decided that the desire to hold her hand must be a symptom of his deprivation: lack of physical touch, of sex for months and months. But such thoughts were best left parked; he didn't need more complications in his ... complicated life.

15

Helen was dancing with Finn Kilbane in a large high ceilinged room, under coloured lights, arms around each other. Other couples danced around them, the only one she recognised was Isla dancing with Peter, her Head of Department in Westgrove. Through the long windows, it was still light, one of those long West of Ireland evenings, the sky still blue, a star just visible. She was so happy to be dancing, hadn't danced for a long time and Finn Kilbane looked happy to be dancing too.

She slowly surfaced to her blank white ceiling, closed her eyes to hold onto the dream, couldn't, instead lay savouring its lightness, brightness.

Finn Kilbane was a good man, that much she knew, he'd been generous and thoughtful, helping her out. He was humorous too and she sensed from his hug last evening that maybe...only maybe... he fancied her which pleased her, because it challenged her sense of the wreck she'd become. Did she fancy him? Her mind and body had been flattened for so long, she didn't know, but did think that before her life crashed, she would have. He was handsome, smart, had nice eyes. Did her body stir at the thought of sex with him? Maybe... but that was crazy thinking. If it went badly, she'd lose one of her only friends on Achill, although wouldn't she at least be taking a step forward into a new life?

She copped onto herself, it was hardly fair to think of Finn as an antidote to misery – an antidepressant or mood supplement. He was his own person, with his own plans, desires, would hardly appreciate being used for medicinal purposes.

As she showered, she realised that the dream and her ruminations were completely different to her usual loops and Christ, if nothing else, wasn't that a good thing?

*

Next day she was again on her way to Dublin, train travel now her highest form of expenditure; she consoled herself that it kept her footprint on the earth lighter than a car would.

At TRIARC she was quickly ensconced, acknowledged now as a regular, which was pleasing. In Rosarii's thesis, she found the copy of *Country of Amethyst*. Three boats were moored at an inlet behind a two storey building, presumably the Amethyst Hotel. The colours were wonderful, the whole scene imbued with a mauve haze, the mauve of amethyst, much valued by princes and healers apparently – the spirit stone.

A Northern Whig review of a 1921 Dublin exhibition by Paul and Grace, noted, that "while slower to mature than Paul,"(she) "had developed a sharper eye, a more acute sense of colour as exemplified by her "Amethyst" picture." Yes!

However, not everyone agreed. An Irish Times reviewer, dismissed *Country of Amethyst* and Paul's *Red Earth* as "crudely executed and un-representational." It pleased her to read that a fellow critic rebuked him, accusing him of having grown so accustomed to "dreary prettiness" that he'd missed the vivid strength of their work. A minor controversy in the Letters Page of The Times followed.

Helen stopped to recall controversies about Art in modern times, Warhol's can of soup, Damian Hirst's cows in formaldehyde, Tracy Emin's or closer to home, the Spire sculpture in O'Connell Street, loved, hated, renamed, *Spike in the Dyke, Stiletto in the Ghetto* and many more. Controversy and Art were still alive.

She read on, Grace's Amethyst painting was praised by AE, for her "use of strident colours justified because of their psychic appeal". What did "psychic appeal" mean?

No idea. She moved purposefully to *Keem Bay,* Achill's jewel in the crown beach. The shore and the close packed village perched on the near side of the hill, had creamy gable walls, and yellow thatch roofs. The choice of colours intrigued Helen, did her choices relate to "psychic appeal"? The painting was distinctly different to the postcards sold everywhere, highlighting the famous turquoise water at Keem. Grace had used a completely different palette, the beach and surroundings hills were mellow autumnal colours: yellow, beige and brown, the sea, pale grey-blue with a smattering of white capped waves. Why?

Further down the page, help came. The work of the Fauvists – who James had mentioned – was relevant. Matisse was one of its leaders. The Fauvists simplified lines, exaggerated perspective and used brilliant but arbitrary colours, to emphasise spontaneity and freshness, over finish. In this way, the imagination was freed from an obligation to imitate nature. Phew. She reread it slowly, and grasped how this was true of the two paintings before her.

The Henrys left Achill in 1919 and moved to Dublin. This jolted Helen, was this a leave-taking for her too, she'd moved to Achill to find Grace Henry, now Grace had gone to Dublin? Would it be harder to imagine Grace in Dublin? Art and Reality were suddenly confusing.

She took a break, had a quick walk around the quadrangle, then some coffee. Students milled about, young men in skinny jeans, young women wearing mini shorts, over black tights and boots, an off-beat look. She sipped and watched for twenty minutes, then confronted her confusion. Grace wanted to move to Dublin, chose it, what was the problem? She could research Grace's Dublin life from Achill. She took hold of herself, she was researching, not reliving, needed to keep a grip on that, walked back to the Library.

The Henrys moved to a flat overlooking Trinity College, from which Grace painted a view of rooftops, under moonlight, in shades of blue. Lovely. However, they found the Dublin artistic milieu conservative, symbolised by the Royal Hibernian Academy's annual exhibition. Paul's views were documented in his biography: he was angered by the prejudice against Modernism, shocked especially, that Impressionism, a major influence across Europe, had failed to cause a ripple in the Dublin Art world. It disappointed him that no artistic equivalent to the Literary Renaissance had happened there. It seemed reasonable to assume that Grace, always interested in European influences, would have shared his views.

In 1920, with Jack Yeats and others, the Henrys set up the Society of Dublin Painters, establishing a venue, where more experimental artists, excluded from official exhibitions, could show work. The names of those exhibiting were now familiar, a roll call of success: Harry Clark, Mary Swanzy, Mainie Jellett ... and again, the role played by women in the Irish avant garde was highlighted. According to one commentator, they spearheaded, "a quiet revolution." James had mentioned a revolution too.

But the path of the Society didn't run smoothly. The foundation of the Free State had brought the theme of national identity to the forefront, so politically and culturally, the Society was out of tune: looking to Europe at a time when Irish culture was more introspective, seeking to define its own identity. Helen's sense of making progress was quickly kicked back into place, by a whole new angle on the subject. Then she remembered James' reference to "tensions" in the Irish art scene, a subject "for another day". Hopefully.

Rosarii Moran noted how Grace's work became more confident and expressive during the 1920's, her use of paint freer and more fluid, using colour to express weather, mood, emotion, in keeping with the style of The Fauves.

Rosarii's commentary about one painting, *Spring in Winter*, was illuminating. A small horse, simply drawn, stood alone in a vivid West of Ireland setting, possibly Pegasus or the mythological horse which took Niamh and Oisín to *Tír na nÓg*. Bare mountains surrounded it, a tumultuous sky above, but the colours were not Irish landscape colours at all. Instead, a turbulent sky is painted in green and white, brown-red tree trunks bore fluffy blossom-like growth, the rocks painted with swirling brush strokes – this vivid background was used to convey passion and, without doubt, captured a mood of agitation.

Some biographical details threw dramatic light on the painting. Grace painted it around the time that her personal life took a different turning. She became involved in a relationship with a mutual friend of hers and Paul's, a man with whom they had been staying in Dublin, a married man called Stephen Gwynne, writer and critic, who apparently accompanied her when she set off travelling.

Helen paused to absorb this. Presumably the relationship had flown in the face of convention in the 1920's, even for artists, and presumably, being friends and part of a small Art circle made it harder for Paul.

Helen was catapulted into familiar territory of her own, her sympathy pulled towards Paul, as the title of the painting dawned, *Spring in Winter*.

It marked a celebration of joy, rebirth – when least expected – in the cold, flat, dullness of winter. Grace risked her marriage for this.

Is that what Shane felt about Chloe?

A sinking feeling took her, she couldn't concentrate, left, walked along Nassau Street, around Merrion Square, back to the National Gallery Café, joining shoppers and tourists, watching them from behind a pane of glass.

"Different…" was what Shane said about Chloe, "it was different." Was that it – rebirth – Spring in Winter?

The pain in her chest was back. She put a hand on it to still her breathing, counted, in-out, over and over, made it to one-hundred-and-eighty, until the gulping eased and slowly passed.

16

By Saturday, the winds had departed and Finn decided to drive the Corraun peninsula to take some photos, tracking the route of the tattie hokers from Cloughmore pier to Westport. Later he could show them to Gawina, which might be of help to her. It would also get him out of the house, offer a different vista, and on the off chance that Helen might fancy it, he rang her. Just back from Dublin, she was pleased at the invite.

"That would be great," she said immediately. "Will I need raingear?

"Need you ask?"

She was waiting at the gate and they set off. In response to her enquiry, he described his dire work scenario, while she was upbeat about her research, having found a very helpful thesis.

The cold fist of December gripped Corraun, nothing moved apart from sheep. He hadn't driven this for a while, and within minutes was struck by the bogginess of the land, also registered a few spanking new holiday homes, all closed up.

He told Helen that Corraun was a favourite haunt in

summers during his teens, with pal, Sean, cycling around in the hope of meeting holiday girls, the new talent.

She smiled, "I remember from my days at the Donegal Gaeltacht, the local lads would line up outside our house."

"We had a scoring competition," he recalled, "how many counties did you kiss?"

She raised eyes to heaven.

"Dead serious! One summer I kissed girls from nine counties, Donegal, Dublin, Clare …can't remember the rest – double points for a foreign girl, England or Europe, triple for America."

"Jesus," she said, "culchie Lotharios."

"You better believe it."

They stopped, to look back at the Sound.

"It seems such a small settlement from here," she said.

Sheep came bleating, hoping for food. He shooed them away, drove on through Beal Feirste, the home of one of the drowned tattie hokers, he was almost sure, was interested to hear that she'd visited the headstone in the graveyard.

He watched for the harbour signpost and took the turn which brought them down to Caladh Mhanais, a small working harbour with pier and boats, looking directly across at Cloughmore. Harbours were like magnets for him, significant for his destiny he hoped.

He pointed out landmarks, their houses, O'Malley's Tower, Cill Damhnait cemetery, the Life Boat Station, only a hop across and wondered what this satisfaction was of looking at a place you knew well from an altogether different angle? She sat, while he got to work, photographing the sister harbours from as many angles as he could, under a moody sky. He was pleased she'd come, they seemed more comfortable with each other each time they met.

They pushed onwards, stopped again at a sign for the Quay, Cé Aith an Aoil, followed a small track and there before them was Clare Island, snoozing in the bay.

"Imagine discovering that for the first time," she said, walked closer, "this is great Finn, I've been so restricted with only the bike, so much I haven't seen."

He leaned over her shoulder to point, "This is the same view as the tattie hokers had from the hookers that day, a photo version of their route is doable, I reckon, even from land."

She nodded, turned slightly, her face brushing his hand, a soft, moist touch. He retrieved his hand, said, "A tricky job to do well though, better photographers round these parts than me."

"That doesn't mean they'd want to do it, whereas you do."

She was right all the same, the job was to capture background shots not exhibition pieces.

A sleety rain started, swamping all views, so they retreated to the van for shelter and hot tea. He badly wanted to get to the Ice House ruins, further along. Built by a Scotsman, Alex Hector, who'd set up a successful salmon fishing venture on Achill and Corraun, preserving fish, and shipping them off.

"Another Scot, like Grace Henry," she said. "How did he make it to Achill?"

"Haven't a notion, but so many Achill people went to Scotland, it's good to hear about reverse traffic!"

The rain got heavier, with no visibility ahead, they were beaten back. At the Sound, they stopped for coffee at his suggestion. He didn't want her to leave, wished he could bring her home, make dinner, drink wine.

Instead he dropped her to her door, suggested a Chianti evening soon.

"You free tomorrow night," she asked, "can't offer dinner, but some nibbles with the wine?"

He was surprised, pleased, detected an air of what... resolution about her?

"Sure," he said. They had a quick hug and she was gone.

*

He cycled to Helen's next evening, a dry, clear night, didn't want to drive home after the wine. She welcomed him, had her hair down, which was longer than he thought. This time they sat by the fire, not at the table, nibbles laid out on a coffee table, the atmosphere more relaxed.

They chatted awhile, he told her he'd be starting on the decorating job next day. "I hate it... but beggars can't be choosers."

"Is that how you feel about your job?"

"All the time." But that old rag and bone discussion bored him, he shifted gear, asked about her.

She mentioned her father's disappointment that she wouldn't be in Spain for Christmas. "I plan to go in Spring, getting off Achill right now daunts me."

"An unusual enough problem, I'd say."

She gave a half-smile.

"I'm worried about my Dad, Fiona doesn't think Spain's working out for him, he's cut off, but won't say so, everything's always grand! I hate that word, the Irish smokescreen." Suddenly a rueful glance, "I haven't seen him for over a year, what with all my woes."

"Are ye close?"

"We are," she said immediately, "as my sister and mother are, so it's even Stevens."

Then she asked about his father.

He dithered; should he speak truthfully or just pass the time? This seemed to happen with Helen, was it her, or the dynamic between them that made casual exchanges difficult? Talk of his father always triggered regrets, of missed opportunities, generally he avoided it.

He gave her the summary: an Achill man through and through, great farmer, died from pneumonia after a sudden illness at sixty-eight, which was terrible for his mother and tough on Kevin who was left with the farm. "Even worse for her when a few years later, Kevin went to Oz to try it out. The land was rented, then when Kevin settled abroad, she sold it off."

Helen nodded, "Very hard on her. Were you close to him?"

Summary clearly wasn't enough – he glanced at her briefly, she was intent. "No. I disappointed him. I'd no *grá* for farming, which was his measure of boys and men. Luckily, Kevin assumed that mantle." He paused, "I was away when he died … so I'd no chance to spend time, maybe, y'know, repair a few bridges."

The mood had slumped, he refilled their glasses, emptying the bottle. "That didn't take long," he said. They sat in silence until he noticed her hand again, on the cushion beside her. "You've lovely hands," he said.

She was startled, "Really?" She took his hand, examined it, "Nice too."

Then he took her hand, as he'd wanted to the last time, stroked it and she followed suit, their eyes locking, until she released her hand from his, to lift her wine glass and he followed suit.

He heard the rain beginning to spatter, bad timing as

usual. "I'd better make a move," he said grimacing, "before it's bucketing."

"Okay," she said. Then, to his great surprise, she said, "Eh, you could stay...if you want?"

He hesitated, unsure of what she meant.

"I've a spare bedroom or a double bed," she added holding his look.

This was so unexpected he hesitated, then spoke carefully, "The double bed would be very nice...if you're sure?"

She leaned towards him to prove it, "We could start with a kiss?" she suggested and moved closer so their lips met. They kissed tentatively, then more deeply, tongues meeting, then after a while decided to go upstairs.

Both were a bit pissed, which got them over initial nerves, both confessed to nerves, which helped, but desire was slowed by her exit to the bathroom to fit her diaphragm and on her return the fumbling removal of clothes, down to t-shirts. In the bed, they lay awkwardly next to each other, like they hadn't done this before.

Helen faced him, "Maybe we should remove tops and start kissing again, see where that gets us?"

A good plan it turned out, offering no way back. The sex happened fast, she guided him inside her, and too fast, after months of deprivation he came, as did she, but more quietly than him.

They lay silently for a minute afterwards, then sweeping her hair back from her face, he asked, "Did that just happen?"

"Were you not there?" she said with a slow grin.

"I wasn't expecting it..." he said, holding eye contact.

"That makes two of us."

Without much chat, they kissed and slipped into sleep, arms entwined. He woke once, she wasn't in the bed, saw a light in the bathroom. He tried to stay awake for her return, but nodded off and the next time he woke, she was fast asleep next to him, the chestnut hair spread out, which he touched lightly.

Then his watch beeped, it was half-seven, he scrambled up and out as quietly as possible, left a note on an envelope:

7.30 am
Lovely evening. Decorating calls, beggars can't be choosers. F xx

On the cycle home, he wondered if the sense of resolution he'd detected in Helen was part of her recovery from a broken heart? If so, did it bother him? He didn't know; but sleeping with her definitely made him feel more hopeful. Despite his dire economic prospects, it suggested – what – possibilities? Then another thought came: without Helen around, Achill would now be a barer place. How had that happened?

17

Helen woke remembering sex with Finn Kilbane, his smell, touch still on her body, still in the bed. In ways it was a blur, both of them a bit pissed, both nervous, but bodies took over, quick but sweet and something else – relief.

She's considered the possibility beforehand, wanting to take a step back into life, but didn't trust herself to do it until she spoke the words. He looked so surprised, getting ready to set off home on his bike. "Are you sure?"

"Yes," she'd said, even surer when she experienced something like a low thrill that she could surprise him and herself, could take a chance on something.

"Let's try it and see how it goes," Alex Bertell had said, but she hadn't dared back then, nor dared for years.

She didn't mind that he'd had to leave for work early, the morning after might have been awkward, nervy, better a bit of space before meeting again. Also she'd woken in the night with an urge to cry – relief, sadness – she wasn't sure – didn't want that to spoil what had happened, slipped into the bathroom until it passed while he slept.

Now she set out for the Sound for groceries, it was dry and cold, good for cycling. She treated herself to coffee and cake in the café and cycled back. She felt something she hadn't felt for a long time – ordinary – not sad, broken. An ordinary woman who'd had a bottle of wine with a nice guy and they'd slept together afterwards. Other people did this all the time. No big deal, no win or lose, no promises, no contract to sign or break.

She cycled past an abandoned house, its garden overrun by large leafed Gunnera – huge rhubarb like plants. They'd arrived, she'd read, as ornamental plants from a part of Chile which had similarities with Achill. Two places she'd never have connected. At first the plant was a novelty, but now it was invasive, shading all plant life underneath it. But how could she dare to judge it – wasn't she another blow-in in search of new ground? She smiled to herself, turned into her laneway, ready now to go over some Grace Henry notes.

*

Isla phoned that evening. Telepathy, Helen had been planning to ring her.

But Isla was odd, edgy.

"Is something wrong?" Helen asked.

Helen heard an intake of breath and then, "Shane had his baby on Friday, Helen."

"Friday?" she said stupidly.

Another intake of breath, "I'm sorry to be the bearer of …"

She felt calm. "I made you promise to tell me, Isla. Remember?"

After a pause Isla said, "I guess it's another milestone passed, Helen?"

"Yeah," she agreed.

"Puts more distance between you both…?"

"True."

Helen couldn't think of useful things to say, sensed Isla's concern building, "Are you OK Helen?" she asked in a worried voice.

She seemed to be. "A bit stunned Isla, not that I didn't know it was coming… but apart from that, I think I'm OK."

Isla wasn't convinced, "I could come the weekend after next…if you'd like?"

Helen thanked her, said she'd be alright, knowing Isla was under work pressure. Before they finished, she asked, "Boy or girl?"

"Boy."

That threw her, in her mind she'd always envisaged a girl.

"You'll come through this Helen," Isla said, "stronger than him."

Later in bed, she recalled Hania harbour, the grapevine's dappling light, the blue ring, one of the few things she still had, the waiter taking their picture, fixing them in time, fell asleep remembering the crimson streaked sunset.

Next morning she felt stiff as if she'd had a bang which had knocked her off balance. She struggled downstairs, made toast and tea, feared she'd caught something, took paracetamol and slept again. When she woke, the day was drawing in and her first thought was: Not a boy.

That was cruel. She'd dreamed of a boy for months – a boy with dark hair, blue eyes, he'd kept her going through the ovulation charts, temperature checks… and then a new snapshot: Shane holding a baby, brown eyed like Chloe, wrapped in a soft blue blanket, freesias, daisies around the bed, Maria, Karl, Paula – a champagne cork popping, *Chin, Chin... Sláinte, Sláinte.*

How? How had this happened to her?

Her breathing tightened, she took air in, breathed it out, she must keep breathing steadily, above everything, keep breathing steadily, in-out, in-out, which she did, but intent on that she couldn't prevent that terrible day launching at her.

Her and Shane in a different café altogether, Holloway Road, heavy vehicles trundling past. Her rage at his affair with Chloe had carried her through, she'd refused his calls, kept teaching, preparing, marking, kept working. She stayed at Isla's, cooked dinners, Kate called, they'd watched TV. She was girded by anger.

Until that Friday afternoon, when he stood waiting outside the school gates. She walked past but he followed, tried to speak to her, so she speeded up.

"A cup of coffee is all I'm asking for," he said.

She couldn't scream or push him off with staff and students looking on. Cornered, she walked quickly towards the Italian place where staff sometimes went for celebration lunches. He followed, kept step with her.

Inside, it was the afternoon dead shift, nobody there but the waiter watching horse racing on a small television behind the counter. He ordered coffee; she sat rigid, silent.

He said he was sorry, over and over, said he understood the hurt she must feel – he'd feel the same in her place. Lies ruin things, he said – then he said he still loved her.

The words ran off her, she was unmoved, removed.

"Why?" was the only thing she asked.

He shook his head, tried to frame words, failed.

"Why?" she spat through her teeth.

He didn't look at her. "I don't know, something happened … it changed things. "

"Something happened?" She didn't comprehend. "What happened?"

He shook his head, "The feelings came out of the blue, were different, I felt different-"

"– different? What the fuck does that mean?"

A shoulder shrug, "I'm so sorry Helen –"

"– you're sorry? After twelve years, you're sorry?"

He stayed silent.

She couldn't stand it. The same sick feeling she'd had the night he'd told her he'd slept with Chloe, the sense of being unmoored, was rising again. She got up.

"Helen, don't go, please, there's something else I have to tell you," and he was gripping her elbow to stop her moving.

"Don't touch me!"

"You must, please."

Something in his voice caught her and she found herself sliding back into the seat, legs weak. If she could, she'd have left, certain now something terrible was coming.

"Chloe's pregnant." His voice was flat.

The words swirled around her: her first thought – what did that have to do with her?

"Pregnant with who?"

His face contorted, "Me."

Now a high wave hurtled towards her. All that had gone before was just a lead up – terrible had not been terrible at all – betrayal had not been betrayal – now it raced at her, fierce, savage.

"You?" Her yelp caught the attention of the waiter.

But she was trapped, because the air was seeping out

of her, a sensation of crumpling in the middle. Her chest tightened, as though her lungs had knotted and she began spluttering for air. Shane was now beside her, but she couldn't breathe because an elastic band was squeezing her lungs and she had no strength to beat him away.

The waiter came over holding a glass of water, not understanding that water was beyond her.

"I… I…." She couldn't manage more than rasps. She was going to die from lack of air.

Shane was telling her not to speak, to take short breaths and then he was counting them for her and she couldn't get away from the waiter and she couldn't get away from Shane. She was going to die of suffocation, right here on Holloway Road,

"Breathe in – out, in – out…"

Stop, she wanted to scream, but couldn't speak.

Suddenly, a slit opened in the elastic band stretched around her lungs, enough for a tiny channel of air to rush through. Her lungs began moaning as she took in air, precious air, and slowly, slowly she stopped dying.

The waiter and Shane had their eyes glued to her, it was impossible to escape, she couldn't move.

Finally she was able to whisper, "Go …away!"

But Shane didn't budge.

A long time later her breathing settled enough to say again, "Go away…leave me alone."

His eyes were desperate, pleading.

"Leave me…" she said and saw his face cave in.

She watched him go, every step of the way, until he backed out of the Café door, then she sat, held up by the back of the bench, because there was no way she could move of her own accord.

"Take your time," the waiter said, moving away but leaving the glass of water.

She sat and sat, the hum of the horse racing behind her, the waiter at the counter, not looking but keeping his eye on her, she knew, while all the time, keeping his distance.

*

For months afterwards, a hollowness took over. It was the crumpling, the jack knifing of her body which undid her. If she had exploded at him, shouted, screamed, hit, she could have saved herself. The pieces would have blown outwards, like shrapnel, towards him. Shane would have carried the debris within him. Instead, she'd saved him from all of that, while he'd saved her from nothing.

Now she stood, hand on her chest, counting breaths, in-out, knowing she must not let her body crumple or jack-knife again. This time, she must not...could not... let him do that to her again.

18

Finn arrived home, tired after a tedious staircase job, to find his mother waiting to show him a large parcel from Australia. Christmas gifts, one for everyone, to go under their Christmas tree. Finn had posted his mother's parcel to Perth a month ago.

"Aren't Kevin and Lou very good?" she said, sounding sad.

He felt for her, "It must be hard for you not seeing them?"

She was tearful, "Not seeing the children grow up pains me." She dabbed her eyes, picked up her knitting.

He nodded, began eating his dinner, knew she wanted something more from him. "Were you and Kevin close after Dad's death?" he heard himself ask.

She stopped knitting to look at him strangely. "Of course we were close. That's an odd thing to ask."

He persisted, wanting to keep the door ajar, "Just wondered because he spent most of his years out with Dad round the farm."

"That's the way it was, Kevin was your father's second in command and a very good one at that." She paused, "Though your father was hard on him."

"Why?" This question also caused her to peer at him.

"Wasn't Kevin a great worker?" he added.

She shook her head slightly, knitting idle again. "Your father was hard to please…things had to be done just so. His father was the same with him, even harder, from what he told me, so it was the only way he knew, I suppose. I used tell him to praise Kevin more, get the best out of him… but it didn't come easy."

Finn had never experienced his grandfather's hard ways, remembered him as a benign presence, playing cards with them, always good for a Puca story.

"Kevin and me were never close, as you know," he said, hoping for God knows what.

She grimaced, didn't like to hear it. "Ye were just different in temperament."

"More than that Mam…" He turned words over in his mind, bully… cruel … but with Kevin's Christmas parcel between them, couldn't. "He was very hard on me."

She pursed her lips, "Well, you were more on the sensitive side, he was a country lad, rough round the edges."

Finn knew this door wasn't open, so left it.

She finished a couple of knitting rows then stood for bed, "Aren't ye grown men now, Finn, time's passed, can't ye put those things aside?" When he didn't answer, she added, "He'll always be your brother Finn."

He nodded, that was the problem. He stayed sitting by the warm range, thinking how time had cured fuck-all between him and Kevin and how Christmas had a way of unleashing old crap. Finn and his mother would be spending it with Maura in Galway for which he was grateful. She was a great hostess and also a great one for family stories. "Remember the time we…" she'd ask, wanting Finn to share

147

their childhood memories with her own kids. He envisaged taking his turn, "Remember the time Kevin tried to drown me..." pictured Maura's horrified face, his mother's heart speeding up, his nephews and niece stunned. Or maybe they wouldn't be? Weren't they fans of the Addams Family?

Leave it, he thought, switched on TV to find a cop thriller where a family feud happened to be at the heart of the crime. Right up his street.

*

Eilis emailed a reminder about the next History Group meeting at Martha's:

> *Don will give feedback on his recent conversation with the Trust administrator.*

Finn wavered, as always, but with nothing better to do, decided to attend.

Martha opened the door with a welcoming smile. Inside, was a full quota of members, enjoying mulled wine and mince pies to get them into the Yuletide mood.

"Non-alcoholic," she said, handing him a glass.

Finn watched the shadowy Minaun cliffs, as Don filled them in.

"The Trust Administrator has told me off the record, that there is "interest" in our memorial project," he said.

Enthusiasm gripped the room, he heard Gawina's "Great," and Michael say, "That's brilliant."

"Don't get carried away," Don warned, "she stressed it wasn't any kind of commitment, it was to encourage us. Also, they only accept submissions of one proposal."

"Well," Maureen said, brightly, she wore a black velvet top, like she'd come from a pre-Christmas do. "If we agree they all have merits, we could put them in a hat and draw one out."

A stunned silence was followed by consternation.

"What?" Martha said, "we're nowhere near that stage."

"That's way too random," Michael added, his voice high.

Then Gawina spoke, sounding offended, "Not just random, that would be reckless, we're not prepared."

Finn knew Maureen liked to stir the pot, useful sometimes, but at other times, like now, it was egocentric and foolish. He wondered if she'd had a glass too many earlier, was struck by the tension in Don's face at her suggestion, he seemed annoyed. Was he beginning to invest in the project or was he just displeased at Maureen's bad manners?

Finn added his view, "I think it's too premature for that approach."

"Choosing should be a collective process," Gawina added, hitting the nail on the head.

"Before we run away with things," Don said, "the Administrator mentioned another option, applying for development funding, which means you get money to pin down your proposal, consult designers, explore costs, carry out local consultation, before you submit anything. They call it Seed money."

"Seed money?" Michael was amazed, "that's a new twist on an old tale hereabouts. Wasn't seed money one of the reasons for tattie hokin?"

Finn caught Martha's eye, knew instantly they were thinking the same thing: this was their only way forward.

She grabbed the reins, "That's an excellent idea. We're

at the starting line with this and it's a big project, I think we should go for that."

"It's not guaranteed we'd get it," Don reminded them, "we'd need a very strong application and be in competition with others, of course."

Both Gawina and Michael expressed concern that the group might lose momentum by doing this, while Martha argued the opposite, it could keep them focused, which Finn and Don agreed with.

"It's a very good idea," Maureen said like she'd suddenly reconnected with the meeting, from another zone.

Nobody responded.

Then Finn thought of Sean. "I could talk informally to a Planner I know, about pros and cons of Development funding and applications?"

"Is he discreet? "Don asked, "we don't want word spreading yet".

"He is and knows his stuff." Finn now began to believe Don was opting in and, if so, he'd be a valuable supporter.

The meeting agreed unanimously to Finn's proposal which restored Christmas cheer to the room.

Outside Gawina was fuming. "Do you think Maureen wanted to destroy our chance, picking out of a hat?"

He shrugged, "She likes stoking flames."

"Likes the power it gives her," Gawina grumbled, but then she cheered herself up at the possibility of development funding which she'd come around to as probably their best bet.

On his drive home, Finn reflected on the meeting. Development funding was their only hope – offered a pathway to a proposal. The group, strong on passion and commitment, needed to up their game on how external funding worked. Good ideas were just the starting point, the devil lay in details, in covering all the bases. Without that, good projects failed, time and again, he'd seen it too many times. When he thought about his own role at the meeting, he was pleased he'd managed to keep enough distance whilst contributing too. Maybe he was learning that balancing act, slow-ly.

His mind wandered to Helen Bradshaw, he'd texted her, but hadn't heard back, wondered about calling at the house on his way home but there were no lights on when he passed, so he left it.

Next day, Ciaran phoned. Finola Kerrigan was told by the Bank they'd have the money in January. "Good," Finn said, relieved.

Ciaran was more cagey, "We won't get excited until we see the cash, Finno," he said, "but at least it's not bad news."

"Sure," Finn said, deciding to take it as a glimmer of good news to get him over Christmas. He knew nothing would come in London in January, perennially a dead time, but if Kerrigan's came through, he'd have a regular income – for a bit.

Another thought then hopped on, what reason not to help with the Development application, if he was around? He knew about that stuff, didn't he?

He could hear his Aunt May say, "Isn't it about time you got stuck in there, Finn!"

Wasn't he the lucky man to have people around who always knew what he should be doing, better than he did himself? What would he do without them? He knew the answer – he'd travel lighter.

19

Helen had to get moving, movement was her only hope: she would cycle, walk, stay out of the house. Kate had rung, said similar things to Isla about Shane's baby, milestones passed ...moving on... putting it behind her... Helen agreed but found the words no help. She knew words wouldn't save her, this battle went deeper, so she must keep people she was close to, at bay, for now. They had faith in words, she didn't. She texted Isla and Kate, thanked them for their support, said she was, "handling it", going to Dublin for a few days and would be in touch soon. Finn also texted – their night together now seemed like something she'd imagined, she replied briefly: *Going to Dublin for few days, talk soon. Hx*

Next morning she repeated the only words that mattered: *I will not let it happen again*, got up, cycled to the bus. In Westport she had breakfast in a café, then hired a bike in a local shop and headed for Westport House where nobody would know her, she'd know nobody and there were large grounds to cycle in.

She spent three hours cycling around parkland stopping at points to look at its impressive trees, most of which she couldn't name, rested by the boating lake where they'd gone once as kids, then along the meandering river. Finally she stopped to look at the house, built in the eighteenth century by well-known architects, it was elegant, solid and she wondered what it would feel like to call that house your home? She'd no idea, didn't care, felt no envy just gratitude for the space around it which kept her moving, free from destructive looping thoughts.

Back at her house, she fell asleep at nine, too exhausted to think or remember.

Next day she woke early, headed out on her bike as soon as the rain stopped, crossed the Davitt Bridge and cycled along the Greenway, passing only a couple of walkers, bikers and a farmer on his tractor. She'd planned to go as far as Mulranny, but she'd tired quickly, knew she wouldn't be able for the return trip so turned back. Nevertheless, she felt energised, free, as she had yesterday, ate, fell into bed at nine and slept. The only person she met was Anne who greeted her as she was going into her house. They had a brief exchange, Helen telling her she was a bit under the weather, needed an early night.

"Mind yourself," Anne advised.

"I will," she said and meant it.

On the third morning, she woke dog tired, her limbs stiff, muscles aching. She'd overdone it, knew she couldn't cycle anywhere today, fell back onto her bed, trapped in her house. She saw a missed call from Fiona, knew she'd heard about Shane's baby, through his sister, her neighbour. Fiona would want to go down the dead end of talk, she didn't ring her back

Suddenly she grabbed a pen and paper, wrote words down: *You bastard, liar, cheat, imposter, you thief of dreams* – then said them aloud. Over and over, she repeated them,

153

her voice getting stronger, louder, until they took on a rhythm and pace, like an incantation – over and over, until her voice strained and it seemed to her that soundwaves might carry her incantation to Shane who'd hear it, stop in his tracks, shaken to his core.

Finally, voice cracked and tired out, she fell asleep.

The sound of knocking at her door woke her, then Anne's voice calling her name. What did she want? She stayed still, didn't answer, got up, had a toasted cheese, hobbling around on sore limbs, went back to lie down. At six, Anne knocked again and Helen knew that she wouldn't go away, would be concerned, might even... call an ambulance or something awful? Shit.

She threw on her dressing gown, went slowly downstairs.

"Are you okay?" Anne asked when she opened the door, "I noticed your curtains were closed."

Helen disliked the thought of Anne watching her windows, said coolly, "I was resting."

"Good," Anne said, then handed her an apple tart she'd baked. "My mother always believed in apple tarts for pick-me-ups."

Helen nodded, wishing Anne away, but she kept standing there. "I'd ask you in Anne, but you might catch this dose," she said.

"Oh, I've withstood a lot worse than that," she said lightly," and Helen had no option but to bring her in, noticing how Anne's eyes swept the room, the unwashed dishes, crumb scattered table. Luckily Helen had enough milk left to offer tea.

When Helen handed her a cup and slice of tart, Anne asked, "What symptoms have you had?"

"Stuffiness, headache – sinusitis, inherited from my father."

They chatted a while until Anne stood to go, hesitated, then asked, "Are you in trouble Helen?"

The bluntness shook her, then annoyed, what business was it of Anne's? She couldn't trust herself to reply without insulting her.

"If a listener would help," Anne said, "I'd be happy to."

Some nerve. "I'll bear it in mind."

Anne got the message, thanked her for the tea, turned to leave.

But suddenly, Helen felt a strong urge to say it aloud, get it out from inside her, to somebody who didn't know her well and out it came. "I got bad news," she said, her voice heavy as a stone.

Anne sat again, waited.

"My ex-husband and his partner had a new baby." Then she added, dully, "Well, not bad news for them, obviously."

Saying it aloud made the words feel icy. She still didn't look at Anne. "We – me and him – had been trying for a baby for nearly a year, then he met her, began a relationship I didn't know about, she got pregnant," her voice wobbled but she regained it, "so he went to live with her."

Her life in a sentence – worthy of a women's weepy.

"That's very hard," Anne said, reaching for Helen's hand.

Helen pulled back, "Sorry Anne, if you take my hand, I'll start crying and I might not stop, like I did when he left. Sorry."

"You've nothing to be sorry for," Anne said. "Crying's a funny thing. When I started nursing, we used to stop people crying, now it's considered a healing response – a change for the better in my view."

Helen felt another wobble, but stayed firm, heard herself say, "I came here to get away from it, didn't want to be around, they live nearby... but it keeps following me." She paused to ease her breathing, "Every time I take a step forward...I get dragged back."

"It's a big, heartbreaking deal Helen," Anne said, "takes a long time to get over something like that."

Time, fucking time, everyone Helen knew talked about time. When, for Christ's sake, would she have done her time? "I'm sick of doing time" she replied, "I want it over, done with, actually I want it rewound, never to have met him, never to have married him! I want those twelve years back, I want never to have known him."

"I understand," Anne said, "only problem is rewinding can't be done."

Helen shrugged, too worn to say another word.

"Why don't you lie down a while on the sofa," Anne said, handing Helen the throw, "and I'll get you some soup."

Soup – what the hell would that do, she thought but she'd hardly eaten, so didn't say no and Anne was back in five minutes, heating tomato soup and buttering brown bread, which Helen was glad to eat.

"Are you on medication?" Anne asked.

Between mouthfuls, she said, "I stopped."

Anne looked worried, "Maybe it would help ...for a bit?"

"I don't want to, it makes me feel...worse." She knew from her nurse's look Anne wasn't convinced. "Makes me groggy... I hate that feeling."

"Well then, you need to take good care of yourself."

"I'm cycling, it's better than chemicals."

"Okay," Anne replied, "but eating helps too."

Helen gave a reluctant smile, thought how kind a person

Anne was, given that they were almost strangers, knew she was lucky to have met her. "Thanks Anne, for the soup and the…listening…" her voice wobbled but she held it, "you're a very generous person."

Anne patted her hand, "You're welcome."

Helen nodded, didn't weep.

That night she dreamt that Shane, herself and a little girl were walking down a winding lane looking for blackberries, searching for the big, sweet ones. Suddenly Helen was alone in the lane, with no sign of the little girl. Her heart froze, she had lost her and began shouting to Shane, further back, but he couldn't hear her. She ran up the lane wildly, desperate with fear and suddenly the child was there, in a ditch reaching for some fat, sweet ones, hanging low. Helen was flooded with relief.

The dream stayed with her all morning and though she'd no idea why, something in it was comforting.

The following day, she walked out the road a bit, limbs still aching. Later when the bell rang at five, she thought it was Anne, instead Finn Kilbane stood there, holding a bag of potatoes and a large, green cabbage.

"Was wondering if you were back from Dublin?" he said, as she led him in.

She decided against lying, "I didn't go, had a sinus thing…"

He looked surprised.

"I took to the bed, slept through it. Tea?" She felt nervous, their night together seemed from another planet altogether. She asked about his work.

He was still painting in a crowded house. "They think

I'm a magician, expect me to walk on air, while they do their usual things."

Suddenly, weary of pretence, she said, "To be honest, I didn't go to Dublin because I had some …difficult news." She paused, composed herself. "My ex-husband had a baby with his new partner, it em," the wobble in her voice broke through "set me back, so instead I decided to keep in motion, cycled around Westport House, the Greenway… until my limbs seized up."

He looked taken aback. "That's a tough one," he said.

She hadn't mentioned Chloe's pregnancy before, that was a closed chapter, half expected him to leave quickly, steer clear of her troubles.

He didn't. "Did you know it was coming?"

"Yeah, but it was hard to talk about," she ran her hands over her dry eyes, "we'd been trying for a baby at the same time as she got pregnant."

"Phew, heavy."

"Yeah."

They sat in silence, which wasn't awkward, more like he was keeping her company, which she appreciated.

"Anything I can do?" he asked.

"Thanks, but Anne next door has done some shopping for me, she's a gift of a neighbour." Then sick of herself, she said, "Enough of me, how's your Mam?"

"Fine, she's made her Christmas cakes and puddings, so taken up knitting again. She says it's back in fashion."

"In London too, you can tell her."

And so they chatted inconsequentially for a bit, which was a relief. When he was leaving, he hugged her, she couldn't withdraw lest he misinterpret it. "If you need coal, whatever, it's easy with the van."

"Thanks so much," she said, wanting to say something about their night together, but nothing came.

Buttoning up his coat, he suddenly said, "Helen, you did nothing wrong to make this happen, remember that."

*

Next morning, the scrawny tree branch leaned towards the glass as though seeking shelter from the cold. She didn't blame it. *You did nothing wrong to make this happen* echoed. She didn't know what Finn meant, but now thought about it. Failure had haunted her after the breakup, failure to conceive, failure to keep Shane's love and for the past year, failure to move on, leave him behind. Had she dragged her sense of failure across the Irish Sea? Is that what Finn perceived? What others perceived? Christ.

Did Shane ever think he failed her: with his lies, his brutal speed of exit, his final hammer blow, setting up house with Chloe nearby? No, he didn't; she was sure of it. He thought their ending was sad, unfortunate, but inevitable once something "different" had taken hold. He'd moved on, leaving Helen behind, weeping and wailing.

A bird call came through the slit of open window – a note of hope – *the thing with feathers*. She put her raingear on and cycled slowly out the road, her destination – anywhere – as far as she could manage. Breathe – push – breathe – push – she commanded her tired body, cycled past wet hedges, dying ferns, and the brown remnants of Montbreesia for ten and a half minutes. It kept her in motion, was better than nothing.

Finn texted: *How are you? Let me know if you need anything.*

She appreciated it, told him she was back on the bike.

Over the week, she continued cycling daily, working around the weather. It was gruelling, tedious, but she knew every inch of ground mattered and slowly her limbs eased, readjusted to the effort, until she got back to the strength she'd had before Isla phoned.

20

With Christmas approaching, Finn's social calendar perked up. Sean rose from the ashes, suggested a drink (no disco) in Westport, so they had pints, talked sport, local news and music, which was good for them both. Then his pal Niall was back from Oz, so a weekend in Dublin with him, Barney and Jamie was organised and they wouldn't take no for an answer.

He visited Helen who looked thin, but less wan, apologised for burdening him with woes.

"I'm glad you told me," he said and meant it. He understood more about her escape to Achill now. Then she mentioned going to Dublin to her sister's around the same time as he'd be up there.

"Do you want to meet in the big smoke?" he asked, the thought of a new setting appealed.

She was unclear about dates, said she'd let him know.

He hoped this wasn't reluctance, didn't ask, it was hardly the time.

In the end, they passed like ships in the night, her travelling up the day he was leaving Dublin, but she surprised him with a phone-call while he was there, wondering how he was enjoying the metropolis? He took this as a good sign.

Once in Dublin, he fell happily into an overdue catch up with old friends. But twenty-four hours of talk, laughs and too much booze, left Finn in need of a quiet day. He wanted to tour the city, which he didn't know very well and decided on a cultural tour, seeking out the city's memorials and taking photos as he went. Kill two birds with one stone, he figured. He invited Barney to come. Niall and Jamie had failed to make breakfast any day, so were non-starters.

"Cultural tour? What's got into you?" Barney demanded, mopping up egg yoke.

"I've pounds to lose after two fried breakfasts and all those pints," Finn replied. "And so do you, if you ask me!"

"Speak your mind why don't you!" Then working through his last mouthful, Barney, asked, "Is this new woman turning your head?"

"What new woman?"

"The one you were talking to last night!"

Jesus walls have ears, Finn thought. "My sister you mean?"

"You don't have a sister called Helen," he said. "Tell me about her and I'll consider going."

"Blackmail?"

Barney nodded.

He told him briefly about Helen, ending with, "She's not long out of a bad marriage breakup, so it's tricky."

Barney nodded, "Tread carefully Finno, the past can bite hard."

"Okay Mr Counsellor, you coming with me?"

"Yep, show me what you know."

Finn had done some homework and learned key things about Dublin memorials: there were a lot of them; mostly of men, made by men; many had been controversial politically or artistically; a few had been unpopular and been moved to safer terrain, the most famous, Nelson's pillar had been blown up. So, raincoats on, he and Barney took a bus from Drumcondra to the centre.

They spent an exhausting few hours looking at a lot of statues, Parnell, James Connolly, Jim Larkin, Cúchulainn amongst others, and finally, with relief, saw a female sculpture, *Two Women*, sitting with shopping bags, in bronze, near the Halfpenny Bridge. Finn liked it instantly, for its ordinariness and the sense of *spraoi* in the women. Later they found Constance Markievicz and Molly Malone.

"Molly looks a bit brassy," Barney observed.

"At least she's there and the sculptor was a woman, I checked, Jeanne Rynhart." He shook his head, "Y'know, an alien arriving here, would assume the population of Dublin was ninety-nine percent men."

"Your new woman's a feminist?"

"Doesn't it bother you with two daughters?" Finn demanded, "we've only seen sculptures of four women."

Barney nodded, "Yeah, it does, problem is you stop noticing."

On O'Connell Street, they gazed up at the Spire, unable to fathom it.

"It's been dubbed, *The Stiletto in the Ghetto*," he told Barney, who chuckled.

Next stop Trinity College grounds where they quickly took in the statues of Edmund Burke and Oliver Goldsmith, then an abstract shape by Henry Moore.

"I've heard of Moore," Barney said, "but what's it supposed to be?"

"Search me!" Finn looked more closely, liked the muscular shapes. "Maybe it doesn't matter?"

They walked on and Bingo – a sculpture called, *Apples and Atoms,* by a woman called Eilis O'Connell.

"I like that," Barney said.

"Me too, it's humorous isn't it? Well done Eilis." He would mention this one to Gawina.

On they went to Stephen's Green where there were a lot of sculptures, including a Henry Moore abstract version of W.B. Yeats.

"Doesn't look anything like him" Barney said.

Finn agreed. By now Barney was flagging, decided he needed an Irish coffee to set him right, a hair of the dog.

Finn was tempted, but knew if he stopped, he'd never continue, made it to the canal, to the Patrick Kavanagh memorial which he was certain Barney would like. It looked like Kavanagh for starters, he thought as he sat beside him on the bench, realised he was warming to Martha's idea of life-size figures of tatie hokers on Achill.

He pushed on, finally found two which knocked him out. *The Children of Lir* by Oisin Kelly in the Garden of Remembrance, made to commemorate the fiftieth anniversary of the 1916 Rising – big, bold, with fantastic shape and movement to it. He knew the story from childhood: four children doomed to become swans for three hundred years by the act of a woman, jealous of their father's affection. It was all there, the children, the swans, but something which amazed him – sorrow – captured in bronze. How did the sculptor manage that?

He fantasised about placing something that strong at Achill Sound, to evoke tattie hokin, but quickly copped on to himself – they'd never get the money.

The other knock-out was the *Famine Monument* along Custom House Quay – six gaunt figures, two women, four men, clutching pathetic bundles, one carrying a child over his shoulders, barefoot, ravaged faces, arriving at the point of departure for the steamer to the United States, the year the famine began in 1846. Sculpted by Rowan Gillespie, Finn found it downright disturbing. It had everything: hunger, desperation, trauma, etched into the faces and bodies. The idea of a group impressed him too, suggested a village, town, community. He reckoned Gawina would call it a sculpture with emotional impact.

*

Back on Achill he got a call from Milo, offering him a free meal voucher, for two, on Saturday night in the Newport restaurant he was managing. "We're trying to boost numbers."

Finn rang Helen to invite her.

"That would be nice," she said.

The place had been refurbished, trendy décor with local artists' work dotted round. Milo welcomed them, sat them by the window.

"Just as well I put my glad rags on," Helen said, registering Finn's smart shirt.

She looked great in a wine dress, with hooped silver earrings; she also said at the outset that she didn't want to talk of her woes, she'd had a bellyful of them. She spoke purposefully, so he didn't argue.

He felt well pleased to be on a night out, having a fancy meal, glass of wine at a candlelit table, sensed from a kind of glitter from her that she felt the same. They agreed that the starter of dips was promising, but the main course didn't live up: slow roast pork with apple and beetroot sauce, had too many things going on.

"Milo could cook the socks off whoever's in that kitchen," Finn whispered.

"Why's he not the chef?"

"They moved back from Manchester with two kids, lucky to get a Manager job."

"So," she said with a wry smile, "our topic tonight is football isn't it, as we did Art last time?"

He wanted to laugh but it was too good an opportunity to miss. "Soccer or GAA?" he enquired.

Her brow furrowed, "Em, probably GAA."

"Well, you must know the tragedy which haunts Mayo football?" he began.

"Just recap it for me?"

"Well they live under a curse…" He watched her intent look, her determination to keep the promise … "but the problem is, there's no craic talking about GAA with someone who knows nothing about it."

She contained her relief, "You sure?"

"Definitely."

Instead he told her about Dublin's memorial sculptures, which fascinated her, then she talked about her recent Grace Henry research, so Art triumphed again.

Happily the dessert, raspberry and lemon tart was delicious, so they could give Milo overall positive feedback.

As they walked back to the van, Helen pointed, "Look at that moon".

It was almost full, a silvery lamp in a cloudless sky.

"Want to watch it on the water at Cloughmore Harbour?" he asked.

She nodded and on the way they competed for the number of songs which included lines about the moon, which Finn won hands down.

"Who'd guess such a romantic heart beats under a gruff exterior?" she said.

"Gruff exterior?" he retorted, "you're just a bad loser."

They parked on the pier and sat watching moonlight streak the water of the Sound.

"Magic," she said.

"I remember being scared of the moon as a child."

"Why?"

"Afraid it would crash to the ground and break."

She smiled, patted his arm, "A sensitive lad."

He grinned, "Yep."

She leaned towards him gave him a swift kiss, pulled back, then he returned the favour, kissed her and quickly they were embracing and kissing.

"Moonlight is an aphrodisiac," she said, taking a breath.

He nodded, kissed her again.

She broke free to ask, "Did you ever have sex in a car?"

"Jesus," he said, surprised. "Will... my answer incriminate me?"

"I'll tell if you tell!"

He shrugged, "Yes, and that's all I'm admitting to."

"Me too."

"Well, there are planks of wood and a bloody big toolbox in the back of this, so I wouldn't recommend it."

She grinned, "My diaphragm's at home ... shall we settle for my bed?"

He turned the ignition on, drove to her house, and

without much talk, or any hesitation, they hastened to the bedroom and had urgent sex.

While she went to the bathroom afterwards, he lay thinking that Helen Bradshaw was a woman of more elements than he'd guessed. He'd assumed she'd be too sad for sex, instead she was light-hearted, jokey this evening.

When she returned he said, "You seem brighter tonight."

"Good," she said. "I'm so feckin tired of being woeful, sad, depressed – it's no life." She spoke seriously, " I want to have a life again."

When she moved into his arms, he stroked her hair. "I'd like to see more of you."

She looked quizzical, "More of me?"

"More often I mean."

She closed her eyes, "I thought you were leaving as soon as?"

"Yes, but when isn't exactly clear. And besides, aren't you also on temporary licence until March at the latest?"

"Yeah."

"Well, since we're both in the waiting room of the train station, perhaps we could spend more time together while we're here?"

She raised her eyebrows, "You've a way with words."

"So they tell me! Is that yes, no?"

Finally, she said, "Yes."

Next morning they drove to Keel and walked the beach together, then back in Shraheens where they kissed and parted for Christmas: she to Edinburgh, he to Galway, after which he'd go walking with Barney and Milo in Connemara.

*

He held onto his upbeat mood all day, only at night did he wonder if he'd been rash suggesting they meet more, given life's uncertainty. But mightn't she be gone before him in March, so why go down that penal path?

For now, they had both opted into living life, instead of letting it drag them along. Surely that was good.

21

Helen was dozing off when the loud, sharp cries rang out. She forced herself to the window, saw Cathy lying screaming on the grassed area, her husband grabbing at her, trying to pull her up. She scanned Anne's house, saw the lights were on upstairs and this time phoned 999. Her voice shook as she told them a woman was being beaten outside her house and that there were children at home.

"We'll send a car out as soon as possible," the Garda said.

"How long will that take?"

A slight pause, "We'll do our best to get a car out quickly."

She threw her coat on, opened the door, saw that Cathy's husband was now trying to pull her by the hair, which she was resisting, flailing at his hands to stop him, screaming all the time.

"Shut the fuck up," he shouted.

Helen was terrified to get too close, willing Anne to appear, began calling out, "Leave her alone, leave her alone."

He looked up sharply, without letting go of Cathy's hair, his face livid, eyes blazing, "Who the fuck asked you?"

But her voice had thrown him, his grip on Cathy's hair loosened, and she began whimpering.

"Get up," he roared.

Cathy's face, visible for the first time, was bloodied, much bloodier than before.

"Leave her alone," Helen shouted again, her mouth dry as paper and suddenly Anne was there, saying in a loud, firm voice, "Your wife's injured, she needs treatment."

He swirled towards Anne, "I've warned you already to mind your own fucking business." Then he was grabbing at Cathy's arm, "Get up," but Cathy, sobbing, made no move, so he let go of her so abruptly her head banged on the ground.

Thank God, it's grass, Helen thought.

"Fuck's sake," he snarled, striding into the house.

Helen and Anne moved towards Cathy, who lay unmoving, crying, crying.

A minute later, he stormed out, opened his car door and half way in, said, "You fuckin bitches haven't heard the end of this!" Then he drove out on a squeal of tyres, past the two women, immobile as statues.

Every movement of the next part of that night is stamped on Helen's mind: they managed to get Cathy inside, covered her with a blanket on the sofa, her injuries obvious, red patches from where she'd been hit, a rapidly rising bruise on her temple, to which Anne applied a frozen pack of peas, her lip split, bloodied. She didn't speak, lay sobbing, face turned away until Róisín and Lena appeared, like two little sprites, white faced, barefoot, probably awake for the whole desperate episode. They rushed forward, wailing and threw themselves on her, "Mam, Mam."

"I'm alright," she said, "I'm alright," covering them with her arms.

Suddenly, Paddy appeared, ashen faced.

"I told him to stay in the house," Anne whispered, "his blood pressure's up," but he refused to leave, set about making tea, with help from Róisín who directed him to cups and teabags.

Half an hour later, blue lights and sirens arrived, bringing an older man and young female Garda. Enough time for Cathy to be lying dead, Helen thought.

Other than to tell them her own and her husband's name, Cathy declined to talk, saying her head was too sore. They took statements from Helen and Anne, they already knew Cathy and her husband, had been called out before, were sympathetic but resigned to the possibility that Cathy wouldn't cooperate. Before now, Helen would have been angry at their resignation, tonight, she felt depressingly resigned herself. An ambulance arrived, the Medic tried to persuade Cathy into it, but she wouldn't budge, she was staying at home with her kids, she kept saying.

Then Anne found her nurse's voice, "That bruise on your head is nasty Cathy, they need to check for concussion." So Anne prevailed, while Lena became hysterical as her mother was helped into the ambulance. "Stop it Lena," Róisín kept telling her sister, to no avail.

Anne lifted Lena into her arms, the child gulped sobs into her chest and clung like a limpet. Helen put her arm around Róisín's shoulders, she didn't shrug her off, but never looked at her. Her little body was stiff as a board, her shoulders too small and slight for this burden.

The Gardai remained until the Social Worker, Miriam, arrived. She knew the girls, would take them to a foster family they'd stayed with before, until contact with their grandmother was established. But no way was Lena letting go of Anne, so Helen made hot chocolate for everyone, Paddy adding a drop of whiskey to his, Anne's and Helen's. Finally, Lena nodded off, and Miriam moved her to the car where she stayed asleep, next to Róisín.

Then it was Helen, Anne and Paddy alone, grey faced. She remembers Paddy saying two and a half hours had passed since the screams had woken them, and suddenly the air oozed out of her, she began shaking, like her scaffolding had loosened.

When Anne insisted she sleep in their house, she didn't argue, obediently got into bed with a hot water bottle. But her brain was firing with rage, at the girls' father's brutality and the power he had wielded over them all, until exhaustion won out and her eyes closed.

*

Two days later Anne and Paddy drove Helen to Keel to deposit her things in her new house and the following day she flew to Edinburgh.

It took a quiet, comfortable Christmas with Isla and her mother, Maisie, to wipe her head clean of the Shraheens nightmare. She was wined, dined, and the sleety cold, with a bitter East wind blowing round the city, gave them the perfect excuse to hole up indoors next to the fire. The house was full of middle class comforts – deep armchairs, oriental rugs, good food, all of which Helen savoured gratefully.

On Christmas Day, after a delicious dinner, Maisie, a retired piano teacher, played some Chopin and Schumann, Isla read from Robbie Burns and Jackie Kay, while Helen sang two Irish songs. The warmth here reminded her of Nellie Kilbane's kitchen, but this time she was able to stay and doze off in the deep embracing Parker-Knoll armchair.

They ventured out for a walk on St Stephen's Day, talked about Grace Henry and the uphill struggle for women artists and on their return Isla told Helen of her relief at seeing her looking well, feared she'd be gaunt!

In the tea room, Helen mentioned Finn's name and Isla's antennae shot out.

"A new beau?"

"No!"

"C'mon, did you sleep with him?"

"Well…a couple of times!"

Isla cut the garish pink iced fancy in halves, handed one half to Helen, said, "I'm glad," looking pleased.

Helen picked at the pink icing, "I'm not sure I should be with any man for a long time yet," she said, "but I like him and it's a way of getting back into life …?"

"For sure Hel, a good fling is like a good holiday, sets you up for the year ahead."

The icing dissolved in Helen's mouth, pure white sugar swilling round. "I'm not sure I know how to handle flings."

Isla squeezed her hand, "You can learn, what's to lose?" She licked her lips clean, "This cake is revoltingly sweet …" she grinned, "and compulsive."

*

The night before she left, Isla mentioned the annual Christmas gathering at Maria and Carl's, the one Helen and Shane used to go to.

Helen forced herself to ask, "Were Shane and Chloe there?"

Isla hesitated, said, "Yeah, with the baby, a sweet wee bairn."

Helen felt the slice of a knife on her skin, but knew this was the price to pay for coming out of hiding and asking.

"Shane asked about you," Isla added, "I said you liked living on Achill and that your research was going well. Okay?"

Helen nodded, both were true.

*

She flew back to Dublin to stay with Fiona for a few days where life seemed more settled. However, Clodagh, grounded over the festive season, wore a permanent hard-done-by look and spent a lot of time in her room.

On the last night, over a brandy, Helen told her sister about an evening in Gibney's shed, by way of defence of Clodagh. Matt Gibney, a couple of years older, did a paper round, so had a bit of money, as well as edge. One Saturday night, his sister, Geraldine, invited Helen and Reena, her pal, into the shed, where Matt and a few others were gathered.

While Michael Jackson blasted in the background, Matt passed three large bottles of Bulmers cider around. Helen had…four slugs maybe, it tasted alright, but much better was the woozy feeling it brought. Pretty soon they were all laughing about nothing. She remembered feeling emboldened, able to bat the chat back and forward with Matt and Richie Malone and how Richie winked at her.

Sitting on tool boxes and paint pots, Gibney's shed was their Shebeen that night. "It was thrilling," Helen said, "my first foray into illicit pleasure."

Robin laughed, but Fiona didn't even smile.

"It's different now Helen," she said, "those days were innocent by comparison."

"Fiona, I teach kids who come into school hung over, I know it's different, but Gibney's didn't kill me nor land me behind bars. Clodagh's story is a modern version of an old tale!"

Fiona refused to consider it.

*

TRIARC had reopened and Helen took herself off there next day. By ten-thirty Helen was back, taking up where she'd left off, a state which seemed to mirror her current life: picking up pieces again.

The ending of the Henrys' marriage was a bitter, drawn out affair. Grace came and went to France, where, possibly on the advice of Mainie Jellett, she studied under André Lhote, a Cubist, with whom many Irish women painters had studied, including Mainie Jellett and Evie Hone. His influence was visible apparently, in her painting, *Still Life with Torso*, but also clear was her interest and willingness to experiment with new techniques.

Meanwhile, Paul was drinking heavily and according to a friend, the failing marriage was like a "bad Strindberg play". The Henrys held their last joint exhibition at their Merrion Row studio in 1926. In 1928, Grace exhibited *Paintings of France and Ireland* in London where only one painting sold and when the Gallery billed Paul for the outstanding debt, it didn't help matters.

An afternoon tea episode in Dublin, 1925, was recounted. Away in France, Grace was unaware of Paul's involvement with a young Art student, Mabel Young, while Mabel claimed to be unaware of Grace's existence. On her return, Paul invited her to meet him and Mabel in a Grafton

Street café! Grace brought a friend, and according to Mabel's account, (the only account available), it was a very strained affair. Paul's biographer recorded Mabel's first impression of Grace, as "sweetness and light "but she sensed, "hard metal under a velvet glove".

This shot Helen back to London on a day when a card fell through her letterbox after Shane had moved into his friend Bart's place and she'd moved back to her flat alone, both taking time out from each other. The card was of a delicate Chinese flower painting, plum blossom …from a plum fairy, Helen thought when she opened it.

Chloe suggested in small, fine handwriting that they meet and talk.

Helen was stunned: Talk – about what? Sharing custody of Shane?

It might help, Chloe wrote.

Help who? You fucking bitch.

She remembered the strange fear which seized her, that her kitchen roof might collapse on top of her, that it wouldn't stay aloft. When she calmed down, Helen knew the fear was triggered by Chloe's confidence oozing from that card, her assumption of importance in Shane's life, after knowing him for what… eight bloody months? Helen, his partner of twelve years, on the other hand, now lived in a state of dread and fear, clinging on … to blind hope that Shane would realise he couldn't live without her. She'd dumped the card in the bin.

A wave of sadness tugged, but she gritted her teeth, made herself return to her reading. Paul went to live with Mabel in Carrigonna Cottage in Wicklow and began proceedings for a "voluntary settlement", the only option in a country with no divorce laws. Grace apparently was still hoping their separation would be temporary and in 1929 returned to Paris, where she painted a portrait of James Joyce. This opportunity represented an artistic coup for her, and the picture of Joyce sitting at a table reading a manuscript was included in a solo exhibition in Dublin in 1930 where she showed one hundred paintings. Helen paused to take that in – one hundred paintings! It was a remarkable tour de force, given her personal circumstances, and "a testament to her powers of concentration," in the writer's view.

Helen checked the time – shit – as always it was running out, the final section unread, but she'd miss her damn train if she'd didn't leave now. And so she parted company with the thesis, scrabbled her stuff together and rushed out to catch a bus to Heuston.

On the train she thought of Grace – love, marriage falling apart, very little money – and she exhibited one hundred paintings. It was beyond impressive. Helen should take a leaf from her book.

*

Keel was dead as a doornail when Helen arrived back, Martha and James in Dublin, their house dark, only one house had lights. Within a day, she was laid low, couldn't hold food down, liquids just about manageable. It scared her, was similar to the nausea she'd had after Shane left. Psychosomatic – her GP said. But why would that hit her here and now? She slept badly, woke from a dream, where she was moving backwards down a tunnel and however hard she tried, couldn't make her legs move forward.

"Sounds like you have a virus," Finn said, when he phoned, advised she visit the doctor.

The thought cheered her, it was probably a normal person's ailment, something medication could fix. "Yeah, I'll go and get something."

But mention of his walking trip in Connemara threw her; she'd forgotten, found herself wishing he wasn't going. Dear Lord, had she arrived at missing him already?

22

Christmas in Galway was *iontach* – *craic, ceol, bia, deoch*. Maura's kids took Finn on walks and evenings everyone played board games or had music sessions. His mother sat back, at Maura's insistence, while she whizzed about with high octane energy, managing everything, Santa Claus included. Awesome – she seemed to thrive being on the run.

"When I'm teaching I've so little time to do this stuff," she said.

Finn insisted she let him load the dishwasher, wash pots, or, hardest of all, cook a meal, but he was determined and his *Pollo al pimiento* went down a treat. Isabel had taught it to him, which made him wonder how she was – with her parents in Alicante celebrating *La Navidad* in that low key way the Spaniards managed? He also wondered if she'd happily replaced him.

He and Declan, his farmer brother-in-law rubbed along easily, recognising they inhabited different worlds, felt no obligation to force anything. Finn took a few longer walks, glad that Maura and his mother seemed content to catch up, visit cousins and the do the Sales in Galway.

Before he left for Clifden to hike with Milo and Barney,

he and Maura sat up late sipping Bushmills. After talk of this and that, she mentioned Kevin's possible visit in Spring and Finn decided to sound her out about Kevin. As older sister and a mother herself, Maura might have some insights. "I've never been able to work him out," he said, "we never got on, so the visit's tricky for me."

She looked surprised. "Really? Well it's a while since we've all seen him, so I think it's good he's coming especially for Mam's sake and my kids are excited about meeting their Aussie cousins."

Fair enough but she'd avoided his comment about them not getting on, wondered if she saw it as picking at old childhood scabs. He tried again. "What kind of relationship did you have with him?"

She chewed her lip, "Well, eldest girl, I was indoors helping Mam, Kevin, eldest boy, was outside helping Dad, we slotted into our roles I suppose, got on okay. You and Sinead, on the other hand, got away with murder!" She grinned at his shrug of protest, "Sinead carved out her special role early – knitting jumpers, crocheting hats, which brought in a bit of money, so she was allowed keep her hands clean." She paused, "And your role as youngest, was being Mam's darling, wasn't it?"

He defended himself, "Outdoor dogsbody more like, sweeping the yard, washing down sheds, equipment." He paused, "I loved the sheep, but Dad wouldn't let me near them, because I was useless." He swirled his golden brew in the glass, saw her watching him closely, "Mam says Dad was hard on Kevin, nothing he did was good enough?"

She nodded, "I'd a sense of that, though didn't see why. Kevin was a great farmer."

"Apparently Dad's father was even harder on him."

She poured them both another nip, "The sins of the fathers... that it?"

"Maybe." He took a sip, decided to say it, "You know when I was eight, I believed he tried to kill me."

"What?" She jolted forward, "That's a very heavy thing to say!"

"It was a very heavy thing he did."

"Ah c'mon Finn, kids can be rough and mean, I know that well, I teach eight year olds and have one."

In response, he told her about the water barrel.

When he finished she sat silent a while, before speaking. "That's cruel, not all kids are cruel, but... he came and got you out, that's important." She let out a big sigh, "Dear Lord, you could have died, but," her face brightened, "he didn't let that happen."

"It could have happened if he'd mistimed it."

She frowned, nodded.

"Do you remember I told you he was always picking on me and you told him off?"

She shook her head, "I don't. Did it help?"

Finn shrugged. "I avoided him after the barrel and once he moved into secondary, he ignored me, until my teens, when he seemed to hate me all over again." He leaned towards her, "This isn't poor me Maura, I'm trying to get my head around it."

She grimaced, "Y'know Finn, I'm not sure it's wise raking over old stuff."

"Really? Is that what educational psychologists recommend to teachers these days... leave it fester?"

She shook her head, "Obviously not. I suppose it's harder to think about when it's close to home."

"What I'm trying to work out," he continued," is why

182

Kevin needed to torment me if I was the useless one. Where was the threat?"

She frowned, "Maybe… it was to do with Mam?"

"Mam?"

"You were Mam's *peata*, the golden haired boy. Sinead and I agree totally on that, but yerra, it doesn't bother us. You were the youngest, a surprise, Mam told me."

"She never told me that," he said. "But Kevin was Dad's favoured son, so why should he mind if Mam kept me close to her apron strings? Didn't it make me even more useless?"

"Maybe…" she poked the fire, "he'd have preferred to be Mam's favourite, resented you?"

"Why so?"

"Wasn't Mam the emotional heart of the house, Dad never knew how to do that stuff, except when she prodded him into it. Maybe Kevin felt you had the better deal."

This was a new thought entirely. Was there truth in it – Kevin wanted to be his mother's favourite, more than his father's and passed on the harsh treatment he got from their father to Finn? "Don't know what I think about that," he said, "that's a new angle."

She shrugged, "Mull it over Finn."

By then, it was obvious she was drooping, time for bed had come. He thanked her for the chat but before heading off, she reverted to cheery mode, "Sure ye'll probably hit it off like a house on fire in the Spring."

"A house on fire – exactly!"

*

Four days hill walking around Clifden with Milo and Barney was exactly what he needed: pushing body and mind, through wind, rain and intermittent sunshine, left him no space for ruminating on either his past or his future, instead pinned him closely to hill, rock, fence, field. Evenings they caught up with each other over food and pints then fell gratefully into bed. He rang Helen who'd had a lovely Christmas but was laid low with a stomach bug, so he urged her to see the doctor.

The day before they left, the rain pelted full force, trapping them indoors. Barney and Milo were content to watch Premiership football, with pints, for the afternoon, Finn wasn't, so he opted to read. But somehow, he couldn't get into his book, his conversation with Maura about Kevin kept intruding.

It felt like a breakthrough to have talked to Maura; so much about Kevin remained buried. He'd told Alison about the barrel incident and Phil once, in a drunken heart to heart, both of them shocked by it, but nobody else. Was it fear or shame? Over time Kevin had become like a mouldy sock he'd shoved safely away in a locked drawer. But it had fallen out of the drawer on Finn's return home – setting off the smell, touch, sound of Kevin again.

Their last summer bust-up was the final blow. It was a precious summer, Finn's Leaving Cert exams over, hopeful about a place in Galway University, the summer days stretching ahead of him. After their day's work around the farm, he and Sean cycled, swam, fished, smoked weed and drank when they could. He could still picture those long blue evenings, sometimes with streaky pink sunsets, other times, a bold orange canvas tinting the waters of the Sound, the fields, houses.

Finn landed a weekend job as a Lounge boy at the Sound, – money of his own – and Sara O'Donnell, his new girlfriend who worked there – Sara of the dark hair and long legs, funny and strong minded. Even Kevin's dirty slagging when he saw the two of them kissing by the bridge, didn't get to him. Finn would be moving away from Kevin's poisonous tongue, one way or another.

When word came of his place in college, his mother made a roast lamb dinner to celebrate, his father handed him an envelope with money and May gave him a card with twenty quid. Then they toasted him with a glass of wine.

"Well done Finn, credit where credit's due," his father said, the only praise he'd ever given him.

Later, Sean met him in their barn to smoke a joint before heading out and soon after, Kevin arrived, so suddenly, Sean almost burned his finger killing the spliff. "Feck it, Kevin, I thought it was your Dad!"

Kevin sniffed the air, "The scholars getting stoned?"

Sean offered him the rescued joint.

"I don't do that shit," he said, lighting a fag. Kevin never hung out with Finn and from the glitter in his eyes, Finn knew he'd drunk more than a glass of wine, he kept a secret stash somewhere. Time to get out of there, he knew Kevin's moods better than his own. "Let's head Sean, the others are waiting."

But Sean was yapping away, even mentioned Sara, "She's hot, isn't she?"

"If you like that kind of thing," Kevin said.

"As though you'd know anything about her," Finn spat out.

"I know she's a cheap ride, I'd steer clear if I was you, Finno!"

"Jealous are ya?"

"Ask Peter, he has the gory details!"

Peter Kane, Kevin's asshole pal, fancied himself as the local stud. Sara wouldn't give him the time of day.

"Don't you have sheep to put to bed?" Finn asked.

Sean had gone silent.

Kevin's eyes flamed, "Better than a girl's job, licking arses, wiping up shit."

Finn knew this was payback for the toast, and a long buried heat seized him, "You're sick, you know that, you try to poison everything," and for the first time since he was eight, he leapt forward to thump him. But Kevin crossed his arms, a barricade against Finn's efforts.

"Truth hurts eh?" Kevin sneered.

"Cool it lads," Sean said, moving to get at Finn but not before Finn shouted, "Fucking bastard you are," landing a punch on Kevin's shoulder, wobbling him, which gave him a chance to land another. Forced to drop his defence, Kevin then hit out and landed a single heavy blow to Finn's chest which bent him double, sucking for air.

"You'll have your father in here," Sean shouted, hauling Finn away.

"Fuck-ing bas-tard," Finn hissed through short breaths. "All you have is sheep to shag."

"Ooh," Kevin mocked, "that really hurt," clenching his fists for the next round.

"Stop," Sean shouted louder, "or I'll feckin leave yis to kill each other."

Finn saw hatred in his brother's eyes, knew Kevin saw the same in his – they might kill each other if left to it.

Kevin turned on his heel, banging the door behind him.

"What the fuck's got into him?" Sean demanded.

"That's who he fuckin is!" Finn replied.

Finn considered it now: their first fight in a long time

and their last. They never got over it. Worst of all, it killed his precious summer. Kevin's presence became a seeping poison, he could barely get through a meal sitting at the same table, so he gave up the Lounge boy job and started in a Castlebar Supermarket, packing shelves, Monday to Friday, "for college money," he said.

His mother noticed his dour mood, asked over dinner, "What's up with you?"

Before he could answer, Kevin said, "Girl trouble," so she left it alone.

He told Sinead he hated Kevin, "Ignore him," she said, "he can be right bitter when he wants, don't let him get to you."

Way too late for that.

The long summer evenings stole away. He was never free when Sara was and she started going out with Cillian O'Malley, which broke his heart. All he had was the odd evening cycle, or swim with Sean and the lads. And he blamed Kevin for it all.

But he saw something different now, the extremity of his own response. He didn't believe what Kevin said about Sara, knew Kevin invented it but he'd ended up sacrificing Sara and his summer anyway. Why? With hindsight, it was stupid, wasteful, driven solely by his need to escape Kevin, his habit of a lifetime.

It depressed him now that the mouldy sock was still potent, could aggravate him all over again, so he shoved it back into its drawer. He'd more important things to think about. He, Milo and Barney were heading out soon for their last supper, some place uptown with food, music and drink, just what body and soul needed.

23

Next morning Helen went to see a Dr Burke, in the Health Centre, seeking a medical solution to a medical problem. She joined a queue where everyone seemed to know each other. She wasn't in form for chat, dived on the reading material – two dog eared copies of *Ireland's Own* and some glossy magazines. One had an eight page colour spread of a celebrity wedding, which had since crashed and burned, amidst another magazine frenzy.

She waited for an hour and a half, was told when she asked, she'd be called in a while. Acceptance seemed the dominant mood – so she listened to the woman next to her describing her arthritis pains. Undoubtedly, it was a burden to bear, so Helen tried counting her blessings. Finally, she was sitting in front of the doctor, wanting only two things: tablets and a quick exit.

"So, you've had these symptoms for a few days?" he asked, peering from behind his bifocals. He was maybe early sixties, dressed in a tweed jacket with a woollen waistcoat, dapper in an old style way, his manner reserved but alert.

She nodded.

"Are you prone to stomach problems?"

"Not generally… but last year after I separated from my husband, eh, ex-husband, I developed a nervous stomach thing."

"Did you have it checked out?"

"Yes, no lumps, ulcers – stress was the verdict."

"I see," he said and suggested a quick check-up, blood pressure, heart, then a urine test, all the time telling her about the difficulty of diagnosing a virus accurately.

She couldn't fault him on his thoroughness.

He took a couple of minutes with the tests then returned to the computer to type in some notes.

"Well, it's not stress," he said.

She was so relieved, "A bug?"

"No, not that either."

She had the sense that he was waiting for something from her, Jesus, was it cancer?

"When was your last period?" he suddenly asked.

"My period? Well, they've been erratic over the past year," she grimaced, "stress related… probably about six, seven weeks ago."

"Right." He made a note

"Well, Miss Bradshaw," he said, "according to the urine test, you're pregnant," and he returned his eyes to his screen.

Her response was instant, "I couldn't be."

He lifted his gaze, wordlessly quizzed her, then spoke. "You haven't had intercourse…?"

"I've used contraception each time, my diaphragm, I took no risks."

He nodded. "The test isn't one hundred per cent accurate at this early stage, I'd advise you to do a second test in a few days. You can obtain a kit at the chemist."

"But I had a period six weeks ago…?"

He nodded. "It can happen in pregnancy, it's not a proper period, but confusing obviously."

She stayed firm, "This has to be a mistake."

"The second test will confirm it one way or another," he repeated, "although your symptoms of nausea, fatigue, are similar to early pregnancy."

The man wasn't listening, didn't get it. "You don't understand. I tried to get pregnant with my husband, ex-husband, for almost a year and couldn't, so how could I...now after sleeping twice with someone else, using contraception?"

"Did you have fertility tests?"

"No..." she felt herself flounder, "I'd been on the pill, we were advised it could take time."

He nodded sympathetically, "Often it does."

"So, how could this happen?"

He paused to pick his words, "If I may ask, was it a different partner?"

"Yes."

"No contraception is one hundred percent safe and without a fertility test it's difficult to conclude anything." He paused, "There are...some imponderables, when it comes to conception Miss Bradshaw, that even Science hasn't yet fathomed."

Imponderables – what a load of shite!

Helen began gathering her coat and bag, anger rising. She wanted out of here, stood abruptly and he stood to guide her to the door. "Whatever the cause," he said calmly, "if vomiting starts, you need to keep taking fluids."

She didn't look at him.

"Come back if you wish."

As if! Helen left the room without a backward glance.

*

She saw him stretching his shoulders at the window watching her as she stepped outside, knew he was thinking she was like all the other women who'd said, "This must be a mistake." Well it was a mistake, she knew, glaring back. He was wrong, wrong. Then he disappeared from the window.

Helen rang a taxi, sat in her sitting room, blinds down, door locked, and raged. The man was an incompetent who should have retired years ago. She could not be pregnant, she had been unable to conceive when she'd wanted to, how could she conceive now, when she'd been careful each time with Finn. The doctor was a feckin eejit.

Five days later, still nauseous, she took herself to Westport, bought some supplies then grimly got a pregnancy kit in a Chemist, before going home. When the lines began to change colour – turning hateful pink – she grabbed the box convinced she was mixing up the colours, but no, there it was: fucking, unbelievable, positive.

She slumped onto the bathroom floor, feeling that someone was playing with her, only peeled herself off when the cold crept into her bones. Then she lay in bed, to heat up, until slowly, all feeling ebbed away.

Later, the winter sun broke through. A yellow shaft landed on her duvet cover and lit one of the cream walls, warming her hand in its path. She began drifting back into sleep, her mind calm, the baby she'd longed for, week after week, had chosen now ... she saw the tiny, dark, round head of the boy she'd carried in her mind for months. He'd chosen now to come and Shane would never know, never, ever, know.

It was dark when she woke, seven on the clock and she floated peacefully for a minute before reality rushed back on a chilly wave. She sat upright. She was losing her mind, babies did not lie waiting in your womb for the right moment. This baby had no link with Shane whatsoever. What was wrong with her? Where had that crazy idea come from? She fell back, the ceiling staring down mockingly.

The truth was much simpler and starker. Somehow, despite taking care, despite taking no risks, despite never considering it, she had conceived with Finn Kilbane the first time … or the second time they'd had sex. Was some God playing a nasty joke? Finn was almost a stranger, a man passing through, they were two people between things, temporarily on Achill, where she had no choices, no options. Christ Almighty! She could not be a mother at this point, nor he a father, she was sure.

She lay flattened, closed her eyes until sleep took her away. She dreamt about a bridge she was trying to cross, large, red, like the San Francisco bridge, then suddenly it changed, became small, wooden, the last part of the wooden slats were rotted, too dangerous to walk over so she needed to turn back, but she froze, too fearful to move, stood getting colder and colder.

She woke abruptly, at four a.m. her mind churning after the dream. One feeling was uppermost, she had to put space between herself and Finn, who was due back in a couple of days, she needed to think clearly and fast.

The plan came to her that evening and next morning she climbed out of the pit and moved on a wave of adrenalin. It was an energy she'd forgotten she could muster, like a school race where you dart out of the traps at the whistle, and looking neither right nor left, stay hell-bent on the finishing line.

Her parents had sent her money for a flight to Alicante as a Christmas gift, she rang and said she'd decided to visit, would see them in a few days, told Fiona the same story, then rang Isla to tell her she was pregnant and would come to London after Spain. Isla was completely flummoxed, unsure whether to commiserate or congratulate until Helen explained.

Two days later, she was on the coach to Dublin airport, Finn still away. They'd exchanged texts, the only lie she'd told him was about her mother being unwell, which technically speaking wasn't exactly a lie.

*

When the plane set down in Alicante Airport, Helen found it hard to believe she'd made it. Down the steps she went, above her, a blue sky, air drier than she'd felt for a long while. *Hola Espana.*

And there her father was, when she walked out of the airport, looking anxious, probably still uncertain that she'd actually come, his face breaking into a wide smile when he saw her, and when they drove to the apartment her mother greeted her with tears. Helen had stayed away too long.

Quickly she became the centre of attention, her father fussing, her mother keeping a close eye, which was nerve wracking at first. She feared her mother's eagle eye would detect she was pregnant, but mercifully, she wasn't throwing up and morning nausea was easier to conceal, by lying in until nine. Her pallor and under-eye shadows were commented on but they fitted with a broken heart, a camouflage she was, for once, grateful for.

On the third day, she began shedding winter skin: a sunny January morning, the sky blue, air warm, she put away her jumper, and by two o'clock, while her parents rested, she was walking along the dried river bed towards the sea, wearing a skirt, top, runners, hat, denim jacket in bag, just in case.

Cala Estaca, a sheltered, sandy, half circle, was quiet except for a group of older people sitting on chairs, by the wall, reading, chatting – North European winter migrants. Nobody was swimming, but she was determined, gave herself no time to hesitate, stripped to her togs and walked into the water. It was calm, cool, pinched her ankles and knees as she waded through the shallows but once she gained waist level, she plunged and swam parallel to the beach, moving as fast as she could. The shock subsided quickly, the temperature manageable, the water probably the same temperature as some summer days at Keel. No cause for complaint.

"*Brava,*" one of the women called out when she re-emerged.

Once dressed, jacket on, it was warm enough to sit watching the Mediterranean go through its motions. She lay back, relief oozing from every pore. She had a sudden rush of regret she hadn't considered this place as her bolt hole instead of Achill, but, being with her parents wouldn't have worked and she'd never have discovered Grace Henry.

Achill winter was such an unpredictable beast: bright, dreary, cold, mild, windy, wet, stunning, depending on which element took hold. It had stretched her, depleted her, and it had no shelf life – might last until April, like a guest who didn't know when to go home. She raised her face to the sun's rays, felt briefly blessed.

Then her thoughts were interrupted by her father ringing to find out what time she'd be back. Back? She'd just got here. "Not sure Dad, I'm going to take a walk."

"Oh," he sounded disappointed, "we plan to eat at six."

She glanced at her watch. It gave her two hours.

She walked around the low cliff to the Mirada Bar overlooking La Zenia beach where only a few people walked or sat. Over coffee she observed the colours – bright acrylics – so completely different to Achill. Achill had wonderful shifting light, Helen now knew – water colour days, sharp blue days, miraculous clouds, but also gloomy grey days, when low hanging clouds killed the day before it began. It struck her now that it was this brightness, these strong colours which Grace Henry sought in her travels to Europe – and afterwards her paintings blazed.

Too soon she had to move, to do what she'd come for, spend time with her parents. Along the river bed, wild fennel plants showed their new feathery leaves, sprouting inexplicably from earth that looked dry as dust.

Over dinner her mother thanked her for coming. "It's such a rare thing to have you," she said, while her father called her brave for swimming.

Brave – twice in one day; she felt like an imposter.

Bob Harris, neighbour and friend, popped in that evening. A retired London cabbie, he'd moved to the sun with his wife seven years before, but after his wife's recent death, was alone. He was a compulsive raconteur, amusing in short doses. Her mother, no mean raconteur herself, swopped stories with him while Helen and her father listened and began to fade. She escaped to her bedroom after due diligence, recognising a new symptom of pregnancy, the heavy pull of tiredness on her body. From her bedroom she heard her father washing glasses in the kitchen, his escape she reckoned, while Bob and her mother talked on.

In bed, she was surrounded by photos of herself and Fiona at different ages, of childhood books, games, fragments of their old home transplanted to Playa Flamenca and she saw again, what a big, risky step her parents had taken, to come here.

Next morning, her father took her to Torrevieja Market, while her mother stayed behind. The Market was bustling and Helen was elated by the sight of plump pink and purple aubergines, pyramids of oranges, glistening fish, and from a small stall, the smell of brewing coffee. She'd missed this. When she suggested a lunch of *calamares*, her father said they should get back, not leave her mother too long, if she didn't mind? She did, but didn't say.

Later, walking towards the sea she thought how Finn would love a blast of the Market, then stopped herself. Thinking about him was courting trouble, she had set herself on her own path and had to stay with it. This decision was hers, because it was not the same for him and never would be: he would not carry the baby, would not give birth and be indelibly linked for life with it. Deep down, she believed he would agree. He and she were passengers in a waiting room – his words – who might not be in touch in a year's time.

Enough, she told herself and quickened her step to the sea, where the plunge would clear her mind of everything but water, water.

24

Back on Achill Finn slumped into post-Christmas blues. Helen was in Spain, the Kerrigans still waiting for the go-ahead date and snow was now forecast. He crossed his fingers, hoped it wouldn't happen, the island usually escaped the worst of it.

He was dead wrong: Sunday he woke to a transformed landscape, the snow had made sculptures of the trees and bushes, covered the fields and paths and under its covering, all was silent. When he went outside he was Peter, walking through the wardrobe into Narnia, and above, the sky laden with heavy clouds, meant more to come. He walked along the road's pristine surface, to test it before mounting his bike. It was light, soft snow, not frozen yet, he took a short spin. Not a soul out, only one car passed.

Over the next two days, snowfalls on icy roads made travelling tricky and the History Group meeting was deferred. An upbeat Gawina phoned, she and Wim had spent a lovely Christmas in Castlebar with friends, were staying until the snow cleared.

He texted Helen: *Covered in snow here. How are you?*
She replied: *All well in 18 degrees!*

He wanted to finish his Corraun photography, but impossible on those roads, so cleared out the shed instead, put up a few shelves, varnished them and began painting the bathroom, a job waiting for months.

Later, an email arrived from Eilis. Not one to let us sit idle Finn thought, but in fact it gave him something to ponder and something to do, caged indoors.

Dear All,
RE: Deferred Meeting:

As timing is of the essence in these matters, I attach a copy of the Application form for Development Funding. A mere 20 pages! Closing date, March 2nd. Funding seems to range from 5000-30,000 euro.

Can everyone peruse it before next meeting, as completing it will be a complicated task.

Thanks
RSVP

Shit, twenty pages, was Finn's first reaction. He skimmed the lengthy form: on the plus side, it didn't seem to require more than preliminary project outlines, but on the minus side, it required lots of information about the Group, its structure, members, CV's, prior activities, copies of press coverage etcetera.

Groan. Did this data about the Group even exist?

He rang Sean, who put his professional Planner hat on. "That's a very ambitious project," was his first reaction.

"Yep. They're ambitious thinkers."

A slight pause. "Right." he said. "Well, as they've never

done a large scale project before, their only hope in hell is to get hold of Development money."

"They know that now, the Trust sometimes gives it, so that's the strategy."

"Well, the nature and location of any Memorial dictates everything – planning permission, regulation, costs, my advice would be – choose very wisely, something achievable, manageable!"

"I'll pass that on," Finn agreed, "but why do they need so much info about the Group members?"

"For funders the Group is as important as the project and yours is a small Group with a big idea, which will worry them," Sean said. "They want to know their money's safe, in competent hands. I'd suggest upgrading the website asap. Make the most of the Group's track record, previous projects, include photos, newspaper coverage, radio or TV coverage and beef up the members' CV's. If they're smart, ambitious people, funders need to see that writ large. No room for modesty or humility in the funding game ... as you well know."

Finn saw a new hill rising for the Group to climb but knew Sean was right. Why would a wealthy Irish-American Trust dole out dollars to a small group, however ambitious, unless they were convinced the Group would manage their investment effectively? In short, the Group needed to blow its own trumpet, they'd done very good work, needed to acknowledge it, advertise it. But ...he sensed it might not be their style. And how the hell could he broach this, without seeming like an upstart? He'd only been around a few months, had little experience in the trenches.

All this thinking made him tired, then restless, so he put it aside, got boots and snow gear on and walked up the hill to clear his head, his boots sinking into soft snow as he went. From the top the Sound waters looked grey and iron cold.

On the way down he thought about Helen again, wished she was around, hoped they'd be able to pick up where they left off. They'd only exchanged a couple of texts since she went, both initiated by him, so he was leaving it to her to send the next one. Then a different thought occurred, maybe her mother had become seriously ill? He hoped not, assumed she'd let him know. Or would she?

That evening he decided to contact Martha about Sean's suggestions, ask her advice about the next steps. As he rang her number it occurred to him that, when in doubt, she always seemed the best person to consult. Did lots of other people see her this way and if so, did she mind?

She didn't seem to mind when he got hold of her, was very interested in Sean's views and immediately suggested that Finn summarise them, not holding back on Sean's professional opinions, then circulate it to all members and see what response came back.

Next morning Finn did that.

Gawina rang in the afternoon which he expected, then Don did, which he didn't expect and finally Martha rang. All four thought Sean's points were valid and something they needed to take on board. After tossing ideas about for a while Martha agreed to draw up a rough outline for a Group Profile.

Over a few days, the three exchanged suggestions and Eilis swung in by compiling a list of the Group's previous events, talks, newspaper coverage, photos, all contained in one neat folder. At the end of this back and forth, they had a template for a Group Profile which could be put to the next meeting and Don had made contact with somebody who could help upgrade their website.

Finn was impressed by the speed of the work, very glad that Don and Eilis had come on board and began to feel a bit more hopeful about their chances. At the very least, they would be giving it their best shot.

But once that flurry of activity was over, he was still snowbound, until his mother, weary of his restlessness, came to the rescue.

"Tom Mac rang to see were we alright," she said, at the dinner. "He says Jamesey Welch could do with another pair of hands to get feed up and down to the sheep."

Jamesey, a bachelor farmer in his seventies, lived further along the road. Finn didn't hesitate, "I wouldn't mind giving a hand. Have you his number?"

"Best talk to Tom Mac." She paused, "Jamesey had a bit of a turn before Christmas, so Tom's worried about him, but God forbid you'd say it to Jamesey himself!"

When Finn phoned Tom, he agreed that help would be good, but offered advice. "You'd need to go at it sideways – Jamesey is a fierce proud man."

Sideways – the native art form.

Tom went to find the phone number, during which time Finn heard a drawer opening, the sound of footering through it for his contact's book. What a lousy system in an emergency, Finn thought, maybe he should mention it to Tom's daughter, Kathleen, sideways, of course. His years in England had blunted his sideways skill-set. Direct questions and answers, the code he'd encountered in Manchester, needed more usage in these parts.

Finally, Tom lifted the phone. "Sure maybe I'll call him myself and tell him you're at a loose end."

After all that footering. "Grand Tom," he said politely, as expected of a local lad.

But it worked; next morning Finn was on the road to Jamesey's house, wellies, three pairs of socks, hat, gloves.

"You look like one of them gentlemen farmers," his mother said.

Jamesey Welch was one of a dying breed: a farmer who'd never budged out of Derreens and now worked his farm alone, the only one of eight children who'd stayed. Finn's mother said that Jamesey had been walking out with a woman who worked in the Co-op when he was a young man, but his parents were still alive, and clearly there was no rush on it. By the time they passed on, so had the Co-op woman – to Birmingham or was it New York?

"And who'd blame her," his mother always said, at the end of that story.

Jamesey made tea for Finn in his bare, tidy kitchen. The range was belting out good heat, Finn was pleased to note, and then, because conversation was sparse, they began taking out feed from the shed and lugging it up the hill. He was as nimble as Finn on the way up, bag on his back, knowing every bump and groove of the hill track. About thirty sheep greeted them, bleating like a welcoming committee.

"Hunger is good sauce," Jamesey declared, checking feet and hooves for any sign of frostbite or infection. "I hope there's no early lambs," he added, "a snow like this would be fierce hard on them."

They did a head count and descended the hill. When he was leaving, Finn said he'd call each day until the snow cleared and although, "Right so," was as much as Jamesey said, Finn knew he was glad of the help.

The whole way back, Finn tried to get his head around the older man's life and his apparent contentment. The isolation, solitude, confounded him – a life with no mate, no sex, no children, not a lot of company. That prospect had driven Kevin away to Australia.

Interestingly, Kevin had settled near Perth where he was now assistant-manager of a fruit farm, supplying retailers with grapes, peaches, kiwis, berries. He sent his mother pictures of laden orchards and cherry pickers harvesting.

His job gave her some solace. "You can take the man out of Achill, but you can't take Achill out of the man," she'd say.

Partly true, but Kevin had truly settled there, with an Australian wife, Lou, a baby boy, Kevin Óg and a three year old girleen, Carla. Engrossed in these meanderings, Finn was home before he knew it, physical work kept gloom about his life at bay and he fell asleep without a bother.

*

The freeze continued. The County Council had sparse infrastructure for gritting and clearing roads – confined it solely to the main ones. The smaller roads became ice rinks, lethal weapons, only tractors and four-wheelers chanced it. The local schools were closed, Derreens remained in the grip of the Ice Queen.

"Hazardous conditions," the forecasters warned, every morning.

When did dangerous become hazardous he wondered grumpily and how the hell did they manage in Finland or Winnipeg?

When the roads thawed enough to risk going to the Sound for supplies, Finn suggested his mother come along for the outing, but she wouldn't budge, too fearful of falling. He went alone. The road was slippery, every bend and rise required careful negotiation but it was better than staying cooped up. Still no word from Helen, no doubt enjoying the sunshine and she probably didn't want to gloat. Meanwhile, his daily stint with Jamesey kept him sane.

Then thaw and ice began to battle it out for a few days until the thaw finally won, to Finn's great relief. Fields and bushes reappeared, sheep came out of hiding. Hazardous conditions, changed back to normal for the time of year, on weather reports.

The only downside was that Jamesey no longer needed Finn. He'd grown to like it, felt useful.

"You'll be needing to get back to your own work now," was how Jamesey put it, after a couple of days thaw.

Finn didn't argue, knew Jamesey wouldn't be comfortable accepting help once the snow melted. It might look like need.

"Call me if you ever want a hand," he said, as they parted on a handshake.

His phone started ringing again; if he was a plumber, he'd rake it in, but there were other repair jobs. Then Ciaran phoned. "The eagle has landed, we start Kerrigans next Monday."

Phew, Finn thought, he'd be a grown up again, with a proper job for … six whole weeks!

His mother was now willing to venture out, so he drove her to May's house in the Valley to stay the week-end. On the way back he drove through Dubhgort and stopped at the beach. He hadn't been up here for a while, was struck by its charm: sandy beach, flat sea, imperious Sliabh Mór sheltering it from above. With his pals he used cycle here on summer days to jump off the pier, and splash round in the water until their lips turned purple and fingers went stiff – the pre-wet suit generation, the hardy boys.

His mother always swore the water was warmer here, debatable, but it was different to other spots on the island. Edward Nangle's Colony up the road had left its mark, an entire settlement, with church, school, hospital, houses. Its development had paved the way for the village to become the first tourist spot, with two hotels at one stage and now, lots of holiday homes. Helen liked Dubhgort too, had walked up from Keel she told him and was fascinated with the story of the settlement.

She was still quiet, no word from her. He didn't know what to make of it, until it crossed his mind that the considerable pleasures of Spain in January, sun, oranges, oleander, might hold her longer. Perhaps she'd decided to stay on and would let him know in time? That would be a blow, but could he blame her if she did?

25

Over the week, changes in her father and mother disturbed Helen. The deterioration in her mother's mobility was marked, she rarely moved without her stick. Nevertheless, she remained fiercely independent, refused offers of help, which meant she sat a lot, inside or outside at the garden table. She was also disinclined to go places, a radical shift for someone who'd always got out and about: Bridge club, Choir, lunch with friends. Helen noticed a walker in the cupboard, wondered why it wasn't used, didn't know how to ask. Despite her immobility, her mother looked well, tanned, and had changed her style to suit the climate: wore dresses in bright colours, which made her look more youthful, even Spanish. Helen sensed she was beginning to belong there.

Her father, on the other hand, had lost weight he could ill afford, his hair had thinned, giving him an older, slightly gaunt look. He seemed restless, constantly fetching and doing, had rearranged the house to suit her mother's needs: widened a door, made a sewing machine corner, built an outdoor table so her mother could pot plants. Months of work: doing, doing.

He also did the shopping now – a sea change from Dublin, where her mother bought everything, including his clothes.

"We're very modern aren't we Tom," her mother joked, "we've swapped roles."

Helen was very pleased he still read and played golf twice weekly, thanks to Fiona's insistence on having a helper, Maria, come in, but she sensed unease within him. Before sleep, the word fading, came to mind. Was her Dad fading? Did he have some hidden illness? Dear God.

*

Next day he went golfing and her mother asked Helen to drive her to the curtain shop, "I'd like your opinion on a fabric for the bedroom."

This was promotion, Helen's taste always inferior to Fiona's and it gave them an outing together. Her mother managed the walk from the car to the shop slowly, and the fabric she favoured, an apple green with a small yellow pattern, was perfect.

"Impeccable taste, Mam."

They went to a café nearby, the clientele all ex-pats, some of whom her mother greeted and once they'd ordered, her mother took Helen's hand. "I want to know exactly how you're feeling Helen. I've been worried sick about you."

Helen felt childishly disappointed that the curtains were just a ruse for a tete-a-tete, which she'd hoped to avoid.

She gave her mother a short version of what she felt – getting away helped, Grace Henry had opened new interest, and Achill locals had been extremely kind, mentioning Anne, Paddy and the Kilbanes.

"I don't know how you've done it," her mother said, unconvinced.

"Mam, you're a Mayo woman, you grew up the other side of the bay," she said. "It's not Alaska!"

"But I was born to it," she said firmly. Then patting her hand she said, "You still look so wan, Helen."

Helen stirred her coffee, nervous her mother might have seen through her pallor, fortunately her focus was elsewhere.

"Shane's not worth pining over," her mother said firmly.

Helen suppressed a sigh of frustration, wanted to spit out, I know, I know, let's talk about blue skies, sunshine – please – instead she replied, "You're right."

"We all got Shane wrong Helen, not just you."

This conversation was unavoidable, Helen's only option to contain it. She nodded.

"Because…" her mother shook her head, "he's one of those men…"

Helen waited.

"Not a bad person, smart, charming, but deep down selfish, suits himself. He has no loyalty at the core. That's why he could leave like that."

The speed of Shane's desertion could be deemed proof positive of her mother's view, so she nodded, didn't say, isn't loyalty different to love.

"You were his world for years Helen, then she became his world and who knows, further down the line…?" She let it hang. "Some men live their lives that way."

Helen batted away a flash of the dismal hopes she'd carried after Shane left, believing he'd regret it, come back – thought of *Spring in Winter*. "It's a theory Mam," she said, knew her mother wanted to be helpful. "I've none myself;

208

it happened, he's gone. And I'm dead weary of thinking, talking about Shane to be honest Mam!"

Her mother frowned. "Well, his time may come, his new woman may pack up and leave when least expected."

"They've a child now."

"When did that ever stop some men?"

Helen was saved by the arrival of Rose, her mother's friend, a merciful distraction.

Later she felt sad that she and her mother had failed to connect. They were like two dancers who knew the steps but rarely managed to bring them together at the same time. It had always been so. Somehow Helen and her father managed better.

That night she had a vivid dream – she was sitting outdoors, holding a girl baby who was calm and still, then the girl was suddenly gone, had disappeared and when she woke it crossed her mind that the dream might be about herself and her mother.

*

On her second last day, Helen and her father went to Elche, the palm tree capital of Europe, one of his favourite places. Her mother had declined, wouldn't be able for it, she said. When Helen suggested they use the fold-up wheelchair, she snapped, "I'm not an invalid!"

On route, Helen broached her mother's refusal with her father. "What's it about Dad? Why won't she use the chair?"

He sighed, "Your mother hasn't accepted her condition."

"But it keeps her housebound?"

"You can't force it."

Silence settled as they drove past Guardamar's tall

apartment blocks, until she asked, "Can anything be done Dad?"

"A Counsellor we went to said that the passage of time may change things." He didn't sound hopeful.

A Counsellor? Fiona hadn't mentioned it, though Helen was sure she'd known. Jesus, they'd been protecting her, while all this was going on.

"I'm sorry I've been so out of the loop..." she began.

"You've had your own troubles," he said, eyes fixed on the road

"What else did the Counsellor say?"

He shrugged, "Acceptance takes time ... it must come from within the person herself, a step on their journey – that kind of thing!"

"But where does that leave you?"

He glanced at her, "Waiting in the wings." Then eyes on the road again, "Or I might take flight to Achill one day, knock on your door?"

It startled her, her father wasn't a joker.

He registered her alarm, "I'll give you notice, don't worry." Then he said, "Helen, I haven't been to Elche for months, can we just have a day out, not talk about troubles?"

And so they visited the Palm Park, walked the narrow streets, had lunch then climbed the Cathedral tower to take in the views, like happy tourists.

On the journey back, she watched the sun fading over the sea, sketching pink brushstrokes on the sky and felt a wave of great tiredness overtake her. She yearned to tell him she was pregnant, to share it, but how could she? He carried too many burdens already.

*

At the airport, her father hugged her goodbye and when she turned to wave, she caught a look in his eyes which stayed with her throughout the slow moving Security Check. When it dawned, she couldn't believe she hadn't recognised it immediately – loneliness – a look which rose from a parched well. Her Dad was lonely, missed home, missed her and Fiona, the grandkids, his old friends, but he'd changed his life and couldn't turn it back. Dear God, for too, too long, she hadn't been paying attention.

Now she was deserting him. Instead of turning back to help him work on her mother's resistance, she kept walking towards the plane. She'd no choice. She had to do what he was doing, batten down, keep on going, keep her appointment at an Abortion Clinic in Richmond in four days' time.

*

London changed everything. At first, it was a whirlwind of food and talk with Isla and Kate – both aware of her pregnancy, both supportive of her plan. Back in their company, the extent to which she'd missed them hit her like a brick falling: the way she could breathe easy about herself again. She talked about her father's woes, the bitter irony of the pregnancy, its impossibility.

They both said, "It's your life Helen, you have to make the choice that's best for you."

A night together at their favourite Greek restaurant lifted her soul, the mezes, calamares, spanakopita tasted wonderful and prompted talk about a fabulous stuffed aubergine dish they'd all once eaten in… was it Hania?

"I've tried to replicate that dish and failed every time," Kate said.

"Ach, It's the soil," Isla said, "you'd have to bring a sack of it home to get that flavour."

It didn't bother her that the city was in the grip of a cold snap from Siberia. Newspapers, television reports were full of frigid images: cowering Yorkshire sheep, frozen pipes and railway tracks, wilting cabbage fields, boxes of gloves replacing dresses on shop shelves. While Isla was at work, Helen walked each day – fast – around Hyde Park and St James's where the ponds were still and slate coloured. She also walked past the church she thought Grace and Paul Henry had married in but it was closed.

Later she and Isla had a catch up session about Helen's progress with Grace Henry, Isla now as enthused about Grace as well.

"They're beginning to discuss a design for the book," she said.

Helen felt panicked. "Design? God I'm not ready yet."

"Don't worry, it's preliminary, they have to do this well in advance to meet deadlines. They're tossing ideas around, especially about the size of the book, always a big issue when there are lots of visuals."

It dawned on Helen that she'd stopped seeing her research as a chapter in a book, she'd become so immersed in Grace's life and work for her own sake, that she'd side-lined it. But listening to Isla talk about page size, font, was a timely reminder of the purpose of the research, to bring Grace to more people and promote her work.

Next day she met Luke and Rachel from Westgrove School, who filled her in on the school's ups and downs, said they wanted her back no later than September. It was very nice to be missed.

That night, she had a dream about a baby girl again, red-gold hair, curly, unlike anybody she knew. She woke with a start, read her book to escape dreams. But next morning she mentioned it to Isla.

"Isn't it common for pregnant women to dream about babies?" Isla asked.

"Is it? But I don't want to be pregnant!"

Isla shrugged, "Your hormones don't know that."

Unusually, that evening she and Isla had a row. They'd just finished dinner when Isla asked, "Do you mind if I play Devil's Advocate?"

Helen shrank back, "Why do you want to do that?"

"Ach, a line of thought came to me." She shrugged, "Forget it, silly idea."

But once said, it was impossible to ignore, "Oh, just spit it out, it's clogging the air anyway."

Isla took a deep breath. "OK. A year ago you were desperate to be pregnant, now you are pregnant and you don't want to be…what's changed?"

The question was ridiculous. "Everything's changed Isla, every feckin thing!"

"But didn't you really want to have a child then –"

"-of course, and…?"

"And now?"

"Now? I'm recovering from depression, live alone on an island in the Atlantic, in a rented house, with little money, hardly know the man …that's now Isla!"

"But…" Isla wasn't backing down, "you have a flat in London, a job you can resume or get maternity leave – if – if you want to have the baby?"

Noise clattered in Helen's head, she couldn't believe this. "You're suggesting I become a single parent?"

Isla shrugged. "I'm being a Devil's Advocate, Helen, naming a possibility?"

"Well it's not helpful! That's a design on paper, bears no connection to my situation. If I return to Achill pregnant, how would I manage alone and what the hell would I tell Finn?"

Isla sat silent a minute. "I see that would be very difficult," she said, "but … all I'm saying is there's another way to have the baby if you want to. You could return to London, and take it from here?"

"London, now?"

She hadn't given it a moment's thought. She stared at Isla, unable to control her anger, "You mean chum it with Shane, Chloe in the local Mother and Baby group?"

"Helen, I'm hardly suggesting that."

They lapsed into stony silence, which Isla broke. "I just wondered if you'd thought of it as an option, that's all?"

"It's not an option!"

"Fair enough. End of discussion."

But it wasn't fair enough, Helen was still angry, "I need some air, "she said rising.

Isla didn't try to stop her.

Outside she tramped pavements, past genteel, lamp lit sitting rooms, busy restaurants, a pub full with a football crowd.

Jesus! Isla's forthrightness, always a mixed blessing, now seemed crass. She had never contemplated having this baby: wrong time, wrong place, wrong man. She'd certainly never contemplated returning to London to have it. The truth was she wasn't remotely ready for London, nor was she prepared to move elsewhere. At her lowest point, she'd vowed to keep her home, her last line of defence; it was still her bottom line.

Nor could she picture telling Finn about the baby; he'd enough on his plate, trying to work out his future. And if she didn't tell him, what about ten years down the line, a child who wants to know who its father is? She hardly knew Finn, he'd be moving on, as would she, in time. They were ships in the night, not parents.

Eventually, worn out walking and ruminating, she returned to the flat. Isla opened the door looking anxious, "Sorry I upset you."

Helen shrugged, went into the sitting room.

"My big mouth gets the better of me," Isla added.

"Don't I know." Then Helen relented, "I'm sure you meant well, etcetera…"

Isla leaned forward, "The road to hell is paved with well-meaning sinners."

Helen mustered a weak smile.

That night a different dream: walking along Keel Beach where the wind was whipping the sea high and the waves pounded. She felt breathless and invigorated at the same time. Suddenly she became aware that she had a baby strapped to her in a cloth carrier, inside her coat. She was worried that the wind would frighten the baby and began hurrying, pushing herself hard towards the dunes to seek shelter, where they hunkered down, out of the winds. She woke feeling stalked.

Much later in the day, stepping off a bus, a thought came for the first time: What if? What if this was her one and only chance to have a baby? Where on earth did that come from and why now? Was this one of those imponderables that daft Doctor mentioned? Then she remembered Anya, a colleague, who had tried for a child for ten years with her partner but conceived only once, recalled a staff celebratory lunch and Anya saying, "Nobody can tell me why I got pregnant this time. It's a mystery and a miracle."

And they'd toasted miracle baby Paolo's health.

Later she mentioned her worry to Kate. "What if …this is my only chance?"

Kate looked shocked. "Given your age, health and that you've conceived this time, the odds are very good."

Reassuring, but not for long. She hadn't got pregnant with Shane, despite best efforts over months, yet he and Chloe had conceived fast, if the story he told her was true. That ruled him out as the one with low fertility. They'd never had tests, were giving it one more month, before taking that road.

So, what if… she had low fertility and this was her only chance? Christ, why had this thought come to plague her now? She tried to kill it with rapid rounds of Hyde Park, one after another, until a new idea popped into her head. She could get a fertility test, but …as she was currently pregnant, they'd think she was mad for even asking.

The night before the abortion, Isla cooked dinner and Helen mentioned it.

"You're fit and healthy, girl, it'll happen again," she said.

But neither Isla nor Kate could know that; nor could Helen.

She woke at dawn, something was different. She looked through the curtain, the street was wet outside, no frost glittered. The predicted thaw had begun and London could relax its clenched fist.

Helen now had two hours to decide.

Isla was right, it had been her heart's desire to have a baby, when her life was someone else's life, then it became a lost dream. If... if this was her only chance, she could apply to return to her job at Easter, and she'd qualify for maternity leave. Isla was right – it was an option, theoretically.

But it involved Shane, Chloe and baby as neighbours, for which she wasn't ready. It would be awful, would cost her too much.

But if this was truly her only chance, was there another option?

A baby on Achill, in a rented house, no job, savings disappearing, a tiny network of help – Christ how was that an option? Who'd take such a gamble?

But what if she made the wrong choice now and that was it?

She had only two hours to make up her mind, two hours to make a monumental decision, to opt for one path or the other.

26

Finn was pleased to receive a text from Helen, telling him she was back on Achill asking him to call in. He went a day later, a bit unsure about what to expect after the break, bearing a white orchid for her new house.

She looked touched by the sun, her hair cut shorter, lighter at the edges and she also looked less skinny, but although she returned his hug, she seemed reserved.

They talked about Spain. He was envious of so many things, especially her swims and the trip to Elche. She tried to answer his queries about the state of the building industry – puzzled by unfinished skeletons blotting the landscape, while new apartments were still being built.

"Probably bought off the plans," he said.

While she made coffee he watched the Minaun cliffs, still and bare. Over coffee, she explained that she'd gone to London for a few days after Spain.

London? She hadn't flagged that before, perhaps it explained her reserve. "Did it make you homesick?"

"In some ways yes."

It was awkward between them, a shift he couldn't name, like a slight breeze cooling the mood.

She threw him a quick glance. "London brought back difficult stuff…"

This wasn't the reunion he'd hoped for. "Oh," he said, to fill the gap.

Another quick glance, "Finn…" she began, then hesitated.

The note in her voice made him tense – shit – was this a Dear John moment?

"I think I should go more slowly…"she said without holding his gaze, "with you…"

"I wouldn't have called our connection… fast." A silence, then in a level voice he asked, "Can I ask why?"

Her next glance was nervous, she added a sod of turf to the fire although it didn't need it. "In case we… y'know, hurt each other."

"Are you saying you think I'll hurt you?"

She shrugged unhelpfully. Was this some reference to what he'd said about Alison one night?

"Well," he added, "it isn't part of my plan."

"I didn't mean to offend you –"

"– I'm not offended, I'm… confused."

"Sorry," she said, straightening her shoulders.

"For?"

"This isn't about what you might do, it's about me – I should have said that." Another pause, then a brief glance, "Being in London shook me up, and I don't know how I feel about-"

"About-?"

"Us."

Water was moving downhill towards him, "You mean me?"

She sort of nodded.

Was that a yes? He waited briefly, thought of just cutting his losses and heading out the door, but curbed his instinct, Alison's voice in his ears, "That's right, Finn, run."

"Did something happen with your ex-husband?" he asked, being so fucking reasonable.

Her eyes widened, "God no."

Another awkward silence which he knew he'd have to break. He felt like he was sixteen, asking Sandra Lavelle why she'd left the Dooagh dance without him. Christ sake! "Are you telling me you'd rather not continue, whatever it is we started?"

She grimaced, like a delicate lady from an historical novel. What the fuck was up with her?

"I think it's for the best," she said in a flat voice.

Now he was angry, "Obviously best for you?"

"Well," she began, throwing a glance his way, "London brought stuff up again."

Those short glances were irritating, she hadn't held his look since he'd arrived. He'd been blanked, a flush of humiliation crept in. He stood up.

"If that's what you want, so be it!"

"I'm sorry Finn, it's me, not you," this time she looked directly at him.

For Christ's sake. "Spare me," he said.

She bit her lip. "London made things very difficult…"

"So you've said several times, though you haven't said why." He paused, "I can take it, whatever it is?" He waited but nothing came, tried one last time. "A few weeks ago we agreed to spend more time together … or did I get that wrong?"

She looked pained, shook her head, "No, you didn't, but the break changed things," she said, sounding like a stranger.

He couldn't fight a shadow, time was up. "Thanks for the coffee and cake," he said coldly.

She slowly rose, "I'm really sorry, Finn."

The last thing he wanted was that shite, he didn't reply, grabbed his coat, headed out the door.

He walked Keel beach, the sole walker. Apart from the push and pull of the tide, and trails of turf smoke rising here and there, nothing moved. He felt shocked, stung, more than he'd expect to be, given the shortness of their connection. The lack of explanation offended him. In his gut he believed something happened in London, something with her ex-husband, but all she had to do was come out, say it, for fuck's sake. Show some guts. They'd only slept together twice, had no contract. Instead, she'd blown him out, like she wanted him to disappear. He thought she'd more character than that. He stared out at the Minaun cliffs, the waves nibbling at their base, the perennial battle of sea and cliff.

I am an island... he hummed into the wind, although he knew it wasn't true.

*

For the following week, a kind of disequilibrium set in which reminded him of when his ears got blocked. He was angry with Helen Bradshaw and with himself, for the way he'd taken her at face value, let her gain a foothold in his unstable life. He was convinced she'd held back on something, if not the husband, maybe she'd reconnected with someone from before? What was the big deal in just coming out and saying it? Did she think he'd crack like a china cup? He hardly knew her, could live without her, for Christ's sake.

What unsettled him most was that he'd misread her; he followed his instinct with people, had faith in it – this time, it failed.

*

Michael's email arrived like a gift:

A Cairde,
My nephew Daragh, is visiting from Leeds and we plan to climb Sliabh Mór this Sunday. You're all welcome to join us. Wear boots, warm socks, hat, gloves, scarf and rain gear. Bring a stick, flask, water and light grub.

Level of walk: medium / Distance: 1 hr.30 – 2hrs / Views: spectacular (God willing) Meet: Deserted village, 10.00

Yes, please, was Finn's instant response.

"But you'll miss Maggie," his mother said on Sunday, when he told her he was going walking. Maggie, his mother's cousin from Cleveland, planned to call for a couple of hours in the afternoon.

"I'll be well back by then," he said, "unless I fall in a gulley."

"You could bring bad luck on yourself, saying things like that."

*

At ten he joined the merry band of eleven people, in the Sunday morning drizzle.

"Ah, sure the drizzle will blow over," Michael said, introducing Daragh, a Geography Masters student in Leeds. He looked too young for a Masters in anything.

Martha, James and Don were also there, looking different in boots and rainwear, but he was pleased to see them in a different setting. Suddenly it crossed his mind that Helen Bradshaw might have come, since she was a neighbour of Martha's now, but a surreptitious glance around reassured him she hadn't. A bullet dodged.

He badly needed a climb, to stretch limbs and get that mountain air flowing through his brain. He hadn't been up Sliabh Mór since he, Sean and Tina, had climbed it one weekend, a few years back.

"Right lads," Michael said taking charge, "Sliabh Mór is 2,200 feet above sea level."

"That's about a mile high Michael," Don said.

"An Irish mile or an English mile?" called a voice from behind.

"*Ciúnas, ciúnas,*" Michael replied, smiling. "*Níl se ró deachair ar cor ar bith!* Right, ground rules – we'll take the lower slopes handy, then as we begin the ridge, we'll walk at our own pace, but nobody walks alone. Keep a close eye on each other." He surveyed the group. "*Ceart go leor?*"

"*Ceart go leor, a mháistir,*" they replied and were on their way.

Finn walked with Martha, James and Don who were quickly into conversation about local news. He dipped in and out, moving ahead, then dropping back to keep pace with them. Martha was alert to the plants underfoot, Don, free from his Treasurer's role, was also keen, so they frequently stopped to pore over something. James, on the other hand, was intent on the views, commenting to Finn about how inspiring it was for painters.

"Did you take it all for granted growing up?" he asked.

"Sure did."

When they gained the Ridge, people followed their own pace, a few, including Daragh, went forging ahead confidently, others grouped in the middle, watched the path below them, while the last few slowly took up the rear. Michael walked with those at the back, Finn went ahead with the middle group, needing to stretch his legs and lungs. After a while, he stopped and waited for the threesome, Martha and Don looking comfortable, James clearly puffed.

"I have to sit a minute," he said, parking on a rock.

Don sat next to him, "Take your ease."

After a rest they progressed along the Ridge, below which cliffs plummeted and Michael called out to all to take care, "*tabhair aire, tabhair aire.*"

Martha and Don were in conversation about the Memorial, Finn overheard Don saying, "…planning could be a nightmare."

Martha sounded buoyant, "Isn't it always?"

Finn tuned in and out, the perfect state – body engaged, mind half there, more intent on watching the views as they came and went through the drizzly haze.

"Did you hear that Finn?" Martha asked. "Don didn't know about the statue to that Achill boxer at Patten's pub! He wants to know more."

"Johnny Kilbane," Finn said, recalling his father's pride at Johnny being part of the Kilbane clan. "The family were Achill people who moved to Cleveland. He was

224

World Featherweight Champ, 1912 to 1923 – eleven years, unbroken record!"

"Some record," James said.

"Yeah, finally he got a statue," Finn said. "There's one in a Cleveland Park too."

"I'll check out who the sculptor it," Martha said, "might come in useful."

When he and Don fell alongside each other, Don said, "So Finn, development money is our only chance isn't it?"

Finn nodded. He respected Don's open mind and his realism.

"Would you be hopeful we might get some?" Don asked, studying him closely.

"Well," he said cagily, "if they're interested in the idea it's encouraging, but it needs a strong application."

"Michael, Martha and Gawina," Don said, "they're some trio when they set their mind to a thing."

Finn grinned, "Yep! Have they brought you on board Don?"

He nodded. "They've certainly made me consider it seriously. It would be great to get some marker on the island for tattie hokers, sometimes I picture a big sculpture at the bridge... but I know that's big money."

"It is".

"And, you have to wonder," Don added, "why we don't have something already, even a display some place?"

"I agree," Finn said. A permanent exhibition of some kind could well be the easiest memorial to achieve, something informative, aesthetically pleasing which could move around the island and the county. But he wasn't going to throw any suggestions into the mix, it would just confuse things.

Not long afterwards, they reached the trig pillar at the Summit and as soon as all had arrived, a cheer went up and photos were taken of all combinations of people, Michael the common denominator. Then lunch packs were produced and the mist suddenly cleared, as if on cue.

"*A Dhaoine uaisle, Oileán Acla,*" Michael declared, with a sweep of his hand and his best Tourist Guide voice. "I give you the spectacular views of the Atlantic Ocean ahead, the sandy beach and village of Dubhgort below and behind us the peak of Croghaun, below which lurk the highest cliffs in Europe."

A round of applause and now Daragh was on his feet, filming views from all angles, Michael reminding him to watch his footing.

"It's spectacular," James said, between bites of apple.

It was. The scale of the vistas had swept Finn's mind clean. They sat, chatted, until Michael, their shepherd, gathered up his flock, as clouds moved in from the sea.

Reluctantly they buttoned up and set off. As always it seemed to take less time on the descent but required more caution and with everyone tired, there was less chat.

They separated at the old graveyard, Michael promising to organise another walk soon, maybe Achill Head next time. Finn got into his car reluctantly, drove home to do his family duty, greet Maggie, his mother's Cleveland cousin, and try to hold onto his euphoria.

27

Helen walked the beach in a state of agitation. Her conversation with Finn Kilbane had run away from her completely, leaving her tongue tied. In London her mind had been clear: she had decided to keep the baby, because it might be her only chance to conceive. It was her choice and she would stand over it. But telling Finn and when to tell him, she'd been grappling with for days. Not telling him at all, she couldn't stand over and believed it would involve her in a patchwork of lies, estranging him, her and the baby for a lifetime.

She had eventually worked out a Plan: finish the relationship with Finn, to level the pitch between them, later, tell him about the pregnancy and he could then decide, free of obligation to her, what role he did or didn't want. He would have freedom to choose as she'd had. This had seemed the fairest way.

Now she saw that her Plan was abstract, she hadn't foreseen his anger, suspicion, leaving her unable to explain what exactly was going on, so the Plan lay in tatters around her feet. Worse, it felt like she'd opened up a chasm between them, that would be very hard to bridge and the next step, actually telling him about the pregnancy, seemed impossible to imagine.

Their conversation had also brought into sharp focus what lay ahead: telling Fiona and her parents, who would not be happy, she knew. Could the timing of a pregnancy be worse? No. Could her circumstances be less suited? No. Would they think her mad, desperate? Yes.

Exhausted by it all, she saw now what she needed to say to Finn and to all of them was: this might be my only chance to have a child, that's why I'm doing it. But nevertheless it daunted.

*

Three days later, the postman's van, the noise of the letterbox, and on the floor, a letter, address handwritten, postmarked Dublin. She let herself fantasise while she made tea – a relative of Grace Henry had tracked her down, wanted to show her photos, correspondence? The tree at the window showed small buds emerging on its branches, washed damp this morning, but still showing. It spurred her on to open the envelope. James Mulherne – possibly the next best thing to a Grace Henry relative.

Dear Helen,

I hope you're keeping well, that the Achill winds don't disturb your sleep and that your research is progressing?

My stay in Dublin has been extended, because a small problem of a few broken roof tiles has mushroomed into a whole section of the roof needing repair! It's quite a shock, but as Martha said, I'm lucky I don't have to go to a moneylender at 200% interest to borrow it. My sister is always a realistic thinker. Fortunately, I've found a good roofer who thinks he'll finish by end of next week.

My reason for writing Helen, is to share some information which I think you'll find interesting. I discovered the Manuscripts Library in Trinity last week, thanks to a tip from Oliver, and went looking for information about a painter I like, Maurice MacGonigal. Did I mention him?

Helen paused, the name didn't ring a bell, but the MS Library did, distantly.

The Library is a treasure trove of letters, manuscripts, above the Long Room, housing original materials, some very old manuscripts you can't access without wearing special gloves. By the way, anybody doing research can get a Reader's Ticket, that's how I got in.

While I was there, I enquired about a Grace Henry file. There was none, but, of course, there was one for Paul Henry, which contains correspondence about their separation which you might find useful.

Jesus, a stone's throw from TRIARC, and she never asked!

Paul's file contained correspondence over years, donated by Mabel Young, including letters to and from solicitors about his separation from Grace, an acrimonious affair, as you know.

By a stroke of luck, I also found an article in the

*file by a journalist, James Winder Good, written in
1921, about the work of Paul and Grace, entitled: 2
Irish Artists – an assessment of their individual styles.
This file might be of some help?
In the meantime, stay well, and see you soon.*

Best wishes, James M.

"Of some help?" she shouted. "It's a meteor shower
James."

She read it again, sent him a text to express her gratitude,
then feeling restless, decided to return to Dublin to finish
off Rosarii's thesis, find out how to access the MS Library
and stay with Fiona overnight. This would get her away
from morose thoughts about Finn Kilbane.

*

She walked slowly from Heuston Station along the Liffey.
The air was cold but dry, cars crawled past, then minutes
later, she overtook them. She kept walking as far as she
could, to where the river neared the sea at John Rogerson's
Quay, then sat watching its passage, until the cold bit hard.

At TRIARC she re-immersed herself in the latter stages
of Grace Henry's life. Between 1930's and 1954 when she
died, she seemed to live a semi-nomadic lifestyle, helped
by the support of a small number of very loyal friends,
especially Lorraine Creed Meredith and Harriet Kirkwood.
In the light of this, her continued commitment to painting
and her resilience in coping with constant financial
problems and no permanent home, seemed remarkable.

Many of her paintings over this time were inspired by

travel to Spain and Italy, encapsulated by their titles, *Red House at Mougins, A Coastal Town in the South of France, Sails at Chioggia, Boats at Chioggia.* Helen loved, *A Coastal Town in the South of France*, with her characteristic curving lines, multiple colours, and what Rosarii Moran called, "energetic brushstrokes." Both of the Chioggia paintings were vibrant and evocative, as was *Dublin Port Scene* – her interest in boats and ports ongoing. During this period she returned to Ireland at regular intervals.

Grace exhibited, *Paintings of Italy*, in London in 1933, participated in the *Four Artists Exhibition* in Dublin in 1935, at which she showed thirty paintings, including those of Chioggia. Thirty paintings amazed Helen, given the upheavals in her life. A reviewer commented that the Mediterranean had intensified her use of colour – red, magenta, cobalt, orange, white, and that she actually "sought colour in her choice of subject."

The idea of pursuing intense, colourful subjects in a period of emotional disturbance made sense to Helen. She studied *Drying Sails at Chioggia*. A boatman had hoisted his orange-yellow sails to stretch out in the sun, in a small harbour, in front of a terracotta building with a red roof. Two small figures stood on a cream pavement watching. Helen lingered over it, noticing how she felt warmed by the colours, had to drag herself away. How essential those colours must have been to Grace at that turbulent time.

In a rare interview with Máirín Allen, in 1942, part of a series about modern artists, Grace talked about the "exhilaration of gay colour and bright light" especially in Italy. Exhilaration was a strong word, but apt, looking at these paintings. Máirín Allen praised her work, for its "poetic sensibility and (her) capacity to experiment".

But, alas, alack, they were throwing Helen out, she was always the last to leave, the last one to leave the party was a joke now between herself and whoever was key holder.

Along the playing fields, she thought about how much she'd give to be watching yellow and orange sails drying at the harbour in Chioggia now, certain that they would lift her spirits and lighten her step.

*

Helen walked aimlessly up Grafton Street, past a fire eating performer, while behind him, a beggar sat in a dirty sleeping bag. She bought books for Fiona's family, then spent an hour and a half in three different bookshops, in the Modern Art Sections, combing for references to Grace. As usual, there were very few, and those were brief, mainly connecting her to Paul. A disgrace.

On the street a young woman was playing guitar and singing, *Gracias a la vida, que me ha dado tanto*, a song Helen had learned in a Spanish class, *Thank you life, for giving me so much*. Back then, her life had seemed so rich. She gave the singer some money, walked on.

To fight off gloom, she forced herself to count blessings: TRIARC, a mothership; Grace Henry, a lifeline; hopefully a healthy baby; Isla and Kate, who'd offered support; Fiona, Anne, her parents who would help, she was sure, when the time came.

What Helen hadn't had time to think about in London was that taking the decision by herself, would leave her to cope with every uncertainty, every worry – by herself.

Later she contemplated telling Fiona she was pregnant, but over family dinner was hardly the time and finding a quiet moment impossible. Instead she went to bed, decided she'd phone from Achill – an easier way to contain that conversation. Before falling asleep she also decided she could no longer put off telling Finn Kilbane that she was pregnant, it weighed too heavily on her now.

28

Driving back from the Sound, Finn's phone rang: *Helen Bradshaw*. What the hell? He let it ring, speculated that she'd a burst pipe or wanted them to stay friends. Then a short message: *could he ring her back*. He didn't.

He'd spoken to Phil last night about prospects of work in London when the Kerrigans' job ended.

"You're top of my list Finno, because you're such a damn good QS, as well as a great mate, but January and February are dead as doornails." He sighed, "Still, Spring's on its way…"he said perking up, but not for long, his voice dipped, "it better bloody well bring some of those green shoots they keep promising us!"

"Green shoots Phil, it's always a bad sign when you get poetic," Finn said.

"Poetry gets popular during Depressions, didn't you know mate?"

*

Next day another call came from Helen Bradshaw, leaving the same message which he also ignored. What was the

234

point? But something was on her mind because on Saturday morning, she left a third message: *I need to talk to you about something important, asap.*

What the fuck could be important? Well he wasn't changing his plan to go to Westport Library, texted reluctantly: *Will call in after 4pm.*

Today he'd set himself to read about the tattie hokers funeral journey from Westport to Achill, on June 16th, 1894. It was an historic occasion – the first time the new Midlands Great West train line was ever used, was to convey the coffins of the tattie hokers to their homeplace, with Achill Sound, the final stop. Officially the new railway line was unopened but a decision was made to open it for this.

The train left Westport Station at ten thirty am with the coffins on board, to begin its mournful journey, accompanied by grieving relatives, survivors, Achill priests, members of the Relief Committee and an R.M. At Newport the platform was thronged with sympathisers then on it went to Rosturk and Tonragee where coffins were received by grief stricken families. At two o'clock it finally reached Achill Sound where huge crowds had gathered and the coffins were transferred to carts to begin the procession to Cill Damhnait Cemetery, black flags marking the way. A thick mist fell and the wind shrieked as though in mourning for the dead. A photo of men and women, all dressed in black, crossing the Sound Bridge, as they accompanied the coffins to their final resting place was striking. In the blurred image, they looked like scarecrows. My God, the grief of it all, Finn thought.

*

On the drive back Finn wondered about the old station area at the Sound as a possible site for a Memorial, recalled a post-famine sculpture of *Emigrants* on Derry Quay, conveying a whole story, fantasised about something similar.

He pulled in to reconnoitre. The setting was great – the bridge, the waters of the Sound underneath, the mountains beyond – and it was the first arrival point for visitors, in cars or after cycling along the Greenway. The old Station Master's house, now a Hostel, was still in use.

He walked up to the old station, which, from the outside, looked fairly sound, but when he peered inside, it was completely fallen in, no floors, timber strewn, stones scattered, the state of the roof dubious. The level of deterioration was shocking, a waste of a fine building. Nevertheless, he photographed the station and its setting, from as many angles as possible.

As he swung north for Keel to see what Helen Bradshaw wanted, reluctance tugged deeply. But she'd been very persistent, so damned if he did or if he didn't. This would be brief.

Their greeting at the door was so strained he immediately regretted calling.

"Tea?" she asked, ushering him in.

"No thanks."

She sat, he stood. The room was shadowy with only side lighting.

"You mentioned something important?" he said, taking the reins.

"Yeah."

He waited, this was her gig.

"There was something I didn't tell you the last time…

because I hadn't worked out the best way..." and she trailed off.

Later, he would remember his short lived satisfaction at this revelation – his instinct had been right, she had concealed something, he'd sensed it in his bones; but this small restoration of faith in his instinct was wiped out by the rest of the awful encounter.

"Something you didn't tell me?" he repeated.

She tried again, "What's happened is..."

He couldn't hack it, "Can you just come out and say it."

"Okay," and after a sharp intake of breath, she said, "I'm pregnant."

He gulped with shock, was it audible, he didn't know nor care, didn't even try to grope for words, knew he wouldn't find any. This he had not anticipated, what-so-ever, this hadn't crossed his mind for a nano second. Why would it? He glanced towards the Minaun cliffs, which stood firm and solid, offering no help. He swallowed carefully, grappling for explanations: she'd begun seeing someone else – in Dublin – while he was seeing her too? A one night stand? "Are congratulations in order?" he asked finding his voice.

She was looking at him strangely.

"No...?" And then a worm was moving round his brain, towards his frontal lobe. He leaned forward. "What are you saying exactly?"

She stared at him, "It's what you think."

"You're pregnant...with me?" These words belonged on another planet.

"Yes," she answered.

He was hit by a truck, had to sit down.

He heard the tick of the kitchen clock counting seconds, had no idea how many, because his mind wasn't cranking up, wasn't making sense of what she'd said ...because she'd used her diaphragm, each time. "How?" he finally asked, voice aghast.

She stiffened, "The usual way." Pause. "I was as shocked as you."

Shocked wasn't the word. The room became totally claustrophobic, the hissing fire the only sound. He felt he'd explode, stood, "I need to get some air, clear my head," he said, "I'll be back shortly..."

She remained silent and out the door he went.

He pounded down the slope, seaward, Fuck, fuck, fuck's sake! At the strand, the gulls went about their daily business, ignorant of his plight. Soon he was half way across the strand, jogging. He remembered there was a hermit's cave in the cliffs, accessible at low tide, it seemed attractive right now.

Once – only once before had this happened – the end of the first year in Manchester. Alison, in the throes of exams began throwing up in the morning, her face white as a sheet. Exam nerves they'd assumed, until she discovered she was pregnant

The feeling was the same – shock and dread. With a year to go on her course, the timing was disastrous for Alison and disastrous for Finn, who wasn't ready for that either. They'd agreed and she'd had an abortion. If she hadn't wanted to do that, what would have happened? He wouldn't have known how to cope with a baby at that point, trapped in Manchester, desperate to move. It terrified him. But he couldn't have left and where would that have brought them?

Suddenly he stopped in his tracks. How many weeks was Helen gone? He hadn't even asked, hadn't asked the most important questions. What do you want to do? Why did he not ask? That could change everything.

He turned, began walking back rapidly, his belief growing that she would not want this pregnancy either. They weren't even together. Why on earth would she? His heart rate started to slow down.

She opened the door, barely looked at him as he followed her in.

His restored instinct told him to tread carefully. "Sorry if that was, abrupt," he said, "I needed air."

She didn't respond, sat in the armchair, the side lamp turning her hair yellow.

This time he sat, "Have you been ill?"

"Morning nausea."

He hesitated, didn't know how to say it, jumped in, "How far…?"

"Em, " a slight hesitation, "twelve weeks."

"Twelve?" How could that be, flashed through his mind?

"I had a false period, they happen it seems, even though you're pregnant. It obscured things," she glanced his way briefly, "then I was away… as you know."

A silence followed, broken only by the hissing and spitting of the fire. He was confused but couldn't grasp why, needed to ask the key question: What do you want to do?

As though anticipating him, she spoke, "I've thought long and hard about it Finn, I want to have this baby."

It was like his chair moved. "Have it?" he echoed.

She was nodding her head, not looking at him.

Anger helped him now. "And when did you decide that?"

She spoke slowly, "When I was in London."

His cloud of confusion was clearing. "That was about three weeks ago and it didn't cross your mind to mention it the last time I was here?"

She flinched, he was glad to see. She was no longer looking away from him, though not at him. "I should have, but –"

"– but what?" His anger was righteous now.

She looked at him directly, her face pale, like Alison's on those mornings, eyes too green. He blocked a twinge of hopelessness.

"Once I decided I wanted to have the baby," her voice was strong suddenly, "I thought it would be better if we weren't …" her mouth twisted, "together, so you wouldn't feel," she shrugged, looked quickly his way, "trapped."

"How does telling me now change that?" he demanded, throwing out his hands.

She shrugged, fumbled for words, couldn't find them.

He pushed on, "Obviously you think it's purely your decision?"

Her response took a while, "In these circumstances – yes."

"These circumstances?"

She chewed her lip briefly, "I didn't know how to include you, we haven't known each other long, how could a decision like this be made… together?"

He hardly knew where to start. She was in control, trailing him behind. "Well, for starters, you could have asked me what I thought, that's not rocket science."

Another shrug, which infuriated him.

"Well, I don't want to have a baby at this point," he said. "I'm not in a position to take that on."

Pause, before she spoke. "I felt the same, booked an abortion in London, that's why I went there, I thought that would be best, for both of us-"

"-thoughtful of you!"

240

"But I changed my mind..." her voice wobbled then found itself, "realised I wanted to go ahead."

His heart sank, he didn't know her at all, she was crazy.

"I'm not looking for anything from you for this baby," she added.

He hated her at that moment. "So why are you telling me?"

"Because..." her voice got thin, "it would be deceitful not to."

"But keeping me in the dark up to now wasn't deceitful?"

"I thought an abortion would be the best option – you were in Galway –"

"– too far for a fucking phone call? That's shite."

She didn't reply; he was getting used to the way she used silence as a weapon. Then another penny dropped. "How long have you known?"

She hesitated, "About four weeks... "

"Four weeks, Jesus!" She was texting him from Spain about the sunshine when she knew this. A bit of wood hissed angrily in the grate, clearly on his side. He stared across the room at her, stunned all over again.

She broke the silence, "You're making it clear that you don't want to have anything to do with the baby," she said stiffly.

His chest tightened. "I don't think I am making myself clear, though you certainly have made yourself very clear, you get it all your own way! Baby, no baby, secret no secret – it's all down to you!"

"It's an extreme decision, I know," her voice was low now.

The heat from the fire felt suffocating, he wanted out, but was boxed into his chair.

Turning towards him she asked stiffly, "So what do you want Finn?"

Her use of his name irked him, but hopelessness was running at him. How the fuck did he get here? He stood. "I'll have to think it over – unilaterally of course," he said, "I haven't had four weeks to consider…like you!" He moved towards the door, left the house without a backward glance.

Outside the sea breeze slapped his face. He welcomed it, gulped the salty air, faced the Minaun Cliffs to clear the haze from his eyes. Christ Almighty, he'd feared an Achill undertow might get him, instead, he faced a freak wave, which could drown him.

29

Battered after her conversation with Finn Kilbane, Helen delayed telling Fiona she was pregnant, but when her sister phoned bright and breezy she'd no alternative but to grit her teeth and say it.

"Pregnant?" Fiona exclaimed like she'd misheard.

She breathed deeper, took a clipped tone. "Yes, obviously unplanned, with someone I had a brief thing with here."

"On Achill?"

"Where else Fiona? I've decided to keep the baby because it may be the only time I get pregnant in my life, given that I didn't conceive with Shane, despite trying hard."

"Jesus, Helen, you were never tested, Shane may have had a problem!"

"Not likely given that Chloe conceived within weeks."

Fiona was briefly silenced, then gathered herself, "Does this man know?"

"Yeah, he's dismayed. But I'm prepared to go it alone."

"Surely not on Achill? I mean where's the nearest hospital even? Wouldn't London be better, or," her tone lifted, glimpsing light in the tunnel, "Dublin … near us?"

"I couldn't afford to live in Dublin Fiona and London's out of the question, for now."

"But you've a lovely flat –"

"– round the corner from Shane, Chloe and baby, which wouldn't be good for my health nor the baby's at this point in time. They're caretaking for a friend, so they'll move eventually, just not soon enough."

A pause, then, "Robin's mother has a spare room."

"Fiona, don't!"

Another silence, Fiona was unusually lost for words, finally asked, "How on earth will you manage on your own Helen?"

"It's not forever. I'll do it a day at a time," she said, determined to show confidence. "I've made a few friends here and Isla and Kate are very supportive."

"But they're in London!" Then with another sigh, "I assume you've made up your mind, don't want my advice?"

"Fiona, I know what I'm doing and I know it will be tough," she said, managing to strike a more confident tone than she felt. If she expressed any fears to Fiona, her sister would dive in, her help sometimes invaluable, other times, controlling, like lodging her with Robin's mother, a woman with her own life to live.

They ended the call, Helen fully aware that her situation was an unfathomable scenario to Fiona, but what they did agree on was to keep the news from their parents for now.

*

The winds had battered the house all night, so she got up early to go and watch the sea. In Barrett's shop a woman mentioned five metre swells in the Bay so she quickened her step.

244

The ocean was churning with foam, waves toppling over each other, gobbling up the strand. She searched for the swell further out, saw a wall of grey water, upright, solid, like an advancing guard, until it turned and toppled into white foam. Exhilarating, and as always, she felt that fleeting desire to run towards that foam, be tossed, turned, washed through, and delivered safely back onto the sand. For the first time she spoke aloud to the baby bump, "This ocean's wonderful, wait until you see it."

Back home she rested, nausea gone, but tiredness now her constant companion. Her mind wandered over the lack of welcome for her baby: Finn – shock-horror; Fiona – stunned dismay. And more to come.

The conversation with Finn had stung badly, he was on the defensive from the minute he arrived. Yes, she'd blocked him out in London because … she'd reconsidered her choice at the last minute, was under massive pressure, so how the hell could she have involved him? Two hours before the Richmond Clinic, a quick call, "Hey Finn, what should I do?"

Would he have welcomed that? She didn't believe so.

Faced with his coldness, she didn't know how to explain the deep longing to have a baby, fuelled by the deep fear that this was her only chance. His moralistic tone was hard to stomach, since she'd taken precautions, not him. Ultimately, he had a way out; he wasn't pregnant, could walk away. Now, he'd become like a stranger.

A visit to TRIARC would lift her out of gloom but she couldn't face Fiona's interrogations. Instead she'd do what she'd been putting off, see the GP, get linked up with the hospital. She was now a Maternity case; hopefully neither shock nor dismay would be part of the professionals' response.

*

Three days later, Fiona rang, her voice tense. Not another plan to save me, was Helen's thought, but it was a different kind of shock altogether.

"Shane's father, Jim, died of a heart attack yesterday," Fiona said, trying to find the right tone.

"Died?" Impossible – Jim was healthy, barely sixty.

"Sheila told me last night. It was some congenital weakness he didn't know about. No illness, no warnings, he'd been out playing golf the day before."

"That's shocking," she said. Jim and Rosemary, Shane's mother, had always been so welcoming to her, countless cups of tea and dinners, during college years.

"Yeah, they're all in bits as you can imagine, and I knew you'd want to know."

"Thanks for ringing Fiona."

She lay on the sofa, recalling the last time she saw Jim. The Christmas before she and Shane split, on a visit home, they'd taken a drive to Glendalough with Jim and Rosemary and afterwards had dinner. Jim was the picture of health. What a terrible, terrible blow.

It was only later, it dawned that there would be a funeral which Fiona hadn't mentioned…walking on eggs around her. But the thought filled her with dread.

She slept badly, woke wearily, dragged back into the old groove … finally, in an effort to take charge of herself, she rang Fiona, asked about it.

"The funeral's Friday morning, Robin and I are going," she said, "we can represent the family." Fiona to the rescue – as always.

But she couldn't let it rest: should she, shouldn't she,

go to the funeral? Jim had no part in the break-up, he and Rosemary sent a card afterwards, expressing their affection for her, hoping to see her when she was home. Ultimately, going to the funeral was to do with Jim and Rosemary and her affection for them, nothing to do with Shane. Could she do it?

*

And so it came to pass, that she travelled to St Paul's Church with Fiona and Robin, where they sat at the back of a large gathering. Fiona gave her the car key so she could leave at any point. Jim's family were assembled up front, too far for her to see anyone, until Shane stepped forward to do a reading.

He wore a suit, black tie, his hair shorter and her first thought was how like himself he looked, how familiar. And then the utter strangeness of him – she had not set eyes on him for… eleven months since that day on Upper Street with Chloe. So long ago; but not so long ago.

A sob clutched at her chest, which she strangled, making it come out as a weird cough, then she concentrated on breathing in-out-in-out. The rest of the Mass washed over her, his brother Stephen's eulogy about a loving, humorous father came from a long distance and she stayed in the church while the family followed Jim's coffin down the aisle, staring straight ahead.

When Fiona and Robin headed to the front to offer condolences to the family, she slipped out the side door. She wanted to speak to Rosemary, but knew she'd be surrounded by people. She'd send her a card.

As she moved away, someone called her name, Rachel, Shane's sister, was coming towards her, eyes swollen, "Helen, thanks so much for coming," she said, hugging her. "Dad was so fond of you."

"And me of him," she said, before somebody else claimed Rachel. Her words warmed Helen, reminded her of why she'd come. She turned, began walking towards the car park, when a voice called, "Helen!"

The voice was unmistakeable, shocking, she continued walking.

The voice got stronger, closer, "Helen!" He was following her quickly.

She must not run, instead, she stopped, stared ahead.

"Helen?" His voice was at her shoulder, breathless.

She turned slowly, and there he was, face pale, wretched. She found the words she'd rehearsed, "I'm very sorry for your loss Shane."

He nodded. "Rachel said you were here…"

His face once so familiar had changed in some way, which chilled her. Months of distance had altered the details, his hair shorter, chin firmer.

He moved a step forward, "You're leaving…?"

Was it a question? A complaint? A flame of anger licked her throat which she swallowed. Wrong time. She leaned her shoulder against the church wall. "Your Dad was a lovely man, I came to say goodbye to him."

He nodded, groped for words, "I can't…take it in, can't believe it."

She nodded slowly. They stood, a gap of three feet between them, an ocean wide. She felt suddenly light-headed, needed to get to the car. "I'm sorry for your loss Shane," she repeated and made to move.

"Helen, please, don't leave." He looked stricken.

"What?" came out sharply.

He flinched slightly, "I never thought he'd go like this, no warning, nothing," he said, voice breaking, seeming to sway slightly which unnerved her.

She stood rooted to the spot, he was talking to himself mainly, then he wiped his eyes. "Would you not… join us in the hotel? The family would like that so much, Dad was very fond of you …"

She couldn't believe it. "You expect that of me?"

He shook his head groping for words.

"When I could expect nothing at all from you?" she continued.

It was like she'd hit him.

"I'm sorry Helen," he said, "I want to say…" he began again.

"No," she said firmly, raising her hand to halt him, couldn't bear it, not now. "I'm sorry for your loss," she said, turned, walked away on legs which shook but kept moving until she reached the car.

He didn't follow.

*

She stayed in Dublin for two days, feelings of sadness, anger assailing her. She cooked dinner, read during the day, in the evening, watched TV with Fiona's family. Mercifully Fiona didn't try to talk about the pregnancy. Helen considered going to TRIARC but couldn't summon up the energy.

On the train West, blue skies turned to grey, dry fields turned to wet ones and by the time she reached Mayo, fields had turned dry again. Mostly she thought of Rosemary, who would have to start all over again, without Jim, hour by hour, day by day, aware of his absence everywhere, the hole in each day, in each night.

She decided to get off in Castlebar to visit Anne in the Gift shop. When she pushed open the door, there she was, behind the counter, unwrapping new stock.

"A sight for sore eyes," Anne said, smiling broadly. Then, looking closer said, "You're looking mighty pale, what's up darlin?"

Helen struggled to get any words out, could only shake her head, so Anne placed the *Gone to Lunch* sign in the door, and lead her to the kitchenette, and while Helen had a cry for the first time, Anne made tea.

Once she heard that Shane had asked Helen to join the family, Anne didn't hold back her annoyance at his selfish expectations. She also thought Helen had acted generously in going to the funeral.

"I went for Jim and Rosemary," she said wiping her tears, "I don't regret it."

"You're way too good for that fella! If the shoe was on the other foot, would he have done it?" Anne demanded

Helen shrugged, "I dunno. He's in bad shape, Shane has no experience of losing anyone."

"Well, he does now."

Helen looked at Anne, always so sure. "Was your heart ever broken Anne?"

"Surely was. James McCarthy from Ballinrobe, let me down something awful, when I first went to Birmingham. He'd a girl in every dancehall and eejit me thought I was the one and only." She gave a short laugh.

"How did you –"

"– find out? A friend, Aileen Welch, told me." She wrinkled her nose. "He denied it so I blamed her, thought she was jealous." She looked out the window towards the fields beyond, "A case of shooting the messenger."

Helen found it reassuring that Anne had once been a love-struck young one.

"As for your ex," Anne said, "good riddance is my advice!"

Helen managed a nod and then told Anne she was pregnant, unplanned, and was going to have the baby.

She saw Anne suppress shock, pause, before asking, "With –?"

"Finn Kilbane, who's shocked and dismayed."

"You want to talk about it?" Anne asked.

Helen shook her head wearily, "Another time, one sad story per visit."

"Okay," Anne said with a small smile, "just one question, how far gone?"

"Twelve and a half weeks."

*

At four o'clock, Helen woke, sensed Sliabh Mór's pitch black presence behind her, Shane's face, staring: "You're leaving?" Incredible, after the way he left her to sink or swim. And she had sunk, for way, way, too long.

Days later, Fiona sent on a card addressed to Helen.

Dear Helen,

Thanks very much for coming to Dad's funeral. The family want you to know how much they appreciate it. I'm sorry if I upset you, I had no right.

Shane.

She lay on the sofa remembering: for months after he left she'd carried a lump, an unspoken hope, one day he'd return, he'd been infatuated, the passion would burn out, ending was an impossibility, too many years, too much life bound them. He would ring, write, come to the door, ask her to forgive him. She dreamed it often – awake, asleep – reached to his side of the bed to find him. Then one Saturday morning on Islington Upper Street, she saw him and Chloe, across the street, hand in hand, carrying shopping, exactly like he and Helen used to do on Saturdays. A knife cut, deep, bloody. Shane had replaced her, wasn't coming back.

He was now in that place of shock, disbelief, pain, the place she knew too well. Now he grasped it, when it was beyond too late.

30

Every morning Finn woke to a lurking shadow: Helen Bradshaw – what to do, what to fucking do! The shell shock for the first week had been a comfort zone, now receding, as his mind whirled. He see-sawed relentlessly: anger at her, anger at himself, back and forth, he could bail out of this situation, she hadn't consulted him at all, had acted alone, he didn't agree with her decision and hadn't she offered him an escape route? If he didn't, he was trapped…into a life he didn't choose.

He rang Phil in London and told him.

"Wow man," was his friend's first response.

"Yeah."

"And it's definitely yours?"

It had never crossed his mind. "She wouldn't lie about that."

Pause. "How do you feel about her?"

"Totally pissed off."

"Right." Finn could picture Phil thinking, his face screwing up. "So man, what are your options?" he asked.

"Options? Stay or go!"

"Bit extreme, Finno."

"Why?"

"Well, isn't there a middle ground? I mean if the two of you aren't involved with each other and don't want to be, you could offer to help financially and keep in touch? That way you're still supporting the baby and you can do that even if you leave. Sort of half-way house?"

Actually it was and it was so damn simple. "Jesus, yeah. My head's been so scrambled, I've never thought of – options." Relief washed over him. "Thanks Phil, you're a real pal."

*

He went to bed feeling lighter, but woke around three with a completely different thought, a fork lightning strike. Helen had been trying to have a baby with her husband for a while, she'd told him so. Was it possible… she deliberately tried to get pregnant with him? Would she do that?

Pieces slotted together, she'd said she was using a diaphragm and he had taken her word for it – fool, then as soon as she was pregnant, she'd ended the relationship. Had she used him? If so…then he could leave, walk away, couldn't he? Maybe that was what she really wanted: "I'm not looking for anything from you for this baby."

But… she'd also said she'd booked an abortion in London, then changed her mind-only her word for that. Then another line of thought raised its head, whatever the truth about the pregnancy, however fair to offer money, he began to feel stuck on the fact of a child – a child of his – living somewhere, a child he wouldn't know, and this seemed weird, unnatural. But the alternative was as bad – mid-term trips to McDonald's, the Zoo, Theme Parks. Christ.

He couldn't work out what choice he had in any of this, needed desperately to talk to someone, someone he could trust, but Sinead was away in China, on a Maternity Care trip – ironically, so who else? Maura was a sympathetic listener, but a practising Catholic, hardly open to reluctant paternity or abortion as an option.

On the drive to work, Martha Mulherne came to mind. She'd lived in England for years, worked as a social worker, must have dealt with these situations; she was open minded and his hunch was she'd be discreet. But they knew nothing about each other's personal lives, she might think it odd, inappropriate?

*

The fear that Helen had used him to get pregnant gnawed at him. He didn't believe she'd do that, one day, the next, he believed that when desperate, people do things they'd not otherwise consider. In the end, he went and asked her.

It was another ghastly exchange. He recalled it now, parked at the Sound, waiting to pick his mother up from the Hairdressers. Her shock at the question was as strong as his had been when she'd revealed the pregnancy.

Did that make them even? Apparently not.

She became the righteous one, mortally offended at his suggestion. They wove in and out, it rose and fell, they stung each other. He remembered bits clearly, others were a blurred jumble. He stood at points while she sat throughout, he left the same way as he had the last time, without a backward glance.

Snatches rang in his head.

"I only have your word for all of this" he'd said, at which she'd flinched and pulled out the appointment card for a London clinic from a drawer.

Other words: "Given the problems I had trying to get pregnant before, I was afraid this might be my only chance at having a baby."

That stumped him completely; somehow she managed to do that over and over. What was he supposed to say to that?

The room closed in, he itched to be gone, but had to lay out his options – pay maintenance or pay maintenance with visits. He sounded like he was laying out a building design, while she withdrew more and more.

The silence after that was interminable, Finn forced to break it, "I'd appreciate some response – this isn't easy for me."

Without looking at him, she said, "We agree on that much, nothing is easy about this." Then her final response had come in an icy voice "I need time to think about that."

His was equally cold, "Can you make it soon, I've a life to plan too."

He stared out at the steel grey sea, unable to get to grips with how he'd landed in this nightmare, and what an eejit he'd been. And underneath it all, the old familiar itch in his feet was back, the option he hadn't mentioned, to leave, go. Phil said last night he could probably give him some work soonish, that Finn could kip with him for a while, but he'd need to prepare his mother for his exit and also the History Group.

One thing looked very clear, he and Helen Bradshaw were now a whisper away from hatred – how the hell could they work anything out between them?

To keep his mind occupied, he read through pieces in his tattie hokin file. In the *Westport Historical Society* article he was struck by a phrase in the Inquest record: "... We consider that the hooker was not properly ballasted when she left Achill and we consider that the hooker was grossly overcrowded." There was, however, no mention of consequences for this – no responsibility taken, no responsibility allotted and no reparation. Why not?

He flicked through another publication, *Bathadh Acla*, produced by an Achill Commemoration Group to mark the centenary of the Clew Bay Drownings when the stone memorial at Westport Quay had been erected. He saw a reference to the scale of the Achill migration, in an article by Anne O'Dowd: S*palpins and Tattie Hokers*.

"By the last decade of the nineteenth century, practically every able-bodied man, woman and child from the island of Achill had spent some time either digging or picking potatoes in Ayrshire or the Lothians."

The scale of it was mind boggling. Tattie hokers migrated because they'd no choice, to ensure the survival of their land and families.

In Síle A. Nic Aodha's article, he discovered an illuminating detail about Achill life at the time: "More profit was made from the sale of eggs than any other industry, except migratory labour. Eggs were exported in thousands by the local dealers who purchased them from the people." In addition, she noted, "Eggs were also used as a bartering commodity, for goods such as tea, sugar, flour etc."

It was a snapshot of the island's economy, captured in an egg!

The Westport Memorial and the graveyard Headstone, both say clearly, "accidentally drowned". This angered him. Tattie hokin was not accidental, it was an organised system involving Scottish potato merchants, local gaffers recruiting young people to dig and pick tons of potatoes, for small money. Their availability was a result of impoverishment over generations, colonial and native. This history should be visible, like the Murrisk memorial makes the Famine visible.

The Trust could argue that there was a Memorial to tattie hokin in Westport and the Group had to anticipate this. Finn didn't accept this, believed they had a strong case notwithstanding. It was based on two elements: – place: establishing a marker on Achill, as an act of remembrance; context: informing/reminding people about the conditions which led to the annual migration. He knew obtaining funding lay in the lap of the Gods ultimately, but meantime they should do their damnedest to get it.

On a free afternoon, he drove around the Corraun peninsula with Gawina, so she could do some sketches for her proposed mural-tapestry. They stopped at points, she sketched, drove on, stopped again.

"It's so close but different to the island," she said, "more wild."

"Yeah, less settled too."

While she sketched, he tramped a bit, imagining it from the viewpoint of the tattie hokers. He would ask Sean about taking his boat out in the Spring – if he was still here.

He told Gawina about the archaeological finds on Corraun, an infant burial ground and the shell middens, the compost mound of long-ago households, which fascinated her. Unfortunately, with light fading, they didn't have time to seek them out.

She had insisted on giving him dinner, in return for driving her. "Black bean casserole and potato gratin, already cooked."

"It's a deal."

On the drive back she suddenly asked, "Are you sad Finn?"

Jesus! He didn't know whether it was her intuition or her Dutch directness which bothered him more. "Why do you ask?"

"Your energy is low," she said, put her warm hand on his arm, "and you look a little … lonely?"

"No secrets with you?"

She grinned, shrugged.

*

Her house was cosy, the stove glimmering, Wim staying with Simon in Murrisk. She offered him a glass of wine, "There's a spare bed if you want to stay over?"

"Sounds good." He badly needed a break from his same-old, same-old.

On the walls were family photos of Wim, Gawina and Simon, Wim's crayon drawings, framed woven pieces of Gawina's work and photos of Simon's metal sculptures. There was a lot of valuable history to lose here, he thought.

"Do you cook at home?" she asked, when they began eating,

"My mother won't let me in the kitchen, so only when she's out. She feeds me well, but traditionally, so it's great to get something veggie."

"I was brought up vegetarian," she said, "learned to cook at an early age."

Finn remembered Alison's sortie into vegetarianism in Manchester, how she'd tried to get him on board and how he'd resisted, "You can't deprive an Achill man of lamb or fish." He sees now it was another battle between them, him refusing to take on Alison's choices. He'd been a slow learner.

Talk turned inevitably to the Memorial; Gawina was optimistic about getting development money, wondered if he'd any views on the proposals.

"The ideas are great," he said honestly, "but it's impossible to say if we'll get development money or how much, which would dictate everything."

She sighed. "I know, but I must hope."

He mentioned his recent reading about the Drownings inquest and his belief that context should be central. "Can context be conveyed by a mural, a sculpture?" he asked.

"Of course, think of the Famine Ship at Murrisk – you don't need a book to grasp its meaning, the ship of skeletal figures tells the story."

"I agree, but most people know about the Irish Famine, they bring that knowledge to it, it's not the same for tattie hokin."

Now her face was intent, "True, but information can be integrated."

He nodded, then feeling like a change of subject, asked, "How are things between you and Simon?"

She sighed heavily.

"Sorry, none of my business-"

"-that's okay," she gave a crooked half smile. "At least you ask. Many Irish don't mention it, talk about the weather instead!"

"It's called going at the thing sideways. In Ireland there's a saying – the long way round is the short way home."

"What does this mean?"

"It means the direct route is not always the best route. Talking about the weather may be the preamble to –"

"– preamble?"

"– the warm up, the lead-in, before getting to the point."

Another crooked half smile. "Hmm, I'll have to remember that." Then her face clouded, "Simon and I have separated. He's now officially involved," she drew the word out, "with a Murrisk woman, Clare." Her face was sad, "Thirteen years over."

"That's very tough."

A cloud of sadness descended over her face. "Yes. Wim doesn't sleep well – lots of calling out – Simon is not here enough, he misses him," then sounding angry, "Simon wanted me to wait while he made up his mind about this woman…or maybe live with both of us?"

"A hell of a lot to ask."

"Too much. He likes to do things always his way," she paused "he's a creative person but selfish too. I didn't know how much." She rubbed her eyes, "I'm sad, angry and so shocked."

"I see why."

They sat in silence until she suddenly stood, "Enough sadness, let's have some cake," and quickly coffee and a scrumptious dark chocolate cake, made by a French baker from Newport, arrived.

"A French baker in Newport?" Finn asked, hadn't a clue about the many creative people who lived on or near his home place, while Gawina knew them all. Did it reflect some native resistance to blow-ins which he'd held onto?

Over coffee she said that she and Simon would divide the house so they could live separately and share looking after Wim. "We have no choice," she said, "all our money is in this."

"What kind of division?"

"I want partition walls, two separate spaces. It will spoil it, but that's my condition."

Finn thought the plan was riddled with problems. Would Simon's new woman move in and Gawina end up living on a landmine? But … what choice had she?

They had a second glass of wine, talked of other things. Suddenly she leaned towards him, "Would you like us to sleep together?"

He suppressed a smile, it was so direct. He found her very attractive, she was sensual, touched his hand, arm, easily, figured sex with her would be enjoyable, but Gawina was a friend, sex often messed that up and her relationship with Simon was in turmoil, so potentially a double mess. Plus…he was still reeling from his debacle with Helen Bradshaw and his paternity, stuff he couldn't bear to talk about yet.

"I find you very attractive," he said truthfully, "but you're a friend, I wouldn't want to spoil that."

She looked puzzled, "Why would it? We both just enjoy ourselves, as friends."

So clear, so straightforward, he was tempted, but knew he couldn't. "I had a short, complicated relationship recently with someone which just ended – I'm licking my wounds y'know?"

"Sorry to hear about that."

When she was showing him to the spare room, she went on her toes to kiss him goodnight and he came close to changing his mind.

"Maybe some other time," she said, as she closed the door gently.

31

Helen travelled to Dublin for Fiona's birthday celebration, bringing with her the only fancy top she had, a silk green Vietnamese dress which she'd bought in Camden Market a few years back, the softness of the fabric lovely. It was loose, would cover her small baby bump, a conversation she wished to avoid with Fiona's friends and mother-in-law. Checking herself in the mirror, she felt up to scratch for the occasion.

At an Italian restaurant, a group of ten gathered, Fiona's family, Robin's mother and four of Fiona's friends. One was Molly Byrne, who grew up on the same road as Helen and Fiona, now unrecognisably glamorous, her curly blond hair falling like sculpted waves to her shoulders. Helen would have passed her in the street. Molly on the other hand recognised her instantly... how should she take that?

A tasty bruschetta and good cannelloni wiped out Helen's anxiety that she'd lost the skill of social interaction, her tongue loosened, she smiled frequently and was shot back to happy memories of celebrations in London. Robin's mother, Breda, talked about her upcoming trip to China in May, the first holiday since her husband's death, three years ago. She had a quiet courage about her, Helen thought, would like to have asked her how she got it, but didn't know how. Looking around the table Helen saw that the gathering was a joyful recognition of Fiona's life, which her sister fully deserved.

But the social whirl didn't stop there, Helen had a surprise call from James, still stuck in Dublin. After queries about her health, he invited her for afternoon tea in the Merrion Hotel to view their Irish art collection. She didn't hesitate, delighted to go and delighted to delay her return to Achill and another encounter with Finn Kilbane.

"My treat," James insisted.

She borrowed Fiona's nice coat and was glad when she saw the uniformed footman at the entrance. Inside, she stood in a high ceilinged foyer staring straight at a vaguely familiar semi-abstract painting, to the right of which were two Jack Yeats works. Further along was a le Brocquy and to the left, a small Paul Henry, *Killary Harbour*, in shades of blue. She'd stepped into a gallery.

In the dining room, a fire was lighting and paintings hung from every wall. She walked around peering at the work, Mainie Jellett's *Madonna & Child*, *Breton Girl* in bold colour by Roderic O'Conor, a dreamy *Aloes* by Leech, then a sombre, striking painting of crows on a tree by Mildred Butler, *Green Eyed Jealousy*. Intriguing – who was Mildred Butler?

On another wall, two paintings by William Scott caught her eye, completely different in style. She liked one, a simplified, flattened, still life, *Frying pan, Fennel. Eggs & Lemons*, the bright lemon centrepiece seemed to … pulsate.

James arrived, wearing a classy tweed coat.

"This place is great," she said.

"My wife Jean introduced me to it," James said, "thought I needed more culture in my life."

That was the first pebble of personal information James had ever told her, a surprising one, given his depth of knowledge about Art.

"It makes sense," he continued, glancing round, "instead of keeping their Art under lock and key, the owners display it. Apparently," he chuckled, "the Duke of Wellington was born here, the great Englishman, Irish by birth! My father, a postman, told us that snippet." He shrugged, "I was reared a couple of miles away, off South Circular Road."

"Not too far from me, in Walkinstown."

He ordered coffee and scones and it struck Helen that James was different here, more outgoing, more at ease. "Any of Grace's work here?" she asked.

"Sadly no, but I've got you a catalogue," and he handed her a glossy booklet. A quick flick confirmed no Grace.

When six small scones arrived, with jam and clotted cream, Helen thought she'd never manage more than two. Dead wrong, it turned out.

"Best scones in Ireland, bar Martha's," James said.

Helen agreed after the first bite – light as air.

James scanned the paintings, said in a rueful voice, "I came very late to Art and History. At school I'd no interest, preferred Geography and Science, codes, formulas, that sort of thing." He raised his eyebrows, "I thought Art was just for the few."

"Which few?"

He considered the question, "The well-to-do few who bought it and the super talented who made it, I suppose. I knew a couple of people who painted, but they always called it a hobby, saw their work as worlds apart from galleries. Then I met Oliver, who forced me into an exhibition at the National Gallery and literally... opened my eyes!"

"Better late than never?"

"Absolutely. What about you Helen, did you study History or Art?"

"No, though I loved History at school, especially at Leaving Cert. I did Art until Junior Cert, stopped because I didn't think I'd enough talent." She grimaced, "The attitude to Art was like you say, only for the super talented, those born with the special gift. Looking back, Art was viewed as more exclusive, than, say, Music, where there was an acceptance of different levels of talent."

He nodded, "Yes, especially painting and sculpture. Nowadays it's all changed, graffiti, murals, videos are all part of it, the definition has widened hugely, often controversially!" They paused for a second scone after which James resumed his line of thought.

"You know I think the friction between the so called radicals and traditionalists in early twentieth century Art has echoes of all this. Oliver and I argue about it."

Helen tried to imagine James in an argument, voice raised, face red, found it hard, he always seemed so measured and reasonable. "What are the differences between you?"

"Phew, the relationship between Art and society, I suppose."

"Sounds hefty."

He grinned, "Not really, Oliver knows much more than I do but I insist on my opinion, which is how we normally end the argument!" He leaned forward, "Do you want a short, crude summary of the historical friction?"

"Yes please."

"Well, Sean Keating and Mainie Jellett are often used as examples of the two camps, because they're so different and represented contrasting outlooks on Art. Keating trained in Ireland where Representational Art was still respected, Jellett in Paris where Modernism reigned, so their paintings reflect these differences."

"Why is that a problem, why not each to their own?"

"Indeed, but it's never that easy. The establishment of the new Irish state is vital background to it all. Keating wanted to find a visual language to express the new national identity, painting the innovative electricity scheme on the Shannon for example, while Jellett, believed Art is completely separate from politics, so was an abstract painter. Art for Art's sake, in her view, it had no national purpose."

"Poles apart?"

"Yes. Friction was furthered by the views of many Art commentators who saw Jellett as pioneering, progressive, Keating as a propagandist, reactionary. Now this is where Oliver and I part ways. He believes that visual Art is and should be separate from any form of national identity, whereas I believe that there's an accepted link between Music or Literature and national identity, so why can't that be true for visual Art too?"

"I see," Helen said. "I remember reading that Jellett rejected Art which copied Nature? If you could take a photograph of it, why paint it?"

"Yes, that's why she was drawn to abstraction."

"So where did Grace fit into all this?"

"Hmm. Oliver says Grace is a Realist painter with Modernist influences, to which she was very open, as we know. She wasn't completely in either camp, as many others weren't either."

Helen thought of *Evening, Achill*, which is recognisably a place, but not completely representational, more an expression of the way she experienced it. She paused, "I've often wondered what the Henrys thought of the 1916 Rising or War of independence, it's not portrayed in their work at all, though it was happening around them. What do you think?"

James nodded, "Paul worked for the Congested Districts Board, knew about the Land League, the Volunteers, but none of that surfaces in his work."

"They didn't see it as the stuff of Art?" she wondered.

"Or their Art? Landscape was the big pull for Paul, but that isn't neutral, landscape has an integral link with society too."

Helen was grappling with this. "I suppose, they were outsiders, blow-ins on Achill, Grace by nationality too …"

"And both by class," he agreed. "Class was a factor in the friction, many of the Irish Modernists came from wealthy backgrounds, trained in Paris and so found themselves in an insecure relationship to the New Irish State. One commentator described it as caught between the Big House and the peasant cabin."

"They felt culturally dislocated?" she asked.

"Probably."

Helen had never considered cultural dislocation in her research. Was it because, like many, she viewed visual artists as existing in a different sphere – above, separate from society, in a way she didn't view writers? Had she carried a view of artistic neutrality in her head throughout her research? Did that matter?

"The friction wasn't helped," James continued, "by the growing conservatism of the New State, nor the conservatism of the Royal Hibernian Academy, a vital outlet for artists. The Modernists had to fight back to promote their Art, set up a separate Gallery which Paul and Grace were involved in."

She nodded, knew about this, thankfully.

"Over time the friction eased, the Irish Art scene was too small for all-out schism. Artists from both camps sat on the same committees, exhibited alongside each other, notably in the first *Irish Exhibition of Living Art*, in 1943 which brought a dash of colour to wartime Dublin, and to which crowds flocked."

"Grace had a painting in that exhibition I think," Helen recalled.

"As did Keating and Jellett."

It was a good point to end on, James suggested, though Helen would happily have carried on. She was relieved to hear he hoped to be back on Achill in a week.

"One problem about being a late convert," James said reaching for his coat, "you get obsessive. Jean believed I tended that way!"

Helen registered another pebble of personal information, said, "That's no problem to me."

"You know," he said buttoning his coat, "every time I'm here, I'm struck by the contrast between the conditions under which Art is often made and those under which it's displayed."

And he left her with that.

Helen sat, ate her third scone, determined to finish off the clotted cream, last tasted on a trip to Devon. Before leaving, she toured the hotel once more, examining the paintings and one magnificent le Brocquy tapestry.

On the bus she mulled over James' comments. Grace spent most of her life in Ireland, adopted it as her home, did that alter her cultural dislocation? Nothing she'd read had explored this. His final comment about the condition under which Art was made versus displayed also provoked thought. In later life, Grace was impoverished, dependent on friends, yet, kept painting. Once bought, her paintings enjoyed the privileges of their owners, hanging in carpeted and stylish houses, or marbled galleries. Was that what he meant?

Wasn't that often the fundamental artistic struggle … keep doing what you want to do, with no guarantee that anyone else will like it or buy it? Grace's life seemed the epitome of that.

*

On Grafton Street, she stood in a shop doorway watching shoppers, performers, schoolkids, moving purposefully around her, going about their business, she, a solitary figure outside of them. She recalled Fiona's question, *How will you manage on your own?* She didn't honestly know.

She pressed her hand now to the baby bump to reassure herself, hold herself steady. It helped, but it brought a strange thought: who's looking after who now?

32

The pelting rain, whistling winds were the music score to their kitchen scene, Finn reading the *Irish Times*, his mother watching the television – abruptly broken by his phone.

Helen Bradshaw. Oh no, he thought, answered reluctantly.

"It's Helen here..." she said, her voice strange, "I'm really sorry to bother you on this night Finn ...but wonder if you could help me?"

He waited.

"I'm sorry to ask you this, but I need to get to Castlebar Hospital urgently ..." the voice was now wobbling.

"Castlebar, on a night like this?"

"It's an emergency, I've had... some bleeding and the hospital said to go in"

Bleeding? He thought bleeding stopped with pregnancy.

"I'm in Martha's house, she rang the hospital and they told me to go to A&E."

Martha's?

"James has offered to drive but... he doesn't know the road well."

Christ, James Mulherne should not drive the road to Castlebar this night.

"Martha will come with me," she added, perhaps to soften the blow.

"I'll come to Martha's now," he said, what else could he do?

He told his mother that Helen had a severe stomach ache and he was going to drive her to the hospital.

"On such a bad night?" she exclaimed. But she helped him with his raincoat, stood at the door, "Take it slowly, mind the road Finn, whatever you do."

On the way to Keel, he knew he was out of his depth again. Floundering, say no or yes, nothing in between with Helen Bradshaw. And so he was in motion, saying yes, to God knows what.

Martha didn't bat an eyelid when she opened the door, just looked glad to see him. Helen, white as chalk, was sitting on the sofa, coat on, bag beside her. She thanked him for coming, but her entire body oozed anxiety to be gone. James hovered, apologised for dragging Finn out on this unmerciful night, and to Finn's relief, all three were heading out of the estate within minutes, James waving them off. Finn drove Martha's car, his van too uncomfortable for the journey.

Martha sat beside him, up front, Helen in the back so she could lie across the seat if needed. She seemed to have moved into a deep silence, unbearable if he and she had been alone. Finn thanked the Gods for Martha.

He drove carefully, through blinding rain and Martha filled him in. Helen had called her in a panic, told her she was pregnant and bleeding. Once the hospital heard about the bleeding, they'd advised her to come in for a check-up.

She glanced his way, "James offered, but Helen thought you'd be best, knowing the roads like the back of your hand." She spoke neutrally, but must have put two and two together.

Helen spoke from the back, in a thin voice, "Bleeding sometimes happens, doesn't it?"

"Certainly it does," Martha replied calmly.

If Finn had been alone with Helen, he wouldn't have had a clue what to say.

They drove onward through the dark, sporadically broken by yellow lights from behind curtained windows, or front door lamps which winked like frail candles. All three were quiet, the only sounds the rain drumming on the car roof and the wipers as they laboured to dispel the rivulets running ceaselessly down the glass – a totally different music score to earlier. Newport was closed up, everyone at home.

Quickly he reached the part of the journey he feared, the bridge which crossed the bend over the river was prone to flooding. The river was fast, swollen, but the bridge manageable and he was able to splash slowly through to the road beyond it.

"Thank God," Martha said in a low voice, obviously fearful too.

Now the silence was taut, as they faced into the last stage. He sensed Helen's desperation, she was sitting up watching through the window, all three now willing the car forward, each bend of the road a marker bringing them closer. And then the lights of houses on the outskirts flashed by, street lights welcomed them and they made their way to the hospital.

Finn dropped Helen and Martha at the door of A&E, saw Martha get a wheelchair to push Helen in and quickly the two women disappeared while he went to park.

When he arrived inside, there was no sign of them, they'd gone through to A&E, so he sat on a plastic chair to wait. Martha appeared after a while, told him Helen was being examined and sat beside him.

There were a few others waiting, an elderly man with a wheezy cough, a woman with a nebuliser, and a pale young man who had a bloodstained bandaged arm. All sat in silence.

"You alright?" Martha asked.

He nodded. "Helen was lucky you and James were around."

"It was very frightening for her."

Knowing he owed her something, he said, "You've probably put it together…?"

She nodded. "Helen didn't say but… yes."

She patted his arm, a gesture of sympathy, but he was too churned up to know how to acknowledge it.

The quiet was broken by the arrival of a man complaining of chest pains and his agitated wife. The man's breathing was labouring. A nurse appeared, handled the agitated woman with forbearance and they were quickly taken off.

After twenty minutes, Martha went to fetch drinks from the machine. He didn't want one, but didn't refuse, and when Martha arrived with paper cups of tea, it warmed his fingers, still stiff from the drive.

Quite a while later, the nurse was in front of them saying they could join Helen inside and Finn followed Martha, his heart thumping. She lay on a stretcher bed, attached to a monitor, looking a bit less pale and gave them a weak smile.

Martha moved to the side of the bed, took her hand, Finn stayed at the foot.

"We've found the heartbeat and it's strong and regular," the nurse said brightly, "so that's a good sign." She smiled at Helen, whose eyes were fixed on her.

"The bleed was not heavy, also a good sign, but we plan to keep Helen here for forty-eight hours, attached to a monitor and if nothing else surfaces, she can go home."

"That's great news," Martha said.

"I've told Helen that she will need bed rest afterwards and as she lives alone, she'll need to sort out some help."

"I can help out," Martha said immediately, "I'm a neighbour."

Finn said nothing. He'd become rigid once it dawned on him that the heartbeat mentioned wasn't Helen's, but the baby's.

When the nurse left, Helen became tearful, "Sorry for all the trouble," she said, wiping tears away, "I'm so relieved."

"Nothing to be sorry about," Martha said, handing her tissues.

Finn stood like a statue.

Then Helen turned to him, "Thanks so much for driving me Finn," she said, her voice struggling, "that was an awful journey."

He shrugged the thanks off, sensed the depth of her fear, had no idea what to say.

"And you and James, Martha, I couldn't have managed without yous."

The nurse was back. "I think the rain is easing finally," she said lifting the blind. "We'll be moving Helen to a ward, so I'm afraid you'll have to leave."

"Will you be okay?" Martha asked Helen.

She gave a tweak of a smile, "Of course. You two should get going before it rains again."

Martha hugged her while Finn, still at the foot of the bed, managed to say, "I'll be in touch tomorrow."

On the drive back, they were mostly silent – exhausted – Martha didn't seem to expect anything of him, thankfully. Before he drove off in his van, she placed her hand on his arm said, "Mind yourself Finn. This kind of thing takes it out of you."

He appreciated the thought.

To his relief, his house was in darkness when he drove up. Despite utter exhaustion, he knew he'd have problems sleeping, poured himself a large Jameson in hopes of inducing it. Instead he tossed, turned, couldn't block out the sound in his head, the sound of a heartbeat, thumping away, holding on with all its tiny might. He was shocked to the core.

*

Next day, he called into the hospital after work. Helen was now in a ward of eight beds and though still pale, seemed brighter. Anne, her neighbour from Shraheens, was there and shook his hand. He was glad to see her, couldn't imagine what conversation he and Helen would manage alone.

"So far so good," Helen said, "no more bleeding and the heartbeat is fine."

"Good," he said, for the want of knowing what else.

Anne went to get tea from the machine, to give them time together, he guessed. Presumably she knew. He noticed the large bunch of flowers on the locker which she'd probably brought. Hospital rituals, another world, he'd come with one hand as long as the other.

"Are they looking after you well?" he asked.

"Very well. They seem very efficient and thorough, I think."

He saw that weights had been lifted from her shoulders.

"I was so worried," she added.

She waited, allowing him to say how he'd felt, but he couldn't manage it, didn't know.

"They plan to discharge me tomorrow," she said, breaking in. "Anne is insisting I stay with her 'til Friday, she has an en-suite guest room to launch in her new house."

"Very decent." This morning, when he woke groggy after the whiskey and lack of sleep, the thought of bed rest had flashed into his mind like a red flag.

"And Martha and James have offered help when I return to Keel."

She said all this quickly – to relieve him of any burden? Was that what she wanted, what he wanted?

He was floundering again. "I can help too, with shopping …"he heard himself say suddenly.

"Really?" but then nervously, "Thank you."

The waters just got deeper. What was she thanking him for – helping to keep the baby alive?

Fortunately Anne was back to save them and he left shortly afterwards.

*

Helen's sojourn at Anne's house gave him a breather, but although he was busy on Kerrigan's extension, work no longer saved him. His head was not his own, thoughts trickled upwards at will. The drive in the rain to the hospital was something he'd have done for any neighbour in distress, part of the islanders' code, hospital miles away. If asked, you helped, if needed, you offered. But that drive was different; it had dragged him further out to sea.

Had it crossed his mind, on the drive, that life would be simpler if Helen miscarried the baby? He didn't think so. It wasn't until he woke next morning, that it occurred. Now he saw that his life would be simpler if that happened, but Helen's wouldn't. He'd witnessed how vital this baby was to her and so she was right – it was very different for her. And another difference dawned, he was on his own with it; she wasn't, she had people around her to call on.

Within a couple of days, he began to feel his options narrowing, the middle ground slipping. If he left soon, he'd be walking away, but how could he stay and have a new life? It was all turning black and white: yes or no, in or out? Then he'd shake himself, pull himself together – he was in shock, that drive to Castlebar and the heartbeat had hammered him, he needed to calm down, get a grip. But at night, before drifting off, he couldn't escape the sound of that heartbeat. No face, no shape, only the rhythmic beat: small, persistent; small, persistent.

33

Helen returned to her house after five days with Anne and Paddy, grateful for their care and company. She feared she'd have languished alone in Keel, after the hospital. Their grandkids were a treat. Vinny, a quiet three year old, roped her into Lego building while Maria, aged eight, told them tales from school about falling out and making up with pals, boring or fun teachers and daily reports about the Easter concert, in which she was playing Bunny Rabbit and one of four singing, *'In your Easter Bonnet'*. Helen was delighted to help her practise, Anne now worn thin with that damn song.

When she returned to Keel, her house seemed so bare and quiet until Isla rang to say she was coming for a weekend to Dublin in ten days' time and would book them both into a hotel. She was adamant, "I won't take no for an answer, it's been too long."

Helen counted her blessings, a healthy baby, Anne, Paddy, Isla, Martha and James, Fiona and… Finn, who was picking up shopping. She also felt stronger, able to walk the beach most days and let the wind clear her head.

Finally, she faced the task she'd deferred for too long, rang her parents to tell them she was pregnant, omitting any mention of the bleed and fudging the number of weeks, so her mother didn't realise she was pregnant in Spain.

"Pregnant?" her mother repeated, voice rising an octave, then followed it with a volley of Who-What-Where questions which Helen struggled to answer as best she could.

"Someone I slept with who lives locally Mam. I took no risks, the contraception failed."

"And what are his intentions?" she demanded.

Helen said they weren't in a relationship but they'd work something out.

"Work something out? For God's sake, what kind of man is he, leaving you to cope with it?"

"It's my decision Mam – please don't make it worse!"

This brought a brief pause, until her mother said, "I assume you're going back to London?"

Helen gave her mother a modified version of what she'd told Fiona – she didn't want to be around the corner from Shane, so might stay on Achill for a while before returning.

"Helen, you've no idea what you're taking on," her mother said, voice now rising two octaves, "having a new baby is massive even with a husband, so doing it alone on an isolated island… you just…can't!" Then her voice brightened, "Why don't you come here, stay with us for a while, we'd love to have you…both!"

Helen, now utterly drained, decided not to contradict anything, agreed to give Spain consideration to shorten the conversation.

Her father spoke to her briefly, was also shocked, but didn't quiz her, instead enquired after the state of her health and if she was "reconciled" to her situation. Reconciled was a good word she told him and she said yes she was.

"If you need any help putting up shelves, I could come over," he added, amazing her.

"That would be great Dad, I'll definitely need help," she said, lest his offer slip away. It dawned on her that coming to Achill would give him a perfect reason for a break and it would be such a lift. Does every cloud really have a silver lining?

*

Fiona was in regular touch, resigned about the pregnancy now, which was better than fighting about it, then one evening Helen had a surprise call from her niece Clodagh congratulating her on the baby, "I'm delighted to be getting another cousin," she said.

Her enthusiasm touched Helen, Clodagh was the first person to be glad about it. Then she quizzed Helen about baby preferences: boy or girl, blue or brown eyes, dark or blonde, curly or straight hair – none of which Helen had thought about, so her responses were disappointing. She also wanted to know about names, at which Helen failed too, but it didn't stop Clodagh pleading with her, "Not Beyoncé, Apple or North …promise Helen, pleeze."

It was very easy to make that promise.

Clodagh' s call cheered her up.

*

Finn arrived with some shopping next day, asked about her state of health and said yes to a cup of tea, for the first time. He insisted on making it then commented on the mound of books lying next to the sofa where she sat.

"A time for those classics?," he asked then.

"*War and Peace* next," she said, "although I'm bleary eyed reading."

But quickly silence hovered and to fill the space, she told him about Anne's five star accommodation and grandkids. He then mentioned the extension he was working on, its progress, but then the silence was back.

He stood, "My mother sends her best regards – I told her you'd had a stomach thing."

"Oh, right."

Now Nellie hovered in the room with them, both knowing she'd have to be told…sometime soon.

After he left, she let out a long breath, realised she'd been walking on hot coals. She didn't need this extra stress, didn't need him visiting like some awkward do-gooder.

The next time he arrived, she didn't offer tea which she reckoned made life easier for both of them.

*

Fiona invited her to Dublin for a break, so she went, glad to relieve Martha and James of cooking and Finn of shopping. Robin congratulated her on the baby, asked no questions, Clodagh was still excited about it all and Helen noticed that she and her mother seemed on better terms.

Later she told Fiona about their Dad's offer to come to Achill.

"Ah, Daddy's girl," Fiona said, put out, "the number of times I've asked him here!"

"Well you're Mammy's girl, so we're quits." Helen said. "Besides, Dad was always one for the sad cases and that fits me."

Fiona conceded, "It would be good if he came, he'd be a real help."

Helen felt comforted that her baby would have cousins, an aunt, uncle, grandparents. They took on an importance she hadn't anticipated. Was this awareness biological or was it because she'd be alone and needed it more?

Next day, she took herself to TRIARC, to peruse a file called *P &G Henry file,* containing copies of paintings from catalogues which a staff member had alerted her to.

It contained two separate files, a large one for Paul and a much smaller one containing copies of Grace's paintings, some tiny. She leafed through, most she'd seen, but there were also a few jewels, Achill paintings she hadn't seen before – a wonderful surprise. She examined one called, *The Rosary,* a young, dark haired woman, sitting inside a cottage, holding a rosary beads, looking to the side, possibly at others not visible? The cottage had a wooden door and a yellow wall, in which there was a small window, reminiscent of Van Gogh's painting of his Arles room. But it was the colour of the woman's clothes which caught her eye: a full length deep orange skirt, over which she wore a wine and cream shawl. Underneath the skirt, rough, brown ankle boots protruded, contrasting with the bright clothes – the boots of a peasant woman, for rough terrain and hard work. The young woman's face was not well defined, more an impression of features, in that style Grace sometimes used, her Fauves-influenced style?

The second painting, *The Shop,* was intriguing: a small group of people inside a fairly large shop where a man stood behind the counter. The shelves seemed well stocked with goods, again suggested rather than defined and on the counter, a small stack of dishes were for sale. But it was the clothing which gripped Helen. A woman faced the counter, in a full, orange skirt over which was a shawl in shades of beige and yellow. Grace's orange women were a revelation, she'd seen the traditional red skirts of the Aran Islands, but not orange. Was the vibrant orange as Grace saw them or as they were?

Two men stood near to the woman, both with walking sticks, dressed in ganseys and trousers, in shades of beige and yellow, with dark hats. The man serving was dressed differently, in a pale brown jacket, trader style, and again, faces were suggested, not defined. The figure of the woman totally dominated the picture, her size and solidity, the colours of her clothing, suggested a powerful female presence.

Helen was impressed with the way the painting brought her inside an everyday setting which was alive, colourful, miles away from the dreary browns and blacks of old photos of rural life. She'd love a print of it, but where to get one?

She went for a bowl of soup at Kilkenny Design, sat next to a couple who seemed to be having a tense conversation about who was doing what in their child's schedules ... football practice recurred, then time factor, traffic... and later in a resentful tone the woman said, "I can't miss the meeting again."

She couldn't stop herself listening. Would she ever face those disagreements with anyone? Ever? Did that make it better or worse? Did it make it lonelier?

On her walk back, a wave of anxiety caught her: her certainty about having the baby didn't protect her against these waves. She paused to look into the window of the sweater shop, counted breaths. In the glass reflection she

284

saw her pale, anxious face, saw a woman who knew nothing about having a baby or looking after one, even less about doing it alone. This anxiety she had to learn to manage, she told herself sternly, then returned to TRIARC.

*

The weekend with Isla was a tonic. She'd booked them into a boring modern hotel in the city centre, but Helen didn't care a damn as she sank gratefully onto the plush bed. A part of her would happily have stayed in the room for the duration, but Isla was having none of it. "You've to show Dublin to me."

They started at Hugh Lane Gallery, to look at two of the Grace paintings, the stunning blue *Evening, Achill* and the *Girl in White,* which Isla was truly impressed by and in the café later, pumped Helen for the details of its origins. Helen told her about white paint techniques, how many other colours were subtly combined, and how the painter Whistler had probably been an important influence. It was a rare moment for Helen to realise how much she'd learned over the past months.

Isla then showed her a proposed design for the Irish Artists book – large size, high spec, the cover painting was being debated currently, Jack B Yeats, Mainie Jellett or Paul Henry were the options.

"I've proposed Grace Henry or Norah McGuinness to get away from the usual crowd, but the Marketing Department says they aren't well known, and that's what it's all about!"

"So being less well known becomes a self-fulfilling prophecy?" Helen asked.

"Absolutely. In publishing, like other businesses, success breeds success, until it doesn't."

"When does that happen?"

"When you get older, less photogenic, or a book bombs after bad reviews, or doesn't sell after good reviews, or the new kids on the block steal the spotlight from the older kids, which is happening faster and faster!"

"Depressing."

"They're planning book launches in various places, it would be great if you'd be one of our speakers," Isla said.

"Me?"

"Why not? You've a great story to tell about discovering Grace and Irish Art. We need that angle Helen."

"Phew," she said, a bit overcome at the thought, but suddenly realised that talking about Grace Henry could be an exciting thing to do.

They had a Korean meal later and next morning took the DART to Howth, walked up Balscadden to the Summit and back down through the village. Oh, the ease and comfort of doing simple things with an old friend, Helen thought, wondering how she could continue to survive without it.

"Any timeline in your head for returning to London?" Isla asked, over afternoon tea.

She shrugged. "No. A new baby will be a whole new existence, so maybe at six months … that would be Springtime, or sooner, if I'm climbing walls! I'm renewing the career break for another year."

"Good." Then Isla spoke hesitantly, "I ran into Shane in the street, he was full of remorse about what he said to you at the church." She raised her eyebrows.

Helen shrugged, didn't ask for more details.

"I don't see much of them these days," Isla added, "seem to move in different circles."

That was good to hear: it would make life easier when Helen returned.

Next day she waved Isla off on the Airport Express, wishing, wishing, she could go with her.

34

Finn ran into Martha in Westport, who suggested a coffee and after a brief chat about the Memorial Application, he decided to take the plunge, "Could I discuss something personal with you Martha…?"

She looked surprised, "If you think … I can be of help?"

Over fresh cappuccinos, he began– awkwardly– explaining that his situation was difficult to talk about with others, because of the small Achill world.

She nodded, so he ploughed on.

"Because of the work you've done, I wondered if you could offer thoughts, advice, about dealing with… unplanned pregnancy?" He paused, "As a friend of Helen, maybe, you'd rather not?"

She shrugged, "I'm willing to listen and comment, if that's what you want?"

He thanked her, then jumped in. "I don't know how much you know but Helen and I had a brief relationship, for a couple of months, the pregnancy was a shock for both of us and we're no longer together. While in London, she made the decision to keep the baby, didn't tell me or discuss it, so I didn't know until afterwards." He paused, "I'm still very angry that she didn't contact me beforehand, but nothing can change that now, so I'm left … still angry, but also at a loss, about how to deal with it."

Martha didn't bat an eyelid, "A very difficult situation for you Finn," she said, no shock, no horror.

He felt huge relief, then quickly listed his options as he saw them – financial support or financial support with ongoing contact.

"Have you discussed this with Helen?"

"Not yet. Obviously the bleed has put everything else on hold."

"Well, in my experience, unplanned pregnancies can trigger complicated emotions and also deep fears about the future."

He nodded, that sounded right.

"Obviously you have to consider what you are able to contribute, in every sense, emotionally, financially, and of course, the time factor."

She paused to sip her coffee, he caught sight of an electrician he knew in the foyer, averted his eyes.

"I suppose," Martha continued, tilting her head to one side, "a way of looking at options, is to ask which would be best for the child?"

That threw him, hadn't thought of it, groped for an answer. "I'm not sure, we may be in different countries in the future…so financial help would work, but maintaining regular contact might not."

She nodded, "There's responsibility on both sides to a child but I know false promises can do great damage."

"False promises?"

"Well promises to visit, pay money, support, promises broken, over and over… everyone left in limbo, so hurtful, especially to children." She paused, "There's a child with a life ahead at the centre of this situation, so both of you will have to be honest about your commitment and pin it down clearly." She paused, "Legal agreements can be drawn up, if it helps?"

He couldn't stop a grimace. "That sounds daunting."

"Sometimes it helps." She glanced at him cautiously. "There's another option I suppose?"

Her glance worried him, "What's that?"

"Shared custody?"

It stunned him, he gathered his thoughts. "I hadn't thought of that as realistic, to be honest," he said.

Again, there was no shock or horror, just a nod. "You'll have to try and work out a path between you and if that becomes impossible Finn, there are Mediation groups who could help. I have phone numbers for good, experienced people."

His heart sank at the thought. "Thanks, I'll bear that in mind."

Now he was conscious of having prevailed upon her time long enough, thanked her for listening, for her advice, added, "It's a big relief Martha, to talk it over with someone else... to feel heard. Thanks a lot."

After Martha left, he sat for a while, feeling less like Mr Bad Guy. She had been sympathetic, non-judgemental, but hadn't skirted around the reality: it would have to be talked through, in detail, by him and Helen, with the child at the centre of the equation – and right now that felt beyond daunting.

*

On the drive back to Keel, Martha mulled it over. She understood it wasn't something Finn could talk to his family about. She was an outsider, however long she stayed, but it had its uses, gave her freedom to say and do things for which locals would draw fire. She was fond of Finn and Helen, hoped they worked things out.

As she slowed through Mulranny, the conversation dragged her back, somewhere else altogether. January, a bitterly cold snap had London under siege and she couldn't get the flat warm with the puny gas fire. There was a concrete quality to London's cold that was different to Achill's damp cold. When Stephen arrived from the hospital, he looked shrunken and she immediately made him a hot port.

He sat sipping, then said, "She took half a bottle of pills."

It was shocking to hear, shocking to see its impact on him and Martha knew for sure: Celia knows, she took the pills because she knows about me and Stephen.

"How is she?" she asked.

He grabbed at her question gratefully. "They pumped her stomach, she's out of danger."

Then he reached for Martha's hand and she let it lie in his. Partners in crime.

The cold brought an awful clarity. It wouldn't change now: Stephen would never be able to leave Celia. Love or Duty? In the end it would amount to the same for him.

A few months later, she moved to a warmer place, a key worker's flat in Wandsworth, where she was gripped by waves of sadness about Stephen for months on end, until slowly, slowly, they ebbed.

*

Phil was urging Finn to come to London for a weekend, "You need different air man, less salt."

He had a point, but Finn couldn't go missing yet given the pressure from the Kerrigan's job and Helen's condition. When she returned from Anne's after the hospital, at Martha's suggestion, he'd laid the fire each morning, brought turf and coal in and picked up shopping in Westport, when needed. One evening he'd stopped for tea with Helen but the whole encounter was so strained, she didn't invite him again, thankfully. Nevertheless, he didn't want to absent himself until his help was no longer needed.

At the following History Group meeting, Maureen was first out of the traps to support the revised Group Profile. "It's great, makes us look as professional as we are."

That makes a nice change, Finn thought.

Don wasn't far after her. "I think it will add considerable weight to our case, well done to Martha, Finn and Gawina."

It looked like it would fly through until opposition came from the most unexpected quarter.

"I loathe all that PR stuff," Michael said vehemently, "it's style over substance. We've to dress up in finery to prove that we have a good case, is that it?"

Finn felt an intake of breath in the room, saw how Michael's admirable integrity could also make him inflexible.

Don took the reasonable approach, "Would you risk losing funding Michael for the sake of putting your best suit on?" he asked.

"I object to being forced into it," Michael said.

Gawina threw Finn a worried look, a split decision wouldn't work on this.

Michael grew more adamant as the debate continued, Finn stayed silent, had no idea how to persuade Michael from his view.

Then Martha tried. "An important memorial is at stake here, you know that better than anyone, Michael. We're committed, hard working locals, we have a track record, why hide that under a bush?"

"I think we can just tell them straight who we are Martha, without a load of bull attached to it."

Gawina and Don tried again, along the lines of Needs Must…but it didn't convince him.

Finally Martha got back in the ring, "Isn't it like the Yanks returning for visits Michael, everyone painted and polished up the place as a matter of pride and as a mark of welcome?"

Michael frowned, but didn't argue.

Martha persisted, "If a bit of polish and a coat of paint gets us what we want – isn't it worth it?"

It wasn't different to what the others said, Finn knew, but her words and credibility might swing it.

Michael hesitated, then said, "Well since ye all want it, I'll accept, but I'd like my views recorded in the Minutes."

Eilis agreed and a collective sigh of relief flitted round the room as the revised Group Profile was approved for submission.

Finally they were able to move to the enjoyable part of the meeting – a short Power Point presentation about public memorials which James Mulherne had offered to compile, at Martha's request.

James began, with an apology. "It's not a professional display…just some ideas and examples," then proceeded to give them a short overview of modern public sculpture with samples of work, Irish and International which Finn found riveting.

The range and variety astounded him: imposing granite, iron, glass, ceramic structures; abstract metal or wood shapes; tapestries weird and wonderful; eye-catching murals; landscaped areas in parks, on cliffs and at the smaller end of the spectrum, fine, intricate designs on whalebone, marble, shell. A chorus of Oohs and Aahs recurred as James went through them.

As striking as the designs, was the infinite variety of materials used: sand, ice, bicycle parts, foam, rubber, cigarette butts, tyres, animal hides. The potential seemed endless. Nobody spoke, all glued to the screen, only Wim who'd come with Gawina, pyjama clad, chattered to himself, his sounds like a sweet off-beat soundtrack.

Much too soon, it ended.

"One observation," James said, as he concluded, "many public sculptures are striking pieces of Art, but from what I've read, equally important is the way the piece relates to its setting."

Form the nods all round, Finn saw that the group understood that.

Over tea and biscuits, the chat buzzed.

"I think sheep hide would be very appropriate around here," Gawina said.

"Imagine a hooker on stilts at Cloughmore, like that sculpture of St Brendan's boat in Kerry?" Martha said.

"Ah yes," Michael said, more like his amicable self again.

It was fabulous, Finn recalled, as was the *Ghost Ship*, by Dorothy Cross, an old lightship repainted to glow at night in Dublin Bay – beautifully eerie – but they were all large scale works needing big, big money.

As Finn was leaving, Martha had a quiet word, "Helen's getting stronger by the day, don't you think?"

He nodded, "Seems so."

A slight pause, then, "And how are you doing Finn?"

He went for it, "Well…things are completely unsorted, parked, I suppose."

"I understand."

As Martha was the only person he could say anything to, he added, "It's not time yet for…any discussions."

"Carrying that is stressful. Y'know, if you want to talk again, I'd be happy to."

He thanked her, but felt now that she was so closely involved with Helen's care it would be more difficult.

Back in the van, he considered what he would like to say to Martha – that he felt jammed between a rock and a hard place – that as Helen was getting better and had help around, he might leave for London for work purposes– that he'd send money, be back when the baby was born, when they could have that tough discussion about the future. What would Martha make of that?

Two days later, he received a carefully worded text from Helen:

The hospital has contacted me with a date for a scan, twenty-fifth of this month.
  If you want to attend, can you let me know. H.

A scan! Christ, floundering again, he finally replied: *Get back to you by Friday.*

Later that evening, Phil texted:

Finno, when your current job finishes, I could give

you fifteen hours a week, (more or less) and our spare bedroom's available to kip. Think on it. Phil.

The irony of the two messages crossing wasn't lost on him, it summed up the cross currents tugging in opposite directions while he tried to tread water.

London was so tempting: not too far; he could send money to Helen and Skype with the History Group. London would give him space – to breathe, think – decide about his future. Didn't he owe that to himself?

35

Spanish music – Miles Davis, *Concierto de Aranjuez* – strong, colourful, flowed over Helen, easing her worries about the scan and negating any necessity to converse with Finn, at the wheel. They were on route to Castlebar Hospital for a scan, a place in danger of becoming a recurring motif in their relationship, alongside awkward strain – which had returned since her recovery. She wished Anne was with her or she was alone, but had felt obliged to ask him. The music suddenly shifted to what sounded like water falling, stilling her mind.

*

"How do you feel about it?" he asked when they parked.

"Nervous."

He looked surprised, "I'm sure it will be fine."

She bit back, how would you know? Then saw that her efforts to include him were making life harder. Certainly for her … and probably for him, so why do it?

Too quickly, they entered the Ultrasound Department and she felt herself go pale. She was told to sip water because she needed a full bladder for the scan. Then they were led into the room where a young woman, called Sara, introduced herself as the Sonographer. Small, thin, looked about eighteen, Sara began explaining the process, glancing from Helen to Finn as though they were some normal couple. Helen focused on the technical details – high frequency sound waves – via a transducer – echoes recorded – transformed into video images of the baby. It sounded impossible.

"Do you want to know gender?" Sara asked.

"No," Helen said quickly, turned to Finn.

"No," he agreed.

She changed into a hospital gown, lay on the bed, Finn stood beside her, she had gel squeezed on her belly, and filled with anxiety, she took hold of his hand. As soon as the screen showed an image, she tightened her grip.

It was a blue and black world, mostly blue, full of floating fluid in throbbing motion. Sara, the wizard, with wand in hand, pointed out and named details, tiny bones of a spinal column, a leg, an arm, a heart pumping blood, fingers, toes, she counted ten, said, " All present and correct," with a smile. And most of all, the thrump-thrump-thrump of the heart like on the night they'd rushed here through the rain, except it sounded stronger and more strident.

Helen felt she was watching an underwater world, like those TV programmes about deep ocean life which she and Fiona loved. Fish, seals, whales, sharks moved through the depths with fluid movements, except with a lot more space. It had fascinated them, that they could see it all, without those creatures knowing they were being watched by two girls in Dublin. Just like this baby had no idea they were watching every detail now.

"Everything looks fine, normal," Sara said, "and the due date seems more or less accurate."

"Everything's normal?" Helen repeated, wiping beads of sweat off her forehead.

"Absolutely."

Her hand relaxed in Finn's for the first time.

"Everything's fine," he said, nodding at her, though they both knew it was a long way from the truth.

*

Back at the house he offered to cook dinner, while she took a walk. As soon as she crested the dunes, she gulped in sea air. Surely this air couldn't consist of the usual elements, nitrogen, oxygen… and whatever the rest were. No, this had something else, was a different kind of cocktail, then remembered her mother and grandmother talking about iodine's healing properties. Damn right. Relief came flooding in – the baby was healthy, the baby was fine.

Finn made pasta and salad, stayed and ate with her, but the atmosphere was loaded with the unspoken and it dawned on Helen that today held no joy for Finn and it was draining the joy she felt. He moved to clear plates, wanting to be away.

She thought about her changing appearance which Fiona, Anne, Martha had remarked on, which she had noticed in the mirror. Her skinny look was fading, body filling out, breasts too, stomach more rounded, she was pregnant looking, all of a sudden. It scared and reassured her in equal measure. She assumed Finn hadn't noticed, his mind elsewhere. Pregnancy was utterly one-sided on the body.

Words hovered in her head, like bits of dynamite, if spoken, but if not spoken they might rust inside. So, she began, "Finn…" his back was to her in the kitchenette, she waited until he turned, "I'm very sorry for the way I messed it up, between us… not telling you, then telling you. It was wrong. I was in an extreme state of confusion, worry, at the time."

"Water under the bridge," he said, turning back to the sink.

But it's not, it's a poisoned stream, she wanted to shout, stopped herself. "Please sit a minute," she said, "this won't take long."

He moved back to the table, sat opposite, and she sensed hurt, anger, which, preoccupied with her own anxieties, she'd underestimated.

"It's not water under the bridge for me," she said slowly. "I wish I'd done it differently," a slight tremor in her voice, which she steadied. A switch had turned on inside, was pushing her to say it, once and for all, now or never. "I enjoyed our relationship…you were kind, helpful to me before all this, we seemed to be getting on well before – all this?"

He looked a bit stunned, shrugged slightly, "That feels like a long time ago."

She took one more leap, "I regret too, that we broke up that way…"

He looked at her warily, which upset her, but she tried not to show it, braced herself to continue, "Do you have… any regrets about us breaking up?"

He seemed to compose himself before speaking. "I don't know anymore. After you cut things off, I shut it down … and then the pregnancy came like a thunderbolt, changing everything for you obviously and for me."

She waited for something more, but it didn't come, instead silence enveloped them.

Finn broke it after a while, "There's something I need to tell you," he ran a hand over his face, "I may be heading to London, for a few months. My friend Phil needs a QS for a bit, the job I'm on will finish soon, so I'll be broke, back to odd jobbing or the dole. I can send you money and be in regular contact ..." he hesitated then continued nervously, "I can come over to help before the baby's born or get here if there are any problems – it's just a hop across the water."

And there it was, clear as day and although she had pushed for something, this wasn't it, and it rocked her. "Oh." Suddenly, a wave of exhaustion hit and she moved to the sofa where she leaned back, wilting.

He looked worried. "I'm sorry," he said, "that was too abrupt and bad timing. I didn't mean to say it today, not after the scan."

She stayed silent, trying to take it in.

He continued, "My life's scrambled anyway, as you know... I need to make some serious decisions, and the space will help me." He watched her when she didn't reply, "I'm sorry if this makes it harder for you."

She found it difficult to speak, this possibility hadn't occurred to her, but why not, she now wondered. "When do you go?"

"I'm going soon for a weekend to suss things out, then once Kerrigan's job is finished, four or five weeks' time."

She knew he was watching her but she'd closed her eyes and kept them closed.

"I want to support the baby," he said, "and I know we need to discuss that, but at the moment I don't know how to do the bit between you and me."

"Makes two of us," she said. Then a longing to lie down overwhelmed her. "I need to rest," she said and stood. At the door she looked back at him, "You can't forgive me for concealing it, is that it?"

He shook his head, "I don't know."

Upstairs she heard him finish the dishes, tidy up, then let himself out into the cold night, closing the door firmly behind him.

From somewhere, tears came, despite her best efforts to prevent them.

*

Next morning she woke sad, listless, wondering if she'd been mad to speak her mind? But the awful strain had driven her on, she'd needed to try to open a door between them and tell him the truth about her regrets. But Finn Kilbane was moving away, to London and that would change everything. There was nothing she could do about that, nothing at all. She was on her own, as she had been in London when she'd decided on this path.

She checked the tree outside the window, buds getting bigger, unstoppable, as her baby appeared to be. She laid her hand on the bump, "You and me, you and me," in a voice which she couldn't quite control.

36

As soon as Finn exited Heathrow airport, the noise, the people on the train, catapulted him into another world, colourful, cosmopolitan, one which had blown his mind on his first trip at eighteen. Finn remembered the feeling he had then – in a place this big and fast, you could be anyone or just nobody, if you wanted.

At Clapham Common Station he surfaced into the bustle of people, shops, pubs, eateries. Things had changed, still cosmopolitan, but more upmarket.

"*London calling,*" he hummed, but the raucous sound of the Clash seemed out of sync here.

Phil and Naomi lived in a yellow brick, bay fronted Edwardian, on a long tree lined street. He tracked the wave of gentrification from familiar clues: magnolia or wisteria in front, wooden blinds and, here and there, the net curtains of the old guard, probably elderly, living out their final years in houses they'd bought years before or council tenants, a hangover from an era when local authorities owned houses like these.

"No nets," was the shorthand he and Phil adopted in the Galway office, for houses occupied by blow-ins, and sure enough, Number 38, Phil's house, was a giveaway – trellised climber, terracotta window box of Spring flowers and wooden blinds.

Naomi welcomed him warmly, made tea then gave him a tour of the house. It had been close to gutted when Finn last saw it, Phil and Naomi camping in her father's house in Wandsworth, surrounded by a wall of boxes.

They'd done a lovely job, created light and space but kept the interesting features, the cornices, old hall tiles and of course, the fireplaces which were polished up. The guest room overlooked the back garden, part decking and part lawn where creepers were leafing and a swing and trampoline stood.

Was a refurbished Edwardian, Finn's road not taken? If he'd taken the job in the London branch as Phil had, instead of going to Manchester with Alison, is this where he'd be now? Possibly, and right now, it looked damn attractive.

Then Phil arrived and was bear hugging him, while Edward, a proper young boy, hung behind his father's leg.

Over dinner, Edward slowly came out of his shell.

"You talk funny," he told Finn in his plummy English accent, product of a costly private school.

"Yerra so do-you-boyo," Finn replied, in Mayo-ese.

"No I don't," he said.

"Oh yes you do…"

And they were away.

Later, Naomi left the two men with the brandy bottle and Santana.

"The house is great," Finn said enviously.

"The Bank owns it," Phil said, "we're caretakers, paying interest only on the mortgage."

Phil had set up on his own six years back and too soon been hit by the downturn. The stress was visible, hair thinning, and that familiar Friday evening dog tired look.

"Still tough?"

"Without the Olympics, I'd be gone, renting a caravan in Wales."

Finn smiled, but knew Naomi's parents would have bailed them out, though Phil would have hated it. He was an obsessive, gave things his all – his obsession with Sheila had brought him to Galway and their friendship had begun through an exchange of obsessions: Finn's hill walking, Phil's music taste.

"Enough of my sob story, how are you man?"

Finn sighed, "In a swamp."

"Not a bog?"

"Ha, ha."

"Humour me man, I've missed you."

"Me too."

Phil studied him, "Y'know, I went into shock when Naomi told me she was pregnant – and that was planned."

"Why?"

"Was I ready? Would I cut it as a Dad…? I mean I trained as a QS, no mention of fatherhood there."

"At least you were in a relationship with her."

He nodded. "I know it's completely different, sorry, just mentioning…" he reached for the brandy, poured two more slugs.

They watched the dying fire until Phil said, "You're doing the right thing, not deserting the kid."

Finn shrugged. "I haven't worked out what not deserting means in practice."

"Explain hombre?"

"I mean I told her I'll support the baby …but what the fuck does that mean? We haven't talked nuts and bolts."

"Spoken like a true QS."

"Feck off." He leaned his head back, let out a sigh. "I don't know what or how to do all this, feel I've landed in a quagmire." He sighed again, "I know I have to get through this next bit, until the baby's born, then sort it out."

Phil frowned, "Sort it out?"

"Fuck's sake, sort out how to do the baby, and then… sort the rest of my life!"

Phil lobbed a cushion at him. "Calm down man. In her defence, this Helen – she could have gone back to London and you'd be none the wiser, she could have lied, said it was somebody else's, maybe she's keeping a door open for you?"

"She blew me out, remember?" Finn rolled the soft brandy round his tongue, "Though she said she regrets it now." He sighed, "Didn't know what to make of that."

"A door ajar?"

"I liked her, y'know. Was a bit in love…she's a mix of frail and strong, found her interesting."

"Why slam the door?"

"It's like she's become someone else, not the Helen Bradshaw I liked, but Helen Bradshaw, pregnant with my baby and me in shock asking, how the fuck did I get here?" He threw up his hands, "So, what's a decent man meant to do, hombre?"

"Help? Support?" Phil grimaced, "You can't fake feelings, if they're not there."

Finn felt something lighten on his shoulders, no, he couldn't fake feelings.

Phil was wilting, so they moved towards bed.

"Finn," he said, turning off lights, "that offer, fifteen hours and a room here stands, if you want it."

"*Go raibh maith agat.* I'm thinking it over."

Next day, the four of them took the bus to the South Bank. Edward, car reared, thrilled to be sitting upstairs on a double decker, was gobbling up every passing sight.

They strolled by the Thames, wider than Finn remembered, passed street performers, including a woman who worked a dozen hula hoops around her small frame and at the end, asked for donations towards her Student loan. Then they listened to an Ethiopian classical guitarist, making liquid sounds, propped at the river wall.

Finn took them to a restaurant where through the large windows Edward could watch the passing cruisers and boats. "More boats, Daddy," he informed Phil each time another one passed.

"We'll have to bring him here more often," Phil said.

"Then you'll have to work less, darling," Naomi said, and Finn heard the seam of frustration in her voice.

With Monday to himself, Finn took the tube to the National Gallery, where he'd booked into a free guided tour of five paintings. A dozen people were led by a yellow bow-tied guide. A twelfth century religious painting was the starter, followed by a huge canvas painted by an acolyte of Michelangelo, the sheer physicality of it remarkable, then a Caravaggio, the avant-garde painter of his time they were informed, which depicted a beardless Christ, sitting in the upper room with two of the disciples. But the tour-de-force was the last one, a study of the boat race on the Venetian canal by Canaletto. Its detail was awesome.

In the Gallery café, it crossed his mind that it was Helen's talk of Grace Henry and Irish Art which had whetted his taste buds for visual art. He owed her for that, difficult to tell her, now that everything was completely strained. Since her recovery, he'd been going through the motions, wearing a fixed expression on his face – exhausting. He accepted that the pregnancy was a shocker for her too – but she accepted it fully now, wanted it. Her relief at the scan said it all. He was in a different place, churning inside, sometimes desperate, unable to see a clear way forward.

She'd completely thrown him last time, saying she regretted they'd broken up. He felt angered, knocked off balance. She was recovering from the bleed so his survival strategy depended on keeping a lid on inner emotions, his task to mind his manners and not demand, yet again: If that's what you feel, why didn't you contact me when you found out you were pregnant?

Outside, he hopped a bus to Hyde Park, wandered around its green expanse. London was somewhere he could start over, but bunking in with Phil's family didn't feel like an option, they'd enough on and he'd feel like a lodger, despite everyone's best efforts.

Had he another option? With the fifteen hours' work, could he afford a room in a shared house? Would it run through his savings in jig time? Should he gamble on it? Christ, uncertainty was still the name of the game – *Blowin' in the wind* – as Dylan put it.

*

Back on Achill, he rang his sister Sinead to break the baby news – his family ally, a woman of the world. Fresh from her trip to China, she was brimming with enthusiasm for its medicine, hard-working people and the "astounding Great Wall."

When he told her about the baby, he felt relief it was finally out – but not for long.

"Finn I thought you were mature enough to avoid unplanned pregnancy," she said sternly.

"Jesus, Sinead!"

"Well then?" She turned lawyer, "I'm shocked."

"Aren't we all!" Pissed off, he said, "Let's leave it there."

"Ah, come on," she said, gathering herself, "so what's your plan?"

Reluctantly and briefly, he explained, probably maintenance and access.

"It's tough making that work, y'know!"

Was Sinead always such a doomsayer? "I thought you saw complicated parental arrangements all the time?"

"Of course I do, that's how I know it's difficult."

"Are you suggesting it's so difficult, I should walk away?"

"No," she said tetchily, "I'm not suggesting that."

It dawned on him that Sinead had picked up that forthright English thing, familiar from his days in Manchester – a blessing when it cut through waffle – but other times, like now, a sting on your skin. What happened to a bit of Irish sideways?

"We'll work it out between us," he said, with false conviction.

"I'm sure you'll do your best."

He felt like one of her patients, wanted away.

But she didn't, "How do you think Mam will react?"

"I doubt she'll be pleased."

"For sure," she said, "but she won't be able to resist a grandchild once it's there."

And that was the only positive note Sinead struck.

*

He went out to check the barn and gates. No stars, the sky a shroud. He felt like an errant male who went about sowing wild seed. Truth was, he felt deeply let down by Sinead, the two of them had bonded in their teens when they'd opted out of going to Mass, secretly at first, then later, telling their parents they no longer believed in Catholicism, and together had faced the family consternation. In recent years, they'd re-allied, as the ones whose lives didn't revolve around weddings, babies – and happy with it. But ... had it stung because she was right? Hadn't he relied on Helen's diaphragm? Guilty, Sinead, guilty as charged! But I thought you were my pal, not my feckin judge. He studied the sky, saw rain in those clouds, went in.

*

Deciding it was better to be hanged for a sheep as a lamb, he rang his sister Maura, giving her a compressed version of the story. Her reaction stunned him.

"That's great news Finn. Aren't you old and bold enough now to be a Dad. And I'm so pleased my kids will have a cousin, on my family's side, living in the Northern Hemisphere."

It took him a few moments to get his head around that. "Eh, slow down, Maura, it's not straightforward. I'm not with this woman."

Pause. "That's a shame," and then, "but you'll be involved with the baby?"

"I will."

"Good. So what's this Helen like?"

He hardly knew what to say, described her briefly.

"She sounds interesting."

A very snap judgement, he thought, but reassuring.

"Y'know, Finn," she added brightly, "needs must."

"What does that mean Maura?"

"It means you'll work out what's best for the baby, between yous," she said in full confidence.

Finn understood now how Maura juggled being a *muinteoir bunscoile*, four kids and marriage to a farmer. Needs must! Why hadn't he thought of that himself?

But ever practical she asked, "When will you tell Mam?"

"Within the week, I suppose," he said reluctantly.

Immediately Maura asked him to alert her beforehand so she could ring afterwards to help absorb the fall-out. His heart sank at her low expectations but he knew in his gut she was right, that her help would be needed.

The two calls left his head spinning. Had he missed something about his sisters? Yes, definitely: he didn't know Maura as well as he thought and Sinead had a distrust of men he'd underestimated. Something else? Was it possible that Sinead felt deserted – the only single one left? Jesus, it hadn't occurred to him before that having a baby might mean you were no longer considered single.

By now he was in no doubt that telling his mother would be like climbing a mountain. They were close … but not close enough to have ever mentioned his sexual life. He'd learned about sex at school, to his mother's relief, he'd sensed. The closest she'd come to it was a warning to be very careful with girls, during his teens, which he understood to mean, don't get anyone pregnant or ye'll both land in big trouble. Well, she was dead right – big trouble it was!

No escape now; this task would be like climbing Croagh Patrick, in his bare feet.

37

Dreams of babies sometimes woke Helen in the night, a baby girl lay gurgling beside her, then a baby boy, cold, next to her, she had fallen asleep, forgotten to clothe him. She read about it, hormonal changes, fears, strange dreams...all normal. Then one night she dreamed she was submerged in water, couldn't get out to grab the baby, crying on the bed. Terrified, she sat up, groped for the baby, found only her dry bedding, no water anywhere, gave a long exhalation of intense relief.

Later, she googled single parenting groups, found several sites, including two in Mayo. She clutched at key phrases, "can seem overwhelming," "be mindful of social and emotional health" and finally, "reach out." So she set about it – downloaded leaflets then spoke to a friendly woman, Aran, who suggested she attend their meetings in Castlebar. "It's so helpful to talk to other women in the same position," she said.

Helen wasn't ready for that yet, but appreciated the offer, said she'd consider it.

When she mentioned her dreams to Fiona, her sister recalled weird dreams of her own during pregnancy, losing the baby in odd places, on a bus, in a supermarket. "Historically women must have feared losing babies all the time," Fiona said, "we're luckier, most babies make it, but I guess it's still in our collective memory."

Helen was reassured but wondered if these dreams were more intense if you were a single parent? As well as the fear of losing the baby, there was the also the fear of the baby losing you she realised. If anything happened to her in labour, what then? She held back from saying this to Fiona, afraid her sister would think she was asking her to take responsibility.

Later Finn sent his statutory text: *How are you? Need anything brought in?*

She sent her statutory reply: *I'm okay. Nothing needed thanx.*

*

Monday morning, she took the train to Dublin, aware she'd been in the doldrums and neglecting Grace Henry. She also knew she didn't want her research to end, but Isla had begun talking deadlines, so she was on the move again.

Tuesday morning she was the first person to arrive in TRIARC, took up reading where she'd left off. The outbreak of war in 1939 had made foreign travel too difficult, so Grace had returned to Dublin where she moved from one abode to another, but continued to paint Dublin and Wicklow scenes, easily accessible to her, and also continued to exhibit in Dublin and London.

In 1940, T. Bodkin, a former Director of the National Gallery, published a book, *Twelve Irish Artists*, which included Paul, Grace, Harry Kernoff, Sean Keating, Maurice

MacGonigal, (bingo – that was the painter James was interested in); these painters, Bodkin believed, represented the Modern Irish School. Grace was the only woman painter included. Helen was interested to see this group placed together in an Irish School of Art, given the tensions between Traditionalists and Modernists which James had mentioned. It suggested more blurred boundaries than might be assumed.

Her London exhibition, a year later, contained a wide variety of subjects and her inclusion in the first Irish Exhibition of Living Art (IELA) in Dublin, 1943, was recognition of her talent.

Grace held her last solo exhibition in Dublin in 1946 where a reviewer noted her "amazing versatility of subject matter and execution." Her achievement was all the more impressive, given her lack of a stable home during these later years. How did she keep motivated in such unsettled, straitened circumstances? Was such firmness of purpose, the iron fist Mabel Young had detected that day during afternoon tea?

During Grace's later years, her friends, Harriet Kirkwood and Lorraine Creed Meredith were extremely loyal supporters, the latter giving her a great deal of financial help, paying for clothing and accommodation in Wicklow, in return for paintings of the landscape. Where are they now, Helen wondered?

Paul lost his sight in 1945 and was unable to continue painting – a massive loss and according to his biographer, hugely isolating. He and Mabel moved to Bray and he began to create a niche for himself in writing and broadcasting.

Unfortunately, there was little information about Grace's last years, leaving a hole in her story. There was reference to her suffering from melancholy, presumably modern day depression. It was sad to read but didn't surprise Helen, given her lack of a home and precarious income.

Grace died in 1954, in a Nursing Home in Clondalkin, following a stroke, aged 84. Her funeral to Mount Jerome in Dublin was paid for by her friend, Mrs Creed Meredith and attended by a small number of people. Paul did not attend.

Helen put her pen down, feeling bereft. Grace is dead, she thought, Grace Henry is dead.

She wandered around town for a while, feeling sad. Searching for Grace had become her mission, a woman whose life had acquired meaning and urgency for her. Where could she find out more she wondered then remembered the MS Library James had told her about. She'd keep digging.

On the bus back to Fiona's, Helen was consoled by the irrefutable existence of Grace's Art. Her paintings suggested her life story; her body of work was her legacy, living on after her death. All the more reason that it should become better known, a task Helen desperately hoped the new book would contribute to.

*

In Fiona's house, Helen noticed how Clodagh was more upbeat, had regained her fourteen year old stroppiness, visible in a spat with her mother about stacking the dishwasher after dinner. Reassuring, Helen thought.

On Saturday, she went with Fiona to Liffey Valley Shopping Centre to buy maternity wear, which veered in style between the subtly disguising and the blatantly proud. Helen was drawn towards the middle, happy now to have a bump but not drawn to declaring it at every turn, so she bought expanding waisted jeans and leggings and a few loose tops to wear over them, all of which Fiona insisted on paying for.

"Why?" Helen demanded.

"Because you're probably not throwing a Baby Shower are you?" Fiona asked.

"What's that?"

Fiona threw up her hands. "An American cultural import... probably not reached Achill yet. These are my gifts to the baby."

Back at the house Clodagh thought the expanding waists were hilarious, hoped she'd never be condemned to wear such awful things! Fiona reprimanded her for being rude but Helen laughed, enjoyed her youthful scorn. Laughs were a rare commodity in recent weeks, it felt like a tonic and her reaction encouraged Fiona to join in.

Dinner was spaghetti bolognese, cooked by Clodagh.

"Time she learned more life skills," her sister whispered.

Helen didn't disagree, wished she'd had more of her own to call on when she needed them.

Before sleep, she thought about how at ease she felt in Fiona's house these days. They seemed happy to have her come and go, without fuss. Was Fiona's becoming a version of home, a place whose door was open to her, a place she badly needed? Was pregnancy teaching her gratitude?

*

Helen was back on the train to Mayo, grappling with new worries provoked by Finn Kilbane's decision to leave. What if… she had another bleed and there was a gale blowing, what if…she fell, needed urgent medical help, what if … the baby came prematurely and there was a storm? Was it possible that she'd harboured unconscious expectations that Finn would eventually step forward for the baby? Maybe. She didn't know.

None of these worries had crossed her mind that day in London. Should she have considered them? How could she have even known about them?

Watching the timeless green Mayo fields flash past brought to mind all the babies born into this landscape, thriving, dying, surviving, her own baby just another one. The thought calmed her.

A few days later, to Helen's amazement, her father flew to Dublin, stayed overnight with Fiona, then drove to Achill in a hired car. He'd arranged for Maria to sleep overnight with their mother and Bob Harris would call every day. For Helen the timing could hardly have been better.

Over their first dinner, Helen stole glances at him, to make sure he wasn't a figment of her imagination. He was keen to get out and about, so over three days they drove around Corraun, the Atlantic Drive, Mulranny and Westport, all of which he thoroughly enjoyed. Helen also slept so much better with him there, her Guardian Angel.

Then he got down to things, rose early, walked the beach before breakfast, after which he rolled up his sleeves and set about assembling flat-packs – a wardrobe and shelves in the baby's room, extra storage in Helen's.

He said he'd be pleased to meet Finn if she wanted. She didn't, nor did she want to see Finn herself and reckoned he wouldn't want to meet her Dad either. So she lied, said he was working away this week. Mercifully her father didn't ask any questions about Finn's commitment, the future, relieving her of trying to answer the unanswerable. Always a man of deeds, not words, her Dad.

She showed him copies of Grace Henry's paintings and he asked about her life and work. Like the rest of the world he'd heard of Paul but not Grace. He surprised her, had a keen eye for colours and quizzed her about Grace's style in *The Rosary, Floods in Ennis,* amongst others, which she tried to explain as the influence of Modernism. *Country of Amethyst* was his favourite so she asked if she could practise on him, as a type of Everyman, before doing a book launch?

"A type of Everyman," he mused, "would that be an insult or a compliment?"

No flies on her Dad. "Compliment of course!"

But his visit was too short and after six days, he was on the road to Dublin to overnight with Fiona, before returning to Spain. Helen felt completely bereft. She understood better how it was the fate of people living on Achill to say goodbye to others, much too often, but grabbed comfort from the fact that he'd actually come, that the lonely look was gone from his eyes while he was with her and that he'd promised to come again.

38

The day started with good news for Finn, an email from Eilis:

Our application for Development Funding has been placed on a longlist of ten projects. Three will receive funding. Decisions to be made soon. Well done all.

Finn sighed with relief but quickly took hold of himself. It was positive feedback, not a result. Gawina texted: *My fingers all crossed.*

He replied: *Mine too.*

*

Despite the hopeful news, a large shadow hung over him which couldn't be shirked any longer: he had to tell his mother about the baby. Dinner over and before his mother moved to the TV, he began to tell her about Helen and the pregnancy. Quickly it became evident it would be a Stations of the Cross for both, each stage harder than the one before. She listened, eyes never leaving his face while he spoke and when he finished, she stared silently, which he recognised as a symptom of shock.

"I know this is very unexpected for you," he said.

"Helen?" she said, shaking her head.

Why on earth hadn't he told her he'd been seeing Helen before so at least that part wasn't brand new?

"But how…?" she asked flailing.

All he could think to do was to repeat it in a shorter version, finishing with, "We'd been seeing each other, it's an accidental pregnancy but I'll be involved with the baby."

She looked deeply upset, which pained him. He groped for anything to lessen it, couldn't find it. Without saying another word, she rose to put the kettle on. When she returned, she was tearful, and angry he sensed.

He'd let her down. "I'm sorry to upset you Mam."

She looked at him doubtfully, didn't speak. She wasn't a silent woman generally, so he was unnerved. At seventy-five she'd survived her fair share of shocks, didn't need this one.

Could it make her ill again? Jesus, should he have waited until Maura could come?

She was dabbing at her eyes with a handkerchief which had a pink flower in the corner and he remembered her embroidering flowers on plain hankies on winter evenings when she tired of knitting. Sometimes she sold them at the Christmas Sale of Work, boxed as gifts. This memory buckled him.

"I always hoped…" she finally said in a wavering voice, "you'd settle down Finn and have children, but I didn't expect …" she faded.

He wanted to say neither did he, but what help would that be?

"Mam, I don't want you to worry about me-"

"-not worry?" she said sharply, showing her old spirit.

"It will work out okay, I'm sure."

"Are you?"

He nodded, although he wasn't. A baby out of wedlock with a woman he wasn't in a relationship with was a bridge too far for her. Who could blame her – wasn't it a bridge too far for him?

They were saved by the signature tune for *Emmerdale,* one of her favourite programmes, which she turned towards, raising the volume. It flashed through his mind that his story was the stuff of *Emmerdale* these days, but the TV was as close as she wanted it. He hated the damn programme, but blessed it tonight, escaped to lock up.

Across the Sound was the hump of Corraun, where Spring was evident: the few bent trees no longer naked, and best of all, the evenings stretching a small bit. He latched onto this, everything moved on, moved forward.

He went in and watched the News with his mother, though neither spoke. When the phone rang at nine-thirty, he knew it was Wonder-Woman Maura and was more than grateful. Afterwards, his mother's eyes were red again but she seemed more composed. She wished him a polite goodnight, then said, "Helen is a good girl."

"Yeah," he replied.

But by Friday, his mother had retreated. He didn't know if she was punishing him, or depressed. He rang Maura. She was worried too, but had gone further and produced a plan.

"It's Cian's eighth birthday next week, and his ankle's still in a boot," she said, "so I thought I'd invite her over to help me, which would get her out of the house and take her mind off it. What do you think?"

He thought it was more than brilliant, without Maura's plan, he and his mother might sink together. "But haven't you enough on your hands?"

"She'll be a help, Cian is driving us all nuts, turned into little Lord Muck! Also, Shay's passing through Westport on Sunday, so he could pick Mam up, if you drop her in."

He was now in total awe of Maura. A silent journey to Galway would be a heavy burden on him and his mother. "*Míle mait agat*, Maura."

*

Monday morning, his mother in Galway, his work on Kerrigans reduced, Finn headed out on a couple of small jobs. He was feeling lighter. Phil had phoned with some news: Matteo, an architect friend, had work to offer, but – always a damn but – he had a QS contracted who would have to work out his time. Unclear for how long, Matteo and the QS were in dispute.

Near but far.

"Come anyway," Phil urged.

Finn was torn, part of him wanted to go, get on with it, another part wouldn't let him. He'd been googling rooms and so far, none matched his budget and he couldn't risk bleeding his savings while waiting around for more work.

His first job of the day was in a house in Tonragee which the owner assured him would be "straightforward." Now where had he heard that before? He was met by a neighbour, Francie Gill, who held the key, and gave him a quick tour of the fancy dormer bungalow, with views towards Nephin and North Mayo. Dubliners owned it, spent summers there and weren't short of money from the quality of the fixtures and fittings. The afternoon was dry, enabling him to replace the rotting garage doors. He was in and out in four and a half hours, paid in cash, and back on the road. Now that's what you call a Nixer!

His second job was outside Louisburgh and proved a total head-wrecker. He'd been inveigled into it by Finola Kerrigan whose cousin, Catherine, needed help with some carpentry, but when he arrived he found a flat-pack disaster. Finn didn't touch flat-packs – not until starvation knocked – and certainly not botched ones. Brand new wall-to-ceiling IKEA bedroom units were coming away from the wall, doors uneven, crooked shelves, "a holy mess" his mother would call it.

He assumed Catherine had done it herself, suggested she hire an IKEA fitter, at which point, she burst into tears, revealed it was her husband who'd insisted on doing it, confident it would be "handy enough." She swabbed her eyes, "Now he's left me to sort it out, wouldn't even stay home to face you."

Jesus, thanks Finola!

Faced with marriage counselling or flat-pack re-assembly, he opted for the latter and spent six tedious hours undoing the mess. Although Catherine paid him generously and thanked him fifty times, a flight to London beckoned brightly.

*

When he walked into the supermarket he bumped straight into Helen, back from Dublin. They both mumbled greetings, she was about to ring a taxi, so he offered her a lift. He sensed her searching for an excuse to refuse, finding it too hard and shortly after, they were sitting stiffly, side by side in his van, talking about weather and anything safe they could clutch at. When he drove into the estate, he dropped the shopping bags inside and probably because she thought she owed him, she asked if he wanted tea. He hesitated but decided a refusal might seem hostile.

He noticed that her walk was different: heavier, presumably an adjustment to carrying more weight – it was all passing him by. When she took her coat off, there was a bump visible even under her large man's jumper.

"Martha is my scone supplier," she said, producing two scones and a pot of tea, then she sat at a distance. "I thought you'd be gone by now?" she asked in a cool voice.

Below the belt. "I wouldn't leave without telling you!"

She didn't respond.

"The London job's a bit messy, it's been delayed!"

A brief nod as she concentrated on her scone.

Suddenly the bell rang, like shattering glass. Anne stepped in carrying a large pot of paint, shook Finn's hand, said she couldn't stop as Paddy had a Doctor's appointment.

"That's a lovely yellow you've picked," she said to Helen, "perfect for the baby's room."

And she was gone, because Finn was there, he knew. Her exit left a dent in the room, which he tried to fill. "You're painting?"

"Yes."

"Surely you shouldn't be …painting?"

She threw him a quick glance. "Pregnancy isn't an illness. I'll do the low bits and Paddy has offered to do the high bits and ceiling."

"You could have… asked me to do it?"

"I could?" her voice bone dry. "Aren't you're leaving for London?"

324

"I'm not gone yet," he shot back then paused, "I'll paint the room, I'm sure Paddy has enough on his plate."

She frowned.

He pushed it, "I'd like to do it."

She shrugged, "Okay," like she thought a refusal might seem hostile. "Paddy is busy and sometimes if the baby's kicking, exertion's awkward."

Kicking? This baby was old enough to kick? Jesus, he knew nothing about a baby's growth.

Soon after, she went upstairs to rest; he stayed to stack up the fire, brought in coal and turf then let himself out.

*

Back home, he heated soup, trying to block out despondency. How were he and Helen Bradshaw going to get through what lay ahead? He sank in front of the TV where *CSI Miami* were tracking down a serial killer He hated the glaring technicolour, perfect grooming and bleached teeth, but tonight it had appeal – total distraction and absolute certainty – the CSI always got their man.

39

Crocuses appeared out the back of Helen's house, butter yellow and bluey mauve, stunning in their delicate beauty, an unexpected gift on a cold morning and above them like an ancient sculpture, was Sliabh Mór. She wanted to stamp this picture on her mind, recognising that despite all her difficulties and early fears, she would never regret coming to live here. Not only had Achill given her refuge when she was desperate, it had inveigled its mysterious way into her heart.

Then a dream from last night pushed in – Shane was in their London flat packing his case, going to a conference as he frequently did and she sat, calmly watching, unperturbed. Other flashes of him changing his baby's nappy, pushing a pram, came randomly and pained her, but since their meeting at the funeral, days passed without his presence; she was distancing from him, inch by inch. Her belief that sorrow was bad for her baby's health had helped, but it was more than that, she had moved into a different life, one in which he had no place.

Realising this shocked her and unexpectedly sadness surfaced. She was letting go of their twelve years together:

student days, travels to Florence, Crete, San Francisco, setting up home in London, years of sex, learning each other's bodies, the wanting, needing… all now over. What should she do with this history – create a folder, a photo album or delete it? When relationships end, where do the lost feelings go – the joy, pleasure, pain, hatred? Would she carry some part of it within her all her life, or would it simply die?

For the first time it dawned that letting go of a broken heart stirred loss, something she'd never have believed a year ago, even six months ago, when letting go was all she craved. Did Shane feel this? Was that why he'd wanted to say sorry at his father's funeral?

Watching small clouds move over Sliabh Mór she wondered if lost relationships might lodge some fragment of themselves on a galaxy far away, finding a spot in the globe's atmosphere.

She turned her mind to Grace Henry, knew she'd been avoiding going to the MS Library to read the marriage separation correspondence between Grace and Paul, uneasy at delving into their private correspondence. All along, she'd focused on Grace's work and life, in its own right, not in relation to Paul. Did she need to know why they'd ended, "very acrimoniously"? It occurred to her that this relationship was lodged, not on a galaxy far away, but in a Trinity Library, available to those interested.

She discussed it with Isla, who thought it was a good idea to at least read it. "Inevitably Grace's life connects with her work," Isla argued, "the letters might throw further light on her paintings. Why ignore them?"

And so, she travelled to Dublin to read the correspondence. The Library was five minutes from

TRIARC and as easily as James had said, she obtained a Reader's Ticket, then found herself sitting next to a man reading a large size manuscript, wearing special gloves. She obtained the Paul Henry file and was asked to handle it as little as possible, since some of the letters were written on flimsy paper.

Before venturing into the letters, she skimmed through the Winder Good article written in 1921, about the work of Paul and Grace, Entitled: *2 Irish Artists*, and made notes, wishing she'd found it months ago. What a difference it would have made to her early research, hours of time and struggle avoided.

Finally she approached the letters. Paul was an inveterate letter writer, who'd left a wide range of correspondence, but she focused on the section concerning his separation from Grace. The drawn out, painful nature of it became quickly clear – all correspondence came through their solicitors, not a single letter was exchanged directly between them and it went on over years!

In 1929, through his solicitor, Paul sought a separation, with a voluntary settlement. He was living in Wicklow with Mabel Young. In response, Grace proposed a separation for "a period of time", and "reconsideration" at the end of that term, since according to Grace's solicitor, Paul's proposal offered "no hope". Paul had moved on, Grace still holding on, it appeared, a thought which brought a cloud of familiarity down over Helen.

She shook it off, read on. Money was also an issue, neither had much, especially Grace, but their shared studio in Merrion Row became the battleground. Grace continued to use it, but Paul objected. She suggested they share it, each confined to their own portion, which he rejected because it would "destroy the entire effect of separation". The situation was further fraught by the role of a servant, employed by Paul, a woman Grace believed was there to keep an eye on her. At one stage, Grace dismissed her then later became involved in a dispute with her, calling the Gardai to have the woman escorted from the premises. All this was a long, long way from artistic collaboration.

In one letter Paul's solicitor stated that the studio was "more necessary for him than her". It was completely unclear how this could be true, since painting was Grace's only source of income other than the small allowance she got from Paul and the Studio a vital work space. Paul's income sources were wider – writing, radio talks, higher sales and prices; presumably this was another reflection of the unequal way in which men and women's artistic needs were regarded.

Backwards and forwards the correspondence went, as they failed to agree on terms, the bitterness evident. These soul mates, bound for years through love and Art, were utterly estranged and fittingly the fight for the Studio became its focus.

Unfortunately for Grace, her feelings for Paul remained strong; by all accounts she missed him dreadfully and in 1934, aged 62, sought a reconciliation, instigating a final court action for restitution of "conjugal rights". Helen had no idea what that meant, but found it hard not to wonder if it was a desperate attempt to turn the clock back? The action failed and her maintenance allowance was reduced. Paul described her as, "an impossible and persistent woman". Painful reading for Helen: would Shane consider her prolonged sadness in the same light?

During this period, Grace's friend, fellow artist, Harriet Kirkwood, contacted Paul on her behalf, clearly angered by his attitude, stating that Grace was devoted to him and that he judged Grace and others very severely.

In response, Paul stated firmly that Grace had left him for another man, "...all of her affection and time...were given to him, over a two year period". He was adamant, they had separated, "...she to live her life, me mine."

After months and months of letters and failure to agree, a legal separation order was finally issued in 1934. A long, slow death Helen thought. May it not be her own fate when she and Shane proceeded to divorce, as no doubt they would have to in the near future.

*

During a brief walk around the playing fields, Helen realised that she'd overlooked a key element in this correspondence – it was donated to the Library by Mabel, who became Paul's second wife, after Grace's death. Grace had no say in this, despite the personal nature of the material, despite the private nature of her hopes and desires for their reconciliation or her anger about the Studio. How would Grace feel about the public availability of her solicitors' letters to Paul being handed over by Mabel?

How would Helen feel if at some future time, Chloe passed on Helen's correspondence to Shane for others to read? Christ, she'd be enraged, and hate her for doing it. This thought left her feeling uneasy – caught in a tangled web. Here she was, reading this correspondence for her research, not knowing what Grace would think about anybody reading it.

In all of Helen's research, the absence of letters from Grace was intensely frustrating, had left Helen speculating over and over about how Grace would describe or recall events. She'd fantasised about stumbling across a wad of her letters, ink pale but legible, bound by fraying ribbon… left in the attic of the Amethyst Hotel of course.

It was the Hollywood ending and the lowly researcher's dream.

*

Back on Achill, Finn Kilbane rang, he was free to prepare the baby's room for painting and give the ceiling an undercoat. She didn't want to see him, left him the key, went for a long walk, had coffee in the Beehive, hoping he'd be gone when she returned. They had nothing to say, except the unsayable. She wanted him gone to London now, wanted to get used to being a single parent.

He was cleaning up when she returned, cup of tea in hand, so she felt obliged to hover. He sat opposite, told her that the History Group had been longlisted for Development funding for the Memorial.

"That's good news," she said politely.

"It would give the project a real chance."

"Sounds good." A short pause and then she asked, "By the way, when are you leaving?"

He looked surprised, a perfect encapsulation of the gap between them.

"Not sure yet."

"The sooner I know the better," she said, tired of the dithering. "I need to make arrangements for the next scan –"

"– when is it?"

Was she his Personal Assistant now? "Twenty-ninth."

"I could probably work around that –"

"– Anne will come," she said, "she's already agreed."

He stared at her, "I can make it one way or another."

"What's the point," she said, unable to contain herself, "there's another scan later, then pre-natal classes, you won't be able to pop back and forth and… it's not what I need, it would be much harder for me that way."

He frowned, "I told you I'd be back in a few months, before the birth, you accepted that."

"Did I? Is that what really happened?" she asked, then pushed on, "anyway, that was then, in the meantime I realized that I need to get on with being a single parent."

His face tightened, "You're not –"

"– oh yes I am," she said. "Everything's changed for me, not for you, your life can continue as you want, go to London or stay, all up to you. It sure isn't like that for me." He looked completely thrown, so she continued, standing up to relieve her twinging back, "I don't imagine you dream of losing babies at night, which happens to pregnant women often, nightmares sometimes and then there's the pressure on my bladder and the constant search for Toilets if I'm outside and right this minute, this baby is pressing on my back, not on yours, so I have to lie down to relieve that or I may fall down." She let out a short breath, "So, it's a totally different reality for the two of us…and if you'll excuse me," she added, her back pinching now, "I'm going to lie down – now."

She left the room as swiftly as she could, not looking at him, barely making it to her bed, before collapsing onto it, back aching, heart thudding. Once she was lying flat, relief was what she felt, relief from back pressure and relief she'd said it, that she'd finally asserted her own reality.

Take yourself to London Finn Kilbane, find your new life, leave me to find mine.

40

Helen's outburst shocked, then angered Finn, kept him tossing and turning in his monk-like single bed which he should have replaced, he now knew. His thoughts whirled – she didn't acknowledge her solo run about the baby which had landed them both in this almost impossible situation and if she now saw herself as a single parent, what room was left for him? He might as well go to London? Is that what she wanted now? She couldn't have it both ways. He needed to tell her that the truth wasn't her sole prerogative and he would, soon.

But the sound of the baby's heartbeat wouldn't go away and after a couple of days brooding, his plan to go and return before the birth, felt shallow. It meant leaving her to the back aches, scans, hospital visits, pre-natal classes and Christ knows what else, while he sent money and flew in for the final performance. Did it make more sense for him to stay around until after the birth when they would work out arrangements for sharing the child?

God, the phrase, sharing the child, brought fear and disbelief…fear of how on earth he would manage and disbelief that he would actually be the father of a child.

His anxious thoughts were interrupted by a text from Eilis: *Hi Finn, Any chance you could call by asap to discuss an important matter.*

He wasn't in the mood for mystery or visits, why couldn't she just explain by text? It crossed his mind that underneath her neat, precise persona, a touch of Miss Marple might exist, though she'd loathe that comparison. He took himself off to do a garden fence estimate in Dubhgort, then drove to their house to get it over with.

Eilis and Don were both home, in no hurry to communicate the urgent business, Don talking about the weather while Eilis made him coffee served with home-made lemon cake. He had to wait until the preliminaries were done before they got down to it.

Eilis took the lead, "We have a proposition to put to you."

Proposition? Finn looked from one to the other – please don't let it be a botched carpentry job he thought.

"We've had direct contact with the Founder of the American Trust," Eilis said, "she rang two nights ago. A formidable lady," she continued, "thinks our Memorial project is worthy of development money."

"That's brilliant," Finn said, his spirits lifting instantly. He'd been afraid to hope.

"She's of the view that Research and Development are essential to test the viability of a memorial," Don said.

Finn nodded in full agreement, though was suddenly wondering why he was being told this separately.

"In short, her committee is willing to give us development money… but it's conditional," Eilis said.

There's always a fly in the ointment. "On what?"

"She wants a Project Co-ordinator appointed to oversee

the process, someone she can liaise with directly," Eilis said, finally getting to the point.

Finn couldn't recall if the application form had mentioned a Co-ordinator but hopefully it wouldn't be a stumbling block for the group.

Then Eilis came clean, "And we think you would be an excellent choice for Co-ordinator, Finn."

What? Like a bolt from the blue, it stunned him. It took him a few seconds to speak, "Me – Project Co-ordinator?"

Eilis grimaced, "The Sponsor's not keen on committees, thinks they're camels, etcetera, though I think camels are remarkable animals. There is a fee for the job of course." She leaned towards him, "Finn, would you consider taking on the position?"

Take on the position, with a fee? This felt like a moment in a football match when a new score suddenly changed the entire direction of the game.

Both were watching him closely, until Don spoke. "You look very taken aback Finn."

He gathered a response, "I think it's great for the group and for the project and makes sense from her point of view, but why me? Others have been working on this a lot longer?"

Eilis was expecting this, "It requires a particular skill set and mobility which most of us don't have. We mentioned it to Martha and Michael, long term members, neither of whom feel the job would suit them, Maureen and Gawina have other jobs, couldn't do it, and to be honest, Don and I have enough on our hands and are less mobile than we used to be."

He let this sink in.

"You have local knowledge," Eilis continued, "and as a

Quantity Surveyor, can bring technical expertise which it badly needs. In fact," she paused, "others suggested you too. You're very well thought of Finn."

Don took up the baton, "The Sponsor, who wishes to remain anonymous for now, suggests a fee of twenty-five grand, plus expenses, to bring a viable proposal forward." Then he added doubtfully, "She reckons a year would do it, not sure it's realistic myself?"

"A year minimum," Finn said, shaking himself back to life, "depending on the nature of the Memorial. In fact, the time needed might influence the choice …?"

"Indeed," Don said. "It's not a large fee, I know, but it's not a full-time job either. I was firm on that – two and a half days, so you could combine it with other work."

Finn's mind was milling about: twenty-five grand was more than he'd earned over the past year. But another year on Achill… what about his new start? His possible London job? Jesus! Finally he spoke, "I appreciate this offer very much, never thought of anything like it coming my way." He paused, kicked to touch. "To be honest, my future plans are up in the air, I'd need time to consider, think it over."

They nodded, "Of course, Finn."

Eilis assumed her serious look, "Just one other point, it would be essential for the Co-ordinator to commit to working closely with the committee, whatever the sponsor says about camels. The committee will choose the final design, after consultation with the community, taking into account the Co-ordinator's advice of course. We've always done things that way." She paused, "Would you agree?"

Finn figured she should know the answer. "I wouldn't want it any other way Eilis."

To clarify, Don then sketched out how the Sponsor

envisaged the role – working with the committee, background research, liaison with designers, artists, local people, County Council, OPW, plus, of course, ongoing liaison with the Sponsor.

He nodded, head still milling.

As he rose to leave, they both shook his hand and Don said, "We'd be delighted if you took it, we'd be with you every step of the way Finn."

*

He walked to the road, the wind from the sea coming at him hard. Lights flickered in nearby houses, he half expected a bolt of lightning over the ocean! For a year, he'd not had a squeak of a decent job and now, two possible half jobs. Was it trade winds bringing some shift in pressure? He looked at the sea for clues, the water was dark, no help there.

Half an Achill job; half a London job: worlds apart, unfortunately.

He felt suddenly knackered, needed to get home. On the drive back he footered among his CDs, settled for Radiohead.

"No alarms ..."

*

In the morning, he reran the conversation in his head, trying to recall every word, couldn't. It was incredible, incredibly good for the Group, they might get a shot at a Memorial and he allowed himself to savour that thought a while.

But, if he was to take it...it would mean another year on Achill, another delay on sorting out his future. Over the course of the day, the turmoil in his head increased and by night he was scourged by it. If he didn't take the job, who would? He couldn't think of anyone available at short notice and if they advertised would it work with an outsider who didn't know the Group or the turf?

If he didn't take it, would the project sink? He shook himself, for God's sake, someone would come forward, a creative type or a community activist, he wasn't that unique but …it could take time. He hadn't thought to ask if the Sponsor wanted a Co-ordinator by a certain date and if they didn't have one could they lose the funding?

Another thought raced in, if he had a work option here and didn't take it, could that be viewed as desertion of Helen Bradshaw and the baby? Is that how she would see it? If so, would she refuse him visits …would they land up in some awful legal wrangle? Jesus! He took himself in hand: calm down.

He kept his turmoil from his mother who'd recently returned from Galway, fighting fit and brighter in spirit. She was full of stories of Maura's kids and they eased back into their evening routines, dinner, chat, TV News. Neither of them mentioned Helen or the baby, both knew it hadn't gone away, that it would have to be faced – just not right now.

He rang Phil to discuss the job offer.

"You'd be great at that man," Phil said immediately, "though the money's a bit crap."

"More than I earned last year."

"Shit. But if it's just a one year contract, you could do it and next year the building game will have cranked up, so you can pick and choose your QS jobs… as long as you pick me eh?"

"I'll consider you of course," Finn said, but knew Phil was right, his job options would be better in a year.

"So what feels right to you man?" Phil suddenly asked.

"If I knew that amigo," Finn replied, "I'd be sorted."

He slept badly, got up early and to distract himself, drove to check on the building work at Kerrigan's house. Ciaran and the lads were going well, giving him no reason to linger, so after a brief cuppa, he drove away.

Just out of Westport, he was back obsessing about the job offer when Kevin popped into his mind. The offer seemed to have triggered something about his brother, like a shadow suddenly appearing at the window, posing some threat to him.

Finn had long ago worked out what was going on that awful night in the barn, when Kevin was vicious not just towards him but towards his girlfriend. Kevin was jealous – Finn was the toast of the house, going to College, getting presents. Kevin's decision to stay and work the farm was never celebrated, no envelope of money was given, no short speech from their father, his succession to the land was completely taken for granted. Finn got that, what he didn't get was why Kevin didn't take it out on his parents for not celebrating him instead of on Finn? Kevin was lethal that night, spewing bile about Sara, someone he hardly knew. A poisoned tongue took time to master, how many hours of his youth had he spent sharpening it, hating Finn?

Before leaving for university, he'd confronted Kevin one last time. He'd rehearsed what to say, tried to keep his voice level. "I know you wanted to get at me that night in the barn, but why did you drag Sara into it, you hardly knew her?"

Kevin snorted, didn't answer.

"It's a simple question," Finn said getting angry.

Kevin grinned, "I always know how to get to you, you're easy whipped, Finno."

"Bullshit," Finn said.

It was their final exchange, sealed their fate.

Now Finn pondered it – was there truth in it, that he was easy whipped by Kevin? After the water barrel, he'd learned to duck and dive around him or hide if it got heavy, which worked, in the main. Was that what he'd done following the fight in the barn? Had he caved in to Kevin again, limped off licking his wounds, hiding behind supermarket shelves? He thought that taking the Castlebar job was an act of defiance, a refusal to have any truck with Kevin, now it looked like the opposite: self-sabotage. He'd forfeited Sara and his last summer of freedom on Achill, to escape him. It was a high price to pay.

He stopped at Mulranny, walked the beach. Did Kevin's shadow still stalk his decisions? Was the habit of escaping him, getting away, still deeply ingrained? If so, how much time had he wasted not seeing this?

*

For the next six days, Finn thrashed his way through a tangled wood searching for a path through it: should he – should he not take the job? At times he felt feverish, waking when he should be asleep, dragging himself up stiff, dry throated, making conversation with his mother which mentioned none of it, his handyman jobs the only relief from the organ in his head, grinding out the same tune, Should he – should he not?

Early mornings he took to the hill, where he met nobody, sucked in the view of the Sound below, the Bay beyond. He stopped at the ancestral burial site, which rock on rock had outlasted storms, invaders, offering a perspective on his woes, if he could but grasp it. He tried but instead his thoughts circled: the timing of the job offer was disturbing, arriving on a current, as the baby became a visible bump, a kicking creature. *Meant to be* ... the locals would say, an outlook he'd always resisted, having no time for predestination. Nevertheless, it worried him that since his return his thoughts often framed themselves in tides, currents, trade winds – another legacy of island life? Well, when he eventually left Achill, he'd move to the middle of a large land mass, Alice Springs in Oz maybe – far from the ocean and its damn volatile elements.

Before trudging home through clumpy heather and soggy bog holes, other thoughts would grab hold: the Memorial job was a gift some would fight tooth and nail for. He believed in the project, could do the job well and combining it with other work could boost his finances. And it was temporary – his time on Achill would be finite. One clear morning when he glimpsed Ashleam Bay from the hill, a new thought came: could the job give him back that lost time on Achill, that precious summer he threw away at eighteen?

Slowly, painfully, Helen and the baby became inextricably linked to the Memorial job in a way which threw him. The two began to seem intertwined – if he did the job, he could be around for the baby, if he didn't – was it workable? Helen had dismissed him and his involvement at their last encounter, made it clear how totally her life had been changed, while his hadn't. He accepted the truth of that, but ... he didn't have to accept her view about his involvement. It wasn't for her to decide for him. The baby's heartbeat inhabited him too, had refused to go away, staked its claim slowly, surely and as the father he needed to do the scans, classes, make this baby his, in a way he hadn't done so far. If he didn't do it now, he would have to face it later, when the damage was done and the scars had formed.

This was a monumental step in his life, the biggest yet, he knew; it would bring changes he couldn't yet get his head around, but he believed it was the right thing to do and therefore must do it. He saw no workable alternative. As he headed back down the hill, he hoped to God he wouldn't have to fight Helen Bradshaw through law courts to get there.

41

Martha popped in to see Helen, mentioned a swim on Sunday at Keel beach.

"In the sea?" Helen asked aghast.

"I know, a few brave people swim all year," Martha grimaced, "I'm not one. This is a charity fundraiser some friends are doing, if you fancy joining us?"

She thanked Martha, appreciated the invite but couldn't face it. She'd seen people swimming through the winter, viewed them as a different breed.

But later she found herself wondering if this was exactly the kind of challenge she should take on, to face fears, make herself braver. She googled the safety of sea swimming during pregnancy, apparently it was safe, and good for one's immune system. No get out! Alternatively, she could take a long walk with her clothes on and that would boost her immune system. She settled for a walk to the Deserted Village instead, reread the history boards on display, impressed again at the resilience of the un-mortared stone cottages and the resilience of those who'd lived in them.

But swimming lingered, something about immersing herself in a vast ocean off-season seemed an act of defiance, a test. Would it surprise everyone, friends, family, send out a message that Helen had begun to do unexpected things again?

On Sunday morning she heard voices wafting up the hill from Martha's house where a small group had gathered, kit bags in hands, and giving herself no time to think, she put togs on, stuffed a large towel into a bag, covered herself in a big jumper and warm coat, then legged it out to join them.

"Good on yeh," Martha said, and introduced her to a man called Michael, his wife, daughter and boyfriend and without looking back, she followed them to the beach, where they joined a group of six others, about to head into the water.

A woman walker, all muffled up, shouted, "Rather ye than me."

"Very helpful," Martha scowled.

Helen stayed close to Martha as their small expeditionary force faced the steel-grey ocean. She was propelled to walk towards it by the others, into the shallows where the water bit her ankles, forcing her to hop from foot to foot. It was Baltic. Her calves resisted, the tender skin at the back of her knees recoiled, halting her.

To her right, two bodies submerged, Michael and his wife, followed by daughter and boyfriend. Christ, already down. That left just her and Martha, who gave a loud shout and took the plunge. Helen stayed standing, could turn back, she'd every good reason, a pregnant woman, but the thought of turning back seemed...defeating.

"Go for it, Helen," Martha called, "it's better when you're under."

How could that possibly be true, she thought, but five seconds later, she did the unthinkable, and dunked, kept moving, limbs numb, seeing, hearing nothing, just repeating to herself, move, move, move…

"Well done," Martha shouted from somewhere, but Helen couldn't look, kept moving, until her breath ceased to shudder and ahead she noticed the Minaun cliffs.

She swam to right and left, until Martha shouted, "I'm heading in now, you coming?"

"Yeah," she said, the best suggestion possible.

Wrapped in her towel, rubbing life back into her limbs, Helen watched the veterans, still in the water, swimming around. They were another breed. Her legs had turned blotchy red, she fumbled her clothes back on, shaking all the while.

"We did it," Martha grinned, "three whole minutes," handing Helen a cup of steaming coffee, which helped.

The faces of those around looked cold, but revived. A man called Tim was talking about endorphins, "a natural chemical," being released into the body.

Helen half listened, trying to get socks onto feet which were lumps of woodblock, but slowly life began to move through her, as though a lamp, lit from inside, was turning on. Beyond, she registered the calm bay and the sharp outline of Clare Island and thought – I did it for three minutes.

"Hopefully not your last," Michael said to her and Martha "we'll be here every Sunday morning."

"Appeasement of the ancestors is that it Michael?" Martha demanded

He grinned, "You got it in one."

Later, warmed up, Helen looked at herself in the mirror, her face was ruddy, like an old style country girl. It had been

346

an assault, but energising too and she couldn't deny that her mind felt calmer, understood that those damn endorphins keep winter swimmers going back for more.

She felt the baby move for the first time since before the dip. "What did you make of that?" she asked.

*

She returned to typing up her mish-mash of Grace Henry notes, some cross referenced, others not. There was now a provisional date for the book's production, which gave an air of reality to her task, but the disorder of her work reflected painfully the uneven trajectory of her research: slow start, then surges and troughs, until she eventually hit a middle lane of steady work. It was like holding up a mirror to her wavering commitment.

Recently she'd begun scanning newspaper adverts for Art Sales of Irish twentieth century paintings, and was struck by the dominance of male artists, Jack B Yeats, Harry Kernoff, Paul Henry, Le Brocquy, and others, whose paintings were displayed on the page and whose work was highly priced. She began to listen closely to radio adverts for Art Auctions where the same male names predominated. She found an article about differences in the price of male and female artists' works, Paul's paintings priced much higher than Grace's ever were but also consistently higher priced than other, well-known female contemporaries, Norah McGuinness, Margaret Clarke, Estella Solomons. Artistic value didn't equal monetary value.

Isla said success breeds success, in publishing as well as in visual Art, both were market places, subject to market pressures. It depressed Helen, until she remembered one thing she'd learned from Grace Henry's life: keep doing the work you want to do. It was yourself you answered to, often the hardest critic. With a sigh, she returned to her notes, reminding herself that she had two upcoming deadlines hanging over her: Isla her Editor, and her baby, both relying on her to deliver on time: the first before the second.

Next morning, after a week's silence, a message came from Finn: *I can come and paint tomorrow. Would that suit?*

She replied tersely: *I'll be in Castlebar, key under mat.*

Anne had invited her for dinner, a much appreciated invitation. She and Paddy were happily settled into their new life in Castlebar. Over their meal Anne mentioned that she'd seen Lena and Róisín in the shopping centre with their grandmother and apparently Cathy was renting a flat in the town.

"Good to hear," Helen said, realising that she'd buried her worries about them when she'd moved, unable to bear thinking about it.

"There was no mention of the Headbanger," Anne added, "and I didn't ask."

"Fingers crossed."

"And toes," Paddy added grimly.

It was nine o'clock before Paddy drove her home to Keel and Finn Kilbane was well gone. The baby's room was lovely, a soft yellow. She should thank him in a text, but wasn't up to reopening lines of communication yet.

He, on the other hand, had left a note. *I'd like to talk asap.*

Christ, no more talking. It was done, what more to say?

But the Gods were on his side, two day later he bumped into her outside the shop in Keel.

"Can we talk?" he asked.

"I'm working on the Grace Henry stuff at the moment," she said, "up to my eyeballs."

He didn't budge, "This won't take long."

She walked back to the house like a condemned woman.

*

They sat at a distance, he at the table, Helen in the armchair.

"So?" she asked.

He began to speak like he'd rehearsed it. "The Memorial project has received development money for a year and I've been offered the Co-ordinator's job, which means I'll be staying on Achill for the next year."

It was so unexpected, she couldn't get her head around what he was saying, "Co-ordinator's job? What about the London job?"

"It came out of the blue, so I'm going to do it instead of the London job. It's very good news for the project and… for me."

She sank back into her chair, shaking her head, "I don't understand this –"

"– the development money is tied to the appointment of a Co-ordinator and the group has offered me the job." He faltered, "That way I can become more involved with the baby, go to the scans, the classes and …other things, which fathers do."

She couldn't believe it, at the eleventh hour, he'd found his calling. "That's the first time you've ever described yourself as a father."

He winced, didn't argue.

She looked directly at him, "Is this guilt? Guilt isn't a sound basis for…commitment."

He flushed in anger, but spoke in a controlled voice. "No, it's not guilt. It's taken me time to get here …" he threw her a pointed glance, "and that's not all down to me, but now I want to be involved with this baby because I need to be."

She was flabbergasted, "For weeks on end you've kept your distance from this baby, then decided you'd go to London, now you've decided you're not going and want to be involved? What am I supposed to make of this? It's confused, unreliable …"her voice wobbled, she tightened it, "and it's unfair, this is too big a deal for chopping and changing when the mood takes you."

"That's completely unfair," he replied in a tense voice, "I've not been chopping and changing, I've had no reliable work on Achill, had to seek it elsewhere in order to support the baby, now I have a one year contract."

Helen felt overcome with frustration at having to listen to his career issues. "Well, while you've been sorting out your work plans, I've had to make my own, get used to doing it alone, make contacts, rely on other people… and that's what I've done." She needed to end this conversation. "For Christ's sake, involvement with a baby isn't a switch you can turn on and off. What if this job doesn't work out or something? What then? This is too late Finn, way too late!" She saw his face jolt, didn't care.

After a strained silence, he spoke, "Too late for who? I understand it may be too late for you Helen, and you have cause, but… why is it too late for the baby?"

"You opted out," she said angrily, "you can't just turn the clock back."

"I didn't opt out," he replied, "but more important, the baby's heartbeat inhabits me too, won't let me off." He paused, let out a low sigh, seemed to galvanise himself, "So, how is it best for the baby that I walk away?"

He was like a stranger to Helen, someone who'd had an apparition or fallen off his horse. She threw her hands up, "Where has all this come from, all of a sudden?"

"It's been building slowly, but as we weren't in touch of late you weren't aware of that and now, it's become clear to me."

This enraged her, "Lucky you, having the luxury to take your time."

He bit his lip, didn't reply.

This was too, too much, a wave of exhaustion took her. "I need to rest," she said coldly, "that's what's best for this baby right now," and she walked past him, banging her bedroom door after her.

Lying down, she worked on her breathing, heard the front door close and soon sleep overtook her, wiping it all out.

It was getting dark when she woke, still half in a dream. The same curly haired little girl was picking blackberries with her, bending into the ditch to get the fat ones. She'd dreamed this before, but Shane was there and Helen was panicked, fearful she'd lost the child. This time, it was just Helen and the child, picking and eating blackberries as they went. As before, something in the dream was comforting. So many things she would do with her child, help her walk, ride a bike, swim in the sea, take her to school… milestones in both their lives.

She got up, made food, but the comfort of the dream drained away with recollections of Finn Kilbane's words: *How is it best for the baby that I walk away?* Those milestones could be his too, if he was involved.

But, if he proved unreliable, what about the disappointment and hurt for the child watching through the window for a car which didn't turn up? She had read about the pain caused to children from unreliable parents. Is Finn that kind of man? She would have said no – before – but after recent months, his distancing, his London getaway, she was unsure. Then another thought: if the child is at the centre of all this, does she have the right to exclude him? How would she explain it later to the child – that he'd wanted to be involved but Helen didn't trust him…or wasn't willing to take the risk? What would a child, a teenager, make of that? Christ, was deciding about his involvement her burden to bear as well as everything else?

She made herself some dinner, but had little appetite, her line of thought had killed it. Later she reheated her black bean stew, made herself eat to stay healthy, realising that more and more, these days, she was making decisions, choices, for the baby's sake, not for her own. It felt like changing the focus on a camera lens.

She thought about the relationship she had with her own father – close, essential – had she the right to deny that to her baby? Even if Finn was only a half-decent father, had she the right to deny them that? And underpinning it all was how on earth would she and Finn cope with each other, if he was closely involved?

God almighty, she was being stalked again: with dilemmas, big dilemmas – which rattled and shook her hard-won peace of mind.

42

Finn had no time to consider his next step with Helen Bradshaw as he became inundated by phone calls from History Group members congratulating him. Even Maureen sounded pleased.

Gawina, on the other hand, was tearful, "You're the perfect choice Finn," she said, "I'm so happy for you and us."

A brief meeting was held to confirm his appointment, the mood jubilant. Michael called for a toast: "To Finn, in his new job and to a memorial for all of Achill's tattie hokers."

"Hear, hear."

Their positive response was gratifying, although it was dawning on Finn that managing high hopes would be part of the job.

The following day he had a telephone conversation with the Trust Founder, Mrs Valentina Kelly, a good name for a mystery woman, he thought, one which only he, Don and Eilis were allowed to know.

"Call me Valentina," was her opening line, "you and I need to become acquainted."

She told him at the outset that she was impressed with

his qualifications, experience and references, and once that was out of the way, she talked at him.

A self-made woman, whose parents emigrated from Newport to Cleveland in the thirties, she'd started work in Miller's Fabric shop, as a tidy-upper, aged fifteen. Mrs Miller, the brains of the business, took an interest, moved her out to serve behind the counter. "I was in my element there," she said.

From her outgoing style, Finn could well believe it.

"People made their own stuff in the fifties, dresses, pants, coats, curtains, even their goddam underwear, bales of fabric flew out the door." She became Manageress and eventually, when the business went bust under the impact of cheap imports, she bought the shop at a low price and reopened as a Wedding Sale & Hire shop. "You gotta remember Finn, recessions come and go, but weddings don't, they just scale up or down."

Valentina's story was the stuff of films, a rags-to-riches emigrant tale of the kind which drifted back to Achill sometimes and got picked over by his mother and May. They would relish it.

When they got down to business, the business woman emerged, the switch in tone seamless: provisional start dates, resources, timelines, stage one to be assessed before moving to stage two. Finn liked this structured approach, also her directness. It suited him, and he sensed she was genuinely taken with the Memorial project. When he finished the call, his first thought was, Jesus, it's actually happening.

Later he told his mother he was taking the job.

"You're the right man for it," she said and hugged him – their first hug in some time.

Then she ventured onto tricky ground, "Will that make life easier with the baby?"

"Yeah, it should do," he said, although easier wasn't the word which sprang to mind.

*

A week passed without any contact with Helen. In the face of her silence, he recalled Martha's suggestion of Mediation. Is that where they were headed? Would she agree? Then a more worrying thought – if something was wrong with the baby would she tell him? Surely she would…or…maybe she wouldn't? He was in no-man's land, sent a text: *I hope you're well. I'd like to talk further.* In the meantime, to keep his mind on the new job, he began researching computers, and a better phone.

Four more days of silence from Helen passed. What to do? He decided he'd no choice but to call at her house, then paused, would door stepping her make things worse? She'd probably get angry. Instead, he decided to inform himself about paternity rights, logged onto *Treoir*, an advice agency and was very quickly stunned by what he learned – he'd been living in cloud cuckoo land.

Because they were not married, he had no automatic legal right to custody, guardianship or access to the baby, nor would his name automatically go onto the birth cert. Helen would be the sole parent with custody. His involvement would have to be agreed, negotiated between them or failing that, fought through Court.

He walked round the bedroom to shake off his shock; biology carried no automatic rights. How could that be? Why was it all about marriage in this day and age? Then he berated himself for not having checked this before visiting her last time. His naivety had given him false confidence, a false sense of entitlement which probably made things worse. Presumably Helen was fully aware of all this, so if he barged in, guns blazing, he could ruin everything. He sat down, head pounding, just as he'd become clear about what he wanted – to become a father to this baby – he faced losing it. Was this a punishment for his procrastination by vindictive Gods somewhere?

Next morning he felt less shaken, his mind clearer: his next step must be taken carefully. So he wrote and rewrote, struggling to find the right tone, a short letter, which he dropped through Helen's letterbox next evening, when her lights were out.

Helen,

I recognise that my changed plans must have seemed like a sudden about-turn when we last spoke and one that lacked credibility. I apologise for that. I also accept that my connection with the baby built slowly, which was hard for you.

The change in my feelings about being a father has been happening over a period of time, but as we weren't in close contact, you were not party to this change. The memorial job sealed it, offering me a viable living for at least a year on Achill.

I know what I want – to be as much involved with the baby as possible. I would like to know how you see it, what involvement you think the baby needs from me? I can call to see you if you want.

Finn

That evening, for the first time he let himself remember his early meetings with Helen, their chats, Chianti evenings, sleeping together, their decision to see more of each other… the way she'd been such a welcome new presence in his life, until, without warning, it had all crashed on the rocks.

Two days later a text: *Can you call on Friday around 3pm?*

*

As he was leaving for Keel, his mother said, "I'd like to visit Helen sometime soon – if that would be possible. Would you mention it to her?"

"Sure," he said, dodging any revelations, but wondered if his mother had sussed the trouble between them. She could be uncanny sometimes.

Keel looked like a gem when he drove in, blue sky, cliffs regal, a couple of surfers grappling with the swells. What he'd give for a walk on the beach – later, later.

Helen looked pale but composed, led him in, didn't offer coffee, thankfully. They both sat at a safe distance. Sitting opposite her, he saw how much stronger she'd become, had an air of sureness about her now, although he also detected weariness today.

"I got your note," she began, paused, then continued, "I don't want the rest of my pregnancy or the baby's early months marked by you and me fighting about who needs what the most." She looked at him. "I think what's best for the baby should be at the centre."

"Absolutely," he said, but warily. Those were words, easier said than done.

"I think we should move in steps and stages," she said.

"What steps and stages do you mean?"

"Well," she continued firmly, "neither of us knows where we'll be living by the time the baby is a year old, do we?"

It flashed through his mind that they could both be in London, but it was hardly certain. "Maybe not, but why does that affect things?"

She frowned, "Well, it would surely have a bearing on the kind of commitment...you may be able to make, long term."

This worried him, he needed to pin down what she meant. "Do you mean whether it's custody or guardianship ...?"

She registered that he'd done his research, nodded.

He was fearful of agreeing to anything without getting advice, decided instead to focus on step one, as he saw it, steeling himself before he spoke. "I would...I want to have my name on the birth certificate."

She was looking away, half turned to him, spoke in a stiff voice, "I think every baby has the right to know both parents and this baby certainly deserves that."

Finn had expected a battle, instead this was a mighty gain, one he sensed had cost her time and effort, a significant shift from their last meeting when she'd told him in no uncertain terms it was too late. Why she'd changed he'd no idea, but was grateful, concentrated on holding in a massive sigh of relief he didn't wish to reveal, which was now hurting his chest. Luckily a short silence followed, allowing his breathing to ease.

Helen broke the silence. "Nevertheless, I'm worried," she said, looking directly at him, "because we cannot know which arrangements will work best between us going forward, so we have to… need to…take time before deciding that."

"I accept that it will need working through, in stages, but," he paused then went for it, "my position is much more insecure legally than yours, so that worries me."

She took a while to reply. "I get that," she said, "but I can't see any alternative to going in stages. It's too rash." She paused, "We aren't friends anymore, so it will not be…easy."

Marriage with rights, a modern arranged marriage would make it easy he thought wildly, but knew it was crazy thinking, he must be getting light headed. The truth was that an acre of trust had to be regained between them, which would take time and slog – less dramatic stuff than a fake wedding. "No, not easy," he agreed.

He knew they'd gone as far as they could today, but it had taken him so long to get there, he didn't feel like moving, instead, sat, watching the sky outside, still blue.

Suddenly she leaned her head back on the chair, breathed out heavily.

"Are you okay?" he asked.

"Yeah, just a kick. Ouch …" she said bending forward holding her side.

"What's happening?" he asked.

"A mighty kick," she said, breathing her way through it.

"Can I help?"

She shook her head while he watched her breathe in and out, feeling pained, knowing that he'd excluded himself from the baby's kicks for weeks and weeks. When it had passed, he spoke, "I'd like to know about the next scan and the pre-natal classes."

She looked wary. "Anne said she'd come."

"Why Anne?"

She threw him a sharp glance, "Because you were going to be in London."

He accepted her dig, knew it was fair. "But I won't be in London and I want to be there. I want involvement Helen, need to prepare myself," and to rule out any opposition, "to be a father, a decent one."

He heard her repressed sigh, then after a long pause, she said, "I'll mail you about dates."

He stood reluctantly, had no reason to stay longer, but felt the need for some seal on their conversation. "Should we shake on what we've said today, in the Mayo way?" he asked.

She was taken aback, hesitated, then stood and their hands met, lightly, briefly, in a handshake.

43

I

Keel, a pet summer's day – doors, windows of the mobiles open, bikes, scooters, buggies strewn outside, togs, wet suits pegged on washings lines – the summer birds are back, inhabiting the place like they own it.

Helen and Finn take one of the quiet lanes to the beach, the one alongside the old Amethyst Hotel. Each time she passes, Helen tries for a glimpse of Grace Henry, at an easel, or head lowered over a book, but Grace evades her every time. She consoles herself with the summer flowers which thrive on Achill's salty winds, orange Montbreesia, and its best friend, tall with pink spikes. These two are like teenage girls, in summer dresses, inseparable, gay. Behind them, Gunnera, giant rhubarb-like leaves, brooding, intent on conquest. There's always light and shadow, she thinks, as Grace Henry knew.

Finn has moved ahead, forgetting how slow and heavy her walking is, remembers, drops back, suggests they walk the beach. She'd like to but she's tired, her bladder's heavy, fears she'll wet herself, so tells him to walk on, will see him back at the house. For the past three weeks, he has been staying nights at her house, in the baby's room; his idea, in case the baby comes early or there's an emergency. The offer was hard to refuse, those fears stalked her too. He sometimes cooks dinner, they chat, but not about their tricky past or their future, watch TV. They move in parallel paths, have a joint purpose, his presence now reassuring.

At home she dozes off, floats on a calm, tepid river, grassy banks slide by until something begins dragging her down and she wakes to find herself wet, water trickling down her legs. She has pissed herself, the indignity upsets her, until it dawns: the waters have broken. Suddenly a strong pain forces her to grab hold of the sink. This feels different, not practice pains, has the journey begun? She has prepared hard, has no idea if she's ready.

II

Finn thinks there's nowhere he'd rather be than Keel on a day like this, surf boarders grappling with waves, swimmers avoiding them, sun bathers soaking up the rays. He has his sights on reaching Dookinella but progress is slow so turns back.

"It's started," she says, when he walks in.

"You sure?" The baby's not due for three days.

"The waters have broken… pains started …"

"Should we go to the hospital?"

"God no, not yet! We've to stay here as long as possible, away from tubes and strip lighting, remember?"

He does, had a momentary panic – a bad start.

"The pains are manageable," she says, walking up and down the hall "have some lunch, y'know, fortify yourself."

He makes himself a triple decker sandwich. For days, he's wished for this baby's arrival, now he's shit scared.

She sits across from him, taking small bits of food, "I dreamed I was on a river, getting dragged down, woke to the waters breaking…"

He relaxes, "You'll have to tell me what you … need."

She glances at him, "If I know."

They sit listening to voices from a neighbouring house and the squeals of children on the campsite's Carousel.

Then the pain's back, "Sitting's agony," Helen says, walks the hall. And so it goes, for a long time, walk, sit, walk, sit, the contractions getting longer and more punishing. Finn sometimes walks with her, talks to distract her, supports her while she breathes through pains, alternates Nigel Kennedy's *Four Seasons* with Alicia Keys and Aretha Franklin, as agreed, until four hours later, he rings the hospital.

"Best to come in now," the nurse says.

Martha, their driver, pulls up outside, can't hide her alarm at Helen's contorted face mid-contraction, then quickly they're on the road to Castlebar, the same three as before. Today no rain pounds on the car roof, instead warm air floats in the open windows, perhaps a good omen? Finn sits next to Martha to give Helen space in the back, tries sporadic conversation, his mind on Helen, breathing in and out, making painful sounds intermittently. He briefly wonders what Martha makes of him staying in Helen's, figures she'll be pleased they're cooperating. And they are, they've come a long way, moved from wary, strained, to something less defensive, easier, some middle ground he doesn't analyse; it's enough they've made it this far. Sun or no sun, Finn wishes every mile of the journey over as he did the last time.

III

The Labour Room has white walls and dimmed lights and after an initial exam, Karen, her midwife, tells Helen she's four centimetres dilated.

"Only four...but it's been hours?"

"First births are usually slow Helen."

Helen now feels she's in the claw of a brown bear, tightening, loosening its grip, doesn't know how she'll endure it.

"Let's walk," Finn says, taking her arm, and they're on the move, up and down the room, sometimes the corridor, until the pain halts her and she props against him or the wall. She hears cries, a scream from another room, knows she's entered purgatory, maybe hell.

Short lulls come, she sits, eyes closed, recalls feeding mealie mush to chickens on the Glasseen farm. Helen in her cousin's too-big wellies, helps her Aunt. Chook, chook, chook. But Glasseen is snatched away by a clenching pain, her back begins to open and close, vice-like, in, out. She sinks to her knees, clutching at Finn's arm. He massages her back when it's bearable, counting seconds, saying it will pass – as if he feckin knows!

Relief lasts for such a short time she cries out, "I think my back will break!"

"It's back labour," Karen says, offers gas and air.

But Helen can't lie on a bed, nor sit, can't stay still.

"We can give you an epidural," Karen says.

"Take it if you need it," Finn says.

Then another contraction rolls at Helen and kills all power of thought.

She kneels by the bed, trying to visualize the baby's journey downwards, like they said, moving down a wellington boot, the hardest part, the heel.

Come on baby, come on, she begs.

Then Karen wants her to rest on the bed, "We don't want you to wear yourself out."

Helen would laugh If she could – wear myself out? She's shredded. "Lying down is like being caught in a hunter's trap," she says

"Let's move," Finn says.

And they're back on the prowl in the corridor, Helen leaning on his shoulder for short, merciful rests. They pass a young woman, about eighteen, leaning over the handrail sobbing, while her boyfriend, probably eighteen too, stands looking lost. They're children, Helen thinks, lambs to the slaughter.

She glances out, it has begun raining, and how she wishes she could walk away from this place, rain pouring down her face. "They used to call it confinement," she says.

"What?"

"Labour, confined to hell."

He leans down, "Helen, you're doing great."

Now the world is just pain, no past, future, only now with the odd patch of ease. Finn's there, Karen comes, goes, tells her things while she moves into another sphere.

Then she's on the bed again, the hated bed and Karen saying, "You're nearly there, Helen."

"Where" she asks, "where the river meets the sea?"

"Haven't heard it called that before," Karen smiles.

Finn takes Helen's hand.

But she senses Karen's right, the river's speeding up, rushing, pulling, pushing her along and without Finn's hand she'd be gone on the current.

Then, the magic words, "You need to push."

But suddenly, she's a lifeless rag, how can she push? "I can't…"

"The baby needs your help Helen, just a while longer."

She tries and tries until every cell in her body is forced beyond its limit, her face contorted, and then they're telling her not to push.

"I can't stop."

"Keep the breathing going," Finn repeats his mantra,

"You breathe," she snaps, " you do it!"

"Okay, I'll breathe with you," he says, locking eyes with hers.

Karen again, commanding, "The baby's head is there Helen, now push hard."

She tries, and tries.

"Now again."

Enough is never enough, never.

"One more big push, Helen."

And this time, she pushes until her body begins to crack open.

IV

Finn hears the nurse saying, "It's a girl" and they place her on Helen's belly. He watches Helen fold her arms around a wet head, a bloody scrap of life, tears rolling down her face. They ask Finn to cut the cord, which he barely manages, he's so dazed.

Helen's eyes are closed, in shock or relief, but he leans over to see this scrap of life, stunned that a baby is there.

"You were brilliant" he says to her.

She nods, "So were you."

Karen is on the phone, conferring with another nurse.

Finn feels a tug of fear, as she moves next to them, looking serious.

"What's wrong?" he asks.

"The baby's perfect," Karen says, "but you've had a vaginal tear Helen, which needs stitches."

Helen looks alarmed.

"It happens sometimes, so we need to take you to theatre."

Helen is clutching his arm, "Theatre?"

"Safest place to do the procedure, that's all," Karen says.

Helen is completely distraught, "Could I... die?" she asks.

"No way," Karen says, taking her other hand, "it won't take long, but best to go now."

Helen hands Finn the baby, grips his arm, "Mind her Finn."

"With my life," he says.

Then she's gone, wheeled out on a trolley.

V

Stunned by the speed of it, Finn sits looking at the baby, small, skinny, red faced, head bashed from travel, remembers how his mother used to buy seven pound bags of wheaten flour. This baby is a bag of flour. He watches her blurry eyes flickering, tiny mouth pucker, touches the tiny fingers, all there, nails included, remembers the kicks delivered by tiny heels, elbows, fists, harder than he'd have thought possible from these little limbs.

They hand him a cup of tea, terrible tea, which he drinks gratefully. He can't unclench until Helen returns, forgot to ask how long it takes, needs to find a nurse, but suddenly there's nobody close.

His phone pings, five missed calls, Martha, Fiona, Maura, Helen's mother … Jesus, they're probably up the walls. He sends a text, *Beautiful baby girl, seven pounds. All well.*

He rings Maura, because he must talk to somebody. She's calm, tells him it will be fine, the staff know what they're doing, congratulates him and asks for a picture of the baby. "Savour those first minutes, Finn, they're miraculous."

Maura is the absolutely right person for this moment, he thinks, as he turns to watch the baby, her tiny chest whispering up, down, barely visible. Maura's right: it's miraculous.

He read books, attended classes, watched DVDs, but none of them prepared him for that tortuous journey, for moving between uselessness and usefulness. At points he'd thought he'd rather take the pain himself than watch it. In the end, Helen was alone with the pain.

From nowhere, Pedro, the Alicante van driver comes to mind. That day, he and Pedro were collecting marble stones from a supplier when a white van, drove through the open gates, too fast, just as Pedro, intent on his fag, moved forward slightly. The van tipped his shoulder – lightly – but that and the vibration, wobbled him, and Finn sees it now, Pedro tottering, suspended in space, until, by sheer will power, he tilts himself backwards to safety. If he hadn't the van would have hit him, full on.

Bustle and fuss "*Quieres un medico?*" they kept asking,

"Nada, nada, bien, bien," Pedro kept saying.

Finn drove him home, pale, eyes closed, he got out of the van with only a mumbled *Gracias*.

Very weird, Finn thought then. Not now.

Today Finn was hit by a van, pushed to the edge like

Pedro, understood there might only be seconds between life and death, between a good outcome and a bad one. He had no idea that giving birth was so hard or monumental. How did he not know that?

Now he holds the baby. Until Helen arrives back, he's not certain about life or death.

VI

Helen lies in a different white room, her heart breaking. She wants to weep, howl for being snatched away from her baby, but they need her to stay as still as possible. She tries, watches the clock on the wall, tries to breathe slowly, in-out, counting minutes. It won't take long, they say, two voices murmuring at the foot of the bed.

But every minute counts, to be with her baby. Grainne, for Grace, they've agreed. Then a horrible thought – did she dream a baby?

She tries to ask, but her throat's so dry, tries to move her hands, they're leaden, like the rest of her. Where's Finn, why hasn't he come? Then remembers he had to mind the baby.

"You okay, Helen?" someone asks, "we're finished now, we'll take you to the Recovery room."

"I want my baby," she croaks, her mouth is sandpaper.

"Your baby's with her father, they're coming to see you."

In yet another white room, Helen weeps, counting seconds one-two-three-four… gets to three hundred and fifty, before Finn and Karen, wheeling a baby trolley, walk into the room, both smiling.

Epilogue

Grace stares out the window, coat, hat, gloves on to brace against the early morning chill.

It began misty, now it's clearing. Greens emerge, bright grass, silken ivy, lime leaves on dark branches, and suddenly a brief shaft of sun.

The small window frustrates her, but today it has its use, frames the world. She knows the clouds carry rain, so begins. Rapid strokes, lessons learned on Achill, years before – nothing is wasted. When the rain comes and lashes the window she makes tea, waits. Patience was another lesson, harder learned.

She adds a slice of lemon to the red cup brought from Chioggia. That was life in different colours – yellow, red, orange, terracotta, blinding at first, then brightening heart and soul during hard days.

Ireland became her home. Did she choose it or did it choose her? No matter, the task is the same: to catch, hold, paint as best she can, the thing she was born to do.

What could be simpler? Few tools needed – hand, eye, canvas, paint, brush. What could be harder?

Many have asked – to what purpose all this effort Grace? Mostly she shrugs. Don't they know the answer?

She knows for sure: to paint her sense of the thing, leave her thumb print on it.

Acknowledgements

I want to thank the many people who helped this novel see the light of day.

The Irish Writers Centre, Novel Fair 2017 judges who chose it as one of the winners and spurred me on.

John & Mary MacNamara, for welcoming me and offering valuable insights into Achill life, Scoil Acla and tattie hokin.

Heinrich Boll Cottage Committee for a two week Achill residency giving time & space to finish an early draft.

Rosarii Moran for generous access to her Thesis, *When the Soul Sings,* TCD 2008 which opened a vital door into Grace Henry's life & work.

J.G. Cruickshank's *Grace Henry – The Person and Artist 2010* the only biography I found.

Antoinette Murphy's article, *The Poetic Art of Grace Henry* – written for the Paul & Grace Henry Joint Exhibition 1991, Hugh Lane Gallery.

The Irish Art Research Centre (TRIARC) for access to their resources and a quiet place to work & the Manuscript Library, TCM(*Paul Henry* File), both based at Trinity College Dublin.

S.B Kennedy's *Paul Henry*, 2000, Yale University Press.

Kieran Clarke's article, *Clew Bay Boating Disaster* in *Cathair na Mairt, Westport Historical Society Journal* Vol 6, No. 1, 1986

Síle A. NicAodha for her article *Social History of the Time*, published in *Bathad Acla* 1994 where I also found reference to Anne O'Dowd's book, *Spalpeens and Tattie Hokers* Irish Academy Press 1991.

Music References: John Denver's, *Back Home Again*, *Preludes* by George Gershwin, Simon & Garfunkel, *I am a Rock*, Morrisey's *This Charming Man*, Radiohead's *No Surprises*, The Gloaming's *Samhradh, Samhradh,* Bob Dylan's *Blowin' in the Wind*, Miles Davis' *Concierto de Aranjuez*.

Mary-Jane Holmes, Editor at Fish Publishing for crucial suggestions at the right time & Anne O'Sullivan for helpful input.

Hugh Lane Gallery, for the use of Grace Henry's painting, "*Evening, Achill*".

To my daughter Niamh, sons Eoin & Ronan, sisters Siobhan & Maggie, brother Pat and my long-term friends, Iris & Roz, all of whom encouraged, supported me all the way, even when their patience was sorely tried and to the many other friends who showed unwearied interest in the project.

Finally, a million thanks to Ken Lynam, my partner & First Reader, astute, perceptive, honest in his feedback who kept on believing in this novel.

About the Author

Mary Lennon grew up in Dublin, lived in Spain and then London before returning to Dublin.

She has been writing fiction and poetry for a number of years, published short stories in *Crannog, Culture Matters, Time Lines*, and on radio: *BBC 4 & Sunday Miscellany, RTE Radio 1*. She won First Prize at *Listowel Poetry Competition*, was a runner up winner in the *William Trevor, Roberts* and *Tipperary* short story competitions as well as being shortlisted in a number of others.

While living in London, she co-authored (with Marie McAdam & Joanne O'Brien) *ACROSS THE WATER,* IRISH WOMEN'S LIVES IN BRITAIN, published by Virago Press and widely acclaimed in the UK & Ireland.

She has worked as a Community Worker and Teacher of English & Creative Writing in Colleges, Prison & Adult Education in the UK & Ireland.

This is her first novel. It was chosen as a winner in the Irish Writers Centre, Novel Fair competition 2017.

This book is printed on paper from sustainable sources managed under the Forest Stewardship Council (FSC) scheme.

It has been printed in the UK to reduce transportation miles and their impact upon the environment.

For every new title that Matador publishes, we plant a tree to offset CO_2, partnering with the More Trees scheme.

For more about how Matador offsets its environmental impact, see www.troubador.co.uk/about/